Lost & Found

EMI LOST & FOUND SERIES
BOOK ONE

Photography and Cover Design : Christi Allen Curtis
Photography Assistant : Katrina Boone

Lori L. Otto Publications

Visit our website at: www.loriotto.com
Third Edition: March 2014

The characters and events portrayed in this book are fictitious. Any similarity to real persons, living or dead, is coincidental and not intended by the author.

Printed in the United States of America

DEDICATION

to "em"
for befriending me, for believing in me,
for encouraging me, for pushing me,
and for bringing "anna" to life

BOOK ONE

NATE

E M I

CHAPTER 1

Nine years is a long time to hold on to a feeling– one that I felt for only ten seconds of my life. Logically, I know it was twenty seconds at most, but the impact it left made it seem like forever. If I allow myself to think about that night– and I never do– I can remember how the air in my lungs felt completely effervescent, how my chest tightened around my racing heart, how my skin seemed to feel everything around me. Hands. Lips. A cool, fall breeze. I even thought I could feel the stars sparkling above, prickly and scintillating in their luminescence.

Nine years *is* a long time, but with a feeling like that, I doubt I'll ever let it go completely. It's a shame I don't have a good sense of what actually *caused* that feeling, but my imagination has filled in the blanks left by the drunken oblivion of that night.

I chose stupid ways to rebel in college. Of course, drinking was the norm for most students at school, but my actions back then lingered more toward self-centered and inconsiderate. Had I known I'd see Nate at any time that evening, I never would have consumed as much as I had. To this day, I mostly drink in moderation when we're around one another. A better friend may give up drinking entirely, but even *he* has a little alcohol every now and then. And he doesn't have any friends better than me, nor do I have any that rank above him.

As I wait for Nate, hurriedly getting ready for a night out with his current love interest, I wonder if he makes all women feel the way I felt for those ten glorious seconds. That would explain the long string of girlfriends. But maybe that feeling was fleeting. Maybe it was only meant to happen once, to stir up those emotions and questions for those brief seconds. Maybe other women acted on that fleeting feeling... and then maybe it just resulted in fleeting relationships. After all, they're just emotions. By nature, emotions are not stable, nor are they reliable. They come and go. Just as his girlfriends do. In quick succession. They come and they go...

Does it make any sense at all to continue to search for that feeling? I shrug my shoulders as if I'm answering my own question, having my own conversation with myself. Whether it makes sense or not, I'm on a mission to find it again someday, with someone. I just hope that my pursuit doesn't keep me from seeing things in the periphery. From seeing that what I'm looking for is actually right in front of me.

"Well?" he asks, my eyes focusing on what I would call a blouse on any day. It almost doesn't compute. Men don't wear *blouses*. Nate does not wear *blouses*.

"You're not wearing that." I can't contain my laugh.

"What?" he asks, lingering in the doorway to his bathroom.

"That... that... is it a *shirt*?" I ask, cringing at the light pink button down with... *are those ruffles?* I take a few steps closer to confirm the strange quarter-inch of fabric peeking out from under the center hem.

"Yes, it's a *shirt*," Nate argues, his voice not as confident as it was only seconds before.

"Who picked that out?"

"My personal shopper," he defends his clothing choice. "It's Italian... or French, I don't remember."

"Wait, your personal shopper. Is she a jilted lover?" I ask him.

"She wasn't at the time," he confesses as he takes a long, hard look at himself in the mirror.

"Well, I think it's safe to say she didn't want any other women hitting on her man. You can't wear that. Seriously. I don't know what kind of man would wear that sort of thing. Gay men have much better taste. And straight men would run screaming. Wait, why aren't you running, or screaming?"

"Damn it, Emi," he says, frustrated, practically tearing the monstrosity of a shirt off of his body. "I don't have time for this." He walks quickly back to his closet and takes a look inside, stretching his back subtly. I hate it when he walks around without his shirt, and decide to tell him so.

"I hate it when you walk around without your shirt on. It... *bothers* me." *And yet, I can't tear my eyes away.*

"I know you do. But did you not just tell me ten seconds ago that I couldn't wear that shirt? You asked for it." He throws the pink thing at me playfully. "What should I wear then?"

"A regular *American* dress shirt, Nate. Don't you have anything like that?" I push aside t-shirt after t-shirt in his closet until I find a pressed white button-down shirt, still in the plastic bag from the cleaners. "Here."

He takes it from me and walks back into the bathroom. "You need a belt, too," I remind him, catching a glimpse of the waistband of his light blue boxers underneath his loose-fitting jeans. "And you'll probably want to wear an undershirt with that," I yell to him.

"What else, *Mom*?" he teases me, crossing the room to his dresser and pulling out a thin, white t-shirt. "And I'm not wearing jeans, don't worry. I'm wearing that." He points to a hanger holding a pair of black pants and a matching jacket.

"Wow, slacks and a coat. Looks suspiciously like a suit... This must be getting serious. Did you get her a corsage, too?"

"Shut it," he warns me with a smile. "Well at least my wardrobe choices are keeping your mind off of... what's his name?"

"David," I remind him for the twentieth time, watching him pull on the tight undershirt as he goes back into the bathroom. I examine the pink *blouse* and put my arms through the sleeves. "Hey, can I wear this?" I cinch the ends at my waist and push my way into the room next to him, looking at myself in the mirror. I flop the cuffs around, trying to find my hands.

He laughs and turns to me, folding up the sleeves until my limbs are revealed. "I thought you wanted him to like you... not run, screaming."

I roll my eyes at him as I lean up against the doorjamb. After a few seconds, the worry from earlier comes back. "Do you think he will?"

"Will what?"

"Run." I sigh heavily, turning to walk back into his guest bedroom. "And scream," I mumble loudly enough for him to hear.

"Why would he do that?" he asks, standing in the doorway. "I mean, aside from the shirt." The sunlight dancing through the large windows makes his brown eyes sparkle. I involuntarily smile.

"What if he doesn't like me?" I ask him.

Nate throws his hands in the air and scoffs at me. "Emi, we've been over this," he says, going into the bathroom. I hear him brushing his teeth a short while later. I collapse back on his guest bed, where I had spent the earlier part of the day watching him paint, rambling on about the date I had tonight. I had intended to do my freelance work, but I couldn't concentrate. Because of my nervous chatter, he hadn't gotten much accomplished, either. He preferred quiet and was always very focused– never very social– when he was painting.

"But we broke up, like, seven years ago. I haven't even seen him in three," I yell to him. "And he was married then. And, like, what if he's fat and bald?"

"You're not that shallow, Emi. You liked him once... enough to give it up to him," he laughs under his breath.

"I wanted to get it over with," I relate to my friend. "He was cute and nice and he wanted me."

"You liked him," he reminds me. "A lot."

"I know I did," I sigh, standing up and walking toward the bathroom. I lean against his hallway wall, watching him get ready. "What if he thinks I'm ugly?"

"Seriously, Em? Look at yourself," he says, pulling me back into the bathroom and holding my shoulders, pointing me in the direction of the mirror. "You're not ugly. There is no way any man, woman or child would think you were ugly." He glares at me before letting me go, tousling his unruly, wet hair with his fingers.

"Mousey, then?"

"Nope."

"Average..." I murmur.

"You're not even that. And, Emi, remember. *He* sought *you* out."

"I know..." I linger. "But what if he takes one look at me tonight and pretends he doesn't know me?"

"Again with this," he sighs, rolling his eyes.

"I never sent him a recent picture. What if he expects me to look just like I did back then? I mean, he doesn't know what I look like these days."

"And he apparently doesn't care. You're just as cute as you were back then, Em. Cuter, even. Trust me." He always knows just what to say.

I did like David, a lot, many years ago. I was surprised to reconnect with him online a few months ago. He found my email through the NYU alumni network. His first few messages were friendly, but distant. Eventually, he told me that he had divorced his wife earlier in the year. I had to admit, I hated to see marriages fail, but I was a little excited that I might get another chance with him.

We were cordial and flirty through messages and phone calls, but he hadn't asked to see me. I was beginning to think he wouldn't until he casually brought up New Year's Eve one day last week. I told him my roommate and I were having a party, so I invited him to come. He accepted the invitation with no hesitation.

"Why are you feeling so insecure tonight?"

"He didn't like me enough back then," I remind Nate.

"The timing was wrong," he mimics my voice. "It wasn't that he didn't like you."

"I know," I pout. "The timing was *all* wrong." David was an over-achiever, like me, very busy with school. His dream was to go to Los Angeles to become a screenwriter, and he focused all of his free-time trying to realize that dream. Eventually, I relented, not wanting to get in the way of his life goals– and selfishly needing more attention than he could give me. I never harbored any resentment. It was a nice relationship while it lasted.

"Well, I'm sure tonight will be fine." He touches my chin briefly on his way to the closet. "Go drink a glass of wine while I finish getting dressed. You didn't even open that bottle from last week."

"Good idea." I keep my back to him, giving him some privacy to dress, as I pour a glass of my favorite red. My curiosity was piqued, but Nate and I were never going to be anything more than friends. He was attractive– no, scratch that, he was *hot*– but we had an arrangement. I liked our arrangement. He was the best friend I'd ever had.

To tonight, I think to myself, lifting the glass and sipping my drink.

He grabs a bottle of water from the refrigerator after pulling on the rest of his suit. The ends of his black tie hang loosely around his neck.

He takes a long drink of water and points to his necktie.

"Are you ever going to learn to do this yourself? I won't always be here." I set my wine down and begin to arrange the ends into a knot. "And where's the step stool?" He begins to walk backwards to another corner of the kitchen, pulling me along when I don't let go of his neckwear, slowly kicking the stool out to me. I stand on the second step, finding it easier to do this particular task when he isn't towering a foot above me.

"I can," he says. "It just never turns out right... and I'd rather it be crooked than lose my patience over something that's going to be undone in a matter of hours." He smugly raises one eyebrow.

"Right," I say, tightening the knot– tight– against his neck. He coughs dramatically and pulls it a little looser.

His hand draws up to my face, stopping abruptly, his finger lingering inches from my mouth. "Um, you have a little wine on your top lip." He stares at it while I stare back at him. I lick it from my lips and smile with a slight blush.

"Thanks."

"Thank you, Emi," he says after clearing his throat, clutching the knot once more. "How do I look?"

"Your hair's a mess."

"You always say that's a good thing," he says, confused.

"Yeah it is," I sigh. I'd never met another man who could pull off that look in any setting, amongst any crowd. Women everywhere he went would fall at his feet... hence the fact that he was *never* without one. "You look fine."

"Just fine?"

"Good. Great. Amazing. All of the above," I say nonchalantly. He was the epitome of handsome, and I know every detail of him like I know my own– after all, he was often my subject in portraiture class in both high school and college. I know the perfect mix of brown and yellow and white paints that would recreate that messy hair that often covers his light brown eyes. I can haphazardly paint brushstrokes in every direction and it would still look like the perfect head of hair on him. His brows are just a shade darker, his lashes long, outlining a stare so intense at times that it can go right through me. His natural tan coloring always makes me look even paler when we walk side by side. He has a strong jawline with angular cheekbones that exhibit their own natural blush. His nose is well-proportioned to his face, and turned up ever-so-slightly at the tip.

And his lips... I won't even go there. "What were we talking about?" I ask him.

"You were telling me I look amazing."

"Right, so... um, are you going back to her place tonight?" I ask.

"I'm not sure," he answers. "I haven't planned that far. Why?"

"This place is a wreck."

"Well, that's why you need to get your crap and leave," he jokes with me. "The cleaning lady will be here any minute to do her thing."

"Nothing like waiting until the last minute, huh?"

"Well, if she had come this morning, you would have still come over and spread your mess out and made it look like this," he gestures to the room. "My mess is all confined to the guest room." I peek in and see his paint supplies strewn about the small bedroom.

"Wait, you're making her come in on New Year's Eve?"

"It's her job. I pay her well," he reasons.

"I'll pick up my things," I mumble, rolling my eyes at him.

"I know you will. But seriously, I've got to get going if I'm going to make these reservations."

"Were they hard to get?"

"Not for me," he smiles arrogantly.

"Of course not." He starts to pick up my design books, stacking them neatly and putting them in my tote bag. "To-go cup for my drink?" I ask, holding my newly-poured glass of wine.

"You can finish your drink."

"Thank you." I lean against his kitchen island while he takes a seat on the sofa closest to the door, typing something on his phone.

"Hey, are you sure you two can't just stop by tonight? I might need a confidence boost," I plead, knowing he won't bring his girlfriend by, but wanting to ask anyway. I'd never met Laney, and likely never would.

"No, Em, we've got plans." He smiles.

"I know."

"You are going to be just fine," he asserts again, walking over to me as I take the last drink of the wine. "If he's as smart as you say he is, he will fall in love with you and give you a heart-stopping kiss as the clock strikes midnight.

No repeat of last year."

"Don't remind me."

I spent last New Year's Eve, snowed in, with my brother. Wallowing in each other's self-pity, we got completely hammered and both of us passed out as the miserable, previous year exited and the new one flitted in with no fanfare whatsoever.

"Speaking of last year, what's Chris doing tonight?"

"My brother will be entertaining Clara tonight."

"Well, that should be fun for her." It would be. My niece loves my brother and his ability to build giant fortresses in his living room out of couch cushions and sheets. She would pretend to be a princess in her castle and bark orders at him. "We've got to find a girl for him, for next year," Nate says.

"Yeah, I know."

"This is gonna be *your* year, Em," he says after a short, contemplative pause. "I just feel it." He puts his arm around my shoulder and hands me my bag, holding his door open for me. "I'll walk down with you."

We ride down the elevator, just the two of us.

"So, we're still on for tomorrow night, right?" I ask.

"What's tomorrow night?"

I groan loudly in frustration. "*Wicked*, Nate. You promised you'd go with me. I swear, if you stand me up, I'll–"

"I know," he laughs. "I haven't forgotten. A night with witches, I can't wait."

"Surely you're not referring to me..."

"Surely not," he says, ruffling my hair with his hand. "Oh, the spells you cast..." I barely hear him whisper in my ear, a shiver going straight down my spine.

"You're funny," I say sarcastically but nearly out of breath as we exit the elevator. The concierge hands him his keys as Nate opens the doors to his building for me. His car is waiting for him in the drive.

"Just call me," he says as I begin to walk down the sidewalk toward my apartment.

"I will... Like ya, Nate."

"Like ya, Em." He gets into his sporty car, revving the engine and pulling out of the drive quickly. He pulls up beside me and stops abruptly, rolling the window down. "Oh, and burn that shirt for me."

I stroke the ruffle that runs down my center gently and nod to him. As he drives away, I hold the fabric to my nose and breathe in the fresh scent of his fabric softener.

"You left your phone here," Teresa says to me when I get back to our apartment, her voice irritated. "I've been wondering where you were all afternoon. I needed help getting things ready."

"I'm sorry," I tell my roommate. "I was helping Nate get dressed for his date."

"Nate's, of course. I should have known."

"What can I do?"

"At this point, just get ready. People are gonna start showing up in about half an hour." I linger in the kitchen, feeling like I've let her down.

"I really am sorry."

"It's fine, Em," she smiles. "It's all handled. I'm not mad."

"Okay."

"What time did you tell David to be here?" she asks.

"Nine-thirty. I figured I would have had enough to drink to be relaxed, but not so much that I would be completely incoherent."

"Good plan," she confirms. "And if things are going well, but he doesn't seem to have the guts to kiss you, what are you going to do?"

"Take matters into my own hands. I know what to do." We smile at each other. My biggest fear as the year was coming to an end was spending another New Year's Eve alone, un-kissed. She had listened to me worry about this for weeks. It was silly and romantic... but that's me. "I'm going to go shower." I smile to myself, thinking about the kiss that is sure to come tonight. Maybe it *would* be my year.

By ten-thirty, I've decided David's not showing up without a little prompting. I knew in the back of my head that this was a possibility since I hadn't heard anything– email, text, or call– from him in three days. I pull out my phone and check for voicemails again. Nothing.

"Just text him," Teresa yells over the music as she hands me another cosmo on her way back to the living space from our kitchen. "Lure him here. Promise him food, drinks, strip-tease, blow-job, whatever."

"I'm not that desperate," I frown.

"Yeah, you kind of are, Emi." She hugs me. "But I love you." I look at her, a little hurt, but admitting to myself that she's right, even if she's not really sober at the moment. Neither am I.

"Hey, the party's just getting underway. I've saved you a Stella. You still drink those?" I tap my foot nervously, counting the seconds for a response. Still nothing. Fifteen minutes pass. The alcohol lure isn't working... *please, God, don't make me lose all my dignity.*

Thirty minutes later, having given up on David but not willing to give up on the kiss, I scan the room for other options. All the men seem to be partnered up except for two. One is kind of attractive. He catches me looking at him, and I smile and blush, looking away quickly. The other one is... not my type... but the two of them talk, giving me sideways glances as I busy myself with some carrot sticks and one more drink. I peek up from my glass and see Not-My-Type's hand gently stroking Kind-Of-Attractive's chest. *Fuck, seriously?* They entwine their fingers together and laugh. *Probably at me.*

I go out into the hallway, hoping for privacy but just running into a few of our friends making out in front of our neighbor's door. I walk to the stairwell and pull out my phone, my fingers pressing numbers feverishly. The phone rings... rings... rings... *pick up the damn phone, please...* rings... eventually goes to voicemail.

Feeling I have no other options, I send a desperate text.

His response is not just "no" or even "No." It's *"NO." Got it.*

Completely frustrated, I go back inside, wishing that the entire apartment would clear out so I could crawl far under my covers and hide for days and days. Eventually, the countdown comes...

10... 9... 8... 7... 6... fuck me... another year... without... any... 1.

"Happy New Year!" the room shouts in uniform cheer. I look over to my roommate, her lips locked with her boyfriend du jour, his hands all over her ass. *What is so wrong with me?* My breathing becomes shallow, as if I'm starting to hyperventilate. I will not burst out in tears right here in front of God and everyone. *I will not. Fuck, I won't!*

I almost manage to swallow the lump that has formed in my throat as Teresa glances at me from across the room, and my eyes begin to water, giving me away. She smiles sympathetically, leaving her boyfriend behind.

"Happy New Year, Em," she says as she throws her arms around me. She kisses my cheek. "It can only get better from here," she says, smoothing my hair down. "Come on, come get another drink. That fucker isn't worth a single tear. No man is."

I wipe away that single tear that managed to drop down my cheek, but I can't help but think that at least *one* man is...

NATE

CHAPTER 2

"Nate," she whispers in my ear as I feign sleep. I don't want to get up yet, much less continue the fight we started last night. I roll over on my back but keep my eyes closed. It seems too early to let the bright sunlight in.

"Nate?" she says again. I can't tell by her soft voice whether or not she's still angry at me over the conversation we had last night. Admittedly, I'm kind of surprised she's still here at all.

When I don't respond to her words, her lips gently touch my cheek, and make their way to my lips. I taste her lipstick, can smell the freshly applied powder on her skin. Sleepily, I respond.

Waking up to a woman kissing me is pretty exhilarating. Honestly, I like the idea of being the first thing someone thinks about in the morning. With Laney, I'm not. She always gets up, showers, and creates the perfect facade of beauty before I'm even awake. I like it when a woman feels comfortable enough with me to completely be herself, to let me see her natural beauty. Laney and I, we aren't there yet, a month and a half into our relationship. I hope we get there soon. Even on mornings when I wake up first, she spurns any of my advances, no matter how tempting they may be. It's frustrating that none of my reassuring compliments make any difference to her.

Suddenly, I feel her legs straddle mine. I touch them, finding them to be completely bare. As my hands continue to travel up her body, I learn she's naked. I'm fully awake now, opening my eyes to admire her body on top of mine. There is nothing better in the world than morning sex.

I guess I have the answer to my question. I guess she isn't mad after all. "Good morning, baby," I say to her, the effects of a good night's sleep still lingering in my voice. She doesn't return the greeting verbally. She just pulls my boxer shorts down my legs, throwing them carelessly on the floor, positioning herself over me. I guide her slowly, both of us letting out heavy sighs at the feel of one another.

She rocks back and forth as she lightly grazes my chest with her fingernails. My eyes finally look up to meet hers, but she's not watching me. Her eyes are closed, her head angled toward the ceiling. As I put my hands on her waist to pull myself into her deeper, her steady breathing quickly turns into small gasps. Her painted fingernails dig into my skin, the pain somewhat pleasurable. She moves faster and her cries of passion get louder and louder.

I can feel the stirring inside begin, and I roughly pick her up off of me and throw her on her back against the mound of pillows on my bed. She whines, upset that I've stopped before she's had her release.

"I'll make it up to you," I assure her, climbing on top of her, taking her left leg in my hand and kissing her knee before returning to her. She mumbles something unintelligible as her hands grasp the ends of my hair. She quickly finds her pace again as short wisps of air escape her smiling lips. I am completely overcome and give into my desire until I climax, taking her roughly, fast, my need for her feeling suddenly insatiable. Her hands fall limply to the bed as her chest rises and falls quickly.

"I love you, baby," I tell her finally, and the exhaustion quickly sets in. I collapse on top of her, delivering a few kisses to her stained lips. I roll over onto my back and breathe heavily.

"I love you," I repeat to her wearily, glancing over at her and smiling. She normally returns the sentiment, sidles up to me, rests her head on my shoulder and plays with my hair.

But that doesn't happen this morning. Instead, she gets up off the bed and stomps her way to the bathroom, picking up her clothes along the way with purpose.

"Laney?" I call after her. I hear the bathroom door close, and wonder if she might still be angry after all.

Last night was not the best New Year's Eve I've ever had, to say the least. We had gone out to a nice, secluded sushi restaurant for dinner, and then to a crowded club after that. We came back to my loft– freshly cleaned, just for the occasion– around eleven-thirty so we could toast the new year with champagne at my home. It was one of the few nights of the year I actually planned to drink. This year, I was hoping for a very romantic evening. It was shaping up to be just that, and up until that point, the night had been perfect.

My phone rang, and I decided to ignore the call. I was sure it was just my mother. She called me every year on this night shortly before midnight, even though I was typically with a woman and I never answered her call. She would leave a message, wishing me a happy new year, and confirming our plans for lunch on the second. We had the same routine, year after year.

But no message was left, and a few minutes later, I got a text message. Laney happened to check the phone before I could get to it.

"*Is it safe to come over?*" it said, and Laney read it aloud not once, not twice, but three times, her voice getting louder with each repetition. I knew the text message was harmless, knew exactly who it was from, but Laney didn't know the whole story.

"I thought you said that you and Emi were just friends!" she started yelling, throwing the phone onto the sofa across the room. Laney had consumed about seven drinks at that point in the evening, so the irrational reaction didn't come as a surprise to me. I was a little irritated, though, and walked over to the phone, texting back my answer to her question: "*NO.*"

"Laney, I've told you, we *are* just friends. You're being ridiculous."

"Ridiculous?!" she continued. "Then why is she asking to come over to your place at midnight? On New Year's Eve? Friends with *benefits*, maybe? Is that what's going on?"

"No," I answered calmly. "She knows we're together tonight. I have no idea why she'd want to come over." I had hoped– for her sake– that everything was okay at her party, but I knew immediately when I got that text that her night hadn't turned out how she wanted it to. The selfish man inside me smiled a little, though. I don't know why. Emi and I were never going to be anything more than friends. I had accepted that long ago. She was looking for something I was unable to give her.

"I have some ideas," Laney said sarcastically, finishing off both glasses of champagne that I had poured for our toast and crossing her arms in frustration.

"It's not like that with us," I warned my girlfriend. "Her roommate has guys over sometimes, and there's no privacy in their apartment. Sometimes she likes to come over here to get away, that's all."

"She stays the night over here? When *you're* here?!"

"Laney, calm down. This is no big deal. I swear to you, Emi and I are just friends," I explained.

She glared at me in disbelief and was completely silent, waiting for more clarification.

"How many times do I have to remind you that we've been best friends since high school, Lane? We've been through a lot together– as *friends*. Yes, she stays over here sometimes. That's why I have a guest room."

"What do you *do* when she comes over at a quarter till midnight?" she asked, clearly insinuating lascivious acts of passion.

"I don't know, what do most friends do? We work, or talk about things, or watch movies, or do something completely innocent," I pleaded.

"What do you talk about?" she asked, wiping the tears that were forming in her eyes. I sighed heavily and walked over to comfort her. She shrugged away from me, angrier than I had anticipated. The night definitely wasn't going as well as I had hoped.

"Sometimes I bounce some ideas off of her for my next piece. Sometimes we talk about music. Sometimes we bitch about clients. We talk about our families–"

"Do you talk about me?"

Do I say yes or no? Is there a right answer? And if so, what the hell is it? I take a gamble, knowing I have a fifty-fifty shot at getting it right. "Well, yes, Laney, you're a part of my life, of course we talk about you."

"What kind of things do you say?" she slurred, her speech succumbing to all the drinks she had consumed. Had Laney been sober, she wouldn't have cared about all of this, would she? We had talked about Emi before, multiple times, and they were all just fleeting conversations, as this one should have been. This was the alcohol talking.

"Laney... really... maybe we should just go to bed and talk about this in the morning."

"*What kind of things do you say about me?!*" she yelled, emphasizing each and every word. I sighed again. What sort of things do I say about her to Emi? Honestly, I make it a habit to talk very little about my girlfriends to Emi. I had learned my lesson long ago. I used to go on and on about how this girl was the one, and then we'd break up a month later. I repeated it so many times that even *I* got tired of hearing it. I could see the doubt in Emi's eyes after awhile. That even started putting doubt in my own mind.

"I just talk about things we do," I said nonchalantly.

"Like in *bed*?" Her question was so inane that I didn't even want to dignify it with a response. Why waste my breath on that one?

"No, Lane, not things we do in bed," I said, rolling my eyes and taking a seat on the couch. "I do have some sense of decency."

Well, there was that one time, but Emi made it clear she didn't want to hear about it anyway. There was no point in trying to make her jealous, and when I realized that's what I was doing, I never finished the story.

"Then what?"

"I tell her how much fun we have together. I tell her about the restaurants we go to or the exhibits we see."

"And?" she said after a heavy sigh. I could feel her calming down. I tried to soothe her as best as I could, trying to salvage what was left of the night. We had already missed midnight.

"I tell her how beautiful you are." I pulled her on the couch next to me and put my arm around her. She sat up straight, careful not to return my affection.

"And?" she said with these weepy eyes.

"I tell her how much I love you, how much I care about you..."

She blinked and one last tear escaped from her eyes. I brushed it away with my thumb as I took her head in my hands.

"And I tell her how wonderful you make me feel," I whispered in her ear before lightly kissing her forehead.

Her eyes looked even more brown, more beautiful, after she had been crying. When she quietly sighed and looked down, I pulled her head back up so her eyes could meet mine once again.

"Do you know how wonderful you make me feel?" I leaned back in and pressed my lips to her cheek. "Because I know how wonderful I can make you feel." I kissed her ear.

She playfully slapped me away. "Don't try that on me tonight. I'm going to bed." She started to walk away, but I caught her arm and held her back. I kissed her hand, then her wrist.

"Um, no, Nate. You're not getting laid tonight," she said adamantly. As she stumbled toward the bed, she began to undress, leaving her clothes strewn across the floor of my loft. When she was completely naked, she turned around seductively and said, "Good night." With that, she cuddled under the blankets, making sure to take them all, and turned her back to me.

"Really? You're still angry?" I asked in disbelief. I wasn't used to getting turned down.

"I need to think about it," she mumbled. "I have a headache." I was sure that was true and not an excuse.

I was hoping that she would quickly think about it, and then quickly realize how silly she had been. I'd decided to take a hot shower to clear my head. I was hoping she would join me, so the shower lasted longer than normal as I had given her ample opportunity. I toweled off and walked over to the bed, wearing only my boxers. As I crawled on the bed from behind her and kissed her cheek, I tried to get under the covers with her, but she pulled them tighter around her body and, again, told me good night. Point taken.

I got up and went to the small closet to get out a few blankets. I would honor her wishes to not allow me under the covers with her, I would put a brake on my attempts to make love to her, but damned if I was going to sleep on the couch in my own apartment.

After that night, I'm understandably confused this morning. I'm definitely getting mixed signals. She wakes me up for sex, doesn't say a word, and then disappears into the shower. Did she really stomp, or were they just heavy footsteps on my twelfth-story loft's hardwood floors? Is she mad, or am I forgiven? I crawl out of bed and make my way toward the dresser to find a t-shirt, picking up my boxers along the way and sliding them on.   W h e n Laney gets out of the shower, she is wearing the same clothes she had worn last night, even though she had previously left a few items of clothing in my closet for just such an occasion. I'm happy to see the return of the short skirt, since I had spent the entire night imagining what was beneath it, only to be completely shut down after our fight. She looks amazing in it, showing off her long, silky legs as the hem sits at least seven inches above her knees. Those legs look even longer in the black heels that she is wearing. Her breasts never looked quite as beautiful as they do in that shirt. She knows this outfit drove me crazy last night. I had a hard time keeping my hands off of her all night, so of course she'd put those clothes back on.

She's either decided to be a complete tease, or she wants me, too. I know she likes it when I'm driven with desire for her, and I clearly am, my eyes undoubtedly showing my need to have her.

"Tell me you're not mad anymore," I say to her, almost demand.

"I'm not mad anymore," she flirts with me, leaning on the dining room table and pulling up her skirt as she scratches her thigh. I can see that she isn't wearing anything under that skirt, and I know that is my open invitation to take her, now. As I close the distance between us, she entices me further by sitting on the edge of the table, revealing just enough to show me what's waiting for me.

"Make love to me," she orders, as if there is anything else I want to do in this moment.

"Anything," I answer. "Anything you want." When I reach her, she strips me of my clothes, quickly and easily. I remove her top so that I can kiss her breasts. I leave her flirty skirt on, clutching it tightly for better leverage. We make love on the table, undoubtedly awakening my neighbors below me as the feet of the table scuff the wood of the floor, second after second.

Make-up sex might be better than morning sex. I just don't get that very often.

Hours pass as we enjoy each other, our bodies in constant contact as we alternate between lounging around, talking, and making love. She tells me I'm forgiven for what happened last night, and even though I don't quite feel like I'm the one who needs to apologize, I don't argue. Our day spent together turns out to be the perfect start to the new year.

Both exhausted and lying naked on a blanket on the floor, we watch the sun dip below the horizon through my west-facing wall of windows. There are no other buildings around to obstruct the beautiful view my apartment has of Central Park, and therefore, there is no need for curtains or blinds... or clothing, lucky for us.

"Are you hungry?" she asks me as the first of a couple stars comes into view. She pulls herself up off the floor and puts her sexy heels back on. If I wasn't so exhausted, I would grab her by the ankle and pull her back.

"Famished," I sigh, not wanting to get up.

"Let me make you some dinner," she suggests. "What would you like?" I consider her question, but it really doesn't matter to me what she makes. As long as I can lie here a little bit longer, I will eat anything.

"Surprise me." I grab a pillow off my bed and put it under my head, staring at her naked body as she makes her way to the kitchen. This is better than a dream.

A knock on my door startles me awake. It's dim in the apartment, and I can taste the distinct flavor of tomato sauce in the air as I breathe. I struggle to get up off the floor to see who it is. I look through the peephole and see Emi standing there, bundled in a coat with her cute pink knitted cap tied around her head. *Shit.*

"Nate?" she calls out to me.

"It's Emi," I whisper to Laney.

"Uh..." is all I can say through the door. I turn quickly around to find some clothes for both Laney and I to put on, confused. *Do I turn her away? I never turn her away.*

"Is this a bad time?" she yells back at me.

I look back at Laney, hoping to get an answer from her, as I see her walk to the door, still completely naked– except for the heels. She swings the door open in one swift move, to my complete shock and horror. I hold the clothes I had gathered in front of me, embarrassed.

"I'll take that as a yes," Emi says as she quickly averts her eyes and turns to walk away. I hurry to put on some pants and throw a robe at Laney.

"No, come in!" Laney says with false sincerity. I push past her and walk out into the hallway to stop Emi.

"Nate," Laney calls seductively, choosing not to put the robe on and stepping out of the apartment.

"Lane, please put something on, other people live on this floor," I plead with her. "Emi, wait." I can tell that she isn't about to turn around, so I rush to get in front of her. "Stop, will you?" I ask. She covers her eyes, assuming I'm still undressed. I pull her hand from her face, but she can barely look at me. It hurts more than I want it to.

"I'm sorry," Emi says to me. "I tried to call you, like, three times today, and you didn't answer..."

"We were busy," Laney interrupts.

"Obviously," Emi blushes. "Really, I just thought we were going to see the show tonight," she says, still unable to look in my eyes. "It's okay, though, Teresa said she wanted to go... so I'll just call her..." She begins to make her way past me.

The show. Of course. I forgot about the show. Emi had received tickets to *Wicked* for Christmas, and I told her I would go with her. How could I forget? She was so excited about it. It was all she talked about for the past week. *How had I forgotten?*

"No, Emi, um..." I grab her hand before I realize what I am doing. I turn to look at Laney, whose eyes are consumed with more anger than I knew could fill those two beautiful, brown eyes. I run toward her, seeing her intentions, and my arm is the only thing that stops her from slamming the door in my face.

"Shit, Lane!" I holler as I push the door open and grab my wrist. With a little more force, she could have done some serious damage. "What the fuck? I have a show Friday night!" Laney had already been the cause of one cancelled gig. Emi had called me from the club, fifteen minutes after my band was supposed to play, asking where I was. She said my bandmates had been stalling, but were running out of things to play. She said the crowd was getting bored. That night, I had completely lost track of time when Laney surprised me the day before my birthday. It was our second date, and the first time the two of us had made love. I was completely wrapped up in her– quite literally– when Emi had called. I lied and told her I was sick, which looked incredibly suspicious the next day when she, my mother and I met for lunch, and I failed to wipe the look of confusion off my face in time when Emi told me she was glad I was feeling better. I rarely lied to her. I hated doing it.

Laney had been pleased that I had chosen her over my previous commitment that night. After getting off the phone with Emi, thoughts of sex still playing in my head as I spoke with my best friend, I was ready to go again.

The club manager forgave me quickly, knowing I could draw a crowd like few indie artists could. It helped that it was open mic night then. I didn't want to let him down again, though, especially for a broken wrist that would not only impede my musical abilities but also interfere with my work.

I stretch my fingers out a few times, testing my hand. Standing in the doorway, Emi comes up beside me, avoiding Laney and bravely standing in the hallway outside of the front door.

"Is it okay?" she asks with concern.

"It's fine," I say. We both nod and she leaves, no further questions. She really is too good to me.

"Damn it, Lane, can you get over this? We are just friends!" I begin as I close the door to the apartment. I immediately start looking for my phone. I'm sure that if Emi had been calling I would have heard it ring... and I know a follow-up text message will be coming in very soon. I know how Emi works.

"Doesn't look like it," she says, feverishly walking around the apartment, finding her clothes and getting dressed. She even makes her way to the closet and starts pulling out the other shirts and pants that she has left here on prior occasions.

"Well, it's true. I'm not romantically involved with her... I don't know what else to say about it." I continue searching for the phone. Sofa? No. Couch? No. Dresser? No. Under the bed? No.

"No need," she says curtly. I recognize the signs. She is about to dump me. I love her, though, don't I? I have to find a way to prove it to her.

"Don't leave," I instruct, giving up the search and staring humbly at the floor. "Can't we talk about this?" She is silent. After too many seconds pass, I look up at her for a response. She's holding my phone.

"Looking for this?" she asks, precariously dangling it over the now-burning tomato sauce she had been cooking on the stove.

"Laney, don't, please," I beg. "I love you, Laney. Don't you believe me?" Doesn't she know? Didn't I prove it to her, over and over, today? Doesn't she see how passionately I care for her? It is obvious... isn't it?

"Nope," she says as her fingers let loose of my phone, into the tomato sauce. She picks up everything she can carry and walks to the door.

I run to fish my phone out of the sauce, and nearly burn my fingers before noticing what I am doing. I pause for a second, realizing I went after the phone... and not the woman I thought I loved. Big mistake. I look up to see her disgusted face before she marches out of the apartment.

"Laney," I start toward her.

"Don't bother coming after me!" she yells from down the hallway.

Happy Fucking New Year to me. *Shit.*

Turning off the stove and throwing the now-useless phone on the counter, I look around the apartment, the one that had been spotless last night for our special evening. A torrent of passion had swept through the loft in the past couple of hours– and right out the front door. The evidence is all around, blankets and pillows strewn about, items of clothing here and there, a broken lamp on the floor... one of my favorite art pieces hanging crookedly on the wall. Even the couch is shifted about ten feet out of place. Oh well, at least it's starting to feel like home again. I hate the feel of clean living spaces. It's too sterile. It makes me think of the home I grew up in. All of the rooms were very tidy, everything in its place, not a speck of dust to be found. Neutral colors, whites and beiges. A lifeless home, really. My art room was my one comfort in that house. I loved that room, and spent as much time as I could in there as a child. It was the only place in the entire house where I could be a kid.

I go over to the piece that I painted a few years ago and straighten it. I distinctly remember the day I painted it. It was inspired by a different breakup, with a different girl I loved. All of my best work comes when I am in pain. The intensity of my feelings brings it out of me. I suppose the intense love I feel for these women would inspire such work, too, if I wasn't so busy spending that time in bed with them. If there's a choice between making love and painting, though... well, there's no question.

Shit. Why does it keep happening? For a second, I want to call Emi, but realize that she's out with Teresa... and I don't have a phone at the moment.

I make my way to the shower and run the water as hot as possible. I just feel like I need to wash this entire day, this entire experience, this entire relationship off every inch of my skin. Again, I feel like a complete fool. I'm not sure how one man can botch up so many relationships. The look on Laney's face made it pretty clear that this wasn't just a fight. It seemed pretty... *over*... to me. And for such a silly reason. I did nothing to make Laney think I was involved with Emi. We are just friends. Period. Even though I have to remind myself of this sometimes, I never let on to the outside world that she is anything more than a friend to me... because she's not... and she never will be.

I take off my pants and step in the steaming shower. If creativity comes to me when I'm in pain, clarity seems to hit me when I'm in the shower. I stay there until the faucet begins to pour out cool, then cold, water. I step out, wondering what I could have done differently today that would have altered the outcome. To me, Laney really just overreacted, went off the deep end. She has a very passionate streak, that's what really drew me in to her, but that passion isn't so attractive when it comes in the form of jealousy. A deep sigh escapes my lungs. I need to go get a new phone so I can try to call Laney, just explain one last time that there's nothing going on between Emi and me. I can't just let it be over that easy. I love her, don't I? She's worth fighting for... isn't she?

I pull on some jeans and find a clean, white t-shirt stuffed in a drawer. I go to the closet to dig out my red button-down shirt and leather jacket. Keys in hand, I head out to the only phone store still open. Thankfully, they never close... a perfect convenience for guys whose jealous girlfriends douse their electronics in sauce at all hours of the night. A walk on this brisk January night will do me some good, anyway.

After I get the new phone, I realize I really have no way to call Laney. Her number is in the baked phone at home. In fact, the only number I have committed to memory is Emi's. I'll just have to wait for Laney to call me. That is, *if* she decides to call me.

I go to a restaurant near the theater where *Wicked* is being performed and get a bite to eat. Hopefully I can catch Emi before she and Teresa head home. I need to explain myself to her, too.

After a few hours, the streets outside the restaurant become crowded with people, and I know that the show is over. I send Emi a text message, letting her know where I'm at, inviting her to join me for a drink. She shows up a few minutes later, waving goodbye to Teresa at the front door.

"I barely recognized you with your clothes," she greets me from across the quiet restaurant.

"Ha," I scowl. "Emi, I'm sorry about tonight."

"Don't worry about it, Nate. I knew it wasn't your thing."

"But I wanted to go with you, I really did."

"Well... Teresa loved it. It was really good... the ticket was not wasted at all, so don't mention it."

"I guess that's good," I tell her, still feeling bad.

"So what happened?"

"She left, of course."

"I didn't need to ask, then," she said.

"Why do you say that?"

"Red," she answers with a matter-of-fact smile. I roll my eyes at her, but smile back. Emi has a theory about the color red. She insists that I wear it anytime a woman leaves me. I don't do it on purpose, but tonight, my subconscious seems to have sold me out again.

"Right," I sigh.

"Are you alright?"

"I just don't get it... but I'm sure I'll be fine. I wanted to call her, but I don't have her number anymore."

"Did you delete it already? That's not like you." She knows that I keep the numbers of all the woman I've dated stored in my phone. I know it bothers her, but I have my reasons. Reasons that don't matter, realizing I've lost *all* of them now.

"No, she sent the phone swimming in tomato sauce. I don't have her number anywhere else."

"Ahhh... that was rude. What exactly happened? I feel like I walked in on something... although, *what* I walked in on, I have *no* idea."

"She was just upset about something silly. I don't really want to talk about it." How can I talk about it with her? Laney wasn't the first girl to get jealous of Emi. In fact, I got tired of talking about it with her. Anytime our conversations even hint at a relationship between us, everything becomes uncomfortable. It's awkward for both of us, for different reasons only I really understand.

"Okay," she smiles quietly as a waiter comes over to take our order.

"A glass of merlot for her, and water for me," I tell him. "Did you want anything to eat?"

"Nope," she answers. "I'll never eat again after seeing her naked. How will I ever find a man when I have to compete with women like her?"

"Whatever, Em, you're beautiful, too," I affirm to her nonchalantly, a harmless compliment.

"She was like a goddess, though," she tells me, and the vision of Laney– her long legs, leaning over the table in her heels, scratching her thigh, lifting her skirt– this vision lures me in again and I fight off the man in me that starts to make himself known. *Not now. Not with Emi here.* I shift in my seat and pull my jacket closed around my lap, leaning into the table. Focusing on the waiter as he sets our drinks on the table, my body begins to return to its normal state.

"I don't want to talk about her," I mention again.

"Alright," she says, picking up her wine glass. "A toast to not talking about the goddess."

I lift up my water, and we clink our glasses together.

"She was so... um... *bare*. Do guys really like that?"

My brows slightly furrowed, I look up at her, disbelieving that she asked the question. "Are we really talking about that?" My mind wanders to Emi, as I wonder what she must look like. *Fuck...* I scoot my chair closer still to the table, afraid that no article of clothing or piece of furniture will be able to hide my arousal at this point.

"I guess not," she smiles weakly. "You're of no use to me," she jokes. "What good is having a guy friend if you're not going to give me a guy's perspective?"

I tap the table to the drumbeat of the song playing through the tinny sound system, trying to focus on the tempo and figuring out the chord progressions in the melody... trying to ignore her question. I can't. "I prefer natural, but manicured," I mutter, looking down at the table and sighing in resignation. When I finally look up, she smiles and thanks me.

"Shut up," I tell her, hoping to now move on. She motions that she's zipping her lips closed. "Thank you." She nods and sips her wine as her eyes begin to scan the restaurant.

"Oh, Happy New Year," she blurts out.

"Yeah, Happy New Year, Em," I stutter back, realizing we hadn't exchanged our well-wishes for the new year.

"It wasn't so happy," she admits. *Tell me about it.*

"Oh!" *Asshole... inconsiderate bastard...* "How did your date go with David?" I feel bad for not asking sooner.

"He didn't show." She shrugs her shoulders and looks down at the table, tracing the knots in the wood with her fingernails.

"At all?" She shakes her head. "Did he call?" She looks up at me, her sad expression answering for her. "Fucking moron."

"Yeah, I know," she huffs, rolling her eyes and wiping away a tear before it has a chance to form.

I immediately see where her mind has gone. "*Him*, Emi. Not you. He's a fucking moron for standing you up."

"Thanks for saying that."

"It's the truth. And don't dwell on him... you're too good for him. What a pussy," I laugh. "I'm sure he's regretting it now. Just do me a favor and tell me he doesn't get a third chance, because I already hate the guy." I know it's wrong for me to discourage her to pursue a relationship, even if he did fuck up royally... I mean, maybe he had a good excuse... but I can't help myself.

"No third chance. I have my dignity."

"Good girl." I pat her forearm lightly, smiling warmly. Her cheeks turn a bright shade of pink.

After we have a drink, I offer to walk Emi home. Her apartment is a few blocks southeast of mine, so it's practically on my way home. I don't want her out alone this late at night, anyway. She decides to just get a cab instead. When the taxi pulls up, I hand him a twenty and give him her address. She rolls her eyes at me as I open the door for her, but doesn't argue. She knows there's no point.

"You don't want to split the cab?" she asks.

"No, I feel like walking. Like ya, Em," I tell her, closing the door.

"Like you, too," she sings to me her usual response.

CHAPTER 3

I've just stepped out of the shower when I hear my mother's familiar knock on my front door. I hurry to find some clean jeans and throw them on, buttoning them up as I welcome Mom into the apartment.

"I'm not too early, am I?" she asks, holding her arms out to me for a hug. I embrace her and kiss her on the cheek, shaking my head at her as I pull back and smile.

"You look nice, Mom." She had chosen a slimming black dress with a plunging neckline. The diamonds my father had given to her on their first anniversary are polished and seem overly showy today. Her hair is newly-bleached, her make-up perfectly applied.

My mom is stereotypically beautiful. She was the perfect trophy-wife for my father. It wasn't until after he was gone that she truly came into her own, and I'm proud of all she has accomplished.

"You look... wet," she jokes.

"Yeah, sorry. Just a second. Let me grab a towel. Have a seat." She perches on the arm of the sofa as I towel-dry my hair.

"You didn't just get up, did you?" she questions me. "It's after one."

"It's a new years resolution to sleep in, Mom," I explain with a sheepish grin. "You always encourage me to keep my resolutions."

"Maybe that's not such a good one to make, sweetheart. The day's half over!"

"Nah. I'll be up late." She smiles, knowing there's no use in arguing. She walks over to my closet and pulls out a blue button-down shirt and a sports coat, holding them up to me.

"These are nice," she says, although I know she's not making an idle comment. It's a suggestion.

I sigh, resigned. "You're taking me to one of your fancy hang-outs today, huh?"

"It is a special occasion, Nathan." I nod and take the clothes from her, laying them on the bed as I find an undershirt. She sits back down on the sofa. "Cipriani, is that okay? They're holding our table."

"Of course it's fine," I tell her. "Whatever makes you happy, Mom."

"Just getting you to spend this afternoon with me makes me happy. You know that."

"I wouldn't miss it." I pull the jacket over the shirt and run my fingers through my damp hair one last time. "You ready?"

"Ready," she smiles, standing and hugging me once more. She pulls my shirt collar out from under the jacket. "The car's waiting downstairs." Mom never learned to drive and was chauffeured around by her driver or her current husband most of the time. She would take taxis in emergency situations only, but I never knew her to take the subway. On days like today, that was a good thing. I knew she'd be the target of a mugging, never one afraid to show her wealth.

On my way out, I whisper a message in my doorman's ear. "If Laney stops buy, can you get her number?"

"Which one is she?"

I roll my eyes at him in frustration. "Current girlfriend." *Maybe not.
Maybe I should have said the last girl I had over who isn't Emi.* He knows,
though, and nods his head.

"Have a nice afternoon, Mrs. Schraeder. Nate."

"Thanks, Marcus," we say in unison. Mom and I climb into the back of
the town car. I drum out a beat on my knees to a song that had been in my
head until my mom puts her hand over mine to stop me. It was a nervous habit
that she hated, always preferring conversation to me being silent, "lost in my
own head," as she would put it.

"Sorry. How was your New Year's?" I ask her.

"James and I had a nice night. We stayed in." She tells me the details of
their low-key evening at home as we make our way toward the restaurant.

My mother and step-father– although I never really thought of him as
such– never went out on New Year's Eve. I could understand my mother not
wanting to go out, but James was closer in age to me than he was to my mom,
and I never could understand why he didn't like being out on the town
celebrating. Before they married– in fact, before they even met– I would cross
paths with him often at some of the A-list clubs in town. He's nine years older
than me... a nice enough guy, and I know they're in love, no matter how
unconventional their relationship is. He's very different from my father. I
knew she chose him for that reason. It wasn't that she didn't like my father...
being reminded of him would just be too painful for her.

"How was *your* New Year's Eve?" Mom asks me once we are seated at
our regular table.

"Fine," I lie, forcing the corners of my lips to turn up. She glares at me.

"Sweetie, what happened?"

"It's nothing, Mom. Just a stupid fight."

"With Emi?" she asks. I scoff at her assumption. Mom thought of Emi as
the daughter she never had. In her mind, there was no Nate without Emi, and
no Emi without Nate. She was right, of course. I feel the same way...

"No, with Laney..."

"Oh, of course." My mother corrects her posture. "Is everything okay?"

"I'm sure it will be," I assure her with as much confidence as I can feign. "She drank too much and started being really unreasonable. I'm sure it's nothing." Of course it's more than nothing, but I don't really enjoy discussing my failed relationships with my mother anymore. The conversation had begun to bore me, and I could read on her face that she never really took any of my girlfriends seriously. She had other ideas.

"Mrs. Schraeder? Nate? It's nice to see you both here today," the manager greets us at our table. My mother holds her hand out to him.

"Giovanni, thank you for saving our seat. Call me Donna, please, I tell you that every time."

"Of course, Donna. My apologies." He smiles humbly. "Sparkling water?"

"Yes," we both answer. An attractive, blonde waitress delivers our drinks less than a minute later. We place our regular orders with her, as well, and my eyes follow her, study her, as she walks away.

"She's new," Mom comments, getting my attention. I ignore her observation, hoping she didn't notice me staring but sure that she did.

"How are you holding up today, Mom?" I ask, changing the subject.

"I'm okay, sweetheart." She places her hand on mine. "You?"

"I'm good." I don't necessarily need these get-togethers anymore. I've remembered my father in my own ways enough over the years, but I do it for my mother. Celebrating my father at this time of the year is more important than any birthday or holiday to her.

"Your father would have loved this weather today," she starts. "It was just like this on our wedding day."

My parents got married on New Year's Day, twenty-nine years ago. I was born the following November. Growing up, we had celebrated their anniversary as a family every year until he passed. Since then, my mom and I make it a point to have a day together to honor him at the beginning of every year.

"I was going through the attic the other day, and I ran across that painting you had done of you and him." I frown a little, remembering the artwork I had created from a still photo of my father and me. I hadn't seen it since about a week after we buried him. My mother's parents helped her put away many mementos of him because she couldn't bear the pain it caused her to see them every day.

"I remember that one. Did you bring it down?"

"No," she says quietly. "It still made me cry."

"Good," I tell her. That painting is too personal to me. Most portraits I have done are. Those aren't the paintings I display at gallery shows or even in my apartment. My public style is abstract. I've hidden away the portraits, choosing to keep those for me and only me. I know I have an eye for portraiture that most artists dream of having... and I know I would be more "successful" as an artist if I decided to go that route, but it's sharing too much of myself.

"It is so beautiful, though, Nathan. Your father loved you so much."

"Thanks, Mom." I squeeze her hand.

I loved him, too. He could do no wrong in my eyes, even though he apparently had one major flaw. A fatal one, as it turned out.

My mother and father met through my maternal grandfather. Dad was a successful business man, working for my grandpa. He was intelligent, dedicated and focused, and worked his way up through the company quickly. Grandpa always said he saw himself in my father, so on the day he turned 55, he handed over the company to Dad, turning him into the youngest executive the company had ever had at twenty-eight.

Wow. My dad was my age when he began running his own company... and when he met my mother. He had accomplished so much already in his life. I reflect inwardly on what I've done with mine. A fledgling art career. Fleeting romances. Too much idle time on my hands. I wonder what my dad's expectations would have been of me, had he lived to see me become an adult. I wonder if I would be a let down to him, or if he would have accepted the man I've become as my mother has.

Shortly after dad took over, he met my mother. She was only eighteen, a recent high-school graduate who always dreamed of the perfect nuclear family. She wanted a successful husband, two or three children she could raise at home, a nice house... a picket fence... my mom was a dreamer, an idealist. She knew what she wanted and she knew she'd attain it.

Her father encouraged her to apply for a position as a personal secretary for dad, trying to teach his daughter to have a little independence. Begrudgingly, she applied for the job. The interview turned into a romantic dinner, and it was apparently love-at-first-sight. My grandfather couldn't have been happier for his daughter and his protégé. He knew Mom would be in good hands, all her dreams realized. She never worked a single day while my father was alive.

My parents married six months later. Dad swept her off her feet and she had the wedding that every girl dreams of. "That was the most magical day of my life," my mom remembers fondly. She always says that no other day could ever compare to the day that she married my father.

Mom got pregnant quickly, but complications arose, and it turned out I would be the only child she would ever have. My father was delighted to have a son, and instead of being sad about her inability to have additional kids, she focused all of her attention on giving me the perfect life. I was their gift, their little miracle. They lavished me with their love and anything I ever asked for. And my mom spent all of her time with me. I never went without, but I also never took anything for granted. My dad taught me early on that hard work brought us the fortunate life we had. I knew the consequences of all the things we had, too: he sacrificed his time to make sure Mom and I never went without anything. From the outside, we *did* look like the perfect family.

In her eyes, no man would ever compare to him. She had told me that many times over the years. She loved him deeply. His tragic death nearly destroyed her. He had become her life.

This tragic death was caused by his secret life. Well, it was a secret from me. All those late nights in his private study, or away at the office... I just assumed he was that busy. I accepted it; after all, I had no idea it should be any other way. Except for that one day– the day he died– I only have happy memories of my father. After his busy workweek, he reserved the weekends for me and Mom. Every Saturday morning, my mother would wake up early and fix breakfast for us. Cereal was a bad word on weekends. It was always eggs made to order, a choice of either pancakes, Belgium waffles or toast, and a big glass of milk or orange juice. Dad would also have bacon or sausage, but I couldn't stomach either. I still remember the graphic news report on slaughterhouses that stayed imprinted in my mind. I was only five when I saw it, but I never ate meat again after that. There was never any argument. My parents let me be me, all my life.

On those lazy, quiet Saturdays, Dad would consume insane amounts of coffee. Even today, when the aroma of a rich roasted brew hits my nose, images of my father play in my mind. It's bittersweet. I kept thinking that the memories would fade over time with such a common smell, but they never did. I smile to myself at the thought.

"I remember how I would serve you two in bed while you watched cartoons for hours," my mom says. "I loved to see him revel in the joys of your childhood those mornings. He was such a professional most of the time, but with you... he would hold you in his arms and not laugh at the television program, but at your reaction to the shows. It didn't matter how bad his headache was, he would suffer through anything for you. I loved that about him."

"How bad his *hangover* was," I correct her with a wistful smile. She looks away from me briefly, but nods. Even to this day, she doesn't like to admit what he was.

An alcoholic. He was an alcoholic. I never would have believed it until his actions could hide the fact no longer.

"What was your favorite thing to do with Dad on Saturday afternoons?" she asks, focusing once more on the positive aspects of his life.

I ponder all the choices. Every Saturday afternoon, it was just the two of us. Mom would go out with her friends and Dad and I would find various ways to entertain ourselves. In the summer, we'd go swimming in a large pool he had built in our backyard. We were the only people in the neighborhood with a pool. You would think this would have attracted children from all over, but even as a young boy, I was more entertained by my own active imagination. I never really had any real friends until Emi came along in high school.

In the winter, we'd go sledding. On particularly mild days, we'd go for long bike rides. We visited zoos all over the east coast. My dad thought I might be a veterinarian when I grew up. I never really shared with him my artistic endeavors. It wasn't that he didn't care... but drawing and painting were things I enjoyed doing alone, and when my dad made time for me, I wanted to make every second count. I'm glad I spent those Saturdays with him. In the evenings, after a full day together, Dad would retire to his study and I would retreat to my art room. While he "worked," I committed to paper or canvas the memories and feelings of those days in abstract brush strokes and vivid colors.

For a second, I forget my mother had asked me a question.

"My favorite days were when we would feed the ducks and geese at Central Park." From my apartment window, I can see the area where the birds would nip at our feet as they volleyed for bread. I would have paid three times as much for my loft for that view. In those moments together, my dad and I talked about so many things. I was still a child, but he showed me his vulnerable, emotional side. He showed it to no one else, not even Mom. Those afternoons that we shared validated me later in life, and made me more confident in the man that I have grown up to be. I pity those men who feel that having real emotions is a weakness. To me, it makes us all more human.

"And then, on Sundays," my mom cuts in, "well, those were my favorite days. I knew it was important for you two to have your time together on Saturdays, but I loved Sundays the best. I loved getting dressed up and going to church, and then brunch after..." Her eyes begin to tear up and we clasp each other's hands tightly. After brunch, we would sometimes go see movies or go shopping as a family. Other days we'd go for long walks or fly a kite in the park. If the weather wasn't good, we would go to museums.

"I loved it when it rained," I tell her.

"For the museums," she responds with a smile. "You loved the art museums."

"Still do." I smile fully, grateful that I had parents who introduced me to culture and encouraged my interests.

The vast majority of my memories of Dad come from those weekends. It was almost as if he didn't exist in my world during the week. It was my mother who would help me with my homework in the evenings. Our housekeeper cooked meals for the two of us. I didn't miss my father during the week, though. With such a sheltered childhood, I assumed all families operated in the same way.

One April night, when I was ten, I woke up to the sound of my mother screaming. I sat up and huddled in the corner of my bed, against the wall, my blankets pulled up to my chin. I cried, too afraid to get up until her wailing turned into quiet sobs. The phone rang a few times without being answered. My over-active imagination created all sorts of scenarios, each one more horrible to think about than the last. I never heard my father.

I couldn't hear my father. That single thought is what eventually lured me from my bed. Why wasn't my father answering the phone? Or helping her? Could he not hear that she was in pain, hurting, upset? I pulled myself together and decided I needed to help her. Not knowing what was waiting outside of my bedroom door, I picked up a baseball bat that had been given to me by one of my mother's friends. It was the first time I had ever held the bat in my hands, having no interest whatsoever in sports. I gripped it tightly and cracked the door open until I could finally see my mother hunched over on the steps. I could still hear her crying, although it was obvious she was trying to keep her noises to a minimum.

I tiptoed to the top of the steps and watched her, my presence unbeknownst to her. She sat on the very last step with her head in her hands. She was still in her pajamas, her hair messy. I immediately knew something was wrong. No matter what time of day or night, my mother's hair was always perfect, her make-up applied. She always wanted to look her best for Dad.

I peeked into her bedroom before I started taking the stairs down, one by one. My father was not in there. His side of the bed was still made.

"Mom?" I had asked her quietly from a few steps behind her.

She jumped, startled, but didn't turn around. "Nathan," she began, her voice monotone, "can you go back to your room?"

"Mom, what's wrong?" I pressed for more information.

"Nathan." Her voice was more stern. "Grandma will be here in a few minutes. Can you go to your room please until she gets here?"

"Mom, where's Dad?"

She grabbed her legs and buried her head into her knees. She wouldn't answer me, even once I repeated the question.

"Dad?!" I yelled upstairs toward the bedroom they shared, where he should have been, where I already knew he wasn't. Mom started crying harder. I turned around and ran up the stairs, screaming for my father. He didn't answer.

I entered the bedroom and looked around everywhere, as if he would be standing somewhere in a corner, in the closet, under the bed. He was nowhere. I turned around and headed back down the stairs toward his office, the only other place he might be.

"Mom, where's Dad?" I repeated. She sobbed louder, unable to hold her emotions in any longer. "Mom?" I felt the lump in my throat growing, growing so big that I couldn't swallow and tears began streaming down my face. I ran down the stairs past her, but she grabbed my arm before I could round the corner down the hallway that would lead to the study. I dropped the bat immediately and turned around, examining the look in her eyes intently. "Mom, where's Dad?!" I yelled, my face just inches from hers.

She stared at me with a glassy look in her eyes. I put my hands on her cheeks and made her focus on me.

"Where is he?"

"He's gone, Nathan," she said, pulling my hands from her face and holding onto them tightly. I knew immediately that she didn't mean that he had left us. My dad would never leave us. He loved us more than anything. I knew at that very second that he had died. A minute later– or maybe it was an hour, I couldn't tell, as time had stopped when the realization hit– my grandmother walked in the door and ran to my mother and me. She cried heavily as she pulled us close and hugged us tightly. The embrace was warm, but could never comfort me. My grandfather followed in a minute later. He, too, had tears welling in his eyes.

"Donna, baby, I'm so sorry," he said as he sat down on the step with my mother.

"It was him?" my mother asked quietly. I looked at both of them, back and forth, watching him nod and watching more tears push their way out of her eyes.

"*What* was him? *Who* was him? Where's my dad?" I couldn't control my emotions anymore. My grandfather, still strong in his older years, caught me in his arms as I began to collapse. He carried me as if I weighed nothing to my father's study, leaving the women on the steps to console one another. Grandpa sat me down in dad's large leather chair. I looked around the room, a room that was off limits to me, a room that never interested me before. I saw it through new eyes that night.

As Grandpa told me he had just come from the morgue and identified my father's body, he also revealed to me the truth about his alcoholism. The pretty crystal glasses and ewers that lined the cabinet across the room came into focus. The cabinet doors were always locked, and I never even questioned what might be concealed behind them. My grandfather continued to fill in the blanks as I stared with curiosity at that cabinet. My father had died in a car accident. He had driven his sedan into a tree. No other cars were involved, no one else was hurt. I still couldn't comprehend what happened. How could someone just drive into a tree? Had he fallen asleep? Lost his way? I couldn't stop asking him questions. I wouldn't let it go. Finally, Grandpa connected the dots that my innocent brain could not. Dad had been drinking when the accident happened. He was drunk.

Still, I couldn't believe it. I had never seen my father drink. I fought the idea and was convinced he was lying to me. I didn't understand why he would make up something like this. I can remember the rage I felt, the anger that propelled me to run back into the foyer where my mother and grandmother sat. I grabbed that baseball bat and ran back into the office. I busted up every piece of crystal, every glass, the cabinet itself. I broke the doors open and discovered the immense collection of bourbon and whiskey and wine and...

I put my head in my hands just as the food is delivered to our table. I could still remember the expression of shock on my mother's face as she watched me destroy my father's office. I look up to see the waitress giving me a sweet smile. It's almost enough to draw me out of the memory, but not quite.

The adults stood back as I threw every bottle across the room, spilling the contents of each one on the plush carpet and textured walls. The stench in the study was sickening when I was finished. I had cut myself a few times, too, as my bare feet found shards embedded in the rug.

"You're thinking about the glasses, aren't you?" my mother asks, interrupting my reverie. I stare at the delicate flute of ice water in my hand, rubbing the condensation beneath my thumb.

"Yeah."

"They were just glasses." And even as she says it, I can still hear the sadness in her voice. "It didn't compare to losing *him*."

"No, I know."

I would find out years later that I had destroyed the champagne flutes that my parents used to toast at their wedding. They were heirlooms, handed down for generations.

"I'll never stop being sorry for destroying those, though, Mom."

"Don't be silly, Nathan. I was only saving them to give to you for your own wedding. At this rate, you may never have gotten them anyway," she tries to joke with me. "You'd have to pick a girl and keep her."

I roll my eyes but smile anyway. "Yeah, yeah... keep it up and I won't stick around for coffee." It's a hollow threat and she knows it.

My mom reaches across the table and takes my hand into hers. We both bow our heads, each sending our own private message to the man we both loved, before eating our lunch.

As we dine, we're both silent with our thoughts. When I got a little older, I had been so angry with my mother for keeping such a secret from me.

As a child, when Dad was alive, Mom had always been concerned about creating the perfect vision of the perfect family. Alcoholism had no place in that vision. Over the years, as I tried to cope, I learned from her that she didn't realize he was an alcoholic when they first met. She knew he drank often, but he was always so happy-go-lucky that she didn't realize it was a problem— until she realized that he couldn't go through a day without a drink or two, or ten. All those nights he retired to his study, it was to hide his drinking from me.

Dad was a happy drunk, apparently. He was never abusive to Mom or to me, and because of that, my mom never encouraged him to seek help. He seemed to be able to still do his job, and do it well, until the last few months before he died. My grandfather had taken him aside a few times to try to talk some sense into my father. Dad was a good liar, and although he told Grandpa that he was fine, that he could quit— in fact that he had quit— the frequency of his drinking increased. He began to go out to drink instead of drinking at home. This worried my mother, but if any fights arose from it, they kept those from me, as well.

I was angry with my parents for quite some time. Mad at him for dying; mad at her for hiding his alcoholism from me. After a period of rebellion in high school that put my mother through hell, I eventually went to therapy and sorted through the issues. Some time later, I forgave them both. I learned that alcoholism was an illness, and that Dad had just been sick. And I knew that my mother had only the best intentions. She thought she was doing what was right for me. When faced with peer pressure in high school, I thought better of things and decided to never become an alcoholic like my father. If someone as strong as him could be addicted to such a vice, then how could someone like me resist the temptation? I vowed to never drink.

As an adult, though, I became less rigid in my rules. I drink on special occasions, and never to excess. It's not something I find pleasure in, or seek solace in. I don't particularly like the taste, and the smell of hard liquor tends to sicken me, reminding me of the day that I found out he had died.

"Your father was such a good man," Mom says, her voice bringing me back to the present. "He loved you so much," she adds.

"He loved you, too, Mom. You could see it every time he looked at you." I'd never seen two people so in love with one another. They set a good example, the way they revered one another.

"He did love me, I know," she smiles wistfully. "He made me very happy."

"I know."

"You're very different from your father, but you still remind me of him in some ways."

I laugh inwardly. I'm nothing like my father. He was a polished business man. Me? An artist who, on some days, can't bother to brush my own hair or put on a clean shirt. Dad knew what he wanted in life and went for it. I tend to struggle with direction and motivation. I'm single and keep to myself. He was always the center of attention.

"How so?" I ask my mother curiously.

"Your passion for what you do..." she starts. My father loved to work, and his hard work paid off monetarily, just as my grandfather's hard work had paid off when he ran the company. Both men left my mother and me everything when they died. It's not the best way to get money, but it's afforded me a lifestyle that I enjoy. It's also probably hindered any sense of urgency to succeed in many facets of life, professionally or personally.

"...and your capacity to love," my mother continues, smiling. I raise an eyebrow at her.

"You put so much energy into your relationships. And the way you are when you're in love... it reminds me of the way your father was. It reminds me of the way he looked at me. So adoring, so sweet... I know you love with all of your heart, just as your father loved me."

I sigh heavily and fight the urge to roll my eyes. I love too well for my own good.

"I just wish *you* could find one girl to look at so sweetly, so adoringly," she says. As much as honoring my father was a yearly tradition, so, too, was this conversation about my love life, which always ended up with the same question. *What about Emi?* "What do you think about Laney? Am I going to get to meet her?"

I don't let my mother meet very many of my girlfriends. Early in my adult life, I would take women to meet my mother early on, as soon as I started thinking she might be the one. After about ten women, though, I began to hold off on introductions. I put a time limit on the relationship since I seemed to fall in love rather quickly. My own self-imposed rule would require me to be dating a woman for six months before I'd introduce her to my mother. Since I made that decision, Mom had met exactly one woman– and she and I broke up about a month later.

"I don't know, Mom," I answer. I know she won't. I'm fairly certain I'll never see Laney again. After the way she acted last night, I've already begun to accept that she's not right for me.

We finish our meals and order coffee. I watch the waitress– Samantha, her name badge reads– as she walks away. She had smiled at me again, her eyes eager and bright. She was very attractive.

"Well, I'd like to meet her if she's someone special to you. I want you to find someone who makes you as happy as your father made me... and as happy as James makes me now."

"I'll let you know, Mother," I retort, short with her. Through my tone, she knows I don't want to talk about Laney anymore.

"How's Emi?"

"She's doing well. She's been really busy with her freelance stuff," I answer. "I haven't seen much of her lately."

"Is she dating anyone?" she asks less-than-innocently.

"No, not that I know of." Emi dating– such a foreign concept to me. It was funny and sad at the same time. She was so quick to write off men. Rarely were there second dates with her. And it wasn't that she wasn't amiable, attractive, desirable. She was all of those things once people got to know her. Men always asked for another date, but she rarely allowed for them. She was such a dreamer, and she was in search of "the one." She had her one requirement. One standard that I didn't find to be realistic, but it wasn't a topic either of us cared to discuss anymore.

"She's such a sweet girl, Nathan. You know how much I like her."

"I do. And it's never gonna happen, Mom."

"Never say never," she warned playfully. She cut me off before I could argue. "I just don't know why you say that. I'll never understand you two," she says, frustrated.

"Then please just stop trying. She's my best friend. It's fine with me." *It's fine with me for now, anyway.* "I don't think she'll ever be anything more than that."

"Is that because you don't want it? Or because she doesn't want it?"

"It's both," I tell her, sounding more agitated than I mean to, but we've had this exact conversation every year for the past ten years. I know that Emi wants something that I can't give her. I tried. I failed.

50

"Well, you're both silly. If you could see yourselves together, Nathan, you'd–"

Samantha brings our coffees to us.

"Thank you, Samantha," I tell her, lightly touching her hand, glad that she interrupted my mom's train of thought.

"You're welcome," she says with a blush, "Nathan?"

"Just Nate," I correct her, smiling.

"Nate," she nods, her blue eyes staring into mine.

"You can bring our check by any time, dear," my mother instructs her.

"Yes, ma'am," Samantha responds politely, backing away nervously.

"Nathan," Mom says as I turn my attention back to her. "You know I only talk to you like this because I care so much. And I know you make one another happy."

"As all friends should," I answer. "Who'd want to be friends with people who make you miserable?" I mumble sarcastically under my breath.

"I just wish you'd be open to the possibilities."

I shake my head and laugh at her. "That's enough, Mom. She's more than happy to be your 'adopted daughter' without having a romantic relationship with me. She adores you."

"She adores *you*," she counters.

"Not like you insinuate. Trust me."

"But–"

"Mom, come on. Please? Leave this alone. It's not meant to be."

"Okay, Nathan. I'm sorry. Oh, but before I forget, when I spoke with her last week, she mentioned you have a performance on Friday."

"I do. When'd you talk to her?"

"Christmas Eve. She called to wish us a Merry Christmas." *Of course she did.* "Where is your performance?"

"At a dive bar in Brooklyn," I tell her. "It's not a place you'd enjoy, or I would have invited you myself."

"Well, James and I don't have plans..."

"Really, Mom. I think you'd feel really out of place. I promise next time we play at that coffee house you like, I'll let you know."

"Okay." We exchange smiles.

We both sip our drinks in silence until Samantha finally brings the check. She sets it in front of me, but my mother leans over the table and takes it before I have a chance to pay. Samantha's cheeks turn bright red as she watches my mother put cash in the folder. Mom pulls out her copy of the receipt and folds the leather holder closed, handing it back to our waitress.

"Thank you, ma'am," Samantha says, bowing her head and taking the money from my mom. She walks quickly away from the table without meeting my eyes again. I'm a little disappointed.

"You ready?" I ask my mom.

"Sure," she smiles.

Before we get into her car, she stops me and tears her receipt in half.

"I believe this belongs to you, not me," she says, handing the scrap of paper to me and climbing into the back seat. "If things don't work out with Laney."

I look down and see a note written in neat, cursive handwriting. *"Here's my number,"* it says with a phone number beneath. *"I thought you'd like to call me sometime. Sam."*

"She seems a little young for you," my mother adds as I get in the car next to her. It definitely makes for an awkward ride home, but inside, I'm looking forward to calling her anyway.

Once back at my apartment building, Marcus shakes his head at me, communicating to me that Laney didn't stop by. I never thought she would.

CHAPTER 4

On Friday, an hour and a half before the gig, I start to tune my guitar and go over a song I had written lyrics for the summer before college. I started working out the chords and melody a few months ago, feeling nostalgic and melancholy one night. I haven't played it for my bandmates yet, so if I decide to perform it tonight, it'll be acoustic. It's how I envisioned it to be played anyway. Acoustic, in a dimly lit room, just me and her. If Emi does come tonight, I'll strike it from the set list. She said she had some illustrations to finish up on one of her magazine projects. She told me she hoped to make it.

I hope she does– and then mentally kick myself back into reality. I don't know why I struggle with my attraction to Emi when I'm not in a relationship. It's never a problem when I'm seeing someone. I'm always able to direct my full attention and affections to my girlfriend with no trouble. With Laney seemingly out of the picture, my mind again begins to wrangle with the what-ifs. It's not something I like to even consider.

I take a quick shower before going through my closet to find something to wear. Our band's sound has matured over the years that we'd been playing together. When we started, it was a strange infusion of folk and punk, so when we used to play clubs, we'd find our rattiest t-shirts and jeans and our oldest Chuck Taylors to fit the music. Since we've pretty much abandoned the punk aspect, I decide on a burnt orange button-down over a clean, white t-shirt, pressed jeans and some boots I had bought for myself for Christmas. I run my fingers through my hair and grab my brown leather jacket before heading out the door.

The small scrap of paper sits next to my keys and phone. I pick up the innocuous receipt and debate dialing Samantha's number to set up a date with her. I know I need a distraction, but decide to leave the paper on the table as I gather the rest of my things and leave the loft.

Marcus stops me in the lobby.

"Nate, you just missed Laney." I glance outside the glass entranceway, but there's no sign of her. A sense of relief settles over me. Maybe I wasn't as in love with her as I thought.

"Why did she come?"

Marcus walks to the reception desk and picks up a box, and I recognize it as the same one I had given her for Christmas. Inside was a vintage-style Hermes scarf that Emi's sister, Jen, had picked out when the three of us went shopping for holiday gifts. When I open the lid, I see the scarf is still folded up inside.

"She dropped this off?" I ask him.

"She said she wasn't particularly fond of the colors, and thought there might be someone else who would enjoy it more."

"That doesn't sound like Laney," I tell Marcus, imagining the words "particularly fond" coming out of Laney's mouth. They never would.

"I may have worded it a little more politely," he admits. I laugh quietly and nod. "Personally, the color reminds me of Judy's eyes." I'd met his wife, Judy, quite a few times over the seven years he'd worked as the doorman of the building. I could tell that she had been stunning in her youth. I look under the scarf to see if Laney also returned the Louis Vuitton gift card I had given her. *Of course not.*

"I tell you what, Marcus. Why don't you take this home to Judy? A belated Hanukkah gift."

"I couldn't take it," he argues, pushing the box back into my hands.

"Really, Marcus. It's certainly not my style. And I don't have anyone else to give it to."

"But you could get a refund."

I roll my eyes at him. My wealth is no secret to him. "Please take it. It would make me happy to know that *some* woman enjoys it."

Marcus silently wavers, but eventually relents with a smile. He takes the box back. "You're too generous, Nate. And she wasn't good enough for you," he adds, knowing all too well that yet another relationship of mine has come to an abrupt end. "Pretty, but a little shallow."

I shrug my shoulders and begin to walk toward the doors. "You overestimate me," I call back to him. The valet hands me my keys and I get into the car, admittedly driving a little too quickly on my way to Brooklyn.

When I arrive at the bar, I seek out Eric, my drummer, and Jason, my bass player. Both are drinking with women I've never seen before. When they introduce me, I understand that they have all just met, and have made plans to go out for a late dinner after we play. I decline their invitation to join them. On my way to the stage, I glance around, but don't see Emi. I grab a table at the front and drape my jacket over the back of a chair. When a waitress approaches, I order a glass of water and a glass of wine.

"You can set the water on the stage, but leave the wine on the table."

Just in case she shows up.

We start to set up our equipment on stage after meeting briefly with the manager. I apologize again for missing the last gig, but he already seems to have forgotten about it.

"Guys," I address my bandmates. "I've got a new one I think I might want to do a few songs in. It's a slow number. I can do it acoustic."

"You don't trust our improv skills? Jackass," Eric says under his breath, but I know he's kidding.

"If you guys want to join in, that's fine," I tell them, confident in their combined talent.

The drinks arrive in the middle of the first song. The wine sits by itself on the table in front, and I can't stop my eyes from drifting back there every few seconds.

When Emi doesn't show up after the third song, I decide she isn't coming. I turn around to Eric and Jason and give them both a signal that I'd like to perform the new song I had written.

A few bars in, Eric starts in with a light high-hat cymbal beat that provides a perfect understated rhythm to the song. By the middle of the first verse, Jason has figured out a complementary bass line. I smile at the beautiful sound, singing the words I'd penned for her, staring at that full wine glass that I'd ordered for her.

"And at the time, it all felt right
When we first met that fateful night
I held you close, I took you in
You looked at me. Oh, what could've been."

When the chorus begins, I'm startled to see the wine glass move. Consumed by the song, it takes a moment for me to realize what's happened. I hadn't noticed her enter the bar, nor had I seen her sit down right in front of me.

"It should've been me
That tasted the sweet–
But he was the one
Whose–"

My heart skips a beat as I watch Emi sip the wine. She waves at me when my eyes meet hers, and I swallow the words I'd written before any more can escape my lips. I stop playing the guitar abruptly, embarrassed. The guys continue on for a few more seconds, but stop when I wave my hand at them.

"Sorry," I apologize to the audience. "It's a new song we haven't quite rehearsed. I forgot the words," I say with a charming smile and a few strums of my guitar. The audience is kind as they laugh quietly. Emi's brows furrow in confusion. I've never botched a performance before, and she's seen many. I look away quickly, afraid she heard too much already and can read my thoughts.

"Guys, let's move on," I say to Eric and Jason, feeling the heat rise to my cheeks. It's not until the chorus of the next song that I fully recover. I look back over at her and smile, the sweet look on her face reminding me of her enduring friendship that I never want to be without.

"Thank you," she mouths to me after another sip. She takes off her coat to reveal a low-cut sweater that accentuates her chest. She was not blessed with large breasts, but they fit her frame perfectly, beautifully. The pink sweater brings out the rosy color on her pale cheeks, and compliments her strawberry blonde hair perfectly. I, again, find myself looking in the opposite direction before she can catch me ogling her.

During the next song, a pink drink with an umbrella is delivered to Emi's table. The waitress whispers something in her ear and nods to a table of men in the corner. Emi picks up the glass and smiles to one eager man in particular before taking a drink. He waves shyly, and I know he's doomed already. As his friends try to convince him to go over to her table, he tries to shake them off, obviously nervous. One of Emi's biggest turn-offs is a man without confidence. Poor sap. It takes four more songs before he finally gets the nerve to go over to her. I watch the interaction carefully, my fingers strumming the familiar chords with no concentration required, the words coming easily.

He asks if the seat is taken– the seat that my coat is draped over. When

Emi looks at me, I simply raise my eyebrows at her, my expression a little mocking, questioning her assessment of the situation. Her cheeks turn bright pink as she shakes her head and the man sits down next to her. His mannerisms are awkward, and I swear his hand is shaking as he takes a swig from his bottle of cheap beer.

Emi must notice this too, as her fingers gently rest on top of his when he sets his drink down. I can imagine her words to him, soothing, reassuring, telling him not to be nervous. She is always the one to put people at ease. She's a natural. He has no chance with her, I know this instantly, but she's never one to be rude or judgmental, and her friendly smile opens the door to more conversation.

By the end of the set, they're laughing together, but I can see the distance Emi's putting between them by her body language. I can read her so well. I thank the applauding crowd, and then invite another round of praise for Eric and Jason. Emi stands to clap, and the man next to her does the same.

After packing up my guitar and saying goodbye to my friends, I descend the steps and approach Emi's table. She walks past the man to me, giving me a big hug. I take her in my arms and kiss her on the cheek.

"Thanks for coming," I speak softly in her ear. "Who's your friend?"

She pulls away from me, her teeth biting her smiling bottom lip. I've made her blush with my greeting, which is just fine with me.

"Oh, um, Grant?" she says to her new companion. "This is my friend, Nate."

"Nate, nice to meet you," he says as he extends his hand to me. *Weak handshake. Nope, not for Emi.*

"Likewise," I tell him.

"Um, thank you for the drink, Grant," she tells him, gathering her coat and mine. "Are you ready to go, Nate?"

"Go?" I ask her, my face serious.

"To dinner. We have reservations?"

"Do we?" The pitch of my voice is higher than usual as I play with her.

Her back to Grant, she glares with her beautiful, pleading, green eyes.

"We do, remember?"

"Ah, yes. You were going to treat me to dinner. Right."

"Right," she nods. "It was a pleasure to meet you, Grant. And thank you for the drink."

"You already said that," I whisper in her ear as she backs away from the table. She turns quickly and grabs my forearm, dragging me out of the bar. She groans in frustration when we exit into the cold night. I set my guitar down and help her with her coat before putting mine on.

"You... you!" she yells at me, eloquent as always.

"Me, me... I know. I'm sorry. I couldn't help myself."

"Where's your car?" she snaps at me.

I can't help but laugh a little. "Two streets south in a sketchy looking lot." She nods and begins to walk quickly to the north. "South is this way, Em." She groans again and pivots around, running right into Grant as he exits the bar.

"Oh, god, I'm sorry," she says, embarrassed, moving past him. He holds on to her arm to get her attention.

"No, I am. Look, if I had known you had a boyfriend..."

"She doesn't," I tell him, shaking my head. I know I need to shut up by the angry stare on her face. She sighs heavily.

"Look, Grant, you seem really nice, but I'm not really... available..." The three of us stand in awkward silence, Grant and I staring at Emi for her vague explanation.

"Okay," he says plainly.

"Okay," she smiles. "Good night." She picks up my guitar as she walks past me and continues in the direction toward the car. I follow her quickly, attempting to take the guitar from her tight grip.

"I'll get it, Em." She lets go and crosses her arms across her chest. "Emi, I was playing," I plead with her. Her short stature makes it difficult for her to walk angrily ahead of me. She doesn't look at me. "Emi..."

"Jerk," she says.

"I know, I'm sorry," I tell her sincerely. When we get to the street, I guide her toward the lot. She slams my door when she gets in. I try to figure out my next move as I walk slowly to the driver's side. After I get in, I start the car and turn the seat warmers on. "So where are you taking me to dinner?" I ask sheepishly.

Her jaw drops and she turns to look at me slowly in disbelief.

"Home then?" I ask.

A vengeful smile starts to form on her face. She pushes hard against my shoulder. "You're gonna pay for this," she says, barely able to hold in the laughter.

"Okay," I tell her with my winning smile. "I deserve that."

"You do."

"I do. That's what I said."

She rolls her eyes at me, grinning. "See if I ever come to one of your gigs again," she threatens.

"Oh, you never miss them."

"Well, maybe I'll start," she says, prissy.

"Emi," I tell her as I put the car in gear, "I'm really glad you came out tonight. Thank you. It means a lot to me." I nudge her chin playfully with my finger and see her blush again. Before I allow myself to gaze into her seemingly-smitten eyes, I pull out of the parking lot.

I know that my charming ways make her giddy at times, but I know not to go any further than that. We had decided long ago that our friendship should always take precedent over any fleeting romantic feelings. It's not that they didn't exist from time to time. The idea is always out there, sometimes distant, and sometimes not... and there is clearly something between us, but I still have doubts that I could ever be enough for her. She's an idealist, looking for that soulmate. She always seems to look beyond me. And I know she should. From past experience, I know she should.

"What was up with that new song?" Emi asks when I pull up to her apartment building.

"I just forgot the words."

"You seemed entranced by it," she says. "Did you write it?"

"Yeah, a while back."

"Well, I liked what I heard."

"Thanks. It needs some work." A veiled smile hides my real feelings about the song. She tells me good night and gets out of the car. I watch to make sure she gets inside okay, then begin my short drive home thinking about the inspiration behind the song.

One night, more than nine years ago, something happened that told me what I never wanted to know... what I always wanted to forget, but couldn't.

Emi's brother had called me one Friday night. He was drunk, and apparently, so was Emi. He needed someone to pick her up from a party before she got herself in trouble. I was still in high school in New Jersey, and she was in her first semester at NYU, but even then, he knew I would do anything for her.

Anger clouded my eyes when I pulled up in front of the frat house. A stranger's hands were on her cheeks, holding Emi's face close to his. She was trying to move away from him, her hands pressed against his chest. *Or were they gripping his shirt, holding him closer? No, certainly not.* Eventually they stopped kissing, and he held her arm as she slid off the picnic table and stood next to him.

I revved the engine and eventually got the guy's attention... Emi's, too. I got out of the car quickly, and I could tell she finally felt safe enough to move away from him.

"Emi," I said, exhaling as I spoke.

"Hey," she said quietly as I glanced at the frat boy. When she started to cry, she was the only thing in my vision. I couldn't get to her fast enough, but when I finally reached her, I pulled her into my arms, holding on to her, whispering assurances in her ear.

"It's okay, I'm here. Shhh..." She sniffled loudly in my ear. "Are you okay?"

She pulled away and looked up at me, looking sorry and apologetic. She nodded, a motion so subtle I barely caught it. Relieved, I kissed her forehead and pulled her back into my chest before trying to walk her to the car. She was unsteady, clearly drunk. Even with my careful steps, she managed to trip us both. Once I knew she was alright, we laughed quietly.

"Come on, Em," I urged her as I opened the door. She sat down, folding her hands in her lap, obviously obeying me. I pulled the belt across her body, moving her arms out of the way when she wouldn't, and buckled her safely in. I closed the door and smiled at her as she looked up at me, smiling back. I brushed the hair out of her eyes and then felt her hand on the back of my neck, pulling my head to hers.

I shook my head, unsure what she was trying to do. I took her hand in mine, kissed it and placed it back in her lap. I returned to my side of the car and looked back at the guy who still stood motionless next to that table. The anger was immediately back, and I hoped my eyes were communicating it to him as I stared into his. I wondered if Chris knew what had happened in the time that had passed since he called and the time I actually showed up. I wasn't sure that Emi even knew.

I sped away from the frat house quickly, glancing back only once in hopes of seeing the guy's face one more time. He had dark hair, but that was the only physical characteristic I really latched on to, too occupied with taking control of the situation, and I really wanted to remember him... really wanted to go back and let him know it wasn't okay to take advantage of drunk girls—especially the one sitting next to me in my convertible. He had already gone inside, though. *Fucking coward.*

"Did you see him?" Emi asked.

"I didn't get a good enough look. Did he hurt you?" I asked, worried.

"Hurt me?" She sounded like she snorted when she laughed. "God, no, he was beautiful. When he kissed me, it was unreal. Like nothing I've ever felt before in my whole entire life. Nate, I think he's the one."

"No," I laughed back at her. "You're drunk. He definitely was not the one. What would have happened if I hadn't shown up?"

"I don't know," she said, unbuckling her seatbelt when we got to a stop sign. "Good question, let me out and we'll see." She struggled with the door handle, unable to swing the door open. I would always turn the child locks on to piss her off, and I hadn't remembered to enable them after the last time she was in my car. I was thankful for that now. "Let me out," she whined.

"No, Emi," I coaxed her, tried to calm her down. "Sit back down and buckle your seatbelt. I'm taking you to your dorm. Are your roommates there?" I buckled her back in myself, watched an adorable pout form on her sumptuous lips... lips that another man had the pleasure of tasting... lips that I had always wanted to press against my own. She adjusted herself in the car, curling her legs under her body and leaning her shoulder against the seat, while she looked at me with pleading eyes. I touched her face gently with the back of my hand and closed my eyes, imagining a kiss with my best friend. A car horn from behind us snapped me back to attention.

"Fuck off!" Emi yelled to the car.

"Alright," I sighed, taking the corner a little too fast as I raised the convertible top up to protect us from any more trouble. "Behave, Emi."

"He was cute," she said as I rolled up the windows. "The guy at the party was so cute. And perfect. I'm sure I'm in love."

"Cute or not," I argued, "he shouldn't have been taking advantage of you in the condition you're in. How much did you have to drink, anyway?"

She just shook her head, shrugged her shoulders and smiled at me with a dreamy look in her eyes.

"*You're* cute." Her hand reached out and touched my lips and I almost drove into another car at her gesture.

"Hands to yourself, Em," I had whispered to her. "Don't distract me while I'm driving."

"Oh, do I distract you?" she said, removing her seatbelt again. She wrapped her arms around me and kissed my cheek. I had to pull over.

"Emi, listen to me," I started, carelessly parked beside a curb only two blocks from her apartment. I pried her arms from my neck. "Chris thought I was the best option to get you home safely... and you're about to kill us both. Please, sit down, Em."

She crossed her arms across her chest and sat back down with her feet on the floorboard. I buckled her into the car yet again.

"Thank you."

I had to circle her block a few times to find a place to park, and eventually settled on a spot with a two-hour limit. When I finally took the keys from the ignition, I watched as Emi's head slowly slid off the headrest and into the window.

"Ow," she sighed softly, still not fully awake. As I walked to the side of her car, my phone rang.

"Randi, what's up?" I had left my girlfriend abruptly when Chris called.

"Are you coming back?"

"She's in pretty bad shape," I told her.

"Well, you left me in pretty bad shape, too," she responded, her voice sexy.

I chuckled a little. "I'm sorry, baby. I don't think I'll make it back tonight."

"You're staying there?" she asked, panicked.

"For a bit," I explained. "Until I know she's okay, that's all."

"Fuck, Nate, you'll risk getting grounded again for her? This was our first night out in two fucking weeks! It's our social life you're fucking up, you know?"

"Hold up, Randi, I'm not going to get grounded. Mom knows where I'm at. She told me to take care of her."

"So she'll let you spend the night with Emi, but–"

"I'm not spending the night with her, okay?" I argued. "I'm just staying until I know she's okay. Until I make sure her roommates can take care of her.

Plus, it's Emi. You know her. You know it's not like that with her."

"It better not be," she said before hanging up on me. *Nice.*

I cautiously opened the passenger door, ready to catch Emi before she fell out of the car. I wrapped her in my arms and carried her to the front door of her apartment building before leaning her up against the brick wall to take a rest. She was like dead weight in my arms, and I was no athlete in high school. I didn't start working out until college, so that night, I was just some scrawny kid trying to do the gentlemanly thing without dropping her.

A friend of hers I had met a few times recognized us both and managed to sneak us past the resident advisor. I knocked on Emi's apartment door a few times, but no one answered. I eventually dug through her purse until I found the key that let us in.

"Teresa?" I called out into the dark and quiet space. No one answered. "Anyone home?" It was still and silent. I laid Emi on the couch and knocked on both bedroom doors before peeking in. No one was home. "Alright, Emi," I said, lifting her off the sofa.

"I wanna feel it again," Emi mumbled, touching her lips.

"Huh?" Suddenly my imagination began to run wild, and I wondered what that guy really had done to her without her knowledge. "What did he do, Emi?" Her eyes flitted open, looked at me curiously, and then closed again as I carried her to her bed.

I removed her sneakers and, once safely under her covers, I went to her bathroom and grabbed a couple of towels in case she threw up in the night. I spread them on either side of her head, then sat down next to her and watched her slow breathing and her eyes wandering restlessly under her eyelids.

I carefully took her hair out of the rubber bands and calmed the spiky hair gently with my hand. She looked so young and innocent as she slept beside me. I mean, she was. Nineteen, and still a virgin. I couldn't get the image of her kissing that frat guy out of my head, though, but it wasn't anger that I was feeling now. It was sheer curiosity. I wanted to know what it felt like to kiss her. I'd wanted to know that from the day I met her. I guess all I needed to do all along was get her drunk... but then she knew that was never going to happen with me.

I sighed heavily and went into her kitchen and grabbed a bottle of water for her, setting it on the night stand next to her bed. She rolled over on her side and pulled the blankets up to her chin. I stroked her soft hand, wondering if I should leave or stay to make sure she didn't need anything.

When I finally accepted she was sleeping, I arose and grabbed my keys. I leaned over and kissed her cheek softly, a hint of cinnamon lingering in the air. I tucked her hair behind her ear and kneeled down next to her.

Just one kiss... she'd never know... I thought long and hard about what I was thinking of doing. It was no better than what the other guy did, I knew that. But she was passed out... and it was a harmless kiss. A peck, really. My lips barely touching hers. But I had to know how it felt. How she felt.

I moved slowly, watching her eyes intently, ready to pull back if she opened them. She didn't. At the last second, I closed my eyes and softly kissed her. Her lips were cold, and I inherently wanted to warm them, so I moved mine against hers slowly, moistening our lips with my tongue. I felt her hand in my hair before I realized she was kissing me back, her lips parted, the source of the cinnamon discovered as I tasted her chewing gum.

My heart pounding, I pulled away quickly and woke her up.

"What are you doing?" she asked, seemingly unaware.

"Spit out your gum, Em. I, uh, didn't want you to choke on it."

"Oh," she said, pushing the gum out of her mouth with her tongue into my hand.

"Thanks," I laughed nervously. I wrapped it in a tissue and set it next to me. "Um, go back to sleep."

"You're not leaving, are you?" she asked.

"Do you want me to?"

"No. Please stay." She scooted back and lifted up the blankets, welcoming me into the bed next to her. This wasn't the first time we had shared a bed together. There were a few times when boredom had led us to my bed, or hers, but we never did anything but nap together. And even then, we never touched, because I knew I wouldn't be able to hide my attraction to her, and that would have been an incredibly awkward conversation. In fact, every time, I had to sleep with my back to her, and the sleep was usually pretty restless for me. I always woke up before her, and sometimes found myself taking care of matters in the bathroom before she got up. I was a teenage boy, after all.

After kicking off my shoes, I climbed into the bed and turned my back to her. Suddenly her hand was on my shoulder, nudging my back into the bed, and she was sidling up next to me.

"Aren't you hot?" she asked as her hand ran up and down my chest over the wool sweater I had worn. Her eyes were still closed but a pretty smile spread across her lips.

"A little, yeah," I breathed. She gripped the hem of the sweater– and of my undershirt– and pulled them both over my head. I helped to remove them the rest of the way and threw my shirts onto the floor. "You okay?"

"I'm hot, too," she said, and before I knew it, she was unbuckling the overalls and removing both of her shirts, too.

"Emi," I tried to caution her, but once the shirts were off, her lips were on mine, hard and fast. She tossed the overalls over my head, too. *Fuck.*

"Have sex with me," she slurred.

"What?" I asked, trying to make sure I heard her right.

"Have sex with me, Nate. I'm ready. I want to."

My brain was saying no. My hormones had another idea, and my foolish teenaged heart was all in. Still, I tried to fight. "It's not a good idea." Before I could even get the sentence out, she was taking off my pants. I managed to grab my wallet out of the pocket before she had them all the way off. I was relieved to find a few condoms in the side pouch.

"Please?" she asked. Her eyes opened slightly, and it looked like she was having a hard time focusing on me. It was wrong, so fucking wrong.

"Let's slow down," I told her, apparently convinced her. Her actions became less frantic, more restrained. I needed to get control of the situation, the only one in a position to do so. "Emi, you're too drunk," I reasoned, although it pained myself to do it.

"For what?" she asked. "To have sex? That can't happen, can it?"

"It can," I explained, "but that's not what I meant. I think you're too drunk to– ohhhh..." Her fingers brushed against me under the covers, over my boxers. *Too drunk to make this decision, I wanted to say.* I couldn't, though, not with her touching me like that. My lips found hers immediately as her fingers explored my body beneath the sheets. It felt amazing, but it still didn't feel *right*, and I made the conscious decision to keep my hands above her shoulders, cradling her head as we kissed.

"Why don't I feel it?" she whispered as she took a breath. I looked at her curiously. She would have been looking at me the same had her eyes been open. I decided to help her out, took her hand in mine, moved them slowly under my boxers and pressed her fingers harder against me. *There's no way she can't feel that.*

That got her attention and her eyes blinked open in awareness. She gripped me tighter on her own and I let her hand go... let myself get caught up in that moment. "Can you feel it now?" I asked her. "Because it feels amazing to me."

"I feel *that*," she said, emphasizing her word a little too much as she squeezed. I moaned softly in her ear. "That's not what I meant. I want to feel what I felt when you kissed me. I don't feel it."

"What do you mean?" I didn't give her a chance to answer. I just continued to kiss her, hoping to evoke that elusive feeling again.

She pulled both of her hands up to my face and pushed me back gently. Her brow was crinkled in uncertainty. "Earlier tonight, it felt different. It was, like, *everything*," she mumbled, running her fingers through my hair.

That wasn't me.

She closed her eyes again. A few moments passed and I thought she might fall asleep.

She thought that was *me*. I wasn't giving up so soon.

"Tell me how I did it. Tell me how it made you feel."

"I just..." She seemed so unsure all of a sudden. She started shaking her head, mentally trying to put all the pieces together. "It was... I don't know."

"Like this?" I asked, selfishly pulling her hand back beneath the covers as I kissed her again. I had let her touch me over the boxers that time, my conscience starting to intervene because I had known that what I was doing was beyond wrong. I was close, though. I had fantasized about that moment for years, and I knew I wasn't going to last long with her touching me like she was. I could feel the stirring in the depths of my being.

She mumbled something incoherent. Her response to my advances began to lessen. My kisses were no longer returned. Her fingers fell away from my body. She had passed out. What had she said? It sounded like *I don't want this.*

You've got to be fucking kidding me!

"Emi," I tried to nudge her awake. "Emi, what did you say?" It was hopeless. She was out and I was too close to turn back. I squeezed my eyes shut tight and buried my head into the pillow, counting to ten. Then twenty. I was too wound up at that point. I removed myself from her bed and headed to her bathroom to take a shower– and to take care of other pressing issues. I left the door cracked in case she needed to come in... or woke up and wanted to... I was grasping at straws and I knew it, but I still had hope.

Under the stream of hot water, I closed my eyes and lathered up. I wasn't in there for more than two minutes when a woman's voice startled me from less than a foot away.

"My god!" It was Emi's roommate, Teresa. I could tell from her voice alone, but she was also staring through the space left between the shower curtain and the wall.

"What the fuck!?" I pushed the curtain closed quickly, but not before she could take in the full sight of my naked and completely aroused body. *Fuck!*

"That thing is a weapon! I don't think Emi would still be a virgin if she knew you carried that thing around."

"Do you mind?" I asked her, mortified, wishing I had just stayed with Randi instead of getting myself into the situation I had then found myself in.

"You're jacking off in my shower, Nate, honey. I do mind, actually."

"God damn it!" I ran my hands through my hair, getting soap in my eyes.

"Out, kid. Get out of my shower. You and I need to talk." She closed the door, but I could tell she was still in the bathroom with me. I rinsed all the soap off my face and body and turned the water off.

"Can I at least have my boxers?" She pushed back the curtain again and glanced down once more, handing me a towel and my underwear. She pursed her lips and raised her eyebrows, seemingly impressed. I would have felt proud, but at the moment, I couldn't help feeling like the biggest loser alive. I dried off and slid back into my silk shorts. Teresa was sitting on the counter when I came out from behind the shower curtain. "You can't leave a man to his privacy?"

"You're seventeen, Nate. Hardly a man." She always teased me about my age. "But you're certainly built like a man..."

"Alright, can you forget you ever saw me naked, please?"

"Shhh..." she said as she glanced to the bathroom door.

"Emi's out cold. She can't hear us."

"I was more worried about my date. I picked him up at the frat party. I think he's still in the kitchen."

"Can you get me my clothes? I'd like to leave."

"Not so soon," she said. "Let me get a few things straight." I nodded and rolled my eyes. "You and Emi are friends. And Emi is still a virgin. Am I right?"

"Yes, you're right. Is that it?"

"Nope. Why are your clothes on the bedroom floor?"

"She undressed me."

"And why are hers on the bedroom floor?"

"She proceeded to take her clothes off."

"She's drunk." Her statement was meant as a question.

"Yes."

"But nothing happened..."

"No!" I told her emphatically.

"Hence the reason you're in here..." My face turned bright red. I saw it for myself in the mirror.

"Yes."

"You swear nothing happened," she pressed further.

"I swear. We may have kissed, but nothing more. And she won't remember in the morning, so I'd prefer you didn't tell her any of this."

"And if she does?"

"Does what?"

"Remember kissing you in the morning?"

"Well, then she and I will figure that out. As it stands, we're friends and nothing more. But I'd really like to leave. I've got some things to take care of."

"Yes, you do," Teresa said, looking down at my boxers once more.

"Can you stop looking at me, please? Like this isn't embarrassing enough already!"

"Nate, honey, you have nothing to be embarrassed about. Trust me." She leaned in and whispered her next line. "That guy out there, though? He would definitely have something to be embarrassed about."

"I'm out of here," I said, opening the door and retrieving my clothes off the floor. I dressed quickly and grabbed my keys, not bothering to try to wake Emi any more. I hoped that she wouldn't remember anything at all from this night. The stupid frat guy's kiss *or* mine. I hoped the alcohol would erase her entire memory... but I had a feeling that wouldn't happen. I dreaded the morning. I dreaded the conversation that was sure to come.

I glanced at the guy Emi's roommate had brought home, making sure it wasn't the same one that had hit on Emi. Teresa's date had red hair. Definitely not the same guy.

"You won't say anything?" I asked Teresa as she nearly pushed me out the door.

"About *that*?" she joked with me once more, glancing down.

"About *anything*?"

"I won't say anything about anything, honey," she said, and her reassuring voice was finally of comfort to me. "Especially to her brother, who has already doled out one black eye this evening."

"Really? To who?"

"Whom," she corrected me. *Fucking English major.*

"Whatever."

"The guy who kissed her at the party," she'd said.

I couldn't hide my smile. "Good."

I had called Randi on the way down to my car, letting her know I'd be coming over after all. She was thrilled, as was I, anxious to finally get rid of the raging problem that had plagued me since Emi first touched me under the covers. I stayed out all night, too, my mother under the impression I was with Emi.

I totally used Randi that night... and she wouldn't be the first woman I would use to keep my attraction to my best friend in check.

The next morning, Emi had called the house shortly after I returned home. My mother answered, but was none-the-wiser about my whereabouts after talking briefly to her.

"How do you feel?" I asked her.

"Like hell," she admitted. "What the hell was I thinking?"

"I'm not sure, Em," I told her. "I wasn't there for the drinking part. Just the after effects."

"Yeah... can we talk about that?"

"Sure." I felt sick to my stomach at that point.

"What exactly happened last night?" she asked.

"Nothing," I answered immediately, hoping she was truly drawing a blank.

"I know that's not true."

Fuck. I stayed silent for only a second. "Well, then why did you ask?"

"Because I think we need to talk about it."

"Whatever happened," I began, being vague on purpose, "changes nothing between us."

"I wasn't wearing my clothes this morning."

"And..."

"Did we..."

"No, Emi, we did not. You'd know."

"Promise?"

"Emi, you were drunk, what kind of person do you think I am?" *If only she knew...*

"No, I know. I'm sorry. But I think we need to talk about the kiss."

Which one? I thought, unable to narrow it down, but knowing deep down she wasn't talking about any of the kisses we shared. I decided to ask. "Which one?"

"So we did kiss."

"Maybe once."

"Stop being aloof, Nate," she whined. I shut up. "I know what I felt when you kissed me last night. It was unreal."

"No, it wasn't–" I nearly swallowed the words before they came out. "You don't know what you felt. You don't even know what really happened." I knew I needed to tell her it wasn't me, but I didn't want her to rule me out, as she had seemed to try to do the night before.

"I do."

"Emi," I had finally told her, unwilling to face my actions or the unwelcome truth. "You were drunk, and it was a mistake. It shouldn't have happened. I don't think we ever need to talk about it. Ever again."

"But–"

What you felt was for a guy who could never even begin to appreciate who you are and what you mean. He was taking advantage of you! What you felt wasn't for me.

"I'm serious, Emi. I wasn't myself..." I had chosen my next words carefully. "It wasn't really me."

To say any more might have provoked her to find out the truth. Finding out the truth would have meant there was no hope for me in the end.

And I wanted to hold on to hope.

We weren't meant to be together then. We're not now, either. But as she goes through life, boyfriend after boyfriend, searching for that elusive "feeling" she felt one night, I know I may have a chance later, when she lets go of the silly notion that a single kiss could really change everything in her world.

Once upstairs, I pick up the receipt and pull my phone out of my jacket pocket. It's eleven, but I take a chance and dial Samantha's number anyway. Her cheerful voice greets me after one ring.

CHAPTER 5

A pounding on the door startles me as I'm painting one afternoon in late January. I open the door to Emi, her smile wide as she bounces on her toes. She's dressed in tight jeans and a basketball jersey. Her hair is pulled back into two little pigtails at the nape of her neck. *My god, the pigtails.*

"What are you–"

"Come on," she says, excited. "Me and you. Knicks game. Right now. Starts in an hour."

"Emi, you hate basketball."

"No, I don't hate it."

"Yes, you do," I correct her.

"Okay, so I'm not a huge fan, but we're going."

"Every time I take you to a game, you get bored, drink way too much, heckle the players and wind up embarrassing yourself."

"Well, then it's good entertainment for you, anyway. Come on."

"I'm painting," I tell her. Knowing I'll end up going, I take my brush to the sink and begin to rinse it off. I can't say no to her... would never pass up the opportunity to hang out with her.

"Mmmmmm," she says as she crosses the room to inspect the artwork. "It's no good. You need to take a break and come with me."

"Who gave you these tickets?" I ask her.

"That editor I've been working with. The magazine has a suite and he gave me and Teresa four tickets. So we're going. Pronto."

"Do I have time to shower?"

"What part of 'pronto' don't you understand?" she asks, impatient.

"Well, I have to change, at least."

"Go, then!" she laughs, taking a seat on the arm of the couch. I walk to the closet and pull out a long-sleeved t-shirt, checking to make sure there's no paint on it. I take off my work shirt and glance in the mirror, noticing Emi staring at me. It takes her a minute to realize I'm looking back at her.

"See something you like?" I tease her, turning around and causing her to blush a deep crimson. I smile smugly.

"Shut up and get dressed already!" she exclaims as she stands up and walks toward the door.

"Alright, alright. Hair?"

"It looks perfectly messy, let's go."

"Where's your jacket?" I ask her, pulling mine on. The jersey she's wearing has no sleeves with a deep v-neck. It's obvious her bra is helping to enhance her cleavage... her breasts don't typically look so... full...

"I don't have one that goes with this uniform-thingie."

"Take one of mine," I offer her my leather coat.

"Nope," she smiles. "I spent a lot of time putting this look together. Not covering it up."

"It's cold," I try to talk some sense into her.

"Don't I know? I ran over here, after all. I just have to keep moving... so come on!!"

"You ran in those shoes? You've already been drinking, haven't you?" I ask.

"Two glasses. I'm good to go."

"I bet you are," I raise my eyebrows at her, running my hand flirtatiously down her arm.

She looks at me through slanted eyes, slapping my chest. "You're pathetic," she chastises me in jest.

"Like ya, Em," I taunt.

"Yeah, whatever, come on." She leads me out the door, down the hallway to the elevator. She rocks back and forth from her toes to her heels, anxious. *I love it when she's feisty like this.*

When we get to the arena, she allows me to rub her arms to warm her until we get into the suite, at which point she shrugs me off and smiles apologetically. We say hello to Teresa and her editor and a few other guests. Emi orders a glass of wine for herself and water for me. We take a seat in the bleachers in front of the suite as the game begins.

"Nate, you seeing anyone these days?" Teresa asks me.

"Mmmm..." I hedge as Emi's bright eyes look on curiously. "I've been talking to a girl I met a few weeks ago, but it's nothing serious."

"When are you ever going to ask me out?" she asks, a running joke we've had for years. We'd discovered long ago that she was the female version of me.

I just nod and smile. Emi looks away from Teresa, directly at me, and rolls her eyes. She never has liked our teasing about this. Teresa is very much not my type, but even still, Emi has threatened bodily harm if the two of us ever hook up. It likely has something to do with the lack of privacy in their apartment and the incredibly awkward situation that would ensue. I've assured her numerous times that she needn't worry.

"So," Emi says as she takes my elbow in hers, leaning in close to me so our conversation can be heard in the loud arena.

"So?"

"I need some advice." I strain to keep my eyes off her chest... fortunately, her green eyes are completely captivating, her lips soft...

"Let's say you know a girl..."

"I know *many* girls," I answer.

"Right, obviously, but let's say it's one particular girl."

"Is this a girl, or a *woman*, Emi?"

"A woman, but she hates that term." *She* hates that term.

"And is this woman someone I know?"

"She's irrelevant..."

"Okay, an irrelevant woman..."

"No," she laughs. "Stop it. So anyway, this woman..."

"Yes?"

"Let's say you met her under certain circumstances... and she wanted one thing from you, but with the way things panned out, you got the distinct impression that she wanted something else."

"Okay..." *Is she talking about us?*

"How would this girl– this woman– go about correcting this?"

"She shouldn't beat around the bush, and she should just come out and say it. Guys are dense, we need for you to spell things out."

"Okay, yes, that would be the obvious answer... but what if this girl really likes this guy, and he really is just interested in her for the other thing?"

"I'm not following," I tell her. "Dense, remember? Be plain."

"She likes him for one thing... but he sees her differently, based on some things she... did... hypothetically..."

"Right." *What?* "So you don't think the guy and the girl want the same thing?"

"Right. Like, maybe certain circumstances caused this girl to be someone... other than the person she really is... what if the guy just likes the girl he *thinks* she is but not the one she *really* is?"

"Why wouldn't he like the girl she *really* is?"

"I don't know..."

"If the girl is you, I'm sure the guy would really like you, *for you.*" *And if*

78

the guy is me... no, I can't go there.

"This is all hypothetical," she blushes. "Irrelevant girl."

"You are never irrelevant, Emi," I tell her. "If he didn't like you for who you were, he wouldn't be worth your time or trouble, Em. But why don't you think he knows you?"

"Hypothetically?" she plays with me.

"Hypothetically."

"Because she led him to believe she was someone else... that she wanted something else."

"Well, what caused her to lead him on in the first place?"

"Poor judgment," she sighs. "Wine and terribly poor judgment."

"And you're sure the guy likes the girl for this 'something else?'"

"Pretty sure."

"How can you be so sure?"

"He seemed to be enjoying himself... with her..." She blushes again, this time tucking her head into my shoulder.

"I think you'd be surprised, Emi. You should ask him."

"Okay, no," she shakes her head. "That would be too embarrassing. I don't think I could do that... um, *she* could do that."

"Sure you could. Try it." *Just say it.*

"I'd be afraid he wouldn't like me the same way... and then he'd be gone... probably run into the arms of someone better." She laughs lightly under her breath.

"He wouldn't leave you. There's no one *better*." I tuck a strand of hair that had fallen out of her pigtail back behind her ear, losing my breath in the process.

A strange look of awareness flashes through Emi's eyes. Her lips part slightly as she stares at me.

"He's probably on the same page as you," I tell her, my voice hushed. "You just have to tell him, Emi, and find out."

Her cheeks redden for the third time in the conversation as she pulls her arm from mine. "Right. I think I will. I need a drink."

Abruptly, Emi stands up to get another drink. She trips over my feet as she crosses in front of me, falling into my lap, my hand touching her breast as she tumbles into me. *Good lord...*

"Maybe you don't need another," I suggest quietly.

"It's the shoes, idiot," she laughs nervously, "and your big feet."

"Right," I agree with her, unconvinced. *Let the entertainment begin...* Teresa slides into Emi's vacant seat.

"When's your next gig?" she asks.

"Nothing on the calendar yet," I tell her. "But I'll be sure to let you know." We sit together until half-way through the second quarter when I begin to wonder where my best friend has gone. I turn around to scan the room, finding her seated at a bar in the suite talking to a man. He, too, is wearing a Knicks jersey and cap. His posture screams jock, his muscular arms further proof. She's never been into that type. I wonder who he is, what they're talking about.

She's leaning into him, her back straight, chest out. She plays with her damned pigtail, twirling it coyly around her finger. I can see her pronounced dimples all the way across the room. Her laugh stands out among all the other crowd noise.

"Who's that?" I ask, nudging Teresa.

"That's the guy she's been talking to... Colin, I think is his name."

"They're dating?"

"Not exactly," her roommate answers. "They met at a happy hour that the magazine sponsored a few weeks ago. He's a sports writer. Apparently," she says, her voice dramatic, "they made out in his car till the wee hours of the morning."

"Huh." I have no words. "Really."

"Yeah, they've been texting ever since. She wasn't sure he'd show up... I'm glad he did, for her sake."

"Yeah..." I say, running my hand through my hair. *Why am I here?*

"He's a big Knicks fan... hence the outfit tonight. It's her cute cheerleader look."

"I see that," I mumble, unable to tear my eyes away from her. *Were we not just talking about us? About what she wants from me?*

"When are you gonna ask *her* out?" she asks quietly.

"What?" I look at her, startled, the confession of my feelings written all over my face.

"You heard me."

"I don't know what you're talking about," I lie.

"Yeah, keep it up," she says, exasperated. I sit in silence for a few minutes, eventually turning back to the game but just seeing a blur of action in front of me, my eyes not wanting to focus.

"I could never be what she wants," I murmur, a part of me hoping Teresa won't hear me, an equal part wishing she would.

"You don't know that," she argues.

"I do. I'm just her friend. Her fucking best friend. And... she sees something in me that isn't really there." My frustration is obvious.

"I'm not sure," she counters. "I think she knows you well enough to know what you can offer her. And I think she likes what you have to offer."

"I can't offer her enough. She may not realize it, but I do. It doesn't matter how I might feel about her... until she stops looking for a fairytale ending, she won't be happy with me."

"You could convince her to stop looking. If you just accepted how you feel and told her. But you hide your feelings well. You play the friend role masterfully."

"I have to. For now, it's the best I can offer her. And it's served us well all these years. I mean, fuck, look where I'm at right now. She brought me to this game, and she's on a date with another guy. When did I become another one of her *girlfriends*?" I laugh through my sigh. "Am I here for moral support?"

"You're here because she's comfortable around you."

"I'm here as her backup plan. Only if super-jock over there doesn't get to take her back to his place, I'll get to deliver her to your front door, where I will leave her with you and go back to my place, alone." I look back over my shoulder to catch another glimpse. I imagine them together, in the backseat of what I can only assume would be his late-eighties muscle car, paint chipping off the dented bumper... she looks so tiny, so fragile next to his bulky body. She's so much classier than that. How tacky that he took her back to his fucking car, hoping to score with my Emi, to take advantage of her after one too many glasses of wine. Maybe he did... maybe they did, and she wouldn't admit it to Teresa... No, she's not that type. He's not her type... I think I actually taste the bile rising in my throat.

In that moment, Emi looks over from her conversation with the man and smiles warmly at me. She waves us both over to her. My body suddenly feels leaden.

"Come on," Teresa encourages me by pulling on my jacket.

"Nate," Emi says, "I'd like you to meet Colin. Colin, this is my best friend, Nate."

"Good to meet you," he says, standing up to shake my hand. He's got to be 6'6" at least. His grip is strong, crushing on my hand. When he sits back down, he puts his hand at the top of Emi's thigh. She looks down at his hand briefly, noticeably shocked, and she puts her hand on top of it. He's obviously staking his claim on her. I don't like him already. His expression is smug when I look back up at him.

"Tequila shots all around," he orders the bartender.

"That's okay," I tell him.

"I insist."

Teresa passes the shot glasses around to each of us. "To a Knicks win," she says, raising her glass.

Reluctantly, I take the drink as Colin adds his own toast. "To taking the prize." I nearly choke as I swallow, my eyes meeting his as they challenge me. Emi holds a lime wedge up to him. He looks at her, clearly one thing on his mind, as he sucks on it, then licks his lips as she takes it from his mouth.

She licks her fingers after setting the wedge down, and he takes them in his hands and kisses them before sticking his tongue down her throat. He's forceful with her, but she just smiles and looks up at him playfully when he pulls back. *What the fuck am I doing here?*

This is one side of Emi I have never seen before. I've seen her with men, with boyfriends before... but they seemed at least somewhat compatible and always respectful of her. This guy just seems domineering, possessive. *What does she see in him? Does she feel something for him?*

"I'll be back," I whisper to Teresa, not wanting to see any more of the foreplay happening in front of me. I find the nearest bathroom and splash cold water on my face in an effort to calm down. I've never had the urge to fight anyone, even someone she's dating, and I know this guy would beat me to a pulp in two seconds flat.

Colin is standing at the sink next to me when I look up from drying my face, washing his hands.

"She's a wild one, that one," he says to me.

"No," I respond. "She's not. She's sweet and vulnerable and insecure and apparently very confused tonight," I correct him, keeping my posture straight but taking a subtle step away from him. He dries his hands and begins to walk out of the restroom.

"You've obviously never had her," he laughs on his way out the door. I imagine myself running at him, knocking him down with the impact. I can see myself pummeling him, rectifying his incorrect– improper– judgment of Emi. I want to hurt him. But I can barely move. My fists clenched, I replay his words over and over in my head. *You've obviously never had her. A wild one...*

I had wondered if the conversation Emi and I had earlier was about us... had hoped it was, thought it was, even. But things are becoming crystal clear that they were most definitely not.

He knows an Emi that I do not. He knows her as someone that she *is not*.

Her words invade my thoughts now. *She had led him to believe she was someone else. He seemed to be enjoying himself... with her... What was she getting herself into?*

Knowing I have to talk to her, I rush back to the suite. She's telling Teresa goodbye as he stands behind her, kissing her neck... her beautiful, porcelain neck.

"Colin's going to take me home," Emi says as I approach her. I just shake my head, unbelieving.

"Em, can I talk to you for a second?" His big arm across her chest, he pulls her back into his body and takes her earlobe in his mouth.

"We gotta go," he says loudly enough for me to hear. He glances up at me, his glare threatening. She giggles and squirms in his arms, his tongue tickling her neck. *I can't believe I'm watching this happen.*

"Just for a second, okay?" I ask her, not him.

"I'll call you tomorrow," she mouths to me.

I have no doubt that she can see the flash of jealousy in my eyes. Just as I have no doubt of the uncertainty in hers.

He throws his arm around her shoulder as they walk out. His body dwarfs hers, makes her look even more fragile. I just stand, stunned.

"What the fuck?" I ask Teresa, still staring at the emptiness.

"Another shot?" she asks.

"You know I don't want that," I look at her.

"I know you don't *want* it. I think you *need* it." I hate that I do. The need scares me, but I nod to her, and quickly swallow the disgusting drink when she hands it to me.

"One more round," she tells the bartender. I drink again, then sit down on one of the barstools. Emi's roommate pulls another stool closer and sits down next to me.

The alcohol is quick to take affect on my body, more particularly my mind. I don't remember the last time I felt this way– it's probably been years. I sigh loudly and take my head into my hands.

"You okay?" she asks.

"Can't focus," I tell her.

"You're a lightweight," she laughs, putting her hand on my shoulder.

"I don't drink, remember?" I mumble.

"Yes, I do remember." I can hear the smile in her voice. "Another shot," she says to the bartender.

"I–"

"And some water for this guy," she adds. I nod silently.

"Tell me what just happened here," I request of her after our drinks are served.

"You were used, it seems.... you *were* apparently the backup plan. She didn't know if he would show up, and she knew you'd have fun, like you always do. But give her a break, okay? She never lets go like this. It's good for her."

"*He's* good for her?"

"That's not what I said."

"*It* as in... great, yeah. Great," I mumble, taking her shot and downing it, quickly.

"That was mine," she laughs.

"I needed it worse. I'll get you another."

"It's okay. Nate?"

"What?"

"You should tell her there's something better... show her there's someone better."

"That all may be true, but I don't think it's my place to tell her, or to show her. I don't know that I'm that person," I rationalize, then pause. "But him? I mean... *him?* We made fun of pricks like that in high school."

"Pricks like that can have their perks. It's just for fun," Teresa reasons with me. "I don't think they'll be married anytime soon."

"Is that supposed to make me feel better?"

"Nate, she has needs, too."

"Are we really talking about this? About her?"

"Why not? Seems you have some sort of double standard going on. Why do you get to fuck who you want, and not her?"

I laugh at her bluntness, but am quickly reminded of the seriousness of our conversation. "Because it's Emi."

"Emi is an adult, and Emi is not yours. And sorry, but yes, I think it'll do her some good to get laid. This is what she wants right now. And as her friend, I'm going to support her decisions."

"They're bad decisions," I argue.

"They won't hurt anyone."

"They could hurt her."

"She's a big girl, Nate. You have two choices. Go after her, or let her go." She puts her hand on mine, looking sincerely into my eyes. "And since you're not willing to go after her..." I shake my head, not wanting to face the rejection she would likely deliver to me. *I don't want this.* I can still hear her soft voice speaking the words... words that she likely doesn't even remember saying.

"He seems more your type," I tell her casually.

"I'm insulted by that. I like guys with a little more depth. He's very one-dimensional." I run my fingers through my hair.

"Depth," I consider.

"Plus, he's into the little petite girls, that bitch," she jokes. "I'm too much of a woman for him." I scan her body, not overweight by any means, just curvy, beautiful.

"I imagine you're too much of a woman for most men to handle," I smile at her. "You're very pretty. And very sensual," I add with a whisper into her ear.

"Oh, boy," she laughs, leaning in closer to me. "Tell me more."

"You don't need me to tell you. You know you're sexy. All those men Emi tells me about that you bring back to the apartment tell you that all the time. You're trouble on legs, is what you are. Your full lips... your breasts...

your hips..."

"Trouble, huh?" she says breathily.

"Definite trouble." I tug gently on a strand of her long brown hair, wrapping it around my finger, pulling her head closer to mine. "Come back to my place," I suggest. "I want to know what all the fuss is about."

"You're drunk," she smiles, wavering.

"I know. But you know you want to."

"I'm not *your* backup plan." Her eyes, parted lips betray her. "Plus, Emi would kill us both. She'd probably get super-jock to help. And you'd never have a chance with her. *Ever*."

That's all she had to say to clear my head. I stumble as I stand up. "You're right. I'm gonna take off."

"You didn't drive here, did you?"

"Subway."

"Okay... and Nate?"

"What?" I say, frustrated, putting on my coat.

"Just know that saying no to you wasn't the easiest thing I've ever done. But I do it for her."

"Thank you."

"And we don't ever have to talk about *this* again."

"Again, thank you."

I stop by a pub near the arena before going home. The last thing I want to do right now is go home alone. Not when I know she's out there with someone else, know that he's doing things with her that I've only done in my dreams.

I spot an exotic looking woman across the room sitting at a large table with a bunch of other women. It's obvious they've been here awhile based on the amount of empty glasses in front of them. It's impossible to stop looking at her: perfect figure, perfect breasts, perfect smile, light brown skin, long curly black hair, sultry eyes, full lips. She doesn't notice me until one of her friends points me out.

She raises her brow and smiles at me. She stands up and walks to the bar alone. On her way there, she glances over her shoulder at me for the briefest of seconds. I take that as my queue, messing up my hair just a bit before following her.

As she waits for the bartender at the crowded counter, I stand behind her, barely touching her, and whisper in her ear. "I've been watching you all night."

"I hadn't noticed," she teases, turning her body to face me.

"Well, I can't keep my eyes off you. You're easily the most beautiful woman here." I drag my fingers over her neck and bare shoulder. "I'm not sure I can keep my hands off you, either."

She cocks her head, clearly open to my advances.

"What are you drinking?" she asks, adjusting the collar of my jacket and letting her hand lightly graze my chest and stomach before dropping to her side.

"I'm not. I was just about to get out of here."

"I thought you couldn't keep your eyes off me... and you're going to leave? Where are you going?"

"Hopefully somewhere I don't have to keep my hands off you," I say in her ear, kissing her cheek slowly. "Do you live nearby?"

"You don't waste any time, do you?"

"Not when I see something I want. But I can draw this out for you, if you want to play that game."

"I'm not one for games," she smiles. "What's your name?"

"Nate," I extend my hand to her.

"Eva," she says back, shaking it. "Let's get out of here."

I'm a little amazed at how easy that was. The second the door to her apartment closes, we begin tearing each others clothes off, our lips and tongues hungry, needing.

We somehow make it to her king-sized bed. She lies back, her ample breasts accentuating her trim waistline and womanly hips, a true hourglass figure. I crawl onto the bed behind her as she leans on her side, pulling a box of condoms out of her night stand and setting it next to her on the white down comforter, the blanket a beautiful contrast to her dark skin.

I pull one out, but as soon as I do, she takes it from me and pushes me back onto the bed, climbing over me to put it on herself, kissing me along the way. Once it's in place, she kneels over me and turns around on her bed, one leg still on either side of my body. Her long hair, already tangled from the eager work of my hands, falls just below her waistline. I touch her back, then grab her waist firmly as she peers over her shoulder at me, lowering her body onto me, burying myself into her, deeper.

"Oh, shit... fuck... ohhhh," I sigh at the warmth, the tight muscles, the feel of her around me. I guide her hips, but it's clear this woman knows what she's doing. I notice the mirror on the opposing wall, notice her watching us in it. I prop myself up on my elbows, staring in awe at her reflection as she touches herself, her breasts, making arousing sounds, louder and louder, as she nears orgasm. As I feel her constrict around me, I lean up further, pulling her back into my chest, taking her breast in my hand and kissing her neck as she screams obscenities, riding it out. I can't hold out any longer.

"Um... hey." I'm awoken by someone pushing on my chest, my head pounding. I roll away from the disturbance, try to find a position that doesn't make me want to rid my body of all the alcohol I fed it last night.

"Um... I'm sorry," she says. "I don't remember your name." Sleep gone, awareness sets in quickly. *Fuck.*

"Nate," I say, finding it difficult to open my eyes, not wanting to admit what I've done. Finally I do, seeing the beautiful stranger in the unfamiliar apartment. "Oh, god," I say, nauseous, clearly hung over but a bit disgusted with myself as I realize I don't know her name, either. "Shit," I moan, unable to move. "Where am I?"

"You're at my apartment, and you really have to leave."

"What?"

"My boyfriend is on his way over. You have to go, Nate."

"I can't even get up," I tell her.

"Well, you're going to have to. Come on." She starts to push me toward the edge of her bed.

"Fuck," I groan, annoyed, rolling out of her bed, faced with the reflection of both of us, naked, in the mirror. I remember watching her as we had sex last night. My hand aches to cup her breast again. God, she is incredibly sexy. I sit back on the bed, my legs unsteady and my head even worse. I lean over, putting my head in my hands. My mouth starts to water as I feel the distinct need to throw up. I swallow, hard.

"You can't stay, Nate, I'm sorry. He'll be here any minute." She stands up and pulls me up, causing me to stumble into her, my hand getting its wish. "Oh, Nate," she sighs, pulling me to her, to kiss her. "I had an incredible night."

"Yeah, me, too," I say the first thing that comes to mind, just trying to keep my balance. I take a few deep breaths and begin the search in her apartment for my clothes. She pulls on some pajamas, then helps me get dressed, mainly holding my body steady while I try to figure out the mess of shirt sleeves and pant legs. She hands me my phone before unlocking her door.

"I needed that," she says. "Thank you."

"Ummm..." I mumble, the pain in my head making it difficult to form words. "Can I get your number?" I ask, more out of obligation than anything else.

"No," she apologizes. "I have a boyfriend... remember?"

"Right. Okay, then. You're welcome."

She looks through the peephole, then cracks the door and looks down the hallway before guiding me out the door.

"Bye," she says wistfully. I just continue walking in a stupor to the elevator. As I wait for the car to arrive on her floor, I check my phone for any messages.

I had the most amazing night... :D   Thanks for coming with me to the game. Call me later.

Damn her and damn her *amazing night*. I can barely remember anything from last night... I remember the sex was good, but I couldn't describe it as an amazing night with... *God, what was her name?*

The door opens, and a conservative looking man in a suit and glasses exits the car, inspecting me. He's holding a cell phone to his ear. "Eva, baby," he says. "I'm here."

Shit. Eva. Like a coward, I hurry into the elevator and push the button repeatedly to close the doors. *What have I done?*

I barely make it out of her building before doubling over and throwing up in the bushes out front. *Fuck.* Where the fuck am I? I curse the sun, shielding my eyes with my hands as I look upward at the street signs. Am I in the fucking *Bronx*? Seriously? How did I get here? I immediately start flailing my arms at the first available taxi. It pulls over quickly and I stumble into the backseat.

"Eighty-eighth and 5th Ave," I mumble.

"Rough night?" the driver asks. I glance into the rearview mirror and glare at him and his stupid fucking question, the motion making me nauseous. When he abruptly stops at an intersection, I open the door and throw up in the street. "Shit, get out," he orders me, putting the cab in park.

"Seriously, man, I'm fine," I tell him.

"Get out," he repeats. "You're not puking in my cab."

"Fuck you," I mumble to myself as I slowly climb out. I indiscriminately throw a bill in the backseat before slamming the door. The driver peels away from the curb.

I sit down on a nearby stoop and pull my phone out of my pocket.

Her perky voice greets me immediately. "Hey, Nate!"

"Em," I mumble. "Are you busy?"

"Not really," she answers.

"Are you alone?"

"Yes..."

"Can you do me a huge favor?" I ask. Beg.

"Sure, what?"

"I am in the Bronx. And I need to get home. And I'm too sick to do anything but sit on this stoop and look at the cracks in the pavement. The fucking cabbie kicked me out of the car."

"What's wrong?" she asks.

"I'm sick," I gloss over my condition.

"How'd you get to the Bronx?"

"I'll explain everything later." *No, I won't.* "Can you go to my apartment and get my car? And come get me?"

"Nate, I can't drive," she protests.

"You can," I argue. "I helped you study for the driving test... twice because you failed it the first time. I taught you how to parallel park. I made you laugh hysterically when they took your picture and you hated me for years for ruining your ID photo. You *can*."

"But I *don't*," she says.

"Emi, I wouldn't ask you if I could do this myself. Please." I hold the phone away as I throw up again, and get up quickly to stumble away before the person who lives here sees what I did on their steps.

"God," she says. "Did you just hurl?"

"I did."

I hear her sigh on the other end of the phone. "Where exactly are you in the Bronx?"

"Thank you," I gush, giving her the streets of the next intersection. I sit against a building as I wait for her to get there. After what seems like forever, a brief honk gets my attention.

"I guess you don't want to drive," she says after rolling the window down. When she sees me fall over, she opens the door and starts to step out. My car begins to roll.

"Park it, Emi!" I yell at her.

"Fuck!" she squeals, sitting back down and bringing the car to a stop. "I can't drive! I hate your car, I hate it!" she yells as she comes over to where I'm seated.

"Yes, it's the car," I look up at her, silhouetted against the bright sky, again the damn sun making my head feel like a jackhammer is chipping away pieces of my skull.

"Shit, Nate, what's wrong?" She holds out both of her hands to help me stand. "Do you think you're contagious?"

"No." She pulls me to the car, pushes me into the passenger seat.

"Put your seatbelt on," she instructs me. I wouldn't dream of *not* doing that. She's a horrible driver. "How did you get up here?" she asks, pulling away from the curb.

"I'm not real sure," I answer honestly.

"Waaaaait a minute," she says, catching on. "You're hung over?"

"It would seem so."

"That would explain the strange text message I got at four in the morning. You know, Nate, I don't get Shakespeare when I'm wide-awake and completely sober."

"Shakespeare?" I look down at my phone and try to look at my texts, but immediately feel dizzy and sick.

"What did you do after Colin and I left?" she asks.

Fucking Colin. Emi fucking Colin. That's it. "Pull over," I tell her urgently.

"What, here?" she asks, agitated, looking for a place to stop. I hang my head out of the open window and throw up once more.

"Never mind," I tell her, leaning the seat back, closing my eyes.

"How much did you drink?"

"Emi, really, I don't even want to think about it. The thought of it is making me sick."

"Okay," she says, concerned. "We don't have to talk about it. I'm sorry you don't feel well. Do you have any alcohol at home?"

"Of course not, why?"

"The old 'hair of the dog' wives-tale. Maybe I can bring you something on my way to Colin's."

I close my eyes tighter, trying to focus on anything but alcohol and the jackass she went home with... the one she's apparently going to see again today. "No, that's okay."

"Nate, I have to tell you," she begins, filling the silence I was enjoying. "You would not believe me if I told you what happened last night." She taps her fingers in quick succession on the steering wheel.

"Really..." I barely open one of my eyes and peek at her, notice her devious smile, her pronounced dimples. *A wild one...* I may never look at her the same. "Then you probably shouldn't tell me."

"Yeah, probably not," she laughs. "You'd be jealous. But, oh my god, he was–"

"Definitely not," I confirm, interrupting her. "Nope. Don't want to hear it. Can't stomach it."

"You're no fun when you're hung over," she mopes. *I won't want to hear about this when I sober, either.* I debate saying it aloud. I don't even know why she feels compelled to tell me this... I never discuss these things with her.

"Well, it was... wild..." She seems confident and... proud.

"Emi, really." My voice is stern and serious.

"Sorry... I like him..." she says, hurt, as she pulls up to the valet of my apartment building. She again gets out of the car before putting the car in park. As if anticipating it, my reflexes kick in and catch the gearshift. "You made me do this," she spits at me, realizing her error, before slamming the door. She comes around to the passenger side and opens my door.

"I didn't say a word," I say to her. "And thank you for doing this."

"You're welcome," she groans, helping me out of the car. "I guess you need help getting upstairs?"

"I would really appreciate it."

She doesn't speak to me on the way up to the twelfth floor. When I open the door, she goes immediately to my bed and pulls back the comforter and sheets. I lean on the island, watching her from the kitchen, adoring her nurturing ways. *I will never be good enough for her.*

She even fluffs the pillows for me.

"Come on," she says. "Get in whatever state of undress you prefer to sleep in," she jokes with me, her soft side coming out again. "I'm going to get a trash can so you have a proper place to throw up." I take off my jeans and t-shirt and crawl under the blankets in my boxers, covering up. She sets down the waste basket next to the bed. I close my eyes to shield them from the sun, cursing my decision to not buy curtains or blinds for the large windows. The bed feels good.

"I'll be back in a few minutes," she says. "I'm borrowing your keys."

"'kay," I mumble. I start to doze off, then suddenly worry that Emi has taken my car. No, surely she didn't take the car. No. Surely. *Ah, fuck it, who cares?*

I wake up to a rattling sound next to my head. Startled, I jump up to a seated position in bed, immediately regretting it as my head pounds in protest.

"Sorry," Emi whispers, setting down a container of aspirin and a bottle of water on the night stand. "I didn't mean to wake you up." She sits on the edge of the bed, pushing my shoulders back into the pillows.

"You didn't have to do that," I tell her.

"I know. But I've been there. I know exactly how you feel." She smoothes my hair down, her eyes sweet and caring, her smile warm. "I got a six-pack of beer, too. It's in the fridge."

"Ugh," I moan.

"It may help. It always helps me." She leans down and kisses my forehead before placing a cold, wet washcloth on it. "You'll be okay?"

"I think so," I tell her, just wanting to go back to sleep.

"Call me if you need anything," she says softly, standing up. "But only if it's urgent, okay? Your phone's right here." I grab her hand before she leaves.

"Like ya, Em," I tell her, squeezing her hand.

"You're a stupid, stupid man," she blinks innocently, "and you smell horrible... but I like you, too, anyway."

"Gee, thanks." I roll back over in the bed as she closes the door behind her.

The sun is still out when I wake up hours later. I reach over to the night stand and take the aspirin, drink the entire bottle of water. As if I needed another reason not to drink. *Shit. Kill me now.*

I stand under the hot water in the shower, dazed, angry. How could she go home with him? Did she say she likes him? What about him could she possibly like? From my interaction with him, I didn't see a single redeeming quality.

Of course, who am I to talk? I just fucked a woman whose name I didn't even remember. And did I hit on Emi's roommate? Fuck, I did. *Fuck.* Bits and pieces of the night continue to come back to me. I really felt like she had been talking about us when she was asking those questions at the game. What an idiot.

I could never be so lucky. And now, what, she's dating that asshole? She's going to see him today, she said. I should have told her what he said to me in the men's room. I still can. *It's obvious you've never had her.* She'd be pissed, I was sure. She'd break it off, wouldn't she? I should definitely tell her. Definitely.

I remember her smile, though, in the car, and her dimples. Her laughter from last night. She was happy. For whatever reason, she liked him. I really shouldn't interfere. Would I be doing it for her, for her well-being? Or is this just about... me?

Yes, I'm jealous. That's obvious. But he's an ass. She can do so much better. Even if she doesn't want to be with me, she could do *so much better* than him.

To tell or not to tell. Definitely the question. *Wait, didn't she mention Shakespeare? The text...* I hurry to finish my shower and find my phone. Emi hates it when I quote Shakespeare... and I shudder to think what I may have sent her last night.

"But that your trespass now becomes a fee / Mine ransoms yours, and yours must ransom me."

Nice. A revenge fuck? Good thing Emi considers my fascination with the Bard to be elitist. She'll never look that up.

I get dressed after the shower in an effort to get motivated to do something other than going back to bed. My head still hurts, my stomach still unsettled. I decide to turn the television on, but all I can focus on is what happened last night and this morning.

My attraction to Emi. Her pigtails. The asshole who 'had' her, and his arm around her. The tequila shots. *Come home with me.* She turned me down. More alcohol. The beautiful Eva. Us in the mirror. Her boyfriend coming off the elevator. Throwing up, repeatedly.

Disgusted, I remember the beer that Emi had bought. Just one. I take it out, open it, drink it quickly as I stare into the refrigerator. I somehow feel a little better. *Fuck.* One more. I take this one to the couch, stare at the widescreen. Physically better, mentally worse. Why does she do this to me? Why do I do this to myself?

Look at me. What would she ever see in me? I stare at the half-empty bottle of beer, take one more drink and sigh deeply, the feeling it delivers, numbing. Abruptly, I take it to the kitchen and pour it quickly down the sink, realizing I'm finding too much comfort in the alcohol. *Fuck.* I open the other four bottles and empty them into the basin as well.

I go to sit back down just as my phone notifies me of a text message. It could be Emi.

"Would you like to meet me for coffee? I'm just getting off work." Of course it's not Emi; she's with *him.* It's Samantha. I hadn't heard from her in a few days... wasn't sure if this was going anywhere or not. Coffee... could I do coffee? I could try coffee. I could use the diversion, if nothing else.

CHAPTER   6

To say that Samantha is a good distraction is an understatement.   Her upbeat outlook on life has made me a happier person all around, and it's interesting seeing the world through her eyes.

After a few coffee dates with her, just casual meetings that have given us the opportunity to find out things we do and don't have in common, I've finally decided to take her out on a proper date.   I'm intrigued by her.   She seems to have lived a fairly sheltered life, but is curious about everything.

Being new to the city, she's never visited any of the art galleries, so I decide on an evening at the MOMA.   There's a special exhibit that I had been wanting to see of a collection of illustrated concert posters that features one of my favorite bands.   Honestly, the band was one of Emi's favorites, too, and I had hoped to take her, but she had been so busy with Colin that we could never coordinate a time.

As a creative way to ask Sam to accompany me, I had designed and drawn a postcard in the style of the concert posters we would be seeing and had hand-delivered the signed invitation to her at the coffee shop where she works part-time. She gushed over the "art" I gave her, so I was confident she would enjoy the night I had planned.

"How do I look?" she asks at her cramped apartment where we had decided to meet. She lived in Chelsea with three other girls and two cats.

"Beautiful," I tell her, and she does, in a pair of dark, tailored, pin-striped pants and pressed baby blue shirt, the same color of her eyes. The outfit is more conservative than I had expected her to wear. It makes her look much more mature. She certainly doesn't *look* like the young twenty-one-year-old I've been sharing afternoons with. "That color is amazing on you."

"Is it okay to wear tonight?" Her voice is unsure and nervous, such a change from the confident girl I met at the restaurant and have seen a few times since.

"Whatever you're comfortable in," I encourage her. "This night is about us."

"But what is everyone else going to be wearing? I've never been to a special exhibit like this."

"Everyone else?" I ask and laugh to myself. "This is what I'm wearing," I explain, gesturing to my jeans and button-down shirt under my blazer. "Everyone else will likely be wearing service attire. I don't think you understand. When I say this night is about us, I mean it. The museum is closed to other guests."

"Oh," she says in wonder. "How did you do that?"

"My mother is on the Board of Trustees. We've been contributors to the museum since I was a kid. It's always been one of my favorite places to visit."

"That sounds so cool," another voice chimes in. Two of her roommates have been watching us from the couch since I had walked in. "I love art."

"Nate," I introduce myself, moving toward her and extending my hand.

"Casey," the young woman says. "And this is Beth."

"Casey. Beth," I repeat. They both smile and blush in unison as Sam's hand clutches mine.

"Shall we go?" she asks, tugging on my arm lightly.

"Sure." She grabs her bag and leads me to the door.

As we leave the apartment, I hear one of her roommates make a snide comment. "That type *always* goes for girls with no substance." I quickly turn to Sam, who either tuned them out or didn't hear.

I catch the door and peek back in. "Don't wait up, girls," I whisper out of earshot of Sam as I flash them an arrogant smile and shut the door– hard– behind us.

"Fighting with your roomies?"

"No, why?" she asks.

"No reason." I try to shrug off the comment, unsure if I should be more offended for her or for myself. *Girls with no substance...*

"Should we take a cab?" Sam asks.

"No, I'm right here." I open the door to my newly detailed car and help her into the low seat.

"How can you afford to have a car in the city? I wanted to bring mine from Georgia, but the cost to just *park* it was more than my car payment itself!"

"I'm no *starving* artist, Sam," I answer simply, giving her a sideways glance as we make our way to the museum. I hand her my iPod and let her pick the music.

"What do you want to listen to?" she asks.

"Anything you like," I encourage her, curious to know what she would pick.

"But there's so much... and who are all these bands?" *Obviously not into the indie music scene.* "Oh, wait, here's one I know. I love this song..." Seconds later, the recognizable beat of an over-played pop song begins to blare through my sound system. If I'm not mistaken, it was a different girlfriend that put the sexually suggestive song on there in the first place. *She did a strip tease to it in my apartment.* I shake away the thought and sigh internally, but smile at Sam anyway. I need to introduce this girl to some real music.

"I don't believe there will be any posters on display for his concerts," I inform her.

"Yeah, I've been meaning to ask you... what's so special about these posters that they're in the art museum? Couldn't we just go to that novelty poster shop a few blocks over?"

"Uh, no," I laugh. "There's a great art movement across the country. Lots of independent artists design these limited edition gig posters for bands. Mostly independent bands."

"Have you ever done one?"

"One, yes," I tell her.

"Will it be in the show tonight?"

"No. Mom can't buy my way in there," I joke with her. "That would be a dream come true."

"I thought your postcard was amazing. I framed it."

"Thank you. It's a one-of-a-kind."

"I know," she says breathily. "It means a lot to me."

"Well," I hesitate. "I'm glad you like it."

"Is your concert poster at your apartment?" she asks. "Maybe I could see it later." *There's the forward and confident woman I was expecting.*

"Sadly, I don't even have a print. I gave my last one to my best friend as a birthday present."

"He must be a good friend."

"She," I correct her without even thinking. "Uh, yeah, she is."

After sitting in silence as I park the car, Sam continues the conversation. "What's her name?"

"Emi," I tell her.

"What does she do?" she asks as I help her out of the car.

"She's a graphic designer." I begin to lead Sam toward the entrance of the museum.

"Like what you do?"

"Not quite. She has clients who direct her. I do what I want."

"What you do sounds much cooler."

"Well, it's harder to make a living as a fine artist," I explain.

"But you do well?" she asks as she stops walking.

"I get by," I dismiss her question with a kiss to her forehead, hoping to change the subject. I was never comfortable talking about money, or more specifically, how I could afford my lifestyle. "Let's go."

The museum is silent. I can't remember the last time I heard silence. I always have *something* playing. Always. Classical music when I paint, heavy metal when I shower, indie rock when I'm just messing around the apartment, and nature sounds in a constant loop as I sleep.

The silence is nice. The clicking of our shoes echos lightly off the walls as we are individually drawn to different pieces of art in the large room.

"Nate, what does this mean?" Sam's voice startles me. Even though she's barely speaking above a whisper, she seems so loud. I walk over and look at the piece she's staring at.

"This one is about the struggle of everyday life under communist rule in nineteen-sixties China."

"How do you know?" she asks in awe, cocking her head to one side as if trying to get another view.

"See the red– no, not really, Sam, I just made that up," I smile sheepishly, which earns me a slap on the arm. "Hey!"

"That was mean," she pouts. "I was serious."

"Well, then seriously, I don't know what the artist was trying to convey when he painted that. I believe every individual can find his own meaning in art. I don't think there's a right or wrong answer. That's the beauty of it."

"Okay," she answers plainly as she moves to another painting. She shifts her weight to one leg, crosses her arms and studies it with a determined expression on her face.

"So what does it mean?" I ask her after giving her a few minutes. "To you?"

"I'm not creative like you," she finally answers. "I can't even make up a good answer." Her shoulders slump slightly, and I can tell she's frustrated.

"Hey," I whisper into her ear, running my hands down her arms. "Some things are just meant to be adored... to be truly appreciated for their beauty." I kiss her cheek, admiring the artwork on the wall. "I think this may be one of those." I move my arms and begin to move to the next piece, a sculpture about twenty feet away. I look back over to where Sam is simply frozen in place with a smile on her face. "Psst..."

She jerks her head to look at me, then turns her body and walks to me with purpose. She places her hands on my cheeks and pulls my face to hers, kissing me slowly. Even our kiss seems loud.

"I wasn't expecting that," I laugh. Her lips taste of cherry, and are soft and full.

"Do you really think I'm beautiful?" she asks. *Had I said that?* I replay the last conversation and realize what I said and what she has interpreted my meaning to be. I really *was* just talking about the print on the wall, but of course she's beautiful, too. I just think there is likely more to her than just her beauty. Most women would be insulted by that comment.

"Yes, you're beautiful, Samantha." Holding her in my arms, I kiss her again. She shivers lightly. "Are you cold?"

"Nope," she says with a smile. "It's the way you said my name. Say it again."

"Samantha," I repeat.

"It sounds so... *sexy*... when you say it," she giggles.

"Samantha," I say one more time before she pulls me to her again. "You *are* sexy."

"My god, no I'm not," she says, adamant, her eyes studying mine in disbelief. "You, definitely. Me? I'm just a plain little girl from the south."

"You're sexy," I confirm once more. "And there is nothing plain about you, Samantha." She giggles again at the sound of her name. I silence the lilting noise with another kiss.

"Mr. Wilson?" a voice calls from across the gallery. We separate immediately and turn to face the woman calling me. "I'm Lydia. Your dinner will be served in the café in about five minutes. Would you two like something to drink with dinner?" I look to Sam.

"I'll have whatever you're having," she says.

"I'm having water. Please, get whatever you'd like."

"Um... do you have riesling?"

"No, miss, but we have a chardonnay that's a little on the sweet side."

"Okay, I'll try that." Lydia walks away quickly as I take Samantha's hand and lead her toward the dining area. "Why aren't you drinking anything?"

"Just trying to be on my best behavior," I answer flippantly, not wanting to get into any heavy conversation tonight.

"Now why would you want to do a thing like that?" Samantha asks, raising an eyebrow.

"And what are you suggesting? Because my bad behavior can be fairly entertaining..."

"Well, we'll just see about that," she laughs quietly, taking a seat.

"Will we?" I counter, sitting across from her.

After dinner, Sam and I go to the special exhibit area. At my request, the museum had begun playing music by some of the artists whose posters were on display. I was hoping to broaden Samantha's musical horizon.

"Have you seen any of these bands?" she asks.

"A lot of them. That's one of the great things about New York. The city is a stop on everyone's tour."

"Will you take me to a show sometime?"

"Sure," I tell her. "Does that mean I get a second date?"

"There was no question about that," she smiles. She takes my hands and looks me in the eyes, serious, her lashes fluttering quickly. "You can have as many dates as you'd like." I wind a long tendril of her golden hair around my finger before leaning in to kiss her.

She breaks away with a laugh. "God, what is this man whining about, and will someone put him out of his misery?" My hand falls from her chin to my side and I stare at her, wondering if she's serious.

"You're breaking my heart," I tell her. "This is my favorite band... of all time."

"No, it's not."

"Yes," I smile regretfully. "It is."

She bites her lip before apologizing. "Maybe I just didn't give it a chance," she explains.

"It's fine. You don't have to like my music."

"Well, this song... what is he singing about?"

"The singer... the writer... he actually wrote this about a classic piece of art," I begin to explain. She listens intently to the story, lingering on my every word.

On the drive home, Sam finds a playlist of my favorite band, determined to understand what I like about them. By the time we make it to her apartment, I feel a little guilty that I'm a bit exhausted from listening to her theories about what the songs mean.

"Can I walk you up?"

"I hoped you would."

The apartment is quiet and dark when we come in. Sam immediately turns on the television, some cooking show. She turns the volume to a medium level... I can't stand using banal television shows as background noise. It should be something with purpose, at least. For me, it's music, always music. I wonder if I ask her to play something from her iPod, will we be making out to the greatest hits of some boy band? I laugh a little to myself. I've got some things to teach this one about good music. I pat the seat of the couch next to me, and Samantha sits down, her knees tucked under her and her body leaning into mine. Our lips meet at once. Obviously we both have the same idea for how this date should end.

"What are you guys doing tonight?" Emi asks me on the morning of Valentine's Day. I shift the phone to my right ear as my barber concentrates on the left side of my hair. It had become too unruly, even for Emi's taste, apparently. She actually set up the appointment for me after borrowing my phone while we were working at my apartment earlier in the week. I hadn't seen her nor spoken to her since, so when her phone call interrupted my haircut, I made my apologies to the stylist and told him I had to take the call.

"Remember that play they featured in the Times last weekend?"

"The one off-broadway that they said would garner a NC-17 rating if it was a movie?"

"The one and only."

"You're taking her to that? Is she old enough?"

"Shut up. Yes, I'm taking her to that... and then we're going to some new Asian Fusion place."

"I couldn't get tickets to that show," Emi says. "Teresa and I thought about going."

"Tonight?" I ask. "Don't you have a hot date with the superjock?"

"Colin," she stresses his name, "is not into Valentine's Day," she admits quietly.

"What guy isn't into Valentine's Day?" I ask her, distracted by the amount of hair that's being clipped. "It's guaranteed sex..." For a second, I forget who I am talking to and regret saying it aloud. My barber laughs a little in my ear.

"I'm a sure thing any day–"

"I'm not listening to you, Emi." She laughs, leaving me wondering if it's true or just innocent bragging to make sure she has my attention.

"So you think this might be the night with Samantha?" At some point, I had admitted to her the other afternoon that we hadn't slept together yet. She was shocked, knowing my track record.

"Guaranteed," I remind her. "Especially with what I have planned."

"So cliché..."

"I don't care how cliché it is. I want it to happen." I don't know how much longer I can wait. Sam seems so sweet, innocent and demure, but when we've made out, I can see this whole other side of her begging to come out. I can't wait to bring it out of her, either.

A couple of nights, it got close, but she kept stopping things before we could go all the way. And I wanted to so badly. The last time it happened, I left very frustrated, feeling rejected and a little angry. By the time I got home, I had gained a little perspective and felt like an ass for trying to pressure her. When I called her, she was quick to accept my apology, and promised me that my patience would be rewarded.

We hadn't agreed on that reward coming tonight, but I was fairly certain it would.

"So he's really not taking you out?" I ask her, making sure she fully understands how much of a jerk her current boyfriend is.

"He invited me to his place... so I'm going over there. You know, now I don't have to get all dressed up or fight the crowds. It's fine."

"Fine, huh?"

"Yeah."

"So, how was your Valentine's Day, Emi? It was *fine*," I play out the conversation aloud.

"Sure, make fun of me all you want. Not all girls get to date millionaires who can afford sold-out off-broadway shows and insanely priced prix-fixe dinners."

"Millionaires? Or just men who appreciate the women they're with?"

"Alright, this is going nowhere," she avoids my question. "Have a good night, Nate."

"Okay, Em. You have a *fine* night, too." I can hear her groan as she hangs up on me. That was a little harsh of me. I know I should be more encouraging, but she just picks the worst men sometimes. This one just might be *the* worst.

On my way home from the barber shop, I stop by my usual florist to pick up the arrangement I had ordered earlier in the day. Even though it was last minute, and I had requested something unique and non-traditional, I do enough business with them to know they'd not only be able to accommodate me, but they'd get it exactly right. When I see the flowers, I'm impressed as usual.

"Mr. Wilson," the owner says, showing off his wife's artistry. "Is it sufficient?"

"Beyond sufficient," I tell him. Most of the flowers are orchids, and will most certainly set the tone for tonight. "This is perfect." I had paid for the arrangement with my credit card over the phone, but I hand the shopkeeper a couple hundred dollars as a tip, telling him to take his wife somewhere nice.

"Mr. Wilson, I can't accept this."

"Sure you can," I encourage him. "Wasn't there a rush fee? I mean, my inability to plan ahead must come at *some* price. Please, keep it... you know me... you know I'll do this again."

"We're always here to help you, Mr. Wilson."

"It's Nate," I correct him, as I always do. "And thank you for helping me out."

"Thank *you*, Nate." I smile, taking the large vase with me. It's so large, in fact, that I know I won't be able to pick up my suit from the cleaners and carry it all home. When I get back to my building, I ask Marcus if he can have someone retrieve my suit for me, handing him a larger-than-average tip, too. An hour later, the suit is delivered and the maids have come and gone. I'm strategic about everything. I place a little box of candy on the nightstand and put a bottle of white wine in the refrigerator. I turn on the television, flipping through the channels until I find a romantic movie to record, in case I need some help convincing Sam...

...but I doubt I will...

The chauffeur I've hired is waiting for me in the drive when I come downstairs. I knew I might have a few drinks tonight, and I wanted to play it safe... plus, I knew it would impress Sam. And this night is all about impressing her. When we pull up to her apartment, I glance up to her window and briefly catch a glimpse of her as she quickly moves away. She buzzes me in as soon as I ring the doorbell, and is waiting in her open doorway when I make it up to her floor.

"Oh, my God," she gasps. I can barely see her excited expression through the arrangement. "That might just be the most beautiful thing I've ever seen." She takes the vase from me and welcomes me into her apartment.

"I was thinking the exact same thing," I tell her, taking notice of the bright dress that shows off more of her body than I was expecting. Once she sets the vase down, I take her arm and turn her around so I can see the front. "Wow. You look amazing."

"Really?" she asks, nervous, looking down at the dress. It's strapless with sequins of all shades of pink and red, the top part accentuating her full breasts and the long pink silky bow beneath them highlighting her small waist. The skirt part bubbles out, stopping about halfway down her thighs. I follow her bare legs down to silver stiletto heels. "I just wanted to look perfect. I want tonight to be special."

I'm certain the reward's coming tonight.

"You look perfect."

"So do you," she says, smiling. "I like your pink tie." She runs her fingers down it slowly.

"I like yours," I tell her as I threaten to untie the bow.

"It's just for decoration," she laughs.

"Damn," I whisper in her ear, "because I was hoping to take this off of you right now." The sides of her hair are pulled back loosely in a clip, exposing her neck. I kiss her just below her ear, tilting her head to the side and running my fingers through her long, wavy, blonde hair.

"Nate," she whispers back, pushing against me lightly. "We aren't alone." I look around and notice one of her roommates watching us from the couch.

"Casey, was it?" I ask, nodding in her direction.

"I'm Beth," she corrects me.

"Right. Beth, nice to see you again." I clear my throat and walk toward the flower arrangement, plucking a pink orchid from the back. Samantha watches as I snap most of the stem off and tuck the flower next to the clip of her hair. "So, Samantha," I direct my attention back to her. "I didn't think you could look any sexier, baby, but I'm not sure how I'll keep my hands off of you tonight. It's a good thing she's here, or we wouldn't make it out of your apartment." Ignoring her roommate, I run my finger across her collarbone and kiss her just above her heart.

"Then it is a good things she's here," she says, taking a deep breath and walking across the kitchen to get a small purse. "Because I want to know where you're taking me. You said we were going somewhere nice."

"My apartment's nice."

"Nate..." she says in a warning tone as she moves toward the door. "We're going there later," she whispers, turning around ever so slightly so I can see the glint in her eyes and the sexy smile spread across her lips.

"Then let's get this night started." I follow her out the door, then lead her downstairs to the car.

"You hired a driver?" she asks.

"I thought my attention might be elsewhere," I say with a sly smile before shutting the door behind her. The driver holds my door open and I give him directions to the restaurant. I raise the divider between the front and back seats. "I thought right." I lean in to kiss her, anxious to feel her full lips against mine. She holds my face to hers, our kiss long and deep.

"Well, I had hoped this dress would have some effect on you, but I didn't expect this."

"That dress is just begging to come off," I warn her as my finger brushes down her arm and leg, stopping at her knee. "Is that what you had in mind?"

She looks up at me through her lashes and blushes. She nods a little and smiles shyly. "Just not yet. And not here."

"Of course, not here, Sam," I assure her. "I want this night to be special, too."

"Okay," she says, the relief evident in her voice.

"I'm sorry if I'm coming on too strong," I tell her.

"No, it's okay." She squeezes my hand.

"You should know how badly I want you right now, though. This isn't going to be easy."

"Well, *I'm* not easy," she says.

"I know that. I like that about you."

"Thank you," she whispers, her lips closing in on mine again, "for taking it slow. I love that about you."

"You're welcome." We kiss once more before the car pulls up to the restaurant. The driver walks around the car, opening the door for her. I take her hand in mine and lead her into the building.

I'd been by the restaurant earlier in the week to make sure the rave reviews I had read were true, but I wouldn't even have recognized it as the same place. Deep red tapestries are draped between each booth, creating a private experience for each couple. Tapered candles burn in the middle of each table, providing the majority of the light. Thousands of flowers are placed strategically around the restaurant. A pianist plays soft, romantic music near the bar. I watch Samantha as she takes in her surroundings, her dress sparkling wildly in the candlelight. She's easily the most stunning woman here, and I notice many men can't keep their eyes off of her.

"It's incredible," gushes Sam.

"I'm glad you like it." I kiss her cheek before telling the hostess my name. She leads us away from the awaiting crowd in the foyer and seats us in a corner booth.

After dinner and the show, the driver takes us back to my apartment. The newspaper didn't disappoint on its review of the off-broadway show, either. It was quite romantic... sensual, even. If I hadn't already set the tone for the evening, that production would have sealed the deal. There were many couples in the theatre who stole kisses from one another. We weren't the only ones.

"Just a second," Samantha says softly to the driver before he steps out of the car. She leans over me and rolls up the partition again. She takes a deep breath as I look at her curiously.

"What's wrong?"

"Nothing's wrong," she tells me, her hand on my leg. She's quiet for a second before continuing. "Um... can I ask you a question?"

"Of course you can," I tell her, pushing her hair over her shoulder. She bites her bottom lip and looks down, watching my hand stroke hers gently. "Why are you being so shy tonight, Sam? The way you look, you should be the most confident woman in the city."

"I'm just a little nervous."

I laugh to myself. "Don't be nervous, baby. What's your question?"

"Um... do you have any sort of protection?" She giggles quietly and tucks her head into my shoulder.

"Of course I do," I assure her, picking up her head and looking her directly in the eyes, perplexed by her school-girl manner. I have become quite adept at being conveniently discreet about this, because nothing kills a mood quite like fumbling around with condoms. I recognized their necessity long before it was ever an issue, though, and I've always done my part to practice safe sex in my relationships. I kiss her gently. "Are you alright?" I ask her.

"Yes," she blushes.

"Can we go upstairs now?"

"Yes," she says again. As soon as I open my door, the driver scuttles out of the car and rushes to the other side of the car to open the door for Samantha. I hand him a tip before weaving my fingers in between hers and leading her inside.

"Nate," Marcus greets me.

"Shouldn't you be at home with your wife?" I ask him, slowing down to converse with him.

"We're going out of town this weekend."

"Okay, good. Samantha, this is Marcus."

"Samantha, it's a pleasure to meet you." He takes a long-stemmed rose from a large vase and hands it to her.

"Thank you," she says kindly.

"Did you two have a nice evening?"

"It was perfect," she answers, smiling as I put my arm around her and kiss the top of her head.

"I hope you have a good evening, Marcus," I tell him, guiding Samantha toward the elevator.

"You, too. Good night, Nate."

"Bye," Sam says, waving to him as we get inside the lift. I stand behind her and rub her shoulders, feeling her tight muscles.

"Why are you so tense, love?"

"I don't know," she says as she lowers her head, letting me massage her until the elevator reaches my floor.

"Well, that's the first thing we're going to take care of then," I tell her. "I've got to find my girlfriend... because this quiet, demure, tense woman... I don't know her."

She walks inside my loft, slowly looking around. She sets her purse down and turns around quickly to address me. "I'm sorry I'm not myself tonight. I just don't want to do anything to mess things up and I know you have high expectations and I'm just scared that I won't live up to them and you won't like me–"

"Whoa, whoa, whoa..." I stop her string of explanations. "The Sam I know is not insecure about herself. At all. The Sam I know realizes she's the only woman I want to be with. I have no expectations for tonight, baby. None. I hope..." I say honestly. "But I expect nothing."

"Really?"

"Really," I assure her. "And for you to think I won't like you... we've been dating for weeks now. I wouldn't still be seeing you if I didn't like you."

"That's not what I mean. I'm afraid you won't like me after you've... um... *been* with me."

I'm shocked at her statement and realize I need to assuage some serious anxieties. "Sam, baby." I guide her to my couch and sit next to her. "We need to talk." I stand up and pour some wine for both of us, then take it back over to her. "You must have a pretty low opinion of me."

"No, not at all," she says quickly after taking a quick sip of her drink.

"I have genuine feelings for you, Sam. And those feelings don't hinge on how good you are in bed. They're here, now. They won't disappear after we sleep together. You get that, right?"

"I guess." Her shoulders slump, her posture defeated.

"Is that how the men in your past have treated you?" I ask.

She looks up at me through her lashes and shrugs her shoulders.

"I'm not like that. If this was just about sex, I wouldn't have waited this long, okay? You're different. You intrigue me. I've never met anyone like you. I just want to know you better. Know you, fully."

She smiles and blushes before swallowing audibly. "I want to know you... fully... too."

"Okay," I whisper before kissing her cheek. "Good."

"Okay."

"Do you feel better?"

"Yeah."

I test her shoulders again, still feeling tension. "Why don't you turn around, and I'll rub your shoulders a bit. You need to loosen up. Okay?"

"Okay," she agrees, shifting on the couch to turn her back to me. I start with both hands kneading her left shoulder, gradually making my way across to her right side. She finally begins to relax. I move her hair over her right shoulder and kiss her left one slowly. I can feel her sigh, my hands running lightly down her arms. My kisses move slowly across her back.

"That's better," I tell her, my lips lingering against her soft skin. I begin to focus on her neck. When my hands reach hers, she wraps her fingers around them tightly.

"Nate, I'm a virgin," she says hurriedly causing all of my movements to cease.

"What?" I ask her, positive that I didn't hear her correctly.

She lets go of my hands and I sit up straight, waiting for her to turn around. She finally does, then looks me in the eyes and speaks. "I like your haircut." She smiles easily and runs her fingers through my hair.

"Um, thank you," I tell her. "Can we go back a second?"

She looks down at the space between us. "Yes, I said I'm a virgin." She covers her face with her hands.

"Hey." I pry her hands away. "Look at me... Samantha?"

"Now do you understand why I'm afraid you won't like me?"

I put my hand under her chin and force her to look at me. "Are you kidding?"

"No, I really am a virgin," she says. "Why would I make–"

"No, Sam, I believe you. But you think I won't like you because you're a virgin?"

"I have zero experience."

"I'm okay with that," I tell her, almost laughing. "*Very* okay with that."

"Why?" she asks innocently.

I just shake my head. "Wait, how can a woman like you– a siren, honestly– how is it that you've stayed a virgin this long? That doesn't happen."

"Sure it does," she says, perking up a little. "I just wanted it to be with the right person, that's all."

I raise my eyebrows at her. "And I'm that person?"

She takes a deep breath before answering. "I'm in love with you, Nate."

I feel my heart begin to pound in my chest as I smile warily at her. I take her head in my hands and lean in to kiss her. "Okay then," I breathe into her ear, taking her lobe into my mouth.

"Nate–"

"I love you, too, Sam," I interrupt her, knowing the question was coming. She tilts her head back, allowing my tongue to trace down her throat and across her collarbone. I glance up to see her eyes closed, a beautiful smile spreading across her lips. I angle her head back down, smiling back at her. She opens her eyes, and at once all the confidence she'd been hiding from me returns to them. She leans into me, taking my tie in her hands and working out the knot as she kisses me, hard and fast. I remove my jacket quickly as she pulls the tie from my neck. "Let me take you to bed," I suggest, out of breath. "I want you to be comfortable."

"Okay." I take her hand and walk swiftly across the room, unable to hide my excitement to be with her.

"You're sure about this?" I ask her as she unbuttons my shirt.

"I've never been more sure about someone," she says, kneeling on the bed after kicking off her shoes. I barely have my dress shirt off before she pulls me onto the bed with her. I kneel in front of her, letting her hands explore the skin beneath my t-shirt. I pull it over my head quickly, tossing it on the floor. She looks at my chest and slows down, kissing my bare skin reverently. I feel her fingers fidgeting with the button on my pants. She's taking her time, and I almost can't restrain myself from just undressing the rest of the way for her. Instead, I move my hands slowly to the back of her dress and find the zipper. We unzip one another together, our gazes never faltering. I kiss her once more before lifting the dress over her head. She holds her arms up gracefully, then lowers them slowly, her eyes watching me as I study her body.

She smoothes her hair down, then unhooks her bra from the back and sets it on the bed next to us. *This is the confident Sam I know.* "You are driving me crazy," I tell her. She takes my hands in hers and places them on her ample breasts. I cup them in my hands, massaging gently at first. I've felt them over her clothes before, but this is the first time I've felt them with nothing separating us. They are amazing– and amazing *real*– I had wondered... had hoped... As she arches her back, I kiss them, giving equal attention to both.

I feel her touching me beneath my boxer shorts, surprising me. She straightens up when I take her hands into mine and look her in the eyes.

"I'm sorry," she says, her expression truly remorseful.

"No, it's okay," I tell her. "It's nice... but let's focus on you first. Because once you start doing that, I won't want to stop." I smile at her, reassuring her. "And I want to do this at your pace, okay?" She nods. "Good."

I run my hands down her arms again, noticing the orchid still in her hair. I take the clip out, releasing her hair and taking the flower into my hand, holding it up to my nose and breathing it in. I toss it onto the night stand, then comb through her hair with my fingers as I bring her lips to mine again. She leans back, eventually lying down on the bed and taking me with her.

"Tell me about your first time," she requests as I feed her small chocolates in bed. I'm exhausted and can't wait to sleep, but Samantha's mind is obviously racing.

"It's not a romantic story."

"I feel pretty lucky that mine was," she says, smiling brightly and running her fingers through my hair.

"I feel pretty lucky to have shared it with you." Any apprehension I had felt by being her first lover was gone. After what just happened between us, I want to be attached to her. The sex was amazing, and I knew it would only get better. I was still in a euphoric, post-coitus state. I could revel in this feeling forever. It's one of the best feelings in the world.

"So who was she?"

"Her name was Misty Gainor."

"How old were you?"

"Fifteen."

"Wow, you were young," she comments, licking some chocolate from my finger. *God, what a turn on.* I pull her face to mine and kiss her. "How old was she?" she asks, her lips humming against mine.

"Fifteen, as well." Propped up on my elbow, I allow my hand to travel up and down her torso. She eventually moves the chocolates back to the night stand and wraps her fingers in mine.

"Was it her first time, too?"

"No," I laugh, remembering the reputation that Misty had, even before we slept together.

"Tell me about her."

I think back, trying to remember how I saw her through the eyes of that fifteen-year-old boy who was completely infatuated with her... because as the sixteen-year-old "man" I became, the breakup stripped away any kind feelings toward her.

"Where do I start? I went to an all-boys school until high school, so I was pretty curious about the fairer sex by the time I entered the ninth grade. I had a few girlfriends, but they were all 'good girls' and I never got past first base with any of them. I was pretty straight-laced, too, back then. I wanted to do the right thing, make my mom proud. I never wanted to cause her any trouble or any pain... that is, until she started dating a man my sophomore year.

"That was not easy for me to accept. My mom was supposed to love my dad forever, even though he had died years before. I started distancing myself from her and began rebelling against her rules.

"When I first saw Misty, I was sneaking a cigarette in between periods, and she was making out with one of the jocks at my school under the bleachers. She was wearing this impossibly short pleated skirt and combat boots. Her button-down shirt was partially opened, revealing part of her bra. That image of her implanted itself in my head, and I couldn't escape it. She had dark brown hair– long– and the guy she was with pulled on her hair roughly as she moved her body over his.

"I watched them, curious."

"Creepy," Sam comments. Thinking back, I have to agree that it kind of was, and I laugh at her comment.

"Anyway, it looked like he was hurting her... but it certainly didn't sound like it. I remember thinking at the time that I had to get this girl to go out with me, and I was certain that I could treat her better."

"Awww," she coos. "You were always this sweet?"

I roll my eyes. "I guess I was, but girls aren't always receptive to sweet."

"Did she break your heart?"

"Eventually, she did."

"So how did you convince her to break up with her boyfriend?"

"Well, she didn't stay with one guy for very long. That wasn't something I took notice of until after the fact. It was pretty easy to get her attention, though. She loved grunge music, so I just immersed myself in that culture. I got tickets to see Pearl Jam, and she heard about it through the grapevine. She told me she loved them, and I invited her to the show."

"So it happened that night?"

"What kind of a man do you think I am?" I tease her. "No, we didn't have sex that night. But I did learn really quickly that she liked to have her hair pulled. So much for treating her better than the last guy."

"That *was* kind of a turn on," Samantha admits. I raise my eyebrows, and she nods, although the admission doesn't surprise me. Most women I'd been with enjoyed that, but I decide to keep that comment to myself. I had a feeling if we got into the "how many women have you been with" conversation, it would be over between us with an honest answer.

"I'm glad you liked it."

"So back to Misty..."

"Right, Misty..." I continue. "After the concert, we started by meeting up after school at a nearby park. We got to know each other a little, and I was really taken with her. I can see now it was always lust, but at the time, I thought I was in love with her... and I thought she loved me back.

"Eventually we started skipping classes together and making out wherever we could find a little privacy, normally in the back corner of the library. When it started getting really intense, though, we had to find another place."

I sigh heavily and laugh at the memory.

"What?" Sam asks. "Where did you go?"

I laugh again, embarrassed. "Well... during the school day, the buses were left unattended at the far end of the parking lot..."

"Nuh-uh!" she exclaims.

"Yep. I lost my virginity on a school bus... in the very last seat."

Sam bursts out in laughter.

"Not the most comfortable place to have sex, I might add."

"I wouldn't think so."

"But, still, we did it often there. We figured out positions that were more comfortable than others."

"So what happened to Misty?"

"Well... I guess she just got bored with me. After about three months, she dumped me... it completely broke my heart. That's when I swore off love entirely... that's about the time that Emi moved to my school."

"You've known her that long?"

"Yep. She transferred to my high school when her mom left her dad. She had sworn off love, too, so we became inseparable, as friends. We wallowed in each other's misery... and with everything she was going through, she helped me see how unfair I was being to my mother. I straightened up."

"So she was a good influence."

"Still is. But our friendship was built on the complete absence of love. It was just one of the many things we felt we had in common."

"So did it eventually turn into love?"

"With Emi?" I ask.

"Yes."

"No," I tell her, though I'm afraid my wistful smile might give me away. "Emi and I have always just been friends. We vowed to not date anyone through high school. We stuck to it until she graduated. I was a year behind her, and after she was gone, I did see a few girls."

"Did she mind?"

"No, not at all. By that time, she had begun to forgive her parents and had decided that maybe she would find someone to love some day. We just stayed friends through each other's relationships."

"She sounds like a good friend."

"She certainly is," I smile. Sam may be young, may seem young, but she sure is acting more maturely about Emi than Laney ever did.

"So, do you regret Misty Gainor?"

"You mean do I regret losing my virginity to Misty Gainor?"

"Yeah."

"Not at all. She was experienced... she taught me things... things I'll never forget. She's definitely someone I'll never forget."

Samantha lies in bed quiet for a few minutes, playing with the hair on my chest.

"I'm glad my first time was with you," she says, and I have difficulty breathing for a split second, realizing the inextricable bond that was forged tonight. I'll always be someone special to her. She's pretty special to me, too.

"I'm glad I could share this with you," I tell her with a kiss. "Wanna go for a second time?"

She looks at me as her smile grows. She nods slowly, and wraps her arms around me, welcoming me.

CHAPTER 7

"Thanks for meeting me," Emi's brother, Chris, says as we set up on the racquetball court early one Saturday morning. "I can't sit at home and wait any longer."

"What are you waiting for?"

"I've been seeing this woman for a few weeks. I really like her. She, uh, finally stayed over the other night..." I glance at him, and his expression fills in the blanks. "But I haven't seen her since. She's all I can think about."

"Well, Em, here I thought I was spending the morning with your brother."

"Fuck you," he tosses the ball to me. "You don't understand."

"I don't understand women?" I serve the ball– hard– and he swats it back at me. "I know women," I remind him.

"I know. That's why you're here and not any of the decent guys I know."

"Hey, I resent that," I tell him, rolling my eyes. "You listen to your sister too much."

"We have better things to talk about than your sex life," he responds.

"I highly doubt that," I joke with him. "There's really nothing better than my sex life."

"Oh, here we go..." I laugh, continuing our game. "But speaking of which, you still seeing the young blonde?"

"Samantha," I tell him, "and yes."

"Emi says she hasn't seen much of you lately. I'm guessing she's the reason?"

"I will admit that Sam requires a lot of my attention, yes," I answer honestly, "but I don't know if you've met the schmo she started seeing..."

"So you're a fan, are you?"

"You can tell? What's his name? Carter or Colin or Collie... something like that."

"Colin. And yes, I've met him. Briefly. He was at her place last week when I dropped off some books she had left at my apartment."

"First impression?"

"He's big. And his shirt was too tight."

"Yeah, right? He doesn't seem like her type," I hint.

"I don't know, Nate. I honestly don't know him well enough to say one way or another. Plus, what's her type, anyway?" He takes a break from the game to take a drink. He looks at me out of the corner of his eye. "The only guy she's spent any amount of time with is you, and you're just friends. I was beginning to wonder if guys were her thing."

"Shut the fuck up."

He laughs at me defending her. "I just wish she'd find a decent man soon."

"So you don't like him, then?"

"I didn't say that," he groans, starting the game up again. "I'm not going to shut the door on anyone this soon. I'll support any man who wants to date her until he gives me reason not to."

"He's given me reason. I don't like him."

"What? What don't you like about him?"

124

"He's a total dick!" is my first argument... admittedly not a good one. I decide to fill him in on the brief conversation Colin and I had at the basketball game.

"That's real mature."

"Just wait. You know we saw the Knicks together a few weeks ago, right?"

"Yeah, that's where she introduced you two. She told me. What happened?"

"He followed me into the men's room at the arena," I start, looking up at Chris, who is now completely interested in the conversation. "I would have punched him if I had the slightest bit of assurance that he wouldn't break both of my arms off and beat me with them."

"What'd he do?"

"He didn't *do* anything. It's what he *said*. Something like, 'She's a wild one,'" I begin.

"Yikes, do I want to know more?"

"I've never had to defend your sister's honor before, but I did. I mean, out of all the adjectives in the world, 'wild' is not one I would ever use to describe her."

"Yeah, agreed."

"So, after I stood up for her, he told me it was obvious that I hadn't 'had' her. I mean, can you believe that?"

"What? Surely you misunderstood."

I start the game again. "Yeah, I didn't misunderstand. His meaning was quite clear."

"How did you respond? Did you tell her?"

"I wanted to, but once we made it back to the suite, he made it a point to stake his claim on her by putting his hands all over her, glaring at me... you know, for the three minutes they stuck around before going off to wherever and... fuck, it just pisses me off."

He looks at me and laughs, shaking his head. "Don't tell her."

"Why not?"

"Because I just have a hard time believing–"

"It happened–"

"That's fine, so he's a little immature. Maybe he felt threatened by you, I don't know. But let it play out on its own. She hasn't dated anyone in awhile. And she's a pretty good judge of character. There's got to be some redeeming quality about him, right?"

"It's nothing I can see. Nor do I care to."

"You two really are ridiculous, you know that?"

I'm sure he can see through me. He's known me too long and knows me too well. There have been plenty of times that I've let my guard down. I have no doubt he knows how I feel about her, but he'll never say it and he'd never encourage me. I'm sure it's because she feels nothing for me in return.

"Why do you say that?" I decide to ask him anyway as his phone rings from the back of the court.

"Hold on. That's Anna." His smile grows instantly as he sighs, relieved. He runs to his gym bag and answers it. While he's on the phone, I check my emails. Three from Sam. One from my agent. None from Emi. It's been so long since she's dated someone that I don't remember if this is normal. Do we normally go this long without talking? I send her a text, just a friendly reminder that I'm still alive.

"Hey, what do you think about going to dinner with me and Anna?" Chris asks when he gets off the phone. "I'll ask Emi and Colin, too, and we can get to know him a little better. I want you both to meet Anna."

"Sam too?" I'm evenly split between wanting her to go with us and wanting to go alone. I'm just not sure she'll fit in with Chris and Emi.

"Of course."

My phone notifies me of a text message.

"Are you at home? I need a place to go."

"I'll be there in about fifteen minutes. Can't wait to catch up."

"Cool," I respond to Chris. "Emi's on her way to my place, so I'll talk to her. Next weekend?"

"Friday?"

"I'll see if that works for everyone and set something up," I tell him, gathering my things. "You gonna see her? Anna?"

"She wants to meet me for lunch. At my place," he smiles. "I really like this one." He seems genuinely happy, something he hasn't been in a really long time. It's good to see my friend this way.

"Alright. I'll call you later in the week."

"Sounds good. Tell Emi hi."

"Will do."

Emi is walking up to my building as soon as I pull in the drive. I wait for her so we can go upstairs together. She hands me a latte before trying to hug me.

"Careful, I need a shower." She steps back and waves instead.

"Where have you been? Or do I want to know..." Her voice trails off.

"I was with your brother, actually." She raises her eyebrows as we get into the elevator.

"I always knew there was something going on with you two," she teases. "Racquetball?"

"Yeah."

"What was he stressing about this time?" Emi asks, knowing her brother's habits.

"A woman."

"Really?" Emi says, a little shocked, exiting the lift and walking toward my door. "Who?"

"Someone named Anna," I explain, letting her in to the loft. She drops a bag full of her things on the dining room table and takes a seat on the couch. "Have you heard of her?"

"Not a word. I haven't talked to anyone in my family in awhile, though."

"All wrapped up in Collie, huh?"

She glares at me before correcting me. "You're one to talk. Speaking of which, I believe I just met your little Samantha."

I had wondered if that was a possibility. I knew Sam was working this morning at the coffee shop.

"I thought my chai tasted extra sweet. Did you tell her you knew me?"

"She's a bright one. I placed your regular order, and she did this cute little blushy-blinky-thing and said that it was how her boyfriend likes his chai. And then I told her I was pretty sure that it was for her boyfriend."

"Oh, god..." I sigh as I check my phone and see that Samantha has sent me six texts in the last five minutes. "Thanks, Emi. I didn't have time to warn her that we were hanging out." Sam continues to be very understanding of my friendship with Emi, but she is very demanding of my time.

"Well, she seemed okay about it. She was relieved to find out who I was. You've apparently told her about me."

"I have."

"She is young, though, isn't she? How old did you say she is?"

"Twenty-one," I remind her quietly.

"That's right. That means she was..." she pauses, making her thought process obvious, "in the third grade when we met in high school." She cringes a little. "Kinda creepy, no?"

"She's a grown woman now. There is nothing creepy about her."

Emi kicks her feet up onto the coffee table, reaching for the remote. She finds an indie music station and turns the volume up a little.

"So, what brings you out here so early on a Saturday morning?"

"Morning sex," she mutters with disdain.

"I don't know... I don't think Sam would approve of that." I laugh as she glares at me, trying to hide her own smile. "And what do you have against morning sex, Em?" I ask, sipping my latte.

"Nothing if I'm an active participant," she grins slyly. I try to think of other things to get the thought of her and morning sex out of my head. "But I'm not into threesomes, so I had to get out of there."

"So Teresa's found a new guy?"

"She's been seeing him for a few weeks. He's really nice, too. He seems different than the others."

"Wow, all the stars must have aligned to have all of us in relationships. That's never happened."

"No, I don't think it has," she agrees.

"Speaking of which, Chris would like you and Collie–"

"Colin–" she corrects me, sounding genuinely upset.

"Colin, I apologize... would like you to go on a triple date with us. We can meet Anna, and it'll give us all a chance to get to know everyone better. What do you say?"

"Will you learn his name by then?"

I give her a small smile and nod.

"Okay. When?"

"Friday. Can you do that?"

"I think so. I'll just have to see if it's okay with Colin."

"And why wouldn't it be?"

"He prefers it when it's just the two of us." She shrugs but avoids eye contact with me.

"I see. A little possessive?"

"I wouldn't say so. No."

I get up and make my way toward the kitchen to get some water. "You still like him?"

She hesitates a fraction of a second too long. "I do," she nearly sighs.

"Hmmm." I take a drink. "Does he give you that 'loving feeling?'" I ask her in a mocking tone. I'm genuinely curious, though. She gets up and grabs her bag, taking it back to the couch with her, just giving me a momentary glance. "I'll take that as a no."

"Take that as 'it's none of your business.'"

I take it as a no. I can hear the tension in her voice. "Taken. You've got work to do?" I ask casually.

"Yeah."

"Okay, I'm going to go clean up a bit. Make yourself at home."

"Cool."

"Cool."

After my shower, I pull on some pants and a t-shirt to work in. I start to set up my canvas in the guest room after turning on some additional lamps and readying my paint. I look over the sketch I had done earlier in the week in pencil, deciding I still like where the piece is going. I crack the window for ventilation and get to work.

After about a half hour, Emi walks into the room and sets my phone down abruptly on the dresser. "I can't get anything done. You keep getting texts."

"I'm sorry," I tell her, wondering if she's really annoyed. My hands smattered with paint, I don't bother to check my messages. Instead, I turn around to look at her as she's standing a few feet behind me with her arms crossed. "Everything okay?"

"So, who will be accompanying you on this date on Friday?" she asks me. I rinse my brush in a bowl of water and pick a new color, looking away from her.

"Sam," I tell her, continuing with my work. "Who else?" I laugh.

"Who's Audra?"

I groan inwardly, realizing that Emi has seen the texts. "No one."

"I highly doubt that she's no one." I hear the seriousness in her timbre.

"Calm down, Emi. She was once someone. But now, she's just a friend."

"When?"

"I dated her last year. Remember?"

"Nope. I don't remember an Audra."

"It was brief. Kate introduced us, remember?"

"Nope," she reiterates. "Why is she texting you?"

I set my paintbrush down carefully and pick up a rag from the floor, cleaning off my hands. "My, how I love the third degree," I tell her sarcastically.

"Are you cheating on Sam?"

"What do you think?" I ask her, getting angry. I've never cheated on any woman, and have no intention of starting now. I know that would be the quickest way to end our friendship, knowing how her family has been affected by people who have been unfaithful... her father's affair, her brother-in-law's indiscretions... it's caused the women in her family a lot of pain.

"Honestly, I think you are. Judging from the messages. *'It was good to reconnect. Thanks for lunch. When can I see you again?'*"

"I'm glad we've established boundaries of privacy, Emi."

"You left the phone sitting next to me. It kept chiming. She kept texting. What was I supposed to do?"

"Silence it? Ignore it? Not read it."

"Now it sounds like you're hiding something."

"I'm not hiding anything, Emi. We dated last year... we ran into each other on the subway. We decided to have lunch to talk about work. It was fun. She's got a show coming up and she wants me to help her prepare."

"And you're telling me you're not attracted to her?"

"Not in the way you're insinuating."

"So you are."

"Emi, I find lots of women to be attractive. I find *you* attractive, when you're not accusing me of being a complete heel. I can't help that. I do have some modicum of self-control, though. The last thing I want to do is hurt someone I love."

"Someone you love," she repeats.

"What's that supposed to mean?"

"Do you love Sam, Nate? The last I heard, she seems to have become more of a burden to you."

"Emi, I'm trying, and I care about her a lot. Do I know where this is heading? No. But sure, a part of me loves her. I wouldn't still be with her if that weren't true."

"Not hard to figure out which part..."

I roll my eyes at her. "What have I done to change your opinion of me? You're being a little mean."

She nods silently, recognizing her hostility. "You're right, I'm sorry. I just don't understand your definition of love. I guess that's all."

No, she doesn't. She never would. I think our opinions of love are as different as night and day... sometimes I wonder if she is even capable of love. If she knows what it really is.

"Maybe I just have a greater capacity to love," I tease after some of the tension subsides, shrugging my shoulders. "Lots to go around."

"If you *ever* become one of those assholes that cheats–"

"Emi, listen to yourself. Don't you know me at all?"

"I don't know. What do you consider cheating, then?" She asks, exasperated again, more so than I can understand. I just wish we could change the subject.

"Kissing another woman... certainly sleeping with another woman..." I explain. "What's your definition? Hanging out with other women? Talking to other women? Looking? Thinking about them?"

"I don't know, it depends."

"Am I cheating on Sam with you then?"

"No, we're friends."

"Well, what if I were to pursue a friendship with another woman, someone other than you? Someone like, say, Audra? Would that be cheating?"

"Well, I don't think it really matters what I think... but Sam certainly may think so."

"Then why don't you just let Sam be the judge... and you can just be my friend... like normal..."

"Does she know about Audra?"

"She knows she exists. She knows I ran into her last week."

"But she doesn't know you met her for lunch."

"It's not an issue. I didn't *not tell her* because I'm hiding it from her. I just didn't want to end up having a conversation like this one with *her* when there is nothing for her to be afraid of. I am not pursuing Audra.

"What are *you* afraid of?" I ask her.

"I could never forgive you..."

"I would never do it..." She looks at me contemplatively. "Emi, please, don't be mad," I plead. "I don't want to fight with you. I haven't seen you in over a week. I miss you."

"I don't want to fight, either," she turns to face me, frowning, a look of confusion spreading across her brow. If I didn't know her better, I'd think she was... *jealous?* "I'm sorry."

I walk to her and give her a hug, kissing the top of her head. "Like ya, Em." I look down into her unsure eyes.

"Like you, too, Nate," she smiles, looking a little apologetic.

After spending the afternoon together working, Emi is just packing up her things when I hear Sam's familiar knock on the door.

"Wanna stick around a little longer? Get to know her a little better?" I offer.

"No thanks. I need to get ready for my date."

I open the door for Sam, leaning down to kiss her before I let her in. "Emi's on her way out," I whisper in her ear. She scans the apartment quickly until she sees my friend.

"Hi," Sam says brightly. "Did you two have fun today?"

"We got a lot of work done," Emi says, smiling, slinging her bag over her shoulder. "It was nice to meet you, Sam. Probably see you Friday?" Emi asks, directing her attention to me.

"Friday," I tell her, holding the door open for her and then closing it behind her.

"What's Friday?" Sam asks quickly. "I have that night off. I thought we could do something."

I rub her arm in assurance, picking up on her insecurity. "We thought we might go out as a group. Us, Emi and her boyfriend, and Emi's brother and his new girlfriend."

"Oh," she says, relieved. "I'd like that. I want to get to know her better."

"I'd like for you to, too."

"I can tell she's important to you."

"She is. But so are you." I guide her over to the couch. "How was your day?" She sits down, kicking off her shoes and putting them in my lap. I take them in my hands and massage them, continuing with the typical routine we have when she comes over after work.

"Fine," she laments. She proceeds to tell me about different interactions she had with customers. Sometimes I have to focus more than normal to keep up with her chatty conversations. She talks more than most women I've dated, and I'm not always interested in the things she chooses to talk about. She tends to dwell on material things. A coat she liked, a pretty necklace a woman was wearing... shoes she saw in a window. When it comes time to buy her presents, I have no doubt she'll give me plenty of tips.

"This one couple," she starts, "just got engaged last night. They were on the way to Bulgari to get the ring resized. You should have seen it."

"Nice, huh?"

"I've never seen anything like it. The diamond was huge! I mean, the smaller diamonds were bigger than most solitaires I've ever seen. It was really pretty."

I just nod my head, following along with her story.

"He surprised her with it," she continues. "I think I'd like to pick out my own ring. Of course I wouldn't say no to a ring like that," she laughs. "I'd be a fool to."

"A girl who knows what she wants," I comment, leaning in to kiss her.

"I want you, right now," she whispers back to me.

"I can make that happen." We kiss some more on the couch before moving our activities to the bed.

"Nate?" she says after we make love that night.

"Yes, baby," I whisper, barely awake.

"Nate, I love you."

"I love you, too."

"Nate?"

"Yes?"

"Do you love me enough to marry me?" she asks. In the back of my mind, I knew this conversation was coming, but still, I'm not prepared with an answer. Holding her in my arms, I look down at her to meet her blue eyes, her blonde hair messy and obscuring my view.

"I'm not ready to get married," I tell her honestly.

"That's not what I asked."

"I think you will make an incredible wife. Any man will be lucky to have you." I lean down and meet her lips with mine.

"I still don't think you answered my question," she says seriously, but I can hear a hint of playfulness in her tone. "But I just want you to know that I could see myself marrying you." I smile and brush the hair away from her eyes. "Not yet, of course," she adds.

"Of course."

"Why aren't you ready?"

Am I ready? I'm twenty-eight. Most men my age are engaged, married or divorced. I'd like to be committed to one woman for the rest of my life. I don't enjoy going from relationship to relationship.

Maybe that wasn't the best answer. Maybe I'm just not ready to marry *Sam*. I'd had vague notions of myself as a married man, but Sam was not the woman by my side. I don't know why. I care about her. I have fun with her. I just can't see myself growing old with her.

"I'm not sure. I guess I just haven't given it much thought. My relationships typically don't last this long," I laugh quietly.

"Do you think you could start giving it some thought?" she asks me shyly. Is marrying her an idea I could get used to?

"Sure," I assure her. And maybe it is. It's definitely worth considering.

~ * ~

In the following days, I'd done what I told Samantha I'd do. I started thinking more about marriage, and more specifically marrying her. It just wasn't an idea I could easily rectify in my mind. I still think it's too soon to even consider it, but the more I think about it, about her, the more I realize she might not be the right woman for me. She's so young and naïve... and needy.

Still, I don't want to write her off too soon. I'd like to have the opportunity to get some other opinions. The date with Chris, Anna, Emi and Colin should be the perfect chance to get a little perspective from two of my closest friends.

"I'm nervous," Sam whispers in my ear as we wait for the hostess to seat us in the Spanish restaurant I'd chosen.

"Why?" I ask her with a chuckle, wrapping my arm around her bare shoulder. "You look perfect. Everyone's going to love you."

"I hope." I could tell that Sam was putting a lot of pressure on herself tonight. I think she feared that if my friends disapproved, it would be over between us. Even if their opinions weren't favorable, I wasn't ready to end what we had going yet.

"Just be yourself. And I bet everyone's a little nervous anyway, so you'll fit right in," I assure her.

"Right this way, sir," a host signals for us and leads us to the table already occupied by Emi, Chris, Colin and a very pretty Asian woman that I assume is Anna. I smile at Chris and nod my approval. He stands up to greet us, shaking my hand and pulling the chair next to his out for Samantha. As he talks to my girlfriend, I make my way over to his date.

"Anna, I presume?"

"Hi, you must be Nate," she says with a smile that would ease anyone's fears. "It's so good to finally meet you."

"You, as well."

136

Emi's seated next to her, and she stands up to hug me. It's not our normal hug, as her hands barely touch my arms. Colin's too busy eating a chip to even shake my hand. I finally find my way back to the empty chair and take a seat next to Sam. She's introducing herself to Anna and complimenting her on the shirt she's wearing.

"You remember Emi," I mention at the end of their conversation.

"Of course," she says with a small wave across the table at my friend.

"And that's her date, Colin." I refuse to call him her boyfriend.

"Pleasure," he says, stretching his hand over my plate to shake hers.

"I'm Samantha," she says to him. He nods once, returning to his appetizer. *Pleasant guy. Real winner, Em.*

I try to make eye contact with her to see what she thinks about his greeting, but she and Anna are laughing quietly together. Colin taps Emi on the shoulder once and holds a chip in front of her face.

"Taste this, babe," he says to her. I catch myself cringing a second too late. He feeds her the chip, and she looks a little uncomfortable, her eyes meeting mine, then Chris's. I fake a smile at her, then turn my attention to her brother.

"So, Colin," he says, distracting him from feeding her any more food, at least for a few seconds. "Tell me what you do. Emi says you're a writer?"

"Yeah, I write the sports column for the Journey News– LoHud– and I do some freelance now and then for Sports Illustrated." *One time* he wrote an article for his hometown paper, and it was picked up by the well-known magazine. *One time.* I stave off my laughter and keep that fact to myself, not wanting anyone to know that I had done a little research on the guy.

"Any sport in particular?" I ask, joining the conversation.

"Football and baseball, mainly. I played both in college."

"Really? Where?"

"SUNY," he says.

"And what was your major?" I continue.

"Communications," he says.

"Great, when did you graduate?" I already know the answer.

"I didn't," he begins, not an ounce of regret in his voice. "I was drafted to a minor league football team, so I took that gig and ran." He laughs, proud.

"Excellent," I say. "So, what happened with that career?" My tone is admittedly condescending, and he sits up straight in his chair, puffing his chest out.

"He had a leg injury," Emi speaks up as she puts her hand on Colin's. She slants her eyes at me. "His experience at his college newspaper got him the job at LoHud."

"Sounds like an awesome job. What city is that paper in?"

"Rockland... Putnam..." He knows I'm mocking him.

"Right, right. Lots of high school reporting, I guess."

"I hear there's a baseball team in Putnam with a female pitcher," Sam joins in, sensing the tension and trying to diffuse it. "My cousin goes to that school."

"Really?" Colin says, genuinely interested. "I'll have to look into that. That'd make a pretty good story."

Sam smiles brightly, proud.

"I guess you know all about high school sports," Emi pipes in, her attention directed at Sam. "Didn't you just graduate last year?" Emi knows exactly when she graduated.

"No," Sam says, then swallows, picking up on Emi's tone. "I'm a junior at NYU."

"What sorority are you in?"

"I'm not in any sorority," Sam cocks her head slightly when she answers.

"Surprising," Emi mutters under her breath. "I thought all prom queens were automatically drafted into some greek underworld or something."

"You were the prom queen?" Chris's date asks, hanging on to a fact that I wish I had never mentioned to Emi. Anna sounds genuinely interested, though. I like this woman already.

"Yeah, but that was a long time ago." I can tell Sam's embarrassed and doesn't want to talk about it anymore.

"Three years," Emi sighs. "So long ago..."

"I'm sorry," I whisper to my date.

"No, it's fine," she says.

"Do you really want to talk about prom night, Em? Because, boy, do we have a story to tell." She glares at me from across the table. When I look at Chris, he's looking at me with contempt. Emi didn't go to her senior prom out of principle and she had regretted it ever since. That night, she had locked herself in her room and wouldn't come out. Her mother and I sat at the door and tried to talk some sense into her, but it didn't work. It took a phone call from Chris later that night to calm her down. She told me to never bring it up, and I never had until now.

"Why? What happened on your prom night?" Colin asks her.

"Nothing," she mumbles. "And that's the truth."

Colin shifts his focus to me, waiting for me to add to her story.

"You heard the lady." I smile at him mischievously, which is sure to create more questions in his mind. "Wild," I mutter aside, but loud enough for him to hear.

"Anna," Chris jumps in. "Why don't you tell everyone what you do."

"I'm an interior designer," she says with a blush.

"Nate has a great loft that could use a woman's touch," Sam says. "I've been trying to get him to redecorate. I have a lot of ideas. I'd love to talk to you about them!"

"Great!" Anna says. Emi's attention is piqued, her eyes curious.

"Let's not get ahead of ourselves, Sam," I tell her. "Plus, everything there has a purpose. It's all there to highlight the art."

"Oh, right," she says. "I didn't mean–"

"It's okay," I cut her off, not wanting to hurt her feelings. Emi smugly smiles from across the table. "You know, maybe we can work on the guest bedroom together."

"Really?" Sam asks as Emi chokes on her wine.

"Sure." I lean down to kiss her gently. When we part, I glance to see Emi, looking away with purpose, revealing a mark just above her collarbone when her loose shirt slips off her shoulder. My first inclination is to point it out. "Did you scratch yourself or something? There's a large red mark on your neck." *Asshole, marking his territory.*

Instinctively, she immediately draws her hand over the hickey he had left on her delicate pale skin. She knew exactly where it is, and by the blush on cheeks, I'm certain she knows exactly *what* it is, as well.

"I don't know what you're talking about," she lies. "If you'll excuse me, I'll go take a look."

Colin smiles smugly, glaring at me as he downs his third beer.

"Nate," Chris scolds me as Colin stands up, presumably to follow Emi. "Colin, have a seat, I'll handle this," he says. Emi's boyfriend doesn't argue, sitting back down and having another chip. As Chris leaves the table, he whispers over my shoulder, requesting me to follow him.

"I'll be right back, sweetie," I tell Sam as I squeeze her hand.

As we walk toward the bathrooms, he has a hard time keeping his cool. "What are you, *four?* You two are acting like children. You're embarrassing yourselves— and me— in front of a woman I really like. Not to mention the unfortunate dates you both brought along."

"I—"

"Fix this, Nate." He goes into the men's restroom, leaving me in the hallway alone. I wait for Emi to come out of the ladies room. As soon as she sees me, she attempts to push me, trying to move around me, but I block her from getting away. She glares at me angrily.

"This is turning out to be a great night, huh?" I ask her, trying to break the ice. It doesn't work. She steps past me, but stays in the hallway, out of sight of the restaurant diners.

"What is your problem!?"

"Me? What is *your* problem?"

"*You're* my problem," she answers, crossing her arms across her chest.

"Yeah? Well why are you being such a bitch to Sam?"

"Excuse me?" she asks. "Why am I being a *what?*"

"You heard me," I say, lacking the guts to repeat what I had called her.

"Why, Nate," she says innocently, "I'm just trying to get to know her better. I assume you're doing the same by belittling Colin?"

"I have no idea what you're talking about."

"He has a good job, Nate. A steady job. He earns his own money... he wasn't born with a silver spoon up his ass like *some* people I know."

"Wow, my money never bothers you when you get to take advantage of its perks. Are you a little jealous?"

"Shut up, Nate. No way in hell am I jealous." I laugh at her answer.

"So I'm supposed to like him because he has good work ethic? Tell, me, Em, does he have good grammar, too? I know that's a requirement for you. Does he pass your test of they're, their and there?"

"I'm sure he does."

"And I'm sure you're overlooking the obvious. You've lowered your standards to the gutter for this winner. I've read his articles, Emi. They suck."

"Right," she answers.

"I have. Have you? Because if you have, you'd realize they have no sports editor at LoHud, and you would have discovered that he does *not,* in fact, know the difference between they're, their and there."

"I don't care," she argues. "He knows a lot of other things." I can tell by the tone of her voice what she's insinuating.

"Yes, he's left his proof on you," I remind her. "Classy guy. Who needs money when he can give you your very own, personalized, front-facing tramp stamp. Look, it's Emi's red badge of fucking," I say, pulling her shirt sleeve down to prove my point. When I look closer, I notice it's not a hickey after all. It's a fresh bruise. Upon further inspection, I discover another one closer to the nape of her neck.

"Stop," she says, adjusting her shirt.

"What is that, Emi?" I ask, suddenly concerned.

"It's a hickey, just like you thought."

"No, it's not. What the fuck are those?" I pull the sleeve away once more and lightly press my fingers into both.

"Ow," she hisses.

"Are you guys finished over here?" Chris says from behind me. Emi quickly averts her eyes and pulls the sleeve back up again.

"We're fine," she answers him.

"No, Chris, come–" She grips my forearm tightly.

"We're handling things," she smiles at her brother. "We just need another minute or two."

"Please do not make me regret bringing her to meet you. I really want this to work with her." Before I have a chance to speak again, he turns on his heels and returns to the table.

I look back down at Emi, the shock still apparent on my face.

"Did Colin do this?" I brush her shoulder again to remind her of the marks.

"Shut up, Nate, you're completely out of line. You don't know him at all."

"I'm trying to understand him," I pause, realizing my lie. "No, I'm not. I couldn't care less about him, and my god, Emi, if he is hurting you–"

"He's not," she says with a look of disgust on her face. "What just because he's got more muscles than you, you think he beats me?"

"I didn't say that."

"I dropped some books from that shelf in my room," she spits at me. "He had nothing to do with this."

"Then why did you lie and say it was a hickey?"

"It makes for a much better story, doesn't it?"

"Right, of course. Then why didn't you let me have Chris take a look?"

"Because I know his temper, and I know he would jump to conclusions. And I know Colin's strength... my brother wouldn't stand a chance against him."

"Well, what if I decide to take matters into my own hands, then?"

"You wouldn't."

"I might."

"I'd say go for it. You'd be completely in the wrong, and I don't give a shit about what he does to you." I know she's just angry with me... I know she doesn't mean it; even her eyes tell me so.

"Thanks."

"Well, you've been a complete dick all night."

"And you've been the model of civility yourself, Emi."

"You've deserved it."

"Why? What have I done, aside from trying to make you see the guy you're dating for the asshole he really is?"

"That's plenty."

"What do you see in him?"

"You're one to talk. The only thing your Barbie-doll mute has contributed to the conversation is some tidbit about high school."

"You haven't given her a chance to speak!"

"I can see she'll just be one of those women who will sit pleasantly by your side, agreeing with everything you say, going along with everything you do, until she has her hooks in you. Then you'll get to know the real Sam, and it'll be too late to get out."

"What the fuck are you talking about?"

"I can just see her manipulative little mind at work, that's all."

"Whatever. If you just tried to get to know her, you'd see you're completely misjudging her."

"Well, we won't need to worry about that. I don't want to know her."

"That's very mature."

"Doesn't seem like you're into maturity. If you were, you'd date a grown up." She slants her eyes and smiles smugly.

"Alright, I'm done," I tell her, trying to end the argument. "Your brother brought us here to get to know Anna. Let's just try to put this aside for now–"

"Fine," she says.

"Just after I ask Colin about those bruises." I turn to walk toward the table. Either she truly doesn't care about my safety, or she doesn't believe that I will follow through on my threat. I don't think he'll attack me in the restaurant.

I sit down next to Sam as she immediately takes my hand in hers and squeezes it tightly. "So, Colin–"

"Anna, I'm sorry," Emi cuts me off. "I must be having an allergic reaction to some of the food," she explains to her brother's date as she scratches her neck close to the spot I had pointed out to the entire table.

"Oh, that's too bad," Anna says. "I hope you're okay."

"I'm sure it's fine. Probably some herb or something," she mumbles. "But listen, I'll get your number from Chris. Maybe we can meet for drinks one night this week?"

"That'd be great," Anna says.

"Colin," Emi taps her boyfriend on the shoulder as he chews on an appetizer. "Nate was nice enough to offer to drop me off on his way home," she lies to him, "but I was hoping you could take me. I know it's out of your way."

"No, it's fine, babe. Sure. We just ordered, though. Can we wait and have them box it up?"

"Colin, I think we need to go now," she says, her voice urgent. She watches me out of the corner of her eye to make sure I don't say any more.

"I could bring your food by," I offer her, glaring.

"No thank you. We'll find something at home."

"I was looking forward to the lobster," Colin explains, still seated and completely unconcerned with Emi's fake illness.

Emi bites her bottom lip to keep from saying more.

"You should take her now," I tell him, just wanting him out of my eyesight for good. "Plus, maybe it's not a food allergy. Maybe those splotches on her neck are contagious."

"Nate," she warns.

"Wouldn't want them to spread, that's all I'm saying." I stare at Colin as I say this, hoping he understands that I know that they're bruises.

He stands up abruptly and throws his napkin on his plate.

"Goodnight, Emi," Sam calls after my friend. Emi turns around to acknowledge her. "I hope you get better soon. Let us know if you need anything."

"Thanks," Emi says, her smile forced.

Chris finally speaks up after they leave. "I'm sure she'll be fine," he says, addressing his girlfriend. "I've never known her to have any food allergies, though. I'll check on her later."

"So, Nate, tell me about your artwork," Anna says, continuing our dinner as if nothing has happened. She takes a sip of her wine and smiles at me and Sam across the table. I can tell she's going to be good for Chris.

The rest of the evening was just tense between Chris and me. Anna and Sam talked a lot, although the only thing the two found in common was their interest in fashion. Chris would feign interest in their discussion, but shot me glares from across the table constantly.

As we left, he muttered one comment to me. "That's how you fix things?" All the way home, I've been going over the fight with Emi in my head. What did he expect me to do? She's stubborn and wasn't interested in talking anything out. She's the one who chose to leave.

She chose to leave with that prick that apparently held her in some way that left obvious bruises around her neck. It makes me sick just thinking about it. Should I be worried about her now? I am. I wish I could call her.

My anger has returned by the time Sam and I get home, although I'm trying my best to hide it from my girlfriend.

"Can I ask you a question?" Samantha asks when we get back to my apartment.

"Of course," I tell her, taking her jacket from her and kissing the back of her neck, in the same spot I saw the second bruise on Emi. I can't keep dwelling on this.

"I know you said you and Emi never had a relationship..."

I don't really want to talk about her now. "Mmm-hmm..." I tell her with my lips still pressed against her skin. I let my hands travel down her body to her waist and unbuckle the tiny belt. As I take it off of her, I spin her around and pull her into my chest. "What's your question?" I lean down to kiss her willing lips. When we pull away, I gaze into her eyes, trying to communicate my intentions to her.

She shakes her head slightly. "When you look at me like that, I forget everything."

"Good," I respond, kissing her again. Her hands find my hair while mine pull her skirt up. I trace the lace of her thong as she hums quietly in my mouth. I kiss her ears next, and hear her whisper the question in mine.

"Did she ever want a relationship?"

"No," I answer quickly, unfastening her skirt.

"She seemed jealous of me." Her fingers fight with the buttons of my shirt. I pull back again to help her, to gaze into her eyes some more.

"No," I tell her again, pulling the skirt down her legs. She steps out of it as she pushes the shirt from my shoulders and pulls it from my arms. Her lips crash into mine once again while she busies her hands, removing my pants. We part only long enough for me to pull her shirt over her head.

She tries to talk to me as I continue to kiss her.

"Did you ever want a relationship with her?"

"Are we really still talking about this?" I ask her. "No, absolutely not. And the only thing I want right now is you, now."

"Okay," she breathes, moving her lips to my jaw, then to my chest, stomach. She kneels down in front of me, taking my boxers into her hands quickly and yanking them to the ground. A moan escapes my throat as I feel her lips around me.

"Oh, god, Sam," I say quickly, surprised by her actions. She's never done this before... never even hinted that it was something she would or could do.

And fuck, can she do it *well...*

I stop her momentarily and angle her head to me.

"Am I doing it right?"

"Very right," I tell her. "I love you, baby."

"I love you, too," she tells me, kissing the inside of my thigh. "Just tell me before... you know..."

"Okay," I smile at her, putting my hands in her hair and guiding her back to me. I've been deprived of this pleasure for so long that I've forgotten just how much I've missed it. It's easy for me to get lost in it, in her, in my own gratification. My head in a fog, I'm only mindful enough to warn her as I get close.

She backs off gently, taking my hand in hers and walking slowly– too slowly for my taste– to the bed. I rush past her, lying down on the comforter, not bothering with pulling the sheets down. She climbs on top of me quickly, her hands pressed hard into my chest. I watch the rise and fall of her body, her breasts as I grip her hips tightly, guiding her motions. I take her quickly and fully, unable to contain myself any longer.

"Sam," I begin to warn her, but the sounds of her orgasm and the feel of her around me push me completely over the edge. We come together, and she soon collapses to my chest, kissing it reverently.

I pick her head up to look at her pretty, smiling face. I can't help but kiss her again, over and over.

"Thank you," I whisper.

"You're welcome," she answers.

"Where'd you learn to do that?"

"Cosmo."

"Well, thank him, whoever he is," I joke with her. She playfully slaps my chest as I take her in my arms and hold her closely to my chest. As I stroke her blonde hair and listen to her ideas for redecorating the guest room, I finally allow my conscience to acknowledge the one thing I didn't do tonight. I wonder if she knows. I wonder if I should say something. I wonder if it matters anyway.

I decide it doesn't, eventually dozing off as her soft voice lulls me to sleep.

~ * ~

As I amble to Emi's apartment, taking my time, planning my words, I think over the past two and a half weeks.

I hadn't spoken to Emi since then– well, since the morning after the disastrous triple-date. While Sam was showering that Saturday, I had called my friend's apartment to make sure she was okay. I had woken up that morning from a nightmare. In my dream, Colin had beat her to within an inch of her life.

"What?" she had answered her phone curtly.

"Hi."

"Did you need something?" she asked.

"I dreamed he hurt you. I was just checking to make sure you were okay," I explain, a little put off by her attitude. I really didn't feel like she had any reason to be mad at me.

"Did you tell Chris?" she deflected my concern.

"No. Maybe I should have."

"Thanks," she says, her response still terse.

"You didn't answer me. Are you okay?"

"I'm fine, Nate," she scoffed at me.

"Is he there?"

"That's none of your business."

"Well, it will help me gauge the honesty of your answer."

"No, he's not here."

"So you're sure you're okay."

"Stop acting like you care about me," she had said, a comment that caught

148

me off guard.

"Emi," I had sighed into the phone. "What are you talking about? Of course I care about you. What's with you?"

"Just..." she had begun, but never finished. "I need some time to think about things, okay? Things are kind of messed up right now." *As if I didn't know that already.*

"Alright, Emi. That's fine. But I want you to know I care and I'm here for you. And I will worry about you as long as I know you're still seeing him. He's bad news."

"You don't know him." And then she had hung up on me. I had tried to call her twice since then, but she refused to answer or return my voicemails.

I'm sure she'll be surprised to see me today, but I have no one else to go to, and I have to talk to her. I have to get someone else's perspective. Sam didn't understand my need to go see her in particular, but my girlfriend trusted me anyway. *My girlfriend.* What have I gotten myself into?

I notify Emi of my presence with my usual knock. She answers quickly.

"Hey. What are you doing here?" I can't read her demeanor today.

"We need to talk, Emi."

She nods her head, opening the door for me to enter her apartment. I wave quietly to Teresa.

"Do I need the earplugs?" her roommate asks. Emi looks at me expectantly, and I shrug my shoulders, forcing a smile. "You know, on second thought..." Teresa gathers up some papers from her bed and picks up her laptop. "I think I'll go get some coffee."

"Thanks," I tell her.

"No problem." She closes the door quietly, leaving Emi and me alone in their silent apartment.

"What's going on?" she asks.

I exhale heavily and laugh, knowing all too well that nothing I'm about to tell her is funny by any means. "Mind if I sit down?"

"Go ahead." We both take a seat on her bed. I immediately take my head into my hands and begin tugging at my hair. "Must be bad," she says. "An apology shouldn't stress you–"

"Sam's preg–" I interrupt her quickly. I have to clear my throat to get the rest of the word out. "Sorry. Pregnant." I process her words and realize she was expecting an apology. Maybe I should have started with that, but the news I was bringing her would have overshadowed anything else anyway.

I stay still, waiting for Emi to say something. A full minute passes before I look up to see her staring at the wall across the room. Her jaw is taut and I'm pretty sure she's holding her breath.

"Say something."

"Okay," she says, short.

"Okay? That's all you're gonna say? Okay?"

"What the fuck am I supposed to say, Nate? Should I be congratulating you? Did you want me to start planning her shower? What did you expect?"

"I don't know. What are you thinking?" I ask her.

"I'm thinking you're an idiot–"

"I know," I tell her before she can even finish.

"You're sure?" she asks, still unable to look in my direction.

"She took a test at home this morning. She said it's positive."

"She said, or it was?"

"I didn't see it... but it was. She wouldn't lie about something like this."

"If I were you, I'd want to see proof." Just like that, she has me questioning Samantha, even though she's never given me reason to doubt her.

"We'll take another test. But it could have happened–"

"How?" she interrupts. "How could it have happened?"

"How do you think?" I ask her. "We weren't careful." I remember back to that night. I remember how angry I was at Emi. I remember that I wanted to do anything, everything to keep myself from thinking about her. I allowed myself to get completely wrapped up in Samantha.

Emi gets up hurriedly and walks to the kitchen, grabbing a bottle of wine from the metal rack above her sink. After pouring herself a glass, she takes a seat on a barstool, her back to me.

I walk over to her and put my hand on her shoulder. "Emi, please talk to me."

She shrugs away, picking up her wine and walking back over to the window. "I can't even begin to figure out what to say to you. Really, idiot is the only word that comes to mind. Fucking idiot."

"Emi, be fair. It was an accident."

"Pretty big one, though, Nate, don't you think?"

"Of course." I swallow hard, wondering if this conversation would have gone any better had we been on better terms in the first place.

"Well, I guess that's it," she says plainly. Even with her back to me, even though she's trying to hide her emotions from me, I can tell she's crying.

"What's it?" I again approach her from behind and try to comfort her, finding her reaction odd. Shouldn't this be the other way around?

"I hope you love her, Nate." She flinches when I touch her arm. "Get your hands off me."

"What is your problem, Emi?"

"My problem?" she asks, agitated and wiping tears away. "I don't have a problem. This is all your problem. I'm washing my hands of this."

"Emi, come on. You're my best friend, I need you."

"You've got Sam now."

"I need her, too. But I can't do this without you."

She scoffs at me. "Well, why didn't you consult me before? I would have told you not to get her pregnant. But I thought you probably had that under control. You managed not to get any of the *other ones* pregnant. I just assumed you had the safe sex thing figured out by now."

"Okay, I didn't come here for a lecture."

"Then why did you come?"

"I don't know what to do."

"Step one," she says harshly. "Go to the drug store and buy another test. Or better yet, take her to a doctor."

"I will–"

"Step two, decide if you love her." I expect her rant to continue to step three, but when it doesn't, I look over to her. She's staring at me now, the tears gone, her face hard and uncaring. "Do you?"

I glare back at her with measured restraint. "I could."

"That's great, Nate. It's the vow all women want to hear. *I could love you. You've kind of forced my hand, Sam,*" she says, mocking my voice, "*but yeah, I think I could love you.*"

"Will you just stop with the fucking sarcasm, Em?" She's really trying my patience.

"I'm afraid I don't have a lot more to contribute to this conversation, Nate. I could go back to calling you a fucking idiot, if you'd like–"

"Not particularly, no. It's not helpful at all."

"What kind of help can I give? I sold the time machine last week. And I used up my last genie wish to get these new shoes."

"Talk me through this. I'm not looking for a miracle. Just a little compassion or understanding or something."

"Well, I don't understand how you got yourself into this situation."

"It wasn't planned."

"I never thought it was. I know you're smarter than that. I doubt she is," she mumbles as an afterthought. "How is she handling the news?"

"Better than I expected."

"Let me guess, she's ring shopping now, right?"

I look away, knowing she can read me.

"She's talking about getting married, isn't she?"

"She had talked about it before, so what?"

"What?" she laughs. "When?"

"A month ago, I don't know. I told her I wasn't ready."

"She brought it up, though?"

"Yes."

"And how did this conception happen?"

"What?"

"How did it come about that you were completely irresponsible and got her pregnant? Especially knowing that she's hearing wedding bells in the distance." *Well, Emi, I was pissed at you for defending that Neanderthal you're sleeping with, and I had to get that frustration out somehow.* The aggressive way I approached Sam that night was fueled by those feelings. Of course I can't tell her this.

"I'm not– I don't–"

"Who was the irresponsible one?"

"No one. No one is at fault. We both were." I think back to that night, remembering how Samantha had turned the tables on me and had taken charge. It was such a turn on. There wasn't an ounce of rational thinking happening in my mind once that happened– not that there was a whole lot to start with, anyway.

"Did she know at the time the risk she was taking? I guess she's not on the pill?"

"No."

"No to which question?"

"No, she's not on the pill."

"And you knew that?"

"Yes."

"And she knew you weren't wearing a condom?"

"Of course she knew."

"Well why didn't you take action? And pull out?"

My face gets hot, having never really discussed such things with her. "I don't want to talk about the mechanics of my sex life with you."

"Grow the fuck up, Nate."

"Alright, I wasn't in any position to pull out."

Emi groans loudly. "She fucking planned this," she says.

"No–"

"Don't be naïve... I never did trust that girl. She looked at you and never saw past your money."

"*She's* in love with *me*."

"Sure she is. Nate, she doesn't even know you."

"Of course she does. How could she not?"

"You've only been seeing her for two months! That's not enough time to tell whether or not you want to spend a lifetime with a person."

"That's hilarious, coming from you, Miss I-kissed-a-guy-once-and-felt-sunshine-and-ponies-and-nothing-else-will-ever-live-up-to-that."

"Fuck you. Don't throw that back at me."

"Move past it, then."

"Don't make this about me. You came here for a reason. What do you want me to do?"

"Well, I'm not sure now, because I certainly can't get *relationship* advice from you."

She raises her eyebrows, clearly angry. "Yeah, and what does that mean?" She sets her glass down forcefully. I'm amazed it didn't break as the wine sloshes over the side and onto the dresser I was leaning against. I move before the liquid reaches me. "What do you think I'm doing with Colin?"

"I have no earthly idea why you're with that asshole. You're clearly not in a relationship... you're in a high school drama class, playing the part of someone you're not. You think Sam doesn't know me? Well Colin doesn't know the first thing about you."

"You don't know him or anything about us."

"You're right, but I know his type... and I sure as hell don't know who this woman in front of me is anymore. You're dating a walking advertisement for steroids, dressing up for him like some teen-aged preppy whore–"

"Excuse me?" she yells, standing in front of me, frozen.

"Yeah. that's not you. Your over-done makeup and your breasts spilling out of your shirts and your tight jeans and those fucking ribbons in your hair..." My aggression propels me forward, toward her, causes her to move backwards, away from me. She stops when she reaches the wall.

"So what if I want to dress differently? It's how he likes me to look, who gives a shit?"

"You should, Emi, you're acting like someone I don't even know!"

"How so?" she asks.

"For starters, the Emi I know doesn't fuck in the backseat of cars!"

"What?!" She seems surprised that I know, her eyes confirming the truth I didn't want to admit. "For your information, I don't *fuck* anywhere."

"Yes, because it's all about *making love* with him, right?" I ridicule her.

She looks away to respond. "Like you'd know *anything* about that–"

"Tell me, Emi," I continue, pulling her forcefully to me and turning her around, taking her hair in my hands. "Does he hold on to these pigtails when he takes you from behind?" I nudge into her, immediately feeling myself begin to get harder. *Fuck.* One of my hands lets go of her hair and sweeps down her arm, settling on her hip.

She swings around and slaps me with all the force her small body can throw at me. I take her arms in my hands, restraining her from hitting me again and pulling her toward me, her lips so close to mine. She breathes heavily, her eyes shifting back and forth from mine.

Time stands still in that moment. I react without thinking.

I press my lips hard against hers, holding her head to mine. She freezes for a couple of seconds, then pushes me away, but only a few inches. She looks at me with a furrowed brow, her eyes curious and confused. She swallows and leans back into me, initiating another kiss.

Is this my chance?

I kiss her passionately, letting my feelings for her pour out into our embrace. Her hands form fists, clenching tightly to my t-shirt and holding me close to her. My lips move quickly to her chin, then to her neck. She closes her eyes and leans her head back into my awaiting hands. She sighs as I feel her fingers fall to the waistline of my jeans, lingering.

What the hell are we doing?

A million thoughts race through my head, but are immediately interrupted when she breaks away abruptly, pushing hard against my chest and shaking her head. She blinks away tears from her eyes as she stumbles back a few steps.

I reach out to steady her and pull her back toward me. I want to kiss her again– *fuck, what am I thinking?* I lean into her once more, but this time, she looks to the side, avoiding me. "Get away, Nate." She turns her back to me and stares out the window. "Don't you ever do that again to me. Ever!"

"God, Emi, tell me what you want from me," I plead with her, frustrated.

"Not this," she's barely able to choke out. *Not this.* I recall her stating that exact sentiment that night in college. *I don't want this.* It's happening all over again.

"You didn't feel it, did you?" I ask her harshly, easily reading her thoughts as if they were written on her face. She doesn't have to answer. I move closer, observing tears streaming down her cheeks. "Because it wasn't real, Emi," I tell her, leaning closer, trying to reason with her, referring to the ever-elusive mystical kiss that she has never been able to recreate.

"It was!" she argues loudly as I take a step back. "I know what I felt!"

"When are you going to figure out that love is more than a physical reaction to one fucking kiss!? It's been *nine years!*"

Again, she doesn't answer me.

"Just give up the search," I press on, but she remains quiet. I kneel down, meeting her eye-to-eye. She tries to move away from me, but I hold her close, my hands on her shoulders.

"Leave me alone!" she eventually screams, clearly confused and afraid, pushing against me but unable to get away. Her cheeks grow red.

"Emi, what is going on with you? Why are you so pissed at me?"

"Because everything is changing," she cries. "You've changed. We can't even have a normal conversation with one another anymore without one of us offending the other. It's exhausting. I'm tired." She puts her hands over her teary eyes, weeping softly.

"I'm sorry–"

"Why did you kiss me, Nate?" she whispers.

Honestly, I can't explain why I did it. I didn't have words to express my feelings in that moment, and I certainly don't now. I wanted her to feel something for me, but she didn't. She *doesn't*. "I don't know." I finally drop my hands and let her go.

She walks back over to her bed and sits down. She speaks, but doesn't look at me directly. "You've got a pregnant girlfriend who's probably trying on white dresses right now. And I don't like her, Nate, I really don't."

"I'm sorry, Emi." I walk toward her door, knowing it's past time for me to leave.

"Where do I fit in?" she asks, stopping me. I stare at my feet, afraid to look into her eyes. I can't stand to see her cry anymore.

"I don't know," I tell her honestly.

"I don't, either." All I *do* know is that this wasn't how any of this was supposed to happen. I start to walk back toward her, wanting to figure things out, but she stops me. "Get out, Nate," she says quietly. "Please go home."

"Alright." I know I don't have a say in this. I shut the door behind me and stand outside, unable to move.

"I hate you, Nate," I hear her mumble aloud. I open the door and walk back in to her apartment.

"Emi–"

"Get the fuck out, Nate!" She throws a pillow at me and buries her head in another one.

"I'm sorry," I tell her again.

"It's not good enough."

"I know." She stands up and marches toward me, pushing me out into the hallway and slamming the door in my face. The locks fasten quickly.

In a daze, I walk to the stairwell at the end of the hall and open the door. The lone lightbulb flickers above me, barely lighting my way down the steps. I sit down on the second landing, taking in the silence and solitude. I tug at my hair in frustration.

What the fuck just happened? Did I kiss her? Did I just tell her I fathered a child with another woman and kiss her, all in the same five-minute period? What the fuck is wrong with me? Why wouldn't she hate me?

And why did I kiss her? And why did it have to feel so fucking right? I was already unsure of what to do before, but now I'm completely confused. Why did I allow myself to act on those feelings? I've refrained for years, and now, when I have no choice but to be committed to a woman I don't think I fully love, now is when I decide to kiss her?

Do I tell Sam?

Didn't I, by my own definition, just cheat on her?

No, no, it wasn't like that. It was an act of passion, but I did it out of anger, not love. It's not the same thing. *It's not.* I keep telling myself this. *It's not.* The gravity of the situation seeps in.

I'm going to be a father.

I'm not ready, not now. And not with Samantha as the mother. When I pictured what my future family would look like, it did not include my current girlfriend. Instead, they were small children with porcelain skin, strawberry blonde hair, and deep dimples in their cheeks... their mother, the woman I have just left in tears a few floors above.

CHAPTER   8

I can't believe I just spent one-hundred-and-seventy-five dollars on baby shoes. One lone pair of faux-suede baby shoes.

"Would you like them gift-wrapped, sir?" the saleswoman asks.

"No, that won't be necessary," Sam says. She links her arm with mine and takes the shopping bag, careful not to mess up her newly-manicured nails. "Don't you think those would be okay for a boy or a girl?" she asks as we exit back into the mall.

"Well, they're pink, so..."

"No, they're lavender. Boys can wear lavender."

"Okay," I laugh. "Whatever you say, dear."

"Okay, dear." We'd been acting out this happy couple thing all day. All week, really. Samantha was so excited about this baby, it was all she talked about. She was already signing up for registries, picking out all the things we would need. She had taken measurements of the guest room, her ideas for redecorating now revolving around the state-of-the-art nursery we would have.

I told her I wasn't ready to tell anyone yet, and even though that caused a bit of a fight, she refrained from calling Anna and sharing our news prematurely.

She had been begging me all week to take her shopping, and I finally relented today. She was the happiest I had ever seen her.

"Oh, look at these, Nate," she says, peering in the window of a jewelry store. I glance at the sign. *Cartier*. *Sure*. She points to an intricate pair of earrings. "Aren't they beautiful?"

"They are," I agree.

"Can we go in?"

"Sure." I smile and open the door for her. And how much is this shopping trip going to cost me? How much will my guilt make me spend on this situation?

Sam strides across the store to the sales person. "We'd like to..." She stops mid-sentence and looks down at the locked case in front of her. "Wow." I walk closer to see what she's found.

Engagement rings.

Of course.

How the hell do I get out of this one?

She looks up at me, her eyes hopeful. "Look at that, Nate. It's perfect."

"Which one?" I ask, playing along to save face.

"The brilliant-cut diamond with baguettes on either side. That's in the Déclaration d'Amour collection, isn't it?" she asks the sales man.

He is more than obliging to open the case and pull out the ring she was talking about. "This one?" He flashes the diamond under the lights. I feel light-headed. I don't want to marry her. I know I got myself into this situation, but I don't have to marry her. We can stay together for now, raise the baby together, that's fine. Maybe I'll grow to love her more. Maybe someday we will get married. But today, I don't want to marry her.

"It's so pretty."

"Would you like to see it on?"

"No, I couldn't," she answers.

"It's very pretty, though, Sam," I tell her, taking her hand and attempting to pull her away from the case full of large diamonds, each and every one symbolizing forever for some couple or another. Not us. Not now, anyway.

"I guess it won't hurt to see what it looks like on, though, right, Nate?"

I smile wearily at the salesman as I lean in to whisper in Sam's ear. "I think we're jumping the gun a bit, don't you?"

"I don't know. Are we?" she asks, pulling me back to the case. "Let's just see what it looks like." She drops my hand and lets the salesman slip the ring on her finger. I swallow hard, feeling like someone's cut off the flow of oxygen to my lungs. "Nate, come look."

I walk slowly to her, giving the salesman an evil eye on the way. He's too busy complimenting her on the ring to notice. "It's very pretty."

"I don't know," she says. "Maybe a princess cut diamond would be better. Like that one. What do you think?"

"You know what I think," I tell her, moderately frustrated, feeling beads of sweat forming on my forehead in the heavily lit shop. "I'm going to go get some air."

"Are you coming back?"

"I'll be right outside. Take your time."

"Okay," she smiles. "Can you take these with you?" She hands me the three shopping bags she had been carrying, so now I have eight. We were already buying maternity clothes and toys and pillows and a bunch of other things that I felt were unnecessary so soon. An engagement ring would be icing on *that* cake. I don't even want to know how much I've spent. I've never had to worry about a budget, because there's always been more than enough money in the bank for my meager needs... but this could get bad really fast.

Maybe Emi was right about Sam after all. I feel like she would have been just as happy if I had sent her away with only my wallet. Happier, even.

I sit down on a bench next to a play area, putting the bags on the ground by my feet. I watch the kids play on the miniature furniture, and wish my life could be that simple again. And instead, soon I'm going to have one of my own to raise. I put my head in my hands and sigh.

"Are you okay?" Sam asks after about ten minutes of shopping.

"Yeah." I stand up and gather the bags. "Are you ready?"

"I think so," she says, taking a few totes away from me. "Just so you know, the pear-shaped one is definitely the one," she adds as we walk toward the exit.

"Good to know," I tell her with a forced smile.

All the way home, all I can think about is how much I don't want this to be happening. I pull into a Duane Reade parking lot quickly.

"What are we doing?" she asks.

"I just need to pick something up," I tell her. "Did you need anything while we're here?"

"A soda?" she asks.

"I don't think that's good for the baby," I tell her. "How about some water, or juice?"

"It can be caffeine-free," she says. "But I'd really like a soda."

"Alright," I concede. "I'll be right back."

When we get home, I wait until she's removed all of the items we'd purchased at the mall from their bags before handing her the one from the drug store. "I want to take a test, together," I tell her. She peeks inside and pulls out two pregnancy tests.

"You don't believe me?" she asks.

"It's not that I don't believe you, baby, I just can't believe this is happening. I just need some solid proof, that's all. I need something to make this real. At this point, I just can't believe it's happening." I stop myself from nervously ranting on. I feel like I'm on the verge of a breakdown.

"Okay, sweetie, okay," she says. "I get it." Her voice is sweet and assuring as she places her hand on mine. "I'll go take it right now."

"Thank you," I exhale, feeling a little relief for the first time today. "I got two different kinds, in case we can't figure one out or something."

"It's not rocket science," she says. "But okay."

"Okay."

"I'll just be a minute." She walks to my bathroom and shuts the door behind her. I grab some water from the fridge and pace around the kitchen. Five minutes go by.

"Is everything okay in there, Sam?" I ask from outside the door.

"Yeah," she says, but her voice is different.

"Sam, what's going on?"

She opens the door for me and sits back down on the edge of the jacuzzi. She's holding two sticks in her hands, holding them out to me.

"I don't know what this means, Sam," I tell her. "Is the blue good or bad?"

"It's not the color that means anything."

"Oh. Well, then is the minus sign good or bad?"

"It depends on what you're calling *good* and *bad*," she says, her voice elevated. "What would be *bad*, Nate?"

"Sam, I'm not ready to be a father," I tell her, noticing the error in my wording. "I'm really hoping that the minus sign means negative. That you're not pregnant. Is that what it means?"

She nods her head and starts to cry, but I can't help but feel completely elated. I'm an ass, I know. I'd jump up and down if she wasn't in the room.

"Sam, baby, I'm sorry, but it's for the best."

"Are you gonna break up with me now?" she sobs.

"What?" I ask her. I hadn't thought about that. I don't want to marry her right now, that much I know, but there's something between us. "No, Sam, baby. I'm happy you're not pregnant, but we don't have to break up because of it. I still want to see you."

"Do you still love me?" she asks.

"Of course I do."

"I wasn't lying," she says as she stands up and moves past me out of the bathroom. "I swear the test I took before was positive."

"I believe you. It's okay. You always hear about these things being wrong."

"Well, how do we know these aren't wrong?"

My heart stops beating for a second.

"Well, we can go to a doctor and have him do blood tests. In fact, I think we should do that. Do you have a doctor like that?"

She shakes her head. "Not here."

"Well, we can go to Planned Parenthood or something. I think there's one on the west side."

"Okay," she agrees.

"Okay?"

"Okay." I grab my keys from the kitchen island. "Now?" she asks.

"Sure, now. Don't you want to know, for sure?"

"Yeah, I guess so."

"Okay." I help her with her jacket and take her hand in mine, giving her a kiss before leaving the loft.

I drop her off at her apartment after our visit to the doctor's office. She wanted to be alone, and I completely understand.

"I guess we'll have to take all that stuff back," she says with a frown.

"It's not important. If you want to keep it, you can. If you want me to take it back, I will. It's up to you."

"Well. If you don't mind, I'd like the shoes and the teddy bear. I'm sure we'll have a need for them someday."

"I'll put those aside," I offer, ignoring her last statement. "I can return the rest?"

"I guess, yeah."

"Okay. Well, baby, go get some sleep, okay? I know this has been an exhausting day for you."

"Will you call me later?"

164

"Of course. Love you," I tell her with a kiss.

"I love you, too." She sweeps my hair to the side, staring at me for a moment before closing her door.

All the way home, all I can think about is how I'm going to tell Emi. How I'm going to talk to her at all, in fact. I'd left her alone since the fight, but I think this news will change things, and put us back on the path to our strange version of normal. I miss her so much... and wonder if she misses me at all.

I just don't know how that kiss is going to affect what we have. In her mind, I've cheated on Sam with that one, tiny, thoughtless action. She's definitely lost some trust in me. I don't need her to tell me that to know that. I know her and how she thinks.

God, when was the last time things were good between us? It feels like months.

Only an hour after I get home, I can't contain myself any longer.

"Sam's not pregnant," I text her, knowing she wouldn't answer my call.

"That's good news, I guess," she finally responds.

"It is," I confirm quickly. After ten minutes, I stop waiting for a response. *"When can we talk, Emi?"*

"I'm busy." Busy. With him, I wonder? Is she truly busy, or just blowing me off? Because I get the distinct impression that it's the latter.

"Emi, I can't stand this anymore."

"Well, how do you think I feel?" she responds quickly.

"I don't know. You won't tell me. You won't talk to me."

"Are you still seeing her?"

"Yes. When will you not be busy?"

"Does she know we kissed?" I could answer with a no, but I feel like so much more needs to be said, and explained. So much more than I want to send over a fucking text message. I try to call her, but as I expected, she declines my call.

"When will you have some time for me?" I give up, texting her again.

"After you've told her the truth." I don't see the point in telling Sam, though. It would only hurt her... needlessly, at this point.

"I'm sorry, Emi."

"Why can't you tell her?"

"Why should I?" I answer her quickly. *"It was impulsive. It didn't mean anything. It would just make her angry with you, and I don't want that. It wasn't your fault."* I regret sending it as soon as I hit the button. It was harsh. It was borderline mean. And it *did* mean something, to me at least... but I don't want to put my heart out there to be hurt by her. I already know she felt nothing. She told me so herself.

"Leave me alone, Nate."

"That's not going to fix things," I tell her. An hour goes by, with nothing. *"Let me know when you're ready to try to fix things."*

I never hear from her. It leaves me pondering my last text. What will fix things between us, anyway? I honestly have no idea. This isn't just about telling Sam we kissed. There's a lot more behind this that we both need to sort through.

A few weeks later– on Emi's birthday, in fact– as Sam and I are doing dishes after dinner one night, I decide to have the conversation I've been plotting since the day I found out she wasn't pregnant. I know she can sense something is coming. We've been drifting apart ever since, and she's seemed resigned all day, although neither of us have been brave enough to bring it up.

I have to do what's right. By Emi's standard, and ultimately, by my own. I'm not that guy. And since I did feel something, it compounds my need to be honest with Sam.

"Sam, I have something I need to tell you." I take the last plate from her and dry it off, putting it safely in the cabinet. "Come sit down with me?"

"Okay," she says cautiously. She picks up the glass of wine I had poured for her and takes it into the living area. We both breathe heavy sighs together, and lightly laugh after. I'm sure it's the last time either of us will smile tonight.

"I kissed Emi," I tell her, steeling myself to look in her eyes, to see her reaction, to face it head-on.

"I know," she says levelly.

"You know?"

"Yeah. I um... if you're going to let me play with your phone, you should probably delete texts you might not want me to read."

"Sam... shit, I'm sorry."

"It's okay," she says quickly, taking my hand in hers. "I was mad at first. I don't know the details... and I've decided I don't want to know. But the fact that it didn't mean anything to you... well, that means *everything* to me. That's *all* I need to know."

I stare at her, my mouth agape.

"You just kissed, right?"

"Yes," I exhale.

"Once?"

"Yeah, it was one night. We were figh–"

"I don't want to know. Really. I forgive you."

It wasn't supposed to be this easy. It can't be.

"Just promise me it won't happen again."

I nod to her slowly. "It won't."

"Okay," she smiles. Actually smiles. "I'm really happy you told me. If you hadn't, then I would have worried."

"Why are you making this so easy on me? Shouldn't you be mad?"

"Because I love you, Nate. And I know you feel the same way about me. Sometimes things just happen, to test us. This was a test, and we passed." She sips her wine. "If we can make it past this, well. We can probably make it past anything... don't you think?"

"Well, we've made it through a lot already," I chuckle softly.

"We have," she agrees. "I think we're ready to move forward, Nate."

I raise my eyebrows, curiously. "And what did you have in mind?"

She smiles softly. "Remember that pear-shaped diamond?" My stomach drops.

"Yes?" I refuse to jump to any conclusions.

"I want to marry you, Nate. And I want you to make the same commitment to me. I think we're both ready."

"No, I'm not."

"You don't have to go out tomorrow and buy it," she laughs, patting my leg. "But I'd like to know that it's coming. That's all." She makes no hesitation at all when she says this. She's that confident that this is what I want, too.

But it's not. It's so far from what I want that I can't let this go on any longer.

"It's not," I tell her softly. "It's not coming."

Her brows furrow in confusion. "I don't understand."

"I like what we have here, Sam, I do. We have a good time together. I care about you. But I can't see myself marrying you. I've tried."

"I think you're just scared of the idea of marriage."

"That's just it, I'm not. It's what I'd like someday. But I don't see myself growing old with you. I just... don't."

"How can you say that?" she says, finally starting to get angry.

"Because it's the truth. I don't want to lead you on."

"And how can you be so sure?"

"I just am." *I know what I feel for Emi. And it's not what I feel for you.* I can barely admit it to myself, much less Sam. "You just have to believe me."

"Believe you?" she scoffs loudly, wiping her nose and getting up off the couch. "How can I believe *anything* you say to me? Or anything you've *ever* said? What if I had been pregnant?!"

"You're not," I tell her rationally.

"But if I was?"

"I can't create feelings that... aren't there..." I swallow slowly, knowing that's going to hurt. "I'm sorry. Everything just happened so fast."

"You're gonna regret this," she says. "I'll be that one that got away. And Nate, you will be sorry."

I just nod my head in understanding.

"I gave you my virginity, Nate."

"I wasn't in it for that, Sam, and you know it. I cared about you."

"Past tense, cared?"

"Sam, nothing I say is going to make this any easier. I'm not good at this. We can string this out and fight about it, or you can let me take you home. Either way, my mind is made up, and the outcome will be the same."

"I'm not going anywhere with you. Marcus will get me a cab."

"He will," I assure her.

"So that's it. You mess around with me for months, and I don't even get to try to convince you to stay with me? It's not fair."

"Sam..."

"No, that's fine. I'm not wasting any more time on you. I get guys' numbers all the time at work. I don't need you."

"Good," I tell her stoically. "I'm glad."

She nearly screams in frustration. "You're not supposed to be *glad*. You're supposed to be *jealous*. You're supposed to realize what you're going to be missing."

"Sam, come on. This is enough. Why are you doing this to yourself?"

"Because we're meant for one another, that's why. How can you not see that?"

"I just don't."

"Fine," she says, finally grabbing her things.

"I'll notify Marcus."

"Fine," she repeats.

"Goodbye, Sam."

"Screw you, Nate."

My eyes closed, I try to process my feelings. I can't get beyond the thought of Emi. I decide to go and see her right away.

"Happy birthday, Emi," I tell her, my voice strained as I try to read her. She just glares at me blankly.

"Yeah, it's really happy, thanks," she mumbles. "You can't just keep coming over like this," she warns me as she opens the door to her apartment.

"Well, then, you'll have to start taking my phone calls. Or at least returning them." I walk into her apartment and sit on her bed.

"I will when I'm ready," she says, following me to her bed and wrapping her hand around my upper arm, pulling me back up. "Why do you keep pushing things?"

"What are you doing?"

"We can go for a walk, but I don't really want you over here, invading my space." I stop in my tracks and just stare behind her. "Come on."

"Invading your space?"

"Yeah."

"I guess I didn't realize there was such a division here. I apologize."

"Come on," she says again, clearly annoyed and signaling for me to follow her into the hallway. "You're not calling the shots."

"As if I *ever* have," I mumble after her, hating her tone and wishing she would soften it just a little. In my mind, this was supposed to be much easier.

Once we get outside, she starts walking down her street and turns south on 1st Avenue. She finally addresses me as a gusty warm wind blows in our faces.

"What's going on?" Her question sounds so general, so casual.

"I told Sam about our kiss today."

"The guilt finally got to you, huh?"

"Look," I tell her, taking her by the shoulder and spinning her around to face me. I push her hair back behind her ear, holding it against her head since the wind refuses to let up. I keep my other hand on her shoulder. "Let's cut it out with the sarcasm, please. We're never going to get anywhere if you keep talking to me like that."

"Well where would you like things to go, Nate?"

"I want things to get better between us, Emi. I think you want that, too."

"I do," she says plainly, her jaw still set. "I just don't know how that can happen."

"I have some ideas." She searches my eyes and simply nods her head. I drop my hands and begin walking again slowly. She keeps pace easily. "Sam and I broke up," I tell her.

"Shocking." I look down at her from the corner of my eye. "You're right, I'm sorry," she concedes.

"Thank you."

"So she dumped you."

"No," I tell her, still surprised with Sam's response. "She *forgave* me."

"Wow," Emi says. "That's not what I expected."

"Well, she said that she wouldn't be mad, as long as the kiss didn't mean anything."

"And lucky for us, it didn't, right?" She stares straight ahead when she says this. I get the distinct feeling she's simply quoting my words. She starts picking at her nails nervously.

"That's just it."

"What's just it?"

I take a deep breath and walk a few more paces before stopping at a red light. My attention focused on the pedestrian signal, I begin to talk. "I *did* feel something." The light signals us to walk, so I step out into the intersection, waiting for her to speak. It's not until I get to the other side that I realize she didn't cross the street with me. She's just staring at me from the other side, the red light keeping us apart again.

Her eyes don't blink, and even with the distance, I can see her breaths quicken as her shoulders move with each inhale, exhale.

"You felt something?" she yells from across the street. A few people around us pretend to not pay attention, but they're too close to avoid it.

"Yeah!" I speak loudly back to her. "I did." I hope she can hear my confirmation over the traffic, but the words nearly get stuck in my throat as my heart throbs in my ears. "I do."

"And why are you telling me this now?" The light changes again and people begin to cross, but Emi stays planted on her corner, and I don't realize she's not coming toward me until it's too late. I look both ways, but traffic is coming, so I remain on the curb, waiting for the next light.

"Are you coming across?" I holler to her.

"No!" she says quickly.

"Okay, well, wait there." She starts to shake her head, slowly at first, then faster. She starts to turn away from me. "No, wait! Emi!" I call out. Her gait is bewildered as she stumbles away from the street. I start running as soon as the light signals me to.

"Go get her!" a woman shouts from behind me. I *do* feel like I'm suddenly in a movie. Only when I get to the other side, Emi's not waiting for me with open arms. They're actually crossed in front of her chest as she continues walking in the other direction.

I'm short of breath when I get to her. "Wait," I breathe. "Please."

"Why?" she says as she glares angrily at me.

"Because I'm trying to tell you something. I've been wanting to tell you this for– well, forever."

She laughs– *laughs*– at me.

"Whatever, Nate." She rolls her eyes and walks ahead. "Save your breath."

"What? No!"

"When did you say you and Sam broke up?"

"Today. Just an hour or so ago."

"And you're telling me this now, why?"

"Because it couldn't wait!"

"More like *you* couldn't wait. You just can't stand to be alone, can you, Nate? So you go to the next woman you think you have a chance with, right? Have you run out of women, Nate? Have you fucked the whole city already, and I'm the *only one left?*"

"God, Emi, no."

"I'm not a placeholder, Nate. I'm not the bookmark that waits for the next chapter of your life to come along. I'm a human being. I thought I was your friend."

I swallow hard, disbelieving how this conversation has turned out. "You are. I just... I just want you to be *more*. I thought you might feel the same way."

She slants her eyes at me in disgust. "I'm not interested, thank you. I'm not desperate."

"Is it Colin? I'm a better man than him, Emi. I'll prove it to you, every fucking day. I am a better man," I plead with her, holding her hand in mine.

"That's debatable. But no, it's not him. It's me. I have my dignity, Nate, and your fear of being alone isn't going to take that from me."

"That's not what this is at all, Emi!"

"We kissed, Nate. So the fuck what? People kiss every day and live to regret it, just like I do. You said it meant nothing to you. You told me that–"

"I was trying to protect my feelings–"

"By hurting mine?"

"I didn't mean to. Did it? Did it hurt your feelings, because if it did, you must have felt something for me, too."

"No," she says, her posture steeled and her eyes mean. "You are so arrogant. You think the whole world revolves around you, don't you?"

"Actually, no. I feel like it revolves around *you*."

I can hear the surprised sigh escape her lips as her cheeks blush. She swallows hard. "Well, you know I didn't feel anything. So you're wasting your time."

"It's bullshit, Emi."

"No, it's not."

"Then why have you been acting like this?"

"Like what? Depressed? Withdrawn? Colin and I broke up, that's why.

Thanks for asking."

I nod silently. "I'm sorry," I tell her.

"No you're not."

"I'm sorry you're hurting. I'm not sorry you've stopped seeing him, you're right. He was wrong for you."

"And you're not?"

"I don't think... I don't know."

"I know. You need to really think about what you're doing, Nate, and what you're asking. And the consequences of your actions. Everything you've done recently just seems to mess things up. Your confession to me today is just one more."

"I'm just being honest."

"You're just feeling alone."

"I'm not."

"And I'm not going to just jump into your arms and tell you I feel the same. I don't. In fact, I've never been more angry with you than I am right now."

"Why?"

"Because," she begins to cry. "Because you keep messing with my emotions, Nate, for your own personal gain. I just want you to leave me alone."

"No, Emi. Please don't say that." We end up back at her apartment building.

"There are some days that I really hate you," she tells me, the expression of pain taking over every muscle in her face and body.

I shake my head at her words, feeling moisture in my own eyes. "I don't think you do, Emi. I really don't think you do."

"Well then that's for me to figure out. Please don't come by unexpected anymore."

"When can I see you again?"

"I don't know, Nate."

"Can I call you?"

"I'd prefer it if you didn't."

"Don't do this, Emi. Please don't cut me off. Not now."

"I think now's the best time. It seems like you need to really think long and hard about what you've done... and what you're suggesting."

"If that's what you'd like."

"It's what you need."

"Fine," I concede quietly. She nods her head. "Like ya, Em. And again, happy birthday."

A tear drops down her cheek. She wipes it with the back of her hand, turning to walk inside her building. I stare blankly at the empty space she left for a good ten minutes before returning to my own loft.

When I got to my apartment, I expected her to call quickly. I wanted her to come to her senses. Minutes became hours. Hours became days. Days became weeks, and before I knew it a full month had gone by. I tried to reach her many times. In person, by phone, by special delivery, regular mail, email. She wouldn't respond. My friendship with her brother even suffered as he stopped taking my calls, too. I began to feel like I had been cut off by my own family.

CHAPTER 9

The thought to remain single crossed my mind briefly after my recent failures with women. Celibacy had also crossed my mind, although I knew that would never be an option for me. I spent a few weeks just trying to get into a new routine. In an effort to find a new outlet for all of my pent-up frustration, I decide to go jogging every morning in Central Park.

The alarm goes off at six-thirty in the morning. I've long given up on my "sleep late every day" resolution. There are just too many things to do in the daylight hours, and I just don't feel like wasting my life away anymore. I've been unusually productive with my paintings lately, no doubt because of the absence of Emi. Break-ups are one thing. They start off painful but get easier every day. Being apart from Emi just feels worse with every hour. It's been seven weeks... seven insufferable weeks since I last saw her. She doesn't return my calls, won't answer her door. The one time I waited outside her building, she caught one glimpse of me and walked quickly away from me. The look she had given me made it clear not to follow her.

I even wrote her a letter and shoved it under her door, apologizing for my inexplicable behavior.

Dear Emi,

This has gone on for too long. It's fine if you don't have feelings for me like I confessed that I have for you. I don't deserve you, and I'm well aware of that fact. If I could take back everything I've said and done to upset you, I would. I just want things to be normal again. Is there any way to move past this? Anything I can do to make this better? Because I'll do it, Emi. Whatever it is, I will do it, you just have to tell me. You have to talk to me.

I am so sorry. This apology is insufficient, but it's a starting point. Please meet me here, and take the steps to move beyond this fight. I can go back to being friends, if that's what you want. But I can't continue to be nothing to you. You mean too much to me. We've become too much a part of each others' lives. We've become too much a part of each other, period.

I want that other part back, Em. I want you back in my life.

Please call me.

Like ya, Nate

The letter found its way into a pile of paper shreds on my welcome mat the next day. It gave me hope that she at least went out of her way to do that. She hadn't given up on our friendship completely.

I'm at a loss how to show her how very sorry I am, and I don't know how much longer I can do this. I need my friend, even if she wants nothing more from me.

I leave my phone at home while I jog. Any calls can wait until I get home, and really, the only woman in the world that doesn't hate me at the moment is my mother, and since she and James are currently celebrating their anniversary in Paris, that leaves exactly no one to call me.

It's unseasonably warm outside, even for early July. We've been experiencing a heat wave. I like to think that maybe the weather has just put everyone in a foul, unforgiving mood, and that maybe Emi isn't really mad after all. It's a good way to fool myself anyway.

I start my run as usual, at the park entrance by the modern art museum. I'm not five minutes into it when a small dog– a terrier, of some sort– runs past me, leash attached... but no human. It chases a squirrel up a nearby tree and claws at the bark, trying to find a way to get to it. I stop running and make my way toward the dog, grabbing the end of the leash when I'm close enough. I look behind me to see if anyone looks as if they've lost a dog, but everyone seems to simply be going about their own business.

The friendly dog lets me pet it. He starts jumping on me, clearly wanting more attention. He is wearing a collar with a tag. "ROSCOE" is engraved on it above a phone number. If I had my phone, I could call the owner. Instead, I decide to find a park bench close to the sidewalk and sit with the dog. Surely someone will be looking for this dog.

Twenty minutes pass, and just as I decide to start walking back home with the dog, I hear someone calling his name. I can't see where the voice is coming from, but I start walking in that direction. Through a group of trees over a hill, a woman sees the dog and immediately starts running in my direction. "Roscoe!" she yells in relief.

"I take it you know this guy," I say to her as she bends down to pick the dog up into her arms. She has long, straight hair, and she's wearing a velour jogging suit that fits her toned body perfectly.

"Bad dog!" she tells him, her mocha skin glistening in the sun. "Thank you so much. I just knew he'd run in the street and get hit by a car..."

"The squirrels kept him in the park. I think he would have been content to stay and bark up that tree for days." I smile. The woman looks to be about my age, possibly a little older. She's beautiful... she's just what I'm trying to avoid right now.

"Nate," I tell her, offering my hand.

"Kiersten," she says, shaking my hand. "And Roscoe."

"Yes, we've met."

"What can I do to repay you?"

"No, it was my pleasure, really. He's a sweet dog."

"Please, let me do something for you. Lunch? Dinner? A drink?"

"Umm," I smile at her. "Sure."

"Let me get your number. I'll call you and we can grab a drink sometime." I take her phone and type in my information, handing it back to her. "I'll call you," she says. She seems way out of my league, and I doubt she'll ever call.

"Sounds good. You have a good day and hold on tight to little Roscoe." I walk over to pet him one last time on the head.

"Have a good run," she says as she puts Roscoe down and winds his leash around her wrist.

"Thanks." Continuing my run, my mind lingers on the beautiful woman I've just met– and I wonder, and kind of hope, that she *will* call. It's just a casual drink. It doesn't have to be anything more.

~ * ~

A few days later when Kiersten finally calls, my mind is made up that I will meet her. When she suggests a local bar, I suggest a time and plan to arrive a little early. I shower to get the paint off of my arms and out of my hair. I find some nice slacks and a blue button-down shirt to wear over a white t-shirt. I decide to leave both shirts untucked, making sure I look casual. This is just casual. Just a drink.

I make it to the bar a half-hour earlier than I had suggested. I order a soda in a tumbler with ice. By the time Kiersten arrives, the ice will have melted and my drink will *look* like something alcoholic. I hate explaining my history on a first date, but women inevitably ask why I'm not drinking if I order water or anything less-than-*spirited*.

Kiersten sees me immediately as she walks in. She's wearing a very professional-looking suit, and she carries a briefcase. She sits down on the barstool next to mine and orders a club soda.

"Thanks for agreeing to meet me," she says.

"Of course. I couldn't resist." I smiled. "How's Roscoe?"

"He's fine, thank you," she laughs. "We're going back to obedience school this weekend. I guess it didn't take the first time."

"I see." I pick up my tumbler and offer a toast. "To obedient Roscoe."

"To obedient Roscoe." Our glasses clink and we both drink.

"Would you like a glass of wine?" I suggest.

"Oh, no thank you," she answers politely. "I don't drink."

I laugh quietly. "Well, I don't either," I admit. "Soda," I tell her, pointing to my glass.

"Recovering alcoholic, eight years," she says. "You?"

"My dad was an alcoholic... so I just don't make a habit of it," I explain without going into too much detail. "Well, I don't see any point in hanging around here, then," I suggest. "How about some gelato on this warm night?"

"Sounds great," she laughs and we make our way out the door and down the street. "I'm sorry. It's just so socially... *normal...* to meet for drinks that I always just jump to that, assuming that's what everyone wants to do."

"Oh, it's not a big deal. I don't mind being around it."

Kiersten is a 32-year-old human rights lawyer. She was married right out of high school, but her husband soon became abusive and she left him. She started drinking heavily through college until her family convinced her to get help. By the age of twenty-four, she had lived a lifetime. She was determined to turn things around and decided to go to law school. She has made it her mission in life to help those in need. She just seems so good... and selfless.

Even though we seem to have very little in common, the conversation flows easily all evening. She's very centered and knows what she wants in life. She tells me she hasn't found a man that deserves her. I can believe it. I'm pretty sure I don't. Still, when I muster the courage to invite this classy, bright, exotic, beautiful, completely-out-of-my-league woman back to my apartment, she doesn't hesitate.

At the loft, I show her my recent paintings, and she seems very impressed. She discusses them intelligently, commenting on my choice of colors, textures and shapes. I find out that she minored in art as an undergrad. Finally, some common ground. I am blown away by her, and am moved in that moment to take her face in my hands and kiss her, softly. She kisses me back, her lips moving in ways I've never felt before.

I exhale deeply. "Wow, what are we doing?" I ask, running my fingers nervously through my hair.

"Just kissing," she says.

She smiles slyly, closing the gap between us and kissing me again. She knows what she's doing, knows the power she has over me in this moment. I start to unbutton her jacket, but she catches my hand and holds it, not letting me continue. She looks up at me and repeats, "Just kissing."

"Got it," I say, and continue *just* kissing her. We sit on the edge of my bed and kiss for about ten minutes. I am extremely turned on, imagining what other amazing things her lips can do, and I hope in secret that this is just the most incredible *foreplay* of my life.

Sadly, though, it's not. She breaks away from me and looks at her watch. "I've got an early meeting," she tells me. "Can we continue this another time?"

"Just say when and where."

"Tomorrow night, nine o'clock, my place," she says and hands me a card with her information on it. "Don't be late."

"Never." I attempt one last kiss, but she won't let me.

"Tomorrow," she says and smiles. As soon as the door closes behind her, I immediately take a cold shower.

The next morning, I wake up before the alarm goes off. I can't get the day started fast enough. I'm not sure how I'll make it another fifteen hours. I can't wait to see Kiersten, can't wait to continue what we started last night. I'm not sure what she sees in me, though. Sensing my self-doubt, I decide to go ahead and hit the park for my run. I've found I feel better about myself after exercising.

Today is no exception. When I get back, I shower and begin humming a tune while the warm water rinses my body clean. I haven't written a song in over a year, but I'm feeling strangely inspired today. I hop out, dry off, find my boxers and pick up my guitar. I grab a pencil and some paper to write some ideas down. Two hours later, I have a completed song. It's about a woman coming to terms with her feelings for a man who she thinks is all wrong for her... but turns out to be the love of her life... the man only wants her to find love, in the end.

It's not a song for Kiersten, though. It's for Emi. It was a vision of Emi that played in my mind while I created chord progressions and penned lyrics that I was sure I'd never be able to sing in front of an audience. I sigh and pick up the phone to attempt to call her. She still declines my call. I can tell because it only rings once before her chipper voicemail greeting announces itself.

"Em, call me. Please. I am so fucking sorry, Emi, believe me." *This is getting old.*

I pick up my sketch pad and walk over to the window. I begin to draw the view outside in an attempt to distract myself. The ground below seems less bustling than usual. People must be staying inside, avoiding the heat as much as possible. New Yorkers are not cut out for this. I just watch the people below, walking around, two by two. I sigh as I hear my phone beep, notifying me of a text message. I race across the room.

"Someone's interested in a few of your pieces... possibly some commissioned work... let's meet to discuss... I'm in LA now... will call when I'm back in town..." My agent, Kate, rarely contacts me. I'm her least-known client. She loves my work, promotes it often, and represents me well, but there isn't a lot of traditional demand for my non-traditional style. I know she must have found a serious buyer. She doesn't bother me with little things. She typically just handles them on her own.

"Great," I text back. *"Give me a call when you get back."* I haven't done anything on commission in awhile. I find it very difficult, creating things at

the request of other people. They often have specific things in mind that they want. I'm a fine artist... I do what I like... but it's hard to make money that way. I don't need the money, of course, but it always does wonders for my ego when I do. It's nice to affirm that I could support myself some day, if the money ever ran out.

I arrive at Kiersten's building early, eager to see her again. I circle the block a few times killing time. At five till nine, I pull up to the valet and hand them my keys. The doorman of her building notifies her of my arrival, and she comes down to meet me in the foyer.

She's wearing a different velour jogging suit, but looks impeccably put together. Every hair is perfectly in place, her make up is subtle but flawless, her fingernails are painted to match her outfit. My decision to wear some nice jeans and another button down shirt seems to be a good one.

I hug her and kiss her on the cheek, and she does the same. She takes my hand and guides me to the stairway. "I'm just on the third floor," she says, leading the way. I get a good look at her body on the way up. She is flawless. I grab her by the waist before we exit the stairwell and turn her around.

"Remind me why I'm here," I request, and I lean in and steal a kiss from her all-too-willing lips. "That's right," I say, breathless.

I am greeted by Roscoe, who jumps up and scratches my knees until I pick him up. "Hey, buddy," I say to the friendly dog, rubbing him on the head. He licks my face once and I immediately put him back down on the floor. I like dogs just fine, but I don't care to be kissed by them. Now, their owners...

"Would you like some sparkling water?" Kiersten asks.

"That would be great," I tell her, following her into a small kitchen. Her apartment is modest, but very well kept. It's a very modern, clean space, no clutter anywhere. It suits her personality perfectly. She hands me a glass of water and gestures for me to have a seat in her living room. One thing I immediately notice is that she doesn't have a television. She picks up a small remote from across the room, though, and turns on some music. I finally see an unassuming CD player in the corner, but she has small speakers mounted on all the walls. It could be a concert hall in here. The sound is perfect.

Jazz music fills the room. Not the hideous smooth jazz that has flooded the radio waves in recent decades, but the kind that makes me think of a dark, smoky dive, circa 1940. It has definite sexual undertones to it.

"Nice selection," I comment. She brings in a tray of assorted fruit and sets it on the coffee table.

"Hungry?" she asks, picking up a plump strawberry and taking a slow bite out of it. I watch her lips, desiring them on my own, the thought of food the furthest thing from my mind. I can't deny how physically attracted I am to this woman. I just look at her in awe.

And it's not just her physical beauty that is tantalizing me. She carries herself with such confidence, such presence. It's obvious she has no need for a man, especially one like me, but it excites me to know that I am here because she *wants* me here.

"I'm not hungry for *that*," I tell her as she offers me a grape. She laughs.

"Patience, Nathaniel," she says to me. No one ever calls me by my given name, but it sounds so sensual the way she says it... almost breathy... she teases me with a short kiss. "There's more to me than sex."

"Uh," I stumble, looking for words, embarrassed at my behavior. "How was your day?"

"It was nice," she answers, and proceeds to tell me about her morning meeting and the case that she's been working on. She has such passion for her work, and obviously cares deeply for the people she defends. She is a perfect story-teller, too, creating vivid mental images for me as she tells me about her life. Her vocabulary far exceeds that of any other woman I've dated. The perfect enunciation of her words only adds to her appeal.

She tells me that her father was the driving force in her life. He always instilled confidence in her, and pushed her to do better. When she was in college, it was a speech he gave her, voicing his disappointment in the path she was choosing, that made her decide to enter rehab. She always wanted to make him proud. He died of cancer a month after she passed her bar exam.

185

He lived to see her exceed every dream he had for his little girl.

"Sounds like you really loved him," I say.

"Daddy was my life," she smiles.

"So was mine," I lament.

"He is the alcoholic?" she asks, reluctantly.

"Yes, but I didn't know at the time."

"When did you find out?"

"The night he... died," I tell her, clearing my throat.

"Oh, I'm sorry," she blushes. "I didn't realize..."

"No, it's okay," I assure her. "It was a long time ago... nearly twenty years. I was just a kid."

"And your mom?" she asks.

"Mom's still here. Remarried. Very supportive of me," I smile.

"Good."

"Most of the time," I laugh. I see a picture of Kiersten across the room with two small children who look a lot like her. They have perfect, dark complexions, long eyelashes, and amber-colored eyes that match Kiersten's. For a minute, my stomach falls. I get up to take a closer look.

"Cute, aren't they?" she asks.

"Are they your..." I can't even finish the sentence.

"Nieces," she cuts me off. "They're my sister's kids. Alesha and Nessa."

"Sorry, they look so much like you," I laugh.

"A lot of people say that. It makes sense, my sister and I look a lot alike." She pulls out a small album from a bookshelf and shows me a recent picture of the two of them.

"You could be twins," I comment.

"She'd love to hear you say that, she's four years older than me."

"Are you close?"

"Oh, yes. We've grown even closer since my nieces were born. I'm the designated baby sitter, but it's possibly a better job than my lawyer gig," she jokes. "The girls are amazing. Do you like kids?" she asks me.

"Honestly, I haven't spent a lot of time around kids. I was an only child, my parents were the only children in their families... I don't *mind* kids, but at this point, I can't say that I want them."

"That's fair," she says. "I feel the same way... not sure that I want to have my own. Maybe my nieces are good enough for me... or maybe I'll change my mind when I find the right man."

I nod and sip my water, feeling captivated by her. She looks me in the eyes, placing her hand on my chest. I put my arm around her, and she rests her head against me.

"Your heart is racing," she notices.

"I don't know what you're doing to me," I admit. "But I like it." I glance at her clock across the room and I am surprised to see the time. "Is it really midnight?" I ask.

She glances at her watch and is also surprised by the time. "Wow."

"Do you have to get up early?" I ask her.

"Not tomorrow. I'm just working on some briefs at home," she answers. "I'm not ready for you to leave yet," she adds.

"Good. Because I don't want to," and I can feel my heartbeat soar as I lean into her and press my lips to hers. Her fingernails trace soothing circles in my scalp, and I'm completely at ease in her arms. I unzip her jacket to reveal a tight tank top underneath. I kiss her neck, and she settles back against a pillow on her couch.

"Let's take it slow," she requests, and I nod my head in agreement. Her suggestion is soon forgotten as we are both intoxicated by one another. I sit up, allowing her to quickly remove my t-shirt as her lips begin their descent from my mouth, to my neck, my chest, my navel... she pushes me back into the cushions and slowly pulls my boxers off.

Needless to say, I am no longer left wondering what else her lips could do... it was mind-numbing. She doesn't let me return the favor, though, even after she's changed into something more comfortable and we've moved to her bed.

"Tomorrow," she tells me. The suspense might kill me, but I will die happy in anticipation. I try to change her mind as she lies in my arms by telling her what I'd like to do to her, but she remains steadfast in her decision to make me wait.

"It's after midnight," I plead. "It is tomorrow. I don't think I can wait any longer to kiss you," I touch her, lightly, over her cotton pants, "to make your body writhe with pleasure and your voice holler out my name." I smile at the thought and kiss her wondrous lips. "I just want to share this with you."

"Nathaniel, you're awful," she jokes. "Stop making yourself crazy... here, let me get your mind off of it."

I don't fight it, taking advantage of all she's willing to give me. She's far too generous, and I am far too lucky.

Mind-numbing. That's the only phrase I can use to describe it. I literally think that I blacked out for a few seconds.

When I wake up in the morning, I see that Kiersten is sleeping, her apartment very warm. She changed clothes sometime during the night, now simply dressed in a small t-shirt and her panties. Something catches my eye from across the room. Roscoe is sitting by the front door, shaking. I get up slowly, trying not to wake her, and pull on my jeans and my button-up shirt, loosely buttoned. I find Roscoe's leash and snap it to his collar.

Quietly, we exit the apartment. Taking her dog out is the least I can do for her, in exchange for what she did for me last night. *Twice.* I walk him for a few blocks to a coffee shop I've never visited before, and I order two lattes and grab a newspaper. After Roscoe has been taken care of, we go back to her apartment. He walks over to a cupboard in the kitchen and starts sniffing at it. I peek inside to see a bag full of dog food. Spying his bowl in a corner, I pour some food in. He eats it all in a matter of minutes. I carry the coffee to the nightstand and lie back down on the bed, gently. The smell of the coffee wakes Kiersten up shortly before Roscoe finds a way up on the bed and starts attacking her with his tongue. *Lucky dog.*

"Roscoe, do you need to go outside?"

"Already done," I tell Kiersten. "Latte?"

She sits up and stretches, reaching for the coffee. "Wow, thank you."

"Paper?"

"Sure," she says, grabbing the front section from the pile I had laid on the bed. I find the arts section and skim the articles before finding the crossword puzzle. I'm not sure why I torture myself with the Saturday puzzle, but I always try. Never finish.

"V-E-N-T-R-I-C-L-E." Kiersten spells out to me.

"Huh?"

"Ventricle. Thirty-seven down. Then thirty-seven across is 'vortex'." I give her a sideways glance.

"Here, can you finish it?" I pass the page on to her and hand her my pencil.

She laughs. "Honey, I can do these while I sleep. Where's a pen?"

"Now, you don't need to rub it in." She digs in the nightstand and pulls out a pen. She barely has time to read before she starts filling in the squares.

"Wow," I comment. "While you sleep, you say..."

"Yep," she says confidently.

"What about while I do this?" I kiss her wrist and travel up her arm, pushing the t-shirt sleeve back so I could press my lips to her delicate shoulder.

"I'm much stronger than you," she jokes. "That doesn't affect me."

"And this?" I trace her collarbone with my tongue, stopping just below her ear, kissing gently.

"Huh," she says thoughtfully. "No, but you are getting in the way." She nudges me to the side as she continues to write down answers, one word quickly following the other. I start to watch her fill in the blanks, sipping my coffee.

"Impressive," I say when she completes the final word. "I feel emasculated now, but I'm impressed."

She laughs. "You feel emasculated because I finished the puzzle, or because I'm spurning your advances?"

"Both," I tell her. "I know a way you can make it up to me, though."

"Would this help?" she says as she stands up and takes off the t-shirt she was sleeping in, leaving her breasts exposed.

"It would if you came over here," I hold my hand out to her. Instead of coming back to bed, she wads up the t-shirt and throws it in my face.

"Mind if I take a shower?" she asks.

I remain buried under the t-shirt, laughing, frustrated. "No, go ahead," I mumble, the brief vision of her breasts swimming dizzily through my mind. I sigh and get up, moving the mess of newspaper pages off the bed and onto a nearby chair. I walk across the room, touching the window to feel the heat of the day penetrate through. There isn't a cloud in the sky. In the reflection of the window, I see a figure standing across the room. I turn around to see Kiersten wearing a sexy pair of silk boxers that are too big for her body. They barely hang on to her left hip, her hand fighting to keep them up.

"That look is all wrong on you," I laugh, crossing the room to meet her. "Let me help." I pick her up, flipping her over my shoulder, and without the grasp of her hand, the shorts quickly fall to the floor. "Oops." Kiersten nervously giggles but doesn't struggle. I carefully lay her down on the bed.

"Now?" I ask her, kneeling over her, hopeful, her naked body firm, skin smooth, lips moist, eyes calling out to me.

"Yes, Nathaniel, now," she smiles. Anxiously but slowly, I am finally able to return the favor.

When I finish and her breathing finally returns to normal, she comments, "You've had a lot of practice at that, haven't you? Most men don't know a woman's body quite like that."

"Books," I joke. "Water?" I hop up and nearly run to the kitchen, anxious to return to the bed with her.

"Please," she answers, obstructing my view of her unspeakably sexy body with a sheet.

"No, don't hide from me," I plead, crawling on the bed. "We're not finished, are we?" She laughs. I kiss her lips, and then take the sheets between my teeth and tentatively pull them back, revealing her legs, parted and welcoming.

~ * ~

A few days later, after my run, I decide to stop by Emi's apartment again. I knock and wait, but I don't hear anything inside. I don't guess she's home at the moment. I pull out my phone and send a simple text to her. *"Like ya, Em"*. I know I won't get a response, but I still want her to know I am thinking about her.

After a day of inspired painting, I look over everything I've done. I'm feeling strangely conflicted, and it's coming out in my work. I did three pieces this afternoon. They all have elements that are in stark contrast to one another. One's a piece with colors, vibrant orange and a deep blue. Another pairs shapes, one with flowing curves, the other with serrated edges. The other is a mixed media piece, comprised mainly of scraps of silk and sandpaper.

I know it's coming from the inner struggle I'm having: Kiersten versus Emi. What I'm doing with Kiersten versus what I still feel for Emi. Yes, I feel some connection to Kiersten, but my emotions for her still don't rival those that I feel for my best friend. For so long, she has been my dream, my ideal. I don't want to give up on that– on *her*– but every day that passes without her takes me one step further away from that dream. And with Kiersten, things have happened so quickly. I'm sure if I wanted, I could learn to love her.

After cleaning up, I leave to pick her up. We go to the market, selecting some ingredients so she can make dinner for us. I walk a few paces ahead of her to try to catch the elevator for us, our hands full.

"Nate," Marcus greets me warmly. "Emi came by." I stop dead in my tracks.

"What?" I ask him, feeling happier than I have in weeks at this news.

191

"When?"

"Just about a half-hour ago. She said she'd stop by another day."

"Who, baby?" Kiersten asks, catching up to me.

Marcus looks at me apologetically. "No, it's okay," I assure him. "My best friend stopped by," I explain to her nonchalantly, "that's all."

"Oh," she says simply.

"Thanks, Marcus. Have a good night."

"You, too, Nate. Miss," he smiles at Kiersten. After we continue on to the elevator, I realize I should have introduced them to one another, but the thought never even occurred to me.

"She?" Kiersten says as soon as the elevator doors close. *"Her?"*

"Yeah. Her name is Emi." I sense her worry already.

"Emi?"

"Yeah. We've known each other since high school. Just friends."

"Just friends?"

"Yes, Kiersten. Just friends." She's silent until we get upstairs to my loft. "Kiersten?" I ask, closing the door behind us and taking her shopping bags from her.

"I'm not sure I can share you with another woman," she says. I laugh, assuming incorrectly that she's kidding. "I'm serious."

"Oh." More silence as I begin to unload the groceries. "Well, we haven't spoken in, probably two months. I don't think there will be a whole lot of sharing going on."

"Best friends who don't talk for two months?"

"We had a bit of a fight. We just haven't been seeing eye-to-eye on things lately."

"That's too bad," Kiersten says with a tinge of sarcasm in her voice. "Nathaniel, I don't believe that men and women can be friends," she explains. "I don't think it's possible."

"Kiersten, it is... We are... What, you don't have any guys friends?" I laugh a little.

192

"Not a single one." I'm a little shocked by this, but admittedly feel a sense of relief. I understand how she feels, but if she knew the whole story– knew how angry Emi was– she wouldn't be insecure.

"Well, maybe if you tried, you'd realize it's possible," I encourage her.

"That's not gonna work," she says plainly.

"Well, you don't need to worry about her." And even as the words escape my lips, my heart pounds and my mind can't stop wondering why Emi stopped by. I can't wait to find out. "Let's get dinner started," I tell her, not wanting to waste a second of the night. I focus all of my energy into cooking and showing Kiersten plenty of affection while we make dinner. I think I've calmed her down as we sit down to eat.

"Can we talk a little more about your friend?" she asks, taking a bite.

"Of course. My life is an open book."

"I don't really want to know about her."

"Oh, okay... then... what did you want to talk about?"

"Are you going to see her?"

"I'll probably call her... see why she came by. We don't have any definite plans, though."

"I don't like it," she says.

"Really, Kiersten, there's nothing to be jealous about–"

"I am *not* jealous!" she interrupts forcefully.

"Okay," I say quietly, trying to smooth things over. "But I can't not ever see her again. We've been friends for years. I hope we'll be friends for many more..."

"But don't you like being with me?"

"I do," I tell her. And I *do* like being with her. "You shouldn't see her as a threat."

"I'm not saying she is... and I'm not telling you not to talk to her anymore..." she starts.

"Good, because–"

"I'm *asking* you not to, that's all. Just for now... just for me..."

"Kiersten," I retort. "Please, understand–"

"No, Nathaniel, hear me out." She pauses, expecting me to cut in, but I don't. I want to hear her out. "I've been in some bad relationships. A lot of men in my life have treated me badly. I know I seem like a confident woman to you, but in this setting, in a relationship like this, this early on... I don't.. *trust*... like I should.

"I'm not saying you'll never get to see her again. This is just so new. Can you just give me some time, some time to adjust to this relationship, some time to build a little more trust with you? Can't you give me that?"

I'm not sure I can, but I think about it carefully. As we do the dishes, she gives me some space, some time to consider what she's asked. I can tell she's not doing this to be selfish. It's obvious she just wants both of us to focus on *us* right now. And I can't really blame her.

After all, wouldn't this be the perfect opportunity to work on filing Emi away as only a friend? If I distanced myself from her a little more, it would make it so much easier.

"Just try?" she asks, her hands behind her back as she leans against the kitchen counter.

"I'll try," I promise. I need to get my feelings in order, once and for all. I want to learn how to separate those feelings for Emi from my feelings of love for other women; possibly for Kiersten, in particular. I put my hands on the countertop on either side of her hips, my mouth meeting hers for full, deep kisses. We don't leave the kitchen until well into the night, when we're both exhausted and needing of a restful night's sleep.

CHAPTER 10

It's a few weeks before Kate calls me. I've never heard her so animated.

"My plane literally just landed, Nate," she says with excitement. "We need to talk."

"Right, okay... now?"

"No," she says. "I want you to meet me at the corner of 8th and 51st in an hour."

"Alright," I say, my interest piqued.

"Look nice," she suggests. "Fix your hair, at least. You're meeting your client."

"What?" I ask, suddenly nervous.

"You heard me. It's too good, Nate. You won't say no."

"That's no pressure," I retort.

"I'll see you in an hour," she says, smug and confident.

I take a shower and try to find something appropriate to wear. I choose some clean jeans and a white button-down shirt. I pull out a tie, and knot it loosely. I purposefully leave the shirt untucked. Nice, but not too nice. I run my fingers through my wet hair. There's really no point in doing anything to it. It always looks the same.

An hour later, I'm standing on the corner of 8th and 51st in front of a storefront that's undergoing some renovations. I shove my hands in my pockets and wait for Kate's arrival, scanning each taxi as it slows by the curb.

"Nate," she calls me from the doorway of the storefront. "Come in." I follow her in, hugging her and kissing her on the cheek. There's a man standing by an empty bar, about my age, dressed in what looks to be a very expensive suit. "Nate, this is Albert," she says.

I shake his hand. Firm grip. The sign of a good businessman, or so I'm told.

"Nice to finally meet you, Nate," he begins.

"Thanks, uh, likewise."

"You're probably wondering why you're here," he says.

"A little, yeah," I laugh apprehensively.

"Well... you're standing in one of my newest ventures. I'm opening three clubs in the next six months. This one, one in LA and one in Vegas."

"Okay," I nod.

"I don't know if you've heard of Track? Frontbar? Albie's?"

"All of them, actually," I answer, recognizing the names of three of the trendiest spots in New York. "You own those?"

"He does," Kate says. "And this place will be just as well-known as the others in a few short months."

"Nate, would you like a drink?" Albert asks.

"Just some water, if you don't mind."

Albert fixes a glass of ice water and puts a lime in it. He pours himself a glass of scotch.

"So, I saw your work at the Axiom Gallery in LA," he continues. "I think your style is perfect for these clubs. I'd like to hire you to do some custom pieces."

"Did you see any at the Axiom that you liked?"

"All of them, but none of them are large enough," Albert says. "We want full, wall-sized pieces. And we want each to be a little different. Each club will have a personality of its own. The architecture is different in each location."

"Wow, okay," I say, intrigued.

"I want you to come out to LA with me and take a look at the place. That's the first one that will open... you can get some measurements, some ideas... you can even stay there and work on it, if it moves you. We'd put you up in a nice hotel for your stay."

"Sounds like a cool project," I say. "Did you have specific ideas for what you want these pieces to be?"

"Not at all," he says. "All I ask is that they fit with the architecture and feel of the place. I trust your interpretation. Like I said, I liked every piece of yours that I saw."

This is a dream job. The opportunity to do large-format pieces of my own design. Very few restrictions. On display in some of the most high-profile clubs in the country. I can't hide my smile.

"Once you have a good feel for LA, we'll go to Vegas. I promise to show you a good time."

"I'm definitely interested." We discuss how I will be compensated, and it's clearly a once-in-a-lifetime gig. Kate was right, I can't turn it down. I wouldn't. I know it is going to take an inordinate amount of time, concentration, energy... but I can't wait. Kate has already put together contracts and we all sign.

"Can you be in LA by the first week in September?"

"Sure thing."

"Well, I'll be in touch with the arrangements. I'm looking forward to it."

"Likewise," I say, eagerly. I shake his hand, and Kate walks me out the door. I pick her up, swinging her in the air as I hug her.

"A million thank you's aren't enough," I tell her. "This is what I've been waiting for."

"I knew you'd be excited. This is going to be so good for you."

"You're the best. This is amazing."

"Go tell Emi," she laughs as she starts to walk back into the club. My smile fades as I turn away from her.

Emi.   How I would love to go tell Emi this incredible news.   Since Kiersten and I had our conversation, though, I've made good on my promise to her. The first week was the hardest. I never found out why Emi came by. She didn't call or stop by again, presumably leaving the ball in my court, knowing that Marcus would have told me.

Any other time in our lives, it would have been strange to go so long without talking, but since we had been fighting, it felt sort-of... okay... that things just didn't return to the way they used to be.   I assume she feels the same way. It doesn't make me feel any better or make it any easier, though.

Things are going very well with Kiersten.   I am finally able to focus on our relationship, and we are growing stronger as a couple every day.   Still, when I let my mind wander to Emi, those feelings eclipse anything I could hope to feel for anyone else.   And for that, I do my best to simply not think about her.

At this moment, though, feeling so happy that I might explode, the only person I think of and want to talk to is Emi. She has been there for me through all the rough times in my career.   She stood by my side at numerous gallery openings, when less than ten people would show up– most of them our family members.   There was a two-year span when the only thing I sold was a 12" x 12" print. Our high school art teacher bought it.

This is too momentous and my decision is made.   I have to talk to her, have to see her. I run to her apartment. I pound on the door like a mad man.

"Emi, open up! Emi, it's me, Nate! Open up!"

"My god, Nate, what's wrong?" she answers.

"Hi," I stammer, taken aback by her simple beauty that I have missed.

"Hi," she says back, a smile forming on her lips.

"I'm sorry," I tell her immediately, knowing for weeks– no, *months*– that would be the first and most important thing to say to her. So many things to be sorry for, but the void I've allowed to grow between us is what I'm most sorry for now.

"I know," she answers softly. "You've mentioned that."

"Can I come in?"

"Sure." She opens the door a little wider, and I take advantage of the space and her refreshing welcoming attitude. I burst into her apartment, picking her up and carrying her to the nearby couch. I fall back into it, with her on my lap, hugging her tightly against me. "Took you long enough," she laughs.

"Are you okay, Nate?" Anna interrupts from Emi's desk. I hadn't noticed that we weren't alone.

"Anna," I shift Emi slightly, putting a little distance in between our bodies. "I'm sorry to barge in like that."

"No, we're just hanging out," Chris's girlfriend explains. "Right, Em?" My friend nods, her eyes bright but curious.

"Well, I have something to tell Emi, and I couldn't wait."

"Should I go?" Anna asks.

"No, it's news for everyone."

"What is it?" Emi grins.

"You won't believe it, Em."

"Try me..."

"I've been hired to do commissioned work for three huge clubs, in LA, Vegas and here!"

"Oh, wow!" she says, surprised by the news. The smile in her eyes falters slightly, but she regains her composure immediately.

"It's a six-figure deal, Emi! And they're owned by the guy who owns Frontbar! *The* Frontbar! Do you know what kind of people go there?"

"Yes, Nate, Page Six can't stay away from there!"

"I know! I can't believe it!"

"Congratulations, I am so happy for you!" She hugs me, holds me close. I keep my arms around her for as long as she lets me. I won't be the first to let go.

"Thank you, Emi, for everything you've done for me," I whisper in her ear. "It means the world."

"I'm your biggest fan, Nate. And your *first*. Don't forget that."

"Never." She pulls away quickly, sitting up straight on the couch and adjusting her disheveled clothes.

"Well, we should go out and celebrate!" She looks at Anna, who nods excitedly.

"Let's go back to the wine bar," Chris's girlfriend suggests. "Do you like the wine bar down the street?" she asks me.

"Um, not really," I hesitate, putting the breaks on their celebratory plans. Already I'm afraid to tell Kiersten about *this* meeting. She will be incredibly hurt to know I went to Emi first with this news. Or that I went to her at all.

"He doesn't really drink," Emi explains.

"We can go somewhere else," Anna suggests again.

"Oh, I, uh, can't," I tell her. "I'm leaving for LA."

"When? Now?" Emi asks, her expression confused.

"Like, sometime soon, I think. I've got a ton of things to clear up here before I go." I hate being so vague, and lying to her physically hurts me.

"How long will you be gone?" she asks with a slight whine, like she doesn't want me to go.

"A couple months, maybe. I go there, and then to Vegas."

"Seriously? You can't hang out for just a little while? Let me buy you dinner or something, Nate," Emi pleads. "If I'm not going to see you for months..." Her voice is sad.

"Emi," I say quietly, my heart breaking. I glance at Anna who has gotten the hint that we need a little privacy. She concentrates hard on something on Emi's computer screen. "Can we talk for a minute? Maybe in the hallway?" Lord knows there's nowhere to be alone in her apartment.

"Yeah, sure. Anna, we'll be right back." She stands up slowly, removing herself from the couch.

"What is it?" she asks once we're in the hall.

"Emi, I'm seeing someone," I tell her slowly.

"Of course you are," she says as if the wind has been knocked out of her. Her shoulders slump, her body deflates. She swallows before continuing. She tries to smile. "Who is she?"

"She, uh..." I laugh, although nothing I'm about to tell her is funny. "She's a lawyer I met in the park last month. Her name is Kiersten."

"Well, good for you." She pats my arm awkwardly. "I'm happy for you."

"She has asked me to not see you."

"You're kidding, right?"

I smile sheepishly. The hurt in Emi's eyes forces my gaze away from hers. "I wish I was... but just for awhile." As if that makes it any better, any easier for either of us.

"You're not going to though, right? I mean, who is she to ask that of you?"

"I need to," I say apologetically. "I like her. I really need to give this a chance. She's just insecure... she's been hurt, a lot. She has some trust issues."

"Well I guess if you're leaving soon, I wouldn't have the opportunity to see much of you anyway. I mean, as long as we can talk, I'll get over it." She shrugs casually. "We have so much to talk about. But I want to figure this out."

"That's just it, Emi. She's asked me to... I guess... distance myself from you."

"But we're just friends," she searches my eyes for agreement, nodding her head. "Is she going to make you stay away from Chris, and Eric and Jason, too?"

"You know it's not the same."

"Why is it not?" she asks, but knows the answer before I have to say it aloud.

"You're a woman. She doesn't believe that men and women can be friends." *And I can't really argue that point. I don't believe that you and I can really be friends anymore.*

"Prove her wrong!" she says angrily.

"Believe me, Em, I tried to do that, I did. But she needs this right now. I need to do this for her. And you're right, I'll be really busy anyway, so there will already be that natural distance."

"No," she cries in disbelief. "That's not fair, no. Don't I get a say?"

"No, Emi," I answer through the lump in my throat. "Not this time."

"I can't believe she's making you choose!"

"I know," I whisper, looking down at my hands, afraid to look into her eyes any longer.

"But even worse, I can't believe you're doing it. I can't believe you're choosing her!"

"Emi, be fair..."

"Fair?" she chokes out. "What is fair at all about this? You're my best friend. I would never, *ever* consider any boyfriend more important than you."

"You don't know that, Emi. When the right one comes along–"

"The *right one* wouldn't ask such a thing of me."

I have no comeback for this.

"Don't do this," she whispers. "Please, don't, Nate."

"It's just temporary," I remind her, hoping that it's true.

"You're leaving when?"

"In a few weeks."

"Maybe she doesn't have to know," she suggests.

"Emi," I plead. "I don't want to lie to her. Please don't ask me to do that."

"I don't know that I can do this. I mean, we just went nearly three months without talking! Don't you want to work this out? I mean, what did you come over here for?"

"Of course I want to work it out, Em, but now's not the time..."

"What, I'm too late? Because I needed space, you wrote me off entirely?"

"Not at all. But I want to respect her wishes. I need to give her this. Now that I know how you feel, I think things will be okay with us."

"No, they won't!" she argues. "This is not okay. I will not be okay with this, ever!"

"Please, Emi. Please try. Please do this for me. I have to try to make this work with Kiersten. She makes me happy."

"And I just make you miserable," she mumbles.

"No, Emi. It's not like that at all."

"How can she make you happy if she's making you do this?"

"God, Emi, just try to understand this from her side."

"I don't want to." She doesn't want to, but I can tell from her heavy sigh, her slouched posture, that she knows she has to.

"Thank you," I whisper in her ear as she holds on tightly to me. "I need to run, Emi." I can't bear to do this any longer. I can't bear to see her so unhappy. Am I sure this is the right thing to do? And who am I doing this for? If this is supposed to make me happy, why do I feel like absolute shit? "I need to tell Mom the news... and Kiersten..."

"Okay," she swallows hard. "So I was the first?"

"Of course you were," I say.

"I guess I should feel special..."

"You are. My god, Emi, you are, you *know* you are."

"Sure, Nate." She lets go of me and opens the door to her unit, her eyes intently focused on the floor. Anna is standing a few feet away in the kitchen, pouring three glasses of wine. "Good luck, Nate." Her eyes meet mine once more, all emotion gone from them. She backs into her apartment.

"Thanks," I say to her, my eyes lingering, taking in all of her, wondering how long it will be until I see her again. "Bye, Emi." I turn to walk down the hallway toward the elevator.

"Nate?" she calls to me.

"Yeah?"

She stands in the doorway, her eyes locked with mine. "I'm sorry, too."

I take a shaky breath. "Like ya, Em." She just lifts her eyebrows, as if she doesn't truly believe me... as if my words aren't good enough. "I do." She shuts the door quietly. "I do," I whisper again, a confirmation to myself. *And just seeing you reminds me of how much I like you, even though I've done my best to not think about you... and just a few minutes with you brings it all crashing back to me. Fuck.*

I go back to my apartment and call my mom. She is ecstatic, too. She says she couldn't be more proud of me. I turn on my computer, which hasn't seen the light of day in weeks. I only use it for research, and I figure I better do some. Kate has already sent me an email with interior photos of the club in LA. I'm familiar with the architect who designed it, and love his work. This is going to be an amazing experience, I already know it.

I try to focus on the project, but I'm feeling too conflicted. I don't know if I've made the right decision– to choose Kiersten over Emi; to go see Emi; to take this job that will cause a natural rift in all of my relationships anyway. The timing's bad for everyone involved.

Plus, I feel horrible about not telling Kiersten yet about the job. She's going to be upset that she wasn't the first to hear the news, and even more angry when she finds out who *was*. I'm going to need to do something nice for her to make up for it.

I decide to go to a jewelry story a few blocks away. I've been wanting to buy Kiersten something anyway, and now seems like the perfect time. After browsing for a few minutes, I decide on some diamond earrings. The sales associate packages them neatly and wraps them for me. I call her on my way home and tell her that I want to take her out tonight. She says she'll be ready by seven.

I knock on her door a little before seven, and she answers in a stunning turquoise dress that compliments her mocha skin. Her hair is pulled back. She looks perfect. We kiss briefly as she welcomes me into the apartment.

"How was your day?" I ask her.

"It's better now that you're here," she says. "It was a rough day. I met a new client... his story just broke my heart." I look at her, the corners of her lips turned down. I walk over to her and hug her.

"What's in your pocket?" she asks, feeling something pressing against her waist.

"Oh, just a little something," I shrug.

"What?" she smiles.

"Maybe a couple little somethings... to make your day better..." I pull the box out of my pocket and hand it to her. She unwraps it, carefully untying the bow and removing the paper without tearing it. I open the small velvet box, and the diamonds sparkle in the light.

"Nathaniel," she says, "they're beautiful! Can I put them on?"

"Please do," I smile, glad to see her cute dimples and her eyes light up. I feel a little better, knowing I've made someone happy today.

"Is there an occasion for these?"

"Well," I say, kissing her, "I got some good news today."

I tell her about the opportunity, and she says she's happy for me. She's a little apprehensive about me going to LA and Las Vegas, not thrilled that we'll be apart for so long, but she's supportive of the job. I tell her I'm sure I can fly her out for a weekend, if she wants to get away. That seems to make her happier.

"Listen, Kiersten," I start. "I just want to let you know that I, uh, stopped by Emi's today... to tell her about the job. I didn't want you to think I was hiding anything from you... I hope that's okay."

She stands in the kitchen, looking at her feet.

"Kiers–"

"No," she says, cutting me off. "What are these, really?" she asks, touching her earlobes. "Is this guilt?"

"Absolutely not," I tell her, shaking my head.

"I asked you not to see her," she reminds me. "This is just not okay..."

"Come on, Kiersten. This was big news... she's supported my career from day one. I had to share it with her."

"You went behind my back and saw the *one woman* I asked you not to see!"

"Why are you so threatened by her?" I ask, somewhat appalled by her tone, trying one last time to talk some sense into her... to get her to allow me to talk to my best friend again. I can't forget the look on Emi's face, and it's tearing me up inside. "I haven't seen her in months! There is *nothing* going on between us."

"We've been over this, Nate, I don't want to have to explain this again. It's me or her!"

When she puts it like that, it just seems completely unreasonable. "Kiersten, seriously... don't give me ultimatums like this, please. Just trust me."

"No," she says. "It's got to be me or her." My heart breaks as I listen to this even though it's nothing new. I ignorantly thought she might reconsider. As she stands in the kitchen, I walk to her living room and sit down on the couch, my head in my hands.

I don't want to have to make this choice. Knowing Emi's open to reconciling, I can't cut her off completely, can I? Even though I made the promise to Kiersten to try, I never actually believed I'd keep it up– especially after Emi and I had started to talk again. I just figured it would be until she built up some trust in me. She's had a month to do that. The ultimatum makes it quite clear that this is going to be a more permanent decision.

She walks into her room and closes the door. After about fifteen minutes, she comes out, dressed in some plaid cotton pants and a t-shirt. My eyes follow her as she goes back to the kitchen and grabs a soda. She sits down at her dining room table and takes out a file folder, begins to read, avoiding any eye-contact with me.

I go back to considering putting Emi in that "friend" category. It was getting easier every day, until I saw her today. Now, though, Kiersten is demanding that I demote her even further. Will I be able to do it? Do I like Kiersten enough? If I consider that I'll never have a chance with Emi, why would I want to continue to torture myself by talking to her, seeing her, even? I either make this commitment to Kiersten, which I think I'm ready to make, or I destroy a pretty good relationship for a woman I can never have.

If I was ever going to make the break from Em, this was the time. Work would keep me consumed for months. It would be a plausible excuse, for sure. Maybe we would just naturally drift apart. It may be good for me to have some time away from her. Maybe the time apart would be good for her, too. Make her find someone else to rely on. The thought of her finding someone else nearly makes me sick to my stomach. But it is selfish of me, isn't it? She should find someone else. Someone that she could love, who could give her what she wanted. I am clearly not that person for her.

I sigh heavily. This is very likely the toughest decision I've ever been forced to make.

"Kiersten," I begin. She closes her work, which she obviously wasn't able to focus on anyway. "I actually did talk to her today about our situation. I told her that I needed some time away from her. I want to make this work between us, okay?"

"Thank you," she says.

We don't make love that night. She sleeps peacefully as I recount the many memories of Emi... and ponder the thought that there may never be any more. I don't sleep at all.

~ * ~

A week and a half goes by quickly as I ready myself for the temporary move. At Kiersten's one night, my phone vibrates in my pocket while she's making dinner. *Emi.* Inside, I smile, am excited to see that she's calling me, but I can't answer. I decline the call and put the phone back in my pocket. No less than fifteen seconds later, it vibrates another time. Discreetly, I pull it out and look at the caller ID again. *Emi.* I decline the call once more. We go through this one more time before I decide it must be something urgent.

"I left something in my car," I tell Kiersten, grabbing my keys and kissing her on the way out. "I'll be right back." I hurry down the stairs and make my way outside her building where the reception is better.

"Em, what's wrong?" I ask.

"Oh, hey, Nate," she says cheerily.

"Hi. Is everything okay?"

"Yeah, everything's fine," she answers.

"Emi, what did you need?"

"Oh, right," she says, her tone now serious. "Did you know you left one of your sketchbooks over here?"

"When?" I ask, not remembering ever taking one to her place.

"Well, I guess technically I borrowed it one night a few months ago, but nevertheless, I have it. You probably want it back."

"I've got plenty others," I answer. "How are you?" I ask after a few moments of silence pass.

"Fine," she tells me.

"Good," I respond, feeling she's not, but trying to stay as detached as possible. "I have to go, Em, okay?"

"So you don't want to come get it?"

"No, keep it," I encourage her. "I wasn't missing it."

"Okay," she sighs. "Did you see that mixed-media exhibit we were interested in seeing is coming to the Filmont Gallery next week?"

"No, I didn't, Emi. I really do have to go."

"Alright," she says, disappointed. "Bye, Nate."

"Bye."

~ * ~

The following weekend, I get a few more calls from Emi. She doesn't leave any messages, though, and not a single text. I eventually turn my phone off since Kiersten and I are spending the weekend at my apartment. On Sunday afternoon, while Kiersten is knee-deep in a case, I decide to test out a new painting technique I had been working on in the spare bedroom.

"Hey, baby?" Kiersten says from the doorway.

I turn down the music, still staring at the canvas. "Yeah?"

"Someone's here to see you." I quickly spin around to see Emi standing a few feet behind Kiersten, waving at me.

"Emi," I say surprised, glancing immediately back at Kiersten. She glares at me angrily. "What are you doing here?"

"I brought your sketchbook back," she says pertly.

"Em, I told you the other day I didn't need it." I set down my brush and walk past both of them to the kitchen sink to rinse off. "God, um, Kiersten, this is Emi. Emi, Kiersten."

"Yes, we just met," my girlfriend informs me coldly, crossing her arms in front of her chest as I dry my hands.

"When did you tell me you didn't need the sketchbook? I thought you said you *did*," Emi says. She scratches her head.

"No, when I called you back I told you I *didn't* need it," I blurt out, catching myself one second too late.

"You *called* her?" Kiersten asks.

Emi answers "yes" at the same time I respond "no." *Fuck.* "She called me last week, I thought something was wrong."

"So that's a 'yes,' then, isn't it Nathaniel?"

"Nathaniel?" Emi says in a mocking tone.

"Emi, cut it out." I want to argue with Kiersten, but realize it's pointless.

"I thought we had an agreement," my girlfriend adds to me.

"Yes, we did," I tell her. "We do."

"I'm sorry," Emi interrupts as she sets the sketchbook down on the island. "Have I done something to offend you or something, Kiersten?"

"Em..." I warn her. She has no idea what she's getting herself into.

"Actually, yes," she raises her voice. "You are in my boyfriend's home, and there is not *room* for both of us in this apartment."

"Wow, okay," Emi says, unfazed. "Even if I stand over here?" she taunts Kiersten by stumbling into the living room, close to the television. Her inability to stand still in one place lets me know she's been drinking. A lot.

"Emi! What are you doing?" I ask her, biting back a smile. She moves about ten feet in the direction of my bed.

"Is this far enough?" As Kiersten's glare follows Emi around the loft, Emi makes eye contact with me. I can tell she's not going to make this easy.

"*This* is who your best friend is?" Kiersten asks. "*This* is who you were fighting for?"

"You fought for me, Nate?" she asks, stunned. "Really?"

Kiersten whips her head around to me. "He lost," she says.

"Emi, we talked about this," I say to her, recognizing the severity in my girlfriend's voice. She is not finding this funny at all. "Kiersten and I... um..."

"Kiersten and I do not want you here," Kiersten says. "I believe that's what he is trying to say."

"Are you, Nate?" Emi asks. Her eyes plead with me. Kiersten's shoot daggers.

"Yeah, come on, Em." I walk over to her and take her gently by the arm to lead her out.

"Don't *do* this," she whispers to me.

"Emi, please." She yanks her arm away from my grasp.

"I have a few things here I'd like back," she says as her eyes begin to water, her cheeks flush bright red. Kiersten begins to gather her things from the table. I can tell it's going to be one or the other... possibly both.

"Come on, Em," I say, getting frustrated with her. "Kiersten, please, stop. I didn't invite her here, I swear. She's leaving. Right, Emi? You're leaving."

"Right, Nate. Right-o." She pulls open my desk drawer and takes out a few of her swatch books, slamming it shut once she's retrieved her items. Next, she goes to the closet and pulls out a black concert t-shirt.

"That one's mine," I argue.

"No, it's not."

"Yes, yours is the red one. That one." I walk her back over to the closet and pull out her shirt, hold it out to show her the design. "You got it because of the illustration, remember? It reminded you of that street artist we met at Union Station. Remember?" I grasp at the thin threads that still hold us together at this very moment, just waiting for them to snap. This is just like a break-up... *I fucking hate this.*

"I remember," she whispers through tears, walking away and throwing the black shirt back at me. On her way out, she stops at an end table and looks at a small framed painting.

"Emi," I stop her, see her mind calculating.

"That's Clara's," she argues, picking it up.

"We did that together," I tell her about the finger-painting her niece and I had created one afternoon when Emi was babysitting. "She gave it to me for my birthday last year, Emi. She even scrawled my name on it."

"Trust me, she wouldn't want her *Nate-Nate* to have it now." She grabs it and tucks it into her bag, throwing open the door. "Who the fuck are you?" she spits the words at me.

I follow her into the hallway.

"You know what, Kirstie, Kristin, whatever your name is," Emi says, turning on her heels and yelling back into the loft. "I don't know what you've done with my best friend, but this guy? *Nathaniel?* Fine. Take him."

"Stop it," I say to her quietly.

"*Who are you?* And where is the Nate I know?" she screams loudly in frustration, literally stomping her feet. "The Nate I know wouldn't let some woman tell him how it was gonna be. He wouldn't kick his best friend of twelve and a half years out of his apartment!" She puts an emphasis on the word "kick" by kicking the doorjamb, scuffing it with her boot.

"You," she says, pointing at my girlfriend. "You have *ruined* a perfectly good guy. Congratulations. Take your prize. You win."

"You're being a real bitch," I mumble to her as she starts to walk away, having a difficult time understanding her behavior– and an even worse time believing that I just called her that.

"I'm sorry, you're *whose* bitch?" she retorts, squaring off against me in the middle of the hallway. Neither of us move, her eyes challenging mine; mine, hers. Finally, boiling over with anger, I go back into the loft and slam the door shut.

"Fuck!" I yell loudly, throwing the t-shirt on the floor as I navigate my way through the apartment to the window. I watch until I see her leave the building. She struggles to wipe the tears from her eyes as she carries all of her belongings. Marcus follows her, is seemingly trying to talk to her, but she just walks quickly away from him, around the corner, out of my life.

Is this really what I want?

"Sometimes we have to give up things that aren't good for us," Kiersten says calmly, putting her hands on my shoulders and kneading softly. *Emi is bad for you, Nate, because you want her and you can never have her. Move on. It's for the best.*

"Yeah, I know." I hope I'm convincing to her; I'm not so sure I'm convincing myself.

"Thank you," she adds, putting her arms around me. I turn around and take her into my arms, kiss her, hope that I will soon feel better about this decision.

At night, she does everything in her power to keep my mind off of anything but her... and it works, if only temporarily. *Thankfully.*

~ * ~

Over the next week, I continue my research at the apartment. I've done some sketches and feel like I have a pretty good grasp on what I want to do with the LA club. Once I get there, I'll know for sure if it's going to work. I have packed about half of my things. My supplies are boxed up and ready to be shipped. I decide that I'll do the painting in Los Angeles. Shipping costs for a large piece of art would be outrageous, and the worry that I would have to live with while waiting for it to cross the country in the back of a semi is too much for me to bear.

Of course, the more time I spend in LA, the harder it will be on Kiersten and me. I promise to fly her out once, if not more often. I know it's going to be a challenge. I've never been in a long-distance relationship. I'll miss the intimacy, for sure. We have become very close. Ever since the day Emi came by the apartment, Kiersten and I have spent every night together. It's been nice because I haven't had a free moment to think about Emi.

That will all change when I get to LA, though, and don't have the constant distraction of Kiersten's mocha skin, her amber eyes, her firm stomach, her breasts... and her lips... her mind-numbing lips. God, how I'm going to miss her touch. She'll definitely have to visit more than once.

In my rush to leave New York, I'm having to multi-task as much as possible, and tonight, I'm breaking a rule. I'm taking my mother out to dinner so we can say our good-bye before my trek across country. Kiersten will be joining us. I want to spend as much time with her as possible, and I figure, since I've made the decision to be with her, I might as well introduce them this evening. I'm not really even nervous. I know Mom will like Kiersten. She's smart, classy... confident. Everything she would want for me.

Kiersten, on the other hand, is terrified. I pick her up at seven-thirty, and she seems to be completely out-of-sorts.

"Calm down," I laugh easily. "She's harmless. She's gonna like you."

"How do you know?"

"Because *I* do," I remind her. "You look stunning." Her diamond earrings sparkle in the light. She sighs and remains quiet as we drive to Mom's favorite French restaurant. When we arrive, I massage her tense shoulders as she walks in front of me into the restaurant. "You're going to be fine."

Mom is already seated and waves at us to join her at her table. She stands up to hug me first, then my beautiful date. It's an awkward hug. Kiersten is completely stiff, feigning a smile, completely *not* like the woman I know. I kiss her neck and whisper in her ear, "Breathe. It's going to be okay."

"Kiersten, it's a pleasure to meet you," my mother says, completely overjoyed that I've brought a woman to meet her. She couldn't be more welcoming, more accepting.

"Thank you," she answers. "You, too." She shifts uncomfortably in her seat.

"So, Nathan tells me you're a lawyer?"

"Yes, ma'am," Kiersten says. Silence spreads out before us.

"She's a civil rights lawyer," I fill in the blanks for her. "She gets to do some pretty amazing work."

"I would imagine so," Mom says, looking at her with interest. Kiersten just nods and smiles.

This is going to be a long night. I'm not sure where I left my well-spoken, outgoing, confident girlfriend, but I wish I could go find her and bring her here. *Now.*

About halfway through our appetizer course, Mom gives up trying to pull information out of her. She begins asking questions that are directed solely at me.

"Nathan, you haven't mentioned Emily lately," she starts. "How is she doing these days?"

"I'm not sure, Mom," I say quickly. "Hey, didn't you say you were doing that cancer walk this weekend? Are you ready for it?" I change the subject with the first thing that comes to mind.

"That was last weekend," she says with a strange smile. "Remember? You and Emi signed up to walk with me months ago."

"Oh, I'm sorry. I guess we forgot to put it on our calendars. Did James go? Or your friends?"

"No," she answers. "Just Emi. We had a nice talk."

We glare at one another from across the table. It's as if Kiersten isn't even there. Before the dessert course, my date excuses herself to go to the ladies room.

"Mom, why are you doing this? If you talked to Emi, you must know what's going on."

"That's just it, Nate," my mother says, wrinkling her nose. "I have no idea what's going on. That's what I want to find out."

"No, we're not discussing this tonight. This night is about Kiersten. You know it took a lot for me to introduce you two."

"And I'm honored, really, I am," she says. "But she's nothing like I imagined she would be."

"She's really nervous, for some reason," I explain. "She really is amazing... she's all the things I've told you. Maybe it just takes her awhile to warm up to people. And all this talk about Emi isn't helping..."

She glares at me, her eyes full of worry. "Why do you think she is so threatened by your relationship with her?"

"She's not threatened," I tell her, shifting my eyes from hers. "She's had some really bad relationships in the past. It's not Emi that bothers her."

"That's not how Emi sees it."

"I'm not talking about this with you. Just give Kiersten a chance. You'll like her."

"I don't know," she hedges. "Anyone who demands you stay away from your best friend–"

"She isn't *demanding* me to," I correct her. "I've chosen this. Emi and I have been drifting apart for months, anyway, and it's only going to get worse... it's just complicated."

"What do you mean?"

"Well, I'm going to be so busy with this job, and she's really busy, too. We're just going to kind of do our own things for awhile. I think it will be good to put a little distance between us."

"So it's just temporary?" she asks.

"Yeah, I guess," I shrug.

"Well, she seems to think it's pretty permanent," she says to me.

"If Kiersten and I stay together... it may be more permanent, I don't know," I tell her. "We'll cross that bridge when we get there."

"Nate, she's your best friend," she reminds me. "I find this a little strange."

I see Kiersten coming back from the restroom. "This is none of your concern. No more talk of Emi in front of Kiersten," I whisper. Mom raises an eyebrow, seething at me with disappointment. I know she can see right through me.

"Well, then I guess I don't have much more to say. Honey," my mother says to Kiersten as she pushes her chair back abruptly and stands up, "it was a pleasure to meet you." She turns her attention to me. "I'm sorry I have to run, but James is waiting at home."

"Of course," I respond, glaring at her in disbelief. It's one thing for Kiersten to be completely unsocial because her nerves have gotten the best of her. It's another thing entirely for my mother to so rudely excuse herself before the meal is even complete.

"When do you leave, Nathan?" she asks.

"Two days."

"Well, I'll call you tomorrow." She gives me a peck on the cheek and nods to Kiersten.

"Goodbye."

"Bye," Kiersten and I say in unison.

"I am so sorry about my mother," I tell her. "I'm not sure what's wrong with her."

"She didn't like me," Kiersten laughs. "Doesn't take a rocket scientist to figure that out."

"It's not that she doesn't like you," I say. "I don't think she really got a chance to know you. Really, you had nothing to be so nervous about."

"She's very intimidating," she tells me. "The way she was looking at me... was like she was... I don't know... *judging* me."

I scoff at the idea. "She was just trying to read you, that's all... she's not judgmental at all. Besides, there's nothing about you *to* judge. You're perfect." I lean over to kiss her, but she backs away.

"Can we leave?" she asks, clearly irritated.

"Sure, let me get the check."

After we get to my apartment, I do my best to persuade her that my mother did, in fact, like her, and that she has nothing to worry about. I know that Mom will eventually grow to like her, and that Kiersten will eventually warm up to her. I'm not worried about it at all. It's just a matter of time. Once I think I've eased her mind, I take her hand and pull her to the bed.

"I'm not really in the mood," she says stubbornly.

"But we only have two more nights together," I remind her.

"Really, Nate," she states firmly. "I'm not."

"Okay, Kiersten," I concede. "Tomorrow..."

"I think I'd like to go home tonight," she says.

"Are you okay?"

"I'll be fine," she smiles. "I'll make it up to you tomorrow."

"Let me get my keys."

"No, I'll get a cab, don't worry about it."

"Are you sure?"

"I'm positive... I'll see you tomorrow."

"Okay then. I'll miss you," I tell her before my lips find hers, my hand on her cheek.

She smiles. "Good night."

"Bye."

~ * ~

I've got a ton of last-minute things to take care of today. My flight is at ten-thirty tomorrow morning, so everything has to get wrapped up this afternoon. As I'm doing laundry and packing a few last things, someone knocks on my door.

"Honey, it's me," my mother says. I sigh heavily.

"Hello, Mom," I open the door to greet her, my teeth clenched.

"Nathan," she starts. "I don't get a good feeling about her."

"Mom, she's amazing. I've told you that. She was just nervous."

"Well," she continues, not skipping a beat, "what's going on with Emi?"

"I told you–"

"You told me we can't discuss it. Emi told me you were ordered to stay away from her."

"It really wasn't Emi's place to tell you anything," I roll my eyes, resenting my friend for getting my mother involved in our fight.

"So you *were* then?"

"No, Mom," I stutter. If my flawed speech doesn't give me away, the lack of eye-contact does. "It's for the best, okay?"

"Do you really believe that, Nate? You feel good enough about Kiersten to leave Emi behind forever?"

"You don't know her, Mom," I warn.

"Is she insecure because she senses that there is something more to your relationship with Emi?"

"Mom, you don't have any idea what you're talking about."

"I think I have more of an idea than you want to admit. I hate to think that you're dumping your best friend for this woman."

"I really like this woman, Mom."

"But you don't love her, do you, Nathan?" she asks me, in a soothing tone that only a caring mother can deliver. Strangely enough, it's the first time I've realized I've never told Kiersten I loved her outside of my typical, uncontrolled outburst at the height of passion. And she's never said it to me, either. *Do* we love one another?

"You love *Emi*." My mother's words shock me. My heart skips a beat as I stop breathing. I just stare at her, searching for something... an answer, maybe. An explanation for her assumption. I just shake my head. "You do."

218

"It doesn't matter," I tell her as I begin to lose my composure. I pace the room, throwing items into boxes haphazardly. "I can't. I can't let myself feel that way. She doesn't love me. She will *never* love *me*. I can't keep holding out for her. I've got to move on. I *have* moved on." It feels strangely cathartic to admit this aloud, feelings I've kept bottled up for too long.

"Nate..."

"Mom, just *stop!*" I shout. "Kiersten will warm up to you. You'll love her once she lets her guard down. She's good for me, you have to trust my judgment... my decision."

"Why would I love her when you don't?" she asks.

"It's not that I don't. I just..." I don't know what to say.

"Just think about it, Nathan," she insists. "That's all I'm asking. Think about what you're doing to Emily. Think about what you're doing to *yourself*, honey. You just admitted–"

"I admitted nothing. I said I've moved on. My future is with Kiersten." I pause, choosing my next words carefully. "Emi is my past." The statement sounds foreign coming out of my mouth. I turn around to hide my watering eyes and swallow the lump in my throat.

"I love her," I sigh, defeated.

"You love *who*?" she whispers.

I love her. I *love* her. When I think those words, what image do I see? Who is the "her" in that sentence? It's her. It's always been her. It's not possible for it to be love for anyone else, because any form of "love" I've felt for other women has been a mere fraction of how I feel about Emi.

I love *Emi*. And apparently I'm fooling no one but myself.

My mother stands silently behind me. I feel suddenly weak, dizzy. I find the nearest chair and sit down, putting my head between my knees to breathe heavily.

"Nathan, I think you two could make it work."

"Mom, please go."

"Just think about it. And call me when you get to LA." I nod my head again before allowing it to fall in my hands. Mom wraps her arms around me and kisses my cheek. I squeeze her hands in mine before she leaves. Once the door closes behind her, I blink the lingering tears from my eyes.

What does she mean, she thinks we could make it work? Has Emi told her something?

My last night in New York, and I'm planning to spend it with Kiersten. With a woman I've chosen over the girl I love. It doesn't make sense to me. It shouldn't be this way.

But at this point, it is this way. There are so many changes happening in my life that I don't know if tonight is the night to make any more big decisions. I decide to just go with my original plans, and let the night unfold how it will. Why hurt her tonight? The long distance will naturally erode what little relationship we really have.

Picking up the meal we had ordered, I walk the rest of the way to Kiersten's place. I had earlier called my usual florist and cancelled the arrangement I had requested yesterday, but I pick up a simple bouquet of flowers from a street vender a block away from her apartment and carry it with me. She meets me downstairs, graciously taking the flowers from me and guiding me upstairs. She's dressed up for our last night together and her mood is nothing like it was after our disastrous dinner date with Mom.

"You look beautiful," I tell her once we're behind closed doors.

"You like this?" she asks, showing off the short dress.

"I do," I smile, gathering the hem of her skirt in my hands and pulling her to me. Her fingers scraping my scalp, relaxing me, we kiss slowly. I sigh into her embrace. It does feel good to be with her, I can't deny that.

"I bought it for you," she whispers. "I want tonight to be memorable for us. It's got to last awhile, right?"

"Yeah," I answer.

"Let's put our salads in the fridge for now, and start out with a different kind of appetizer. How's that sound?" She takes slow, deliberate steps into the kitchen. I walk up behind her as she leans into the refrigerator, wrapping my arms around her.

"I can't argue with that," I tell her. I push her hair aside as she stands tall in front of me and place a kiss on her neck; another on her shoulder. She grips the counter as I press her against it, letting my lips travel down her back as I unbutton the dress. She picks up her skirt to reveal a string bikini. "Is that for me, too?" I run my hands over her warm skin.

"It's for you to take off," she confirms.

"Mmmm, sexy," I hum against her skin. On any other occasion– hell, *every* other occasion– I would have taken that string in my fist and snapped the garment off of her, but for some reason, I'm not quite as ready to go as I typically am. I slow down and concentrate more on Kiersten.

"I want you to take me like this," she whispers over her shoulder.

"I have other ideas," I explain, turning her around and making my way down her body. When I reach my destination, she doesn't object. She braces herself with her elbows on the countertop and her hands holding on tightly to my hair. Her legs weaken, shake, her voice needy as she calls out my name.

"Oh, god, Nate," she gasps as she pulls on my jacket, signaling for me to stand up.

"You liked that, huh?" I ask, my fingers lingering. She holds one of her hands against mine as her other one finds its way to the front of my pants. I can feel my cheeks blush. I close my eyes and look down, embarrassed and not quite sure what to say.

"You've got a lot going on," Kiersten breaks the silence kindly. "It's understandable. I bet I can make things better." I lean my forehead against hers and pull her skirt back down, kissing her sweetly.

"Let's have dinner," I suggest instead. "My head is just swimming in details. We'll get back to that."

She runs her hand down my body once more before agreeing to my plan.

We grab the salads out of the refrigerator and Kiersten pours us both some Italian soda. After I sit down, Kiersten rearranges the plates so that she's in the seat next to me instead of across from me. Her foot plays with mine. I lean down to kiss her before eating. She props herself on her elbow, watching me with a smile while she takes a few bites of her salad. She runs her hand through my hair.

"So, Donna talks to Emi a lot, huh?" she asks. Emi's the last person I want to think about right now.

"She's like the daughter she never had. They have their own relationship that doesn't really involve me."

"Well," Kiersten says, spearing a cherry tomato with her fork and feeding it to me. "It seems like Emi's trying to make your mom choose sides, if you ask me."

"No," I assure her, blowing off the accusation. "Mom just likes to be involved in my life. She gets a lot of the scoop from Em, that's all. They talk, I can't stop that," I laugh. They'd been friends on their own accord for so long, I never considered how their relationship would suffer. It wouldn't be fair to either of them to ask them to stop. "I can't make them not talk."

"I think if Donna knew how much it bothered you, she would stop talking to her."

That's going on the assumption that it bothers me. It doesn't. I shrug my shoulders in response.

"I mean, if she was a good mother..."

"She is," I assert. "You're right," I concede. I'm sure my mother would stop, but I would never ask that of her.

"Well maybe you can talk to her once you get settled in LA." She kisses my chin, then pulls my face to hers to kiss my lips. Her hand wanders to my lap. I drop my fork loudly, wrapping my arms around her and trying to put all of my energy into our embrace. I'm relieved when her fingers find their way back to my hair, since another part of me doesn't seem to want to cooperate right now.

"Come to bed," she says, standing and taking my hand in hers. "Let me make you forget everything."

"I'm not sure what's happening," I apologize to her.

"Shhhh," she says soothingly. "Just lie down." I willingly comply, allowing her to unfasten the buttons on my shirt. I watch as she makes a production out of each of them, one by one. Her knees on either side of my legs, I trace circles in her skin just beneath her skirt. She leans into me and kisses my temple, then playfully sucks on my earlobe. Typically, this one little move arouses me instantly, but it doesn't tonight. Kiersten undoubtedly notices as she shifts above me, pulling her dress over her head.

Her hands make their way down my bare chest. She undoes my pants and allows her hand to travel beneath my clothing, even though I nervously try to stop her. "It's okay," she assures me as she begins to rub gently. Moving her hands to unclasp her bra, her hips continue to move over me. There is *still* no reaction.

"You're beautiful," I tell her, leaning up to caress her breasts, attempting to coerce something to happen... and hiding what *isn't*.

"Lie back," she says as she hovers over me on her hands and knees. She kisses my lips, then my neck, chest... her hands remove my pants first. She leans in, kisses my navel.

Still nothing. Clearly, this isn't working.

"This is embarrassing," I finally say out loud.

"You've got a lot on your mind," she reminds me. "You're putting too much pressure on yourself. Why don't we talk about things?" She stays positioned on top of me, ready to feel something happen– if and when it does.

"Okay. What do you want to talk about?"

She tries to be subtle in her attempt to arouse me, her hips moving slowly against me. Her eyes lock with mine, her expression perplexed.

"Emi," she answers, her head cocked slightly. She leans over me again, her breasts touching my chest, her tongue tracing my jawline, then my lips. I close my eyes, imagine her, the last time I saw her. *The anger in her eyes... fueled by passion... the sadness. She was on the verge of tears. Her eyes grew greener.*

Emi. My body finally begins to react. *Fuck, Emi.* It doesn't just react, it *betrays* me.

I pull Kiersten's mouth to mine, initiating a deep kiss, an attempt to distract her momentarily. I lift her hips, moving her back, away, in hopes of hiding the physical reaction to her mention of one simple word.

Emi.

She moans and runs her fingers through my hair. I kiss her deeply, trying to commit fully to her foreplay, but my thoughts are still with *Emi. Her soft, strawberry blonde hair.*

My body is reacting to visions of *Emi.* Who knew bringing up her name would bring up... other things? *Fuck.*

"What about her?" I begin to touch Kiersten, turning the focus onto her, away from me.

Emi. The way her lips curl into the perfect smile.

I become more aroused. Kiersten leans back tentatively, testing me, feeling every bit of me against her body.

"Wow, Nathaniel," she says, sitting still. "Huh." She doesn't smile. This isn't her typical reaction. *Fuck.*

"You know what, I don't want to talk about Emi." *Her flawless, creamy skin; the dimples that punctuate her cheeks.* "Let's just focus on you," I suggest, trying to nudge her gently out of my lap and back onto the bed. She doesn't budge, just kneels back on her heels with her hand in my lap, pressing against me. I sit up, kiss her once more. "Not Emi."

Emi. Her name consumes me, the very idea of her, strangely liberating. *Her delicate frame, her small but ample breasts, how I've longed to see them, feel them.* The thought brings me to full attention. *Fuck!*

She moves her hand over me, confirming my fears; likely hers, too. "Kiersten," I whisper, kissing her earlobe. Is there any way in hell she will not connect the two?

"So, Emi..." she continues on her earlier topic. *The sound of her laugh, the smell of her perfume.* I'm definitely ready to go now... and it couldn't come at a less opportune time. *Fuck!* Kiersten removes her hand from me, stands up and crosses the room. She puts her bra back on slowly. "I think we *need* to talk about her."

I glance at my boxers and pull the sheets over me.

"Yeah," I sigh heavily. "Maybe so."

"Do you love me, Nathaniel?"

My mouth drops in an effort to answer, but– not knowing what to say– keeps the sound in.

"Okay..." she says as she finds some jeans in her closet and pulls them on. "Do you love *her*?" My whole body shudders at the thought of her. Of *loving* her. *Loving* her the best way I know how, which hasn't been good enough for anyone else... I would learn how to love *better*, for her.

"Who?" *Her small hips, my hands clinging to them tightly as I pull her body into mine.*

"Emi," she snaps. *Those angry green eyes, matted lashes, furrowed brow. How I long to rid my head of these images of her. How I want to see her smile again. Laugh again. Love... again...*

"No." My answer is quick, but a complete and utter lie. It even sounds like one as it escapes my lips.

"No," she repeats. "So it's purely a sexual thing with her then?"

"What? No!" I laugh nervously. "It's not just sexual."

"Oh, so there is something to this?"

"No, Kiersten, I'm just... it's just..." I can't explain it. Not to her, not now. I can't have *Emi. The pigtails. Stop!* I don't want what I can't have. I don't want *to want* what I can't have. And yet she's all I want. I pull a pillow into my lap, mortified at the physical transformation my body has made since Kiersten said that one little word.

Emi.

"Nathaniel," she says, swallowing hard. "*Do* you love her?" Her eyes search mine, feverishly. I don't answer. "You *do*. From the first time you mentioned her to me, I knew there was something there."

"There's nothing there," I tell her.

"I thought I could change you," she continues, ignoring my response. "But when she was at your loft the other day, I could see it. I could see it in *both* of you."

"Really?" I ask, wanting to know more, and then realizing how idiotic my response is. She grabs the pillow from my lap and throws it at my head.

"Get out," she demands.

Stunned at my non-verbal admission, I stand up, my heart pounding. I love Emi. And Kiersten seems to think she might have feelings for me. I hurry and dress, trying to figure out my next move.

After I've got my clothes back on, I address her directly. "I never meant for this to happen to us," I apologize.

"Us?" she asks. "There was never an *us*. You've always belonged to her."

"I'm sorry."

"I thought I could change that. But I had no chance. You were long gone before we ever met." She pushes me toward the door, unlocking it and opening it. "I can see that now. So get out."

She shoves my shoes and keys into my chest. "I'm sorry," I apologize again and duck when she throws the bouquet of flowers at me.

"Get the fuck out!" Her yell undoubtedly will draw the attention of her neighbors.

"I'm going," I assure her as I step into my shoes and feel the wind off the door in my hair when she slams it.

I want nothing more than to run to Emi and tell her how I feel, what happened... find out if there's any truth to what Kiersten said. *I could see it in both of you.*

But I realize I can't. Not with the taste of Kiersten still on my lips. Not seconds after I've ended this relationship. That's how I fucked things up with her last time. I can't afford to do that again. I can only hope she's willing to give me another chance, but now's not the time to find that out.

Even though this is my last night in Manhattan, I refrain from going to her.

At eight o'clock the next morning, I grab my bags and my guitar and lock up the apartment. I'm excited to have this project in front of me, to have this distraction, but can't help but feel like it's coming at the worst possible time. I don't want to leave New York now. I don't want to leave Emi. But I don't have a choice. The project is too important, and we need some time apart. I need some time apart from her and from all women. I'll find a way to put all my focus on my work for the time being.

I'm tired of hopping from one woman to another, like I'm notorious for doing. I'm tired of Emi seeing me this way. I need some time to get to know myself, to make sure I know what I want... to make sure I'm willing to take this risk with Emi... and if I am, I want to do this the right way. I want to make sure of my feelings for her, even if she can never return them. I can't mess this up again. It is too important. *She* is too important.

Before boarding the plane in the morning, I send one text message.

"Goodbye."

A very clean, very modern, very *new* two-bedroom suite spans in front of me when I get to my hotel room. After setting my bags down, I take in my temporary home and start to get comfortable. The refrigerator is stocked with the basics, as well as a full assortment of sodas and bottled water. A bottle of champagne chills in ice on the coffee table with a note from Albert welcoming me and letting me know that he'll meet me in the hotel bar at eight tonight. I put the champagne in the back of the refrigerator, figuring I'll have no use for it while I'm here.

Most of the boxes I had shipped are already waiting for me in the room. The rest, the ones that contain my paint supplies, should be waiting at the restaurant. After unloading my clothes and belongings into the closets and dressers, I find the framed photo that I had packed at the last minute. It wasn't an afterthought. I just wasn't sure I wanted to have the constant reminder with me. In the end, though, I did. The picture is of me and Emi. Her brother took it last year at her niece's fourth birthday party, which was held at her Mom's house in Jersey. Neither of us aware that Chris was taking the picture, we were huddled together, talking intently, just the two of us, holding cupcakes. Emi's expression was very serious as she spoke, but I had a faint smirk on my face. Although I don't remember what was so gripping about the conversation, I do remember the moment quite clearly. I remember the thoughts going through my head anyway.

Emi had frosting on her upper lip, and I had stopped myself from pointing it out to her, allowing myself to indulge in the daydream of kissing the icing from her lips. Eventually, she discovered it and licked it with her tongue, slapping my shoulder playfully when she realized I hadn't told her it was there.

When Chris posted the photos of the party online, this was the only picture I ordered. Emi had ordered one, as well. I loved that she had a sense of humor about herself. She was never one to take herself very seriously.

I had plenty of other pictures of her, but in none of the others did she ever look so beautiful, and so naturally Emi. I place this one on my nightstand, knowing that it's the last thing I'll see before sleep, and the first thing I'll see when I wake up. It will remind me what all of this is for... her, and the possibility of us.

At eight, I meet Albert downstairs and after a quick drink, we take his car to a trendy restaurant in Hollywood. We are led to a private area in the back where about thirty people are already mingling, drinks in hand. These are apparently his close friends and business partners. I quickly note that the men are outnumbered two-to-one... and that every woman there could be an actress, model or both.

Albert is clearly the life of the party, everyone's friend. He takes me around and introduces me to all of his acquaintances and I do my best to remember all the names. He makes a more thoughtful introduction to one woman in particular.

"Nate, this is my business partner, Shannon. She was our interior designer for the clubs," he says.

"Pleasure to meet you," I say, kissing her on the cheek.

"Likewise," she tells me, glancing at Albert. "You were right," she says to him as an aside, but obviously loud enough for me to hear. Albert just nods and walks toward another group of friends.

She turns her attention back to me saying, "Albert says you will be doing the artwork?"

"Yes, uh, I'm very excited to see the location."

"Will you be going tomorrow?"

"No, the day after," I tell her. She is remarkably attractive; long legs, curly red hair, a nice smile... but something about her eyes seems a little mysterious. Devious, even.

"I may join you for the walk through. I want to hear your ideas."

"Oh, of course."

"Looks like Albert isn't being a very good host. Can I get you anything to drink?" she asks, sipping from her own glass of red wine.

"No, I'm good, thanks."

"It's no problem," she assures me. "Beer? Wine? Scotch? Slow Comfortable Screw?" She pauses, gauging my expression. I recognize this is the name of a drink, and it's impossible to miss the innuendo since she follows the phrase by licking her lips, slowly, while raising an eyebrow. "I can get you anything you want."

"No, really, I'm fine," I affirm, laughing at her audacity.

"If you change your mind..." she trails off, walking toward the bar.

I nod, finishing her sentence, "I will definitely let you know."

Waiters are carrying around trays of hors d'oeuvres, and I snack on a few items, realizing I haven't had anything to eat all day. I weave in and out of conversations with no trouble. I've always found it easy to meet new people... it's the getting to know them and making good friends out of them part that I have problems with. I tend to keep most people at a safe distance. The only exceptions are the women I'm interested in dating.

Shannon makes her way through the crowd and hooks her elbow into mine. "Girlfriend?" she asks.

"Uh, no..." I start, smiling.

"Well, Albert says that your agent told him you were always on the lookout for beautiful women."

"Is that what she says?"

"It's what she told Albert."

"Well, she doesn't really know what she's talking about," I laugh. That must be what it looks like from the outside. Kate typically knows of the people that I date, but I never really go into particular detail with her. The only woman she knows anything about is Emi, and that's just because Emi has been there from the start... gone to all of my shows... supported me all the way. But Kate has always accepted the explanation that Emi and I are just friends.

"Really?" Shannon asks.

"I just got out of a relationship," I tell her. "I'm not really ready for another one."

"Who said anything about a relationship?"

I laugh nervously. "I'm flattered, Shannon, but I'm not... really... interested. You're a beautiful woman, really... it's just... the timing's not right."

"Fair enough," she says, dropping my arm and walking away. After talking to a few more of his friends, I decide to find Albert and let him know I'm going to take a cab back to my hotel.

"No, let me take you back," he insists. "I've got an early day tomorrow, anyway." He thanks everyone for coming and we head out to get the car.

"Shannon not your type?" he asks as soon as we drive away.

"Oh, she's beautiful," I comment. "Just, uh..."

"What's your type? I told you I'd show you a good time while you're here, just let me know what you're looking for."

"Oh, uh..." I'm a little taken aback. "Albert, really, you don't need to go to any trouble. This job's going to keep me plenty busy. I really just need to focus on the work."

"Right, so you're going to forego women for a month?" he laughs. I do fully intend to... surely I've got enough will power to last that long. I'm doing it for Emi. If she's the prize, I know I can do it.

"I don't need the distraction," I assure him. "You want art by the time you open, right?"

"Of course," he says. "Just let me know when you change your mind. I'll find the perfect girl for you. There are plenty to choose from here... whatever your preference."

"Sure, okay, thanks." It's easier than arguing.

"If you're worried about commitment, these girls don't want it."

"Good to know," I say quietly as Albert pulls up to the hotel. "I appreciate it."

"Anything, man," he says. "Okay, so you're gonna settle in tomorrow, right? I'll have a rental brought by. Then we can meet on Thursday to do the walk-through."

"Sounds great, looking forward to it."

"Have a good night," he tells me. "If you change your mind..."

"Of course," I laugh as I get out of the car. "Thanks." It's late and I decide to turn in for the night.

The next morning, I wake up before the sun comes up, still on New York time. I make some coffee and head out on the east-facing balcony of my suite to watch the sunrise. The view of the Hollywood Hills is breathtaking as the early rays welcome the day. I decide to take a picture with my phone and email it to Emi. I know she would appreciate it. I wish she were here to appreciate it with me.

"Good morning from LA" is all my message says. Every cell in my body is telling me to hit the send button. It pulsates, waiting to be clicked, taunting me. I play out the events in my head. I send the picture, she will open it. What will she think of it? Of me sending it? It's an olive branch, a peace

offering, but I have no idea how she'll respond. She never texted me back when I left New York. She must still be angry, and why shouldn't she be? I chose another woman over her. I don't know how to start rebuilding what we had... and I'm not sure there is any way she would be happy to hear from me.

And honestly, what am I trying to gain from it? I've decided the only way to move forward is to convince her to give me a chance as something more than a friend. I won't get that from her. This email, this small gesture, only stands to hurt us both more. I close it, choosing not to save it.

Even staring at the beauty of the city in front of me, I miss my hometown. I miss New York, everything about it. I think about all the places I visit, my local grocery store, the coffee shop, the park, the movie theatre, my apartment, Emi's apartment... it all reminds me of her. Manhattan is my home... but it is Emi, too. Everything about it reminds me of her. Places we've been, things we've done, the sights, the sounds, the smells. I can't imagine being there now, in a city so small, her just a few blocks away, but half a world away. I wonder if I can go back... if I can resume any sort of normal life with her there.

We would undoubtedly run into one another at some point, at some event, party, club, gallery. We would be strangers. We would be two people who had difficulty forming words into meaningful sentences... sentences that wouldn't hurt one another, that wouldn't remind us of our past, that would attach to them no emotions. We would talk about the weather. We would talk about the news. We would talk about anything but us... if we were even able to speak at all.

It's unimaginable to me, to think we'll be in the same city, pretending to not be. I can't let that happen. When I go back, I'll figure out how to fix this. It has to be fixable. I love her too much to be without her. I just have to make it through this time apart from her.

I wonder how I'll make it a day, a week, a month or two without Emi in my life. I know this will be good for me, in the end. They say absence makes the heart grow fonder. I wonder if it will for her. I wonder if she can ever feel the same way about me as I feel about her. It's been nearly thirteen years. The only times she's ever shown a romantic interest in me is when copious amounts of alcohol are involved. I learned quickly from that night her freshman year in college that I wasn't what she was looking for, but still, I hoped she would see in me what I saw in her. *How naïve I was. How eager. How much I wanted her to love me, even then. Still now.*

For me, now, the first step is to figure out who I really am. I have jumped from one relationship to the next for so many years that I'm not sure who Nate– *just Nate*– is anymore. I need to focus on myself, be introspective, learn to find love in other things, like my work or nature or music... or myself. It's not just about romantic love, sexual love. There is so much more to life. And when I think about it, I think Emi knows that side of life so well, knows herself better than most, knows how to find love in the world around her. But she is unfamiliar with the romantic love, the sexual love. It almost seems like we are the missing pieces to each other's life puzzles. Could either of us truly feel whole, without the other?

I smile at the thought. The thought that, together, we can understand the world, but apart, we are each oblivious to half of what's important. How can "we" not be meant to be? It seems so obvious in this moment. I will fix this. This will work. It has to. I'm meant to be with her. I love her and I want to be with her.

I laze around the suite all day, spending a little time sketching and a little time reading. It's been a very long time since I've felt at peace with things. I feel completely unburdened. It's strange... it's as if I've been living some sort of half-truth all my life, like I've never been allowed to be completely honest with myself. I just find comfort in knowing, really knowing, what I want.

At four, the hotel concierge calls to let me know that a rental car has been dropped off for me. I ask him to hold the keys, deciding not to venture out this evening. I order room service and begin to make plans for tomorrow. I begin to think about the project. Since the majority of my inspiration comes from some kind of frustration or pain or void, I know this is going to be epic, having never felt such loss in all of my life. Even with the hopefulness I have for something more with Emi, I know I can channel the sadness that lies beneath into something much bigger, much better than anything I've done before.

I consider my life without her. There is no color in that world. No beauty. No life at all. I'm an artist, I'm supposed to have color and beauty. My life is altered, worse, without those things. I know this isn't my destiny, my fate. *She* is. She *must* be.

I don't know if she'll be receptive to the idea of "us" at all. I don't even know how to bring it up. I know she cares about me, but if I lay it all on the line for her– if I tell her that I'm in love with her– I'm fairly certain she will not immediately love the idea. She may *never* love the idea. If I focus on the pain of her rejection, it will help me in two ways. It will help me create the work I was brought here to do, and it may help to prepare me for an undesirable outcome. It just can't end like that.

Just thinking about her turning me down brings a lump to my throat. How I hope she sees the potential in "us."

The phone rings as I'm about to turn on the television for a distraction. It's my mother. I wonder if I should tell her about Kiersten, about my decision about Emi. I should. It would put her mind at ease, and honestly, I should probably thank her for pointing out the obvious, even though I thought I hid it well. Part of me wants to do that. The other part doesn't want me to tell her she was right. I answer the phone on the fourth ring.

"Mom."

"Nate, honey, you made it to LA okay?" she asks with concern.

"I did. Sorry I didn't call sooner."

"I know you're busy... and I figured you were still angry with me." I should let her off the hook.

"Yeah, I've been busy settling in."

"Nathan, I'm sorry about the other night. Maybe I misspoke. It was a little out of line, I guess."

"No, Mom–"

"I just don't want you making a big mistake. But you're smart enough to figure this out. I shouldn't have gotten involved. I'm sure Kiersten is a nice girl. I know I can be a bit intimidating. I'm sure she was nervous."

"Mom, shut up for a second." She sits in silence, waiting for me to continue. "I think you were right, Mom."

"About?"

"Everything... I'm not sure what to do about it yet, but you are right about my feelings for Emi."

"Nate," she sighs.

"I've always loved her, but it's always been understood that we would never pursue a relationship with one another. So I don't really know what's going to happen."

"What are you going to do about Kiersten?" she asks.

"It's over. She broke it off. She hates me, but it's best that it happened when it did. Eventually I'd have to be honest with myself and accept that what I feel for Em is... well, love," I explain.

"And what did Emi say?"

"She doesn't know anything. I'll talk to her when I get back to New York. I need to let everything settle."

"Settle?" she asks. "What needs to settle? You should call her now and tell her how you feel!"

"Mom, I appreciate your willingness to speak up and offer some guidance, but I've got it from here. I want some time alone. I have to think this through, make sure it's worth the risk of not having her in my life at all if she decides this isn't what she wants."

"I just don't think she'll decide that."

"Well, unless she has come right out and told you that, you can't know. I have to be prepared for anything... and I need to be alright with myself, just in case. Plus, I want to tell her in person."

"I guess I can respect that," she says. "I'm proud of you, Nathan."

"Thanks, Mom. I just hope it all works out."

"So do I, honey."

"Thanks for calling, Mom. I'll do better about keeping in touch."

"Okay." I can hear the smile in her voice. "Have a good time in LA."

"Thanks. Goodnight."

"Night, Nathan."

CHAPTER 11

Four weeks have passed since I arrived in LA. The painting is almost complete, and I'm honestly impressed with the progress I've made. In another day or two, the large mural should be finished. Albert requested that I do a few smaller pieces for private rooms, and I was already able to finish those in my spare time in the hotel. He stopped by a few times to check in, but has given me freedom to create whatever I like. He and Shannon were both very complimentary, feeling that all the pieces accentuated the architecture and design perfectly.

I have avoided talking to Emi in this time period in order to channel the feelings of anxiety into my art. Sometimes the emptiness is too much to bear, but I find I'm most productive when I feel like I've lost her forever. It's gotten to the point that I wonder if I'll have to find a new career if I can ever convince her to love me. I laugh at the thought, because if, by chance, that does happen, I know that the passion between us will inspire me far more than pain and sadness. I know it in my heart.

I've also had a lot of time to just enjoy life by myself. I've read a couple of books, visited half a dozen galleries, driven up the California coast, and written two songs. I'm amazed at how much I've done in the past few weeks... and I still feel certain about my feelings for Emi. Her absence from my life has served me well, but now that the LA restaurant opening is nearing, I want to call her and find out how she's doing. I would really like to see her. It's actually more like a need; I *need* to see her.

Before I leave for work, as I'm plotting my call to her, a text message comes through. *It's her.* My heart palpitates quicker, a smile spreading across my face at the sight of her name on my phone and the realization that we were both thinking of the other.

"I don't know if it's okay to tell you this, but I kiss you."

I let out a small laugh, reading it again. *I don't know if it's okay to tell you this, but I kiss you.* I *kiss* you? Wow. The smile grows, knowing it's a typo but hoping deep down it's a freudian slip. I stare at it for a few more minutes, waiting for her to send a corrected text. It doesn't come.

I dial her number slowly, taking a few deep breaths to calm my nerves. I can't wait to talk to her. Her voice rattles me. She sounds happy. "Nate?" she says through her smile.

"Emi," I sigh. "My god." I don't even know what to say next. It is just so good to hear her.

"Did you get my text message?"

"I did, but I don't really understand it," I tease her.

She's quiet for a few seconds. "Oh. What don't you understand?"

"It's just–"

"You don't miss me..." she cuts me off, mumbling to herself, obviously hurt.

"Oh, god, no, Emi," I quickly tell her, hoping to ease any doubt she is having. "That's not what your text said!"

"What do you mean?"

"It said, 'I don't know if it's okay to tell you this, but I... *kiss*... you.'"

"*Kiss* you?" she asks sheepishly.

"Yes, *kiss* you."

"Oh," she laughs. "Damn fingers get in the way. I *miss* you."

"I know," I tell her. "I figured that's what you meant. I think I would know if you were kissing me."

"Probably..." She's silent, silent for too long.

"Emi?"

"Yeah?"

"What is it?" I ask.

"You didn't say you missed me," she states quietly.

"I didn't?" I ask, caught off-guard. "I thought I did. I do, Emi. I really do miss you. It is so good to hear from you. I was just thinking about calling you when your text came through, actually."

"Really?" she asks.

"Yes, really."

"Why?"

"Just to see–" A loud noise on her end of the line cuts me off. "Where are you?" I ask once the noise is gone.

"Hey, Nate, I hate to cut this short. I didn't think you'd respond, but can I call you later?"

"Yeah, I'll probably be at the restaurant working, but I'll have my phone on. Please... do..."

"Cool," she sighs. "Goodbye, Nate." I hate hearing her say that, and correct her immediately.

"Goodbyes suck, Em. Like ya."

"Okay," she laughs, hanging up shortly after.

Later that evening at the club, the aroma of savory food begins to overtake the smell of paint. The chefs have been busy preparing samples for Albert, Shannon and me to taste. It's the first day I haven't been alone in the space to work, but I still feel free to create, even with the chefs coming in to watch me work as they take breaks. My inspiration– and drive to finish– has been fueled today by the earlier phone call. I've kept my music turned down, not wanting to miss her call tonight.

A distinctive chime alerts me from my phone. *Emi.* Anxious, I wipe the paint from my left hand on my jeans and pull my phone out of my pocket.

"Goodbyes do suck." I sigh heavily, unable to suppress the smile at her text.

"Yeah, they do, Em," I sigh and speak quietly to myself. "Tell me about it." I drop the phone to my side and look up, thanking God for the message from her. The phone chimes again before I can place a call to her.

"I'd rather tell you about how much I prefer hellos."

I stare at the phone, perplexed. It's like she read my mind.

"Okay, then tell me," I respond.

A small pinging noise echoes off the walls of the empty restaurant.

"Hey, Nate." I turn around abruptly, staring directly into the spot lights I've been using in my makeshift studio. I block the glare with my hand and finally see her in the shadows, standing alone by the door with a suitcase at her feet. Wearing a gauzy black dress and black heels, she certainly doesn't look like the woman I know as my friend. Her hair falls in loose curls, framing her big smile and green eyes perfectly. She looks amazing.

We walk quickly to one another, but I stop her before she touches me.

"Wet paint," I explain quickly, pointing at my clothes, my arms.

"I don't care," she laughs with a tear dropping from her eye. "You better hug me."

I pick her up and swing her around a few times before settling her on her feet. "What are you doing here?"

"I just wanted to say hi."

"You were gonna call," I stammer. "Not that I'm not happy to see you," I add quickly.

"Okay, I just wanted to *see* you. *And* say hi. Among other things."

"How did you know where to find me?"

"Kate picked me up from the airport."

"Well, hi, Em," I say happily, pulling her back into me. She clings to me tightly and sniffles into my shirt as I kiss her forehead. When I pull away, the bright light shows just how much wet paint I've managed to get on her. "Hold on."

I run to the sink and grab a clean rag, dampening it and carrying it back over to her. Ignoring the mess I've made of her dress, I focus my attention on the light orange daub on her right cheekbone. From memory, I matched the color of her hair perfectly. I gently wipe it away, along with another tear or two. "How are your hands?" I pick them up and examine them closely, feeling the soft skin under my calloused fingers. I blot some lingering paint from them as well.

"It's breathtaking, Nate." She stares at the painting on the wall behind me, taking a step toward me, her shoulder brushing up against my arm lightly.

I turn around to watch her as she examines my work. The soles of her shoes tap softly on the unfinished concrete floor as she moves closer to the mural. I follow her, staying close to her, not wanting there to be even an inch of distance between us. Not anymore.

Her hand rises, reaching for a wisp of the orange paint. I quickly stop her from touching my work-in-progress. My fingers wrap around her small hand, slowly pulling it back toward her body.

"Careful, it's still wet," I say softly. She drops her hand to her side, and I stroke her arm with my thumb, starting at her shoulder and stopping at her wrist when her other hand closes around it. My breath catches in my throat. I briefly wonder if the air conditioner has been cut off, or if the spot lights just got a lot hotter in here. I can feel a bit of sweat forming on my forehead.

"What inspired you?" Emi asks.

"The breakup," I tell her.

"Yeah," she begins, turning around in front of me and looking down at the space between us. "Your mom told me you two broke up. I'm really sorry."

"Not that breakup," I correct her, lifting her chin so her eyes can look into

241

mine. "I guess ours wasn't really a breakup," I try to explain.

"What do you mean?" I'd never noticed how adorable her eyebrows were. My finger traces one of them, trying to wipe the confused look from her face, but it only worsens as she tries to process the smile breaking across mine.

"That's what it's felt like. Being without you. Thinking of my life without my best friend in it. It's kind of sucked," I admit, still not believing she's here. "It's good to see you, Emi."

"Good," she says, her breath shaky, her eyes looking into mine warily. "It's good to see you, too." She turns back around to examine the painting once more. "Nate, it's the most spectacular thing I've ever seen."

"Then I've clearly accomplished what I set out to do." *Because that's what you are to me.* I put my hands on her shoulders, kneading gently. The faint smell of her shampoo stirs up so many memories I have of her. I hold her still, breathing her in.

"Are there other people here?" she asks me.

"Yeah, the chefs are in the kitchen. Why?"

"I just need to talk to you. I think we need to be alone to have the conversation I want to have."

"Okay." She turns back around. "I kind of have plans tonight," I tell her. "Albert and Shannon– that's the owner and interior designer– they'll be here any minute now for a tasting."

"Oh," she says, nodding. "I can wait–"

"That's not what I meant, Em," I laugh. "Stay. Please, stay. The restaurant seats four." I point to the one, lone table situated by a window overlooking the city. It must have been set up earlier today, as I hadn't seen it before.

"I don't want to impose..."

"You're not. Absolutely not. They've been trying to set me up since I landed at LAX. They'll be happy I have a girl with me tonight. And I'll be happy to not have to talk to them about my preference in hair color, or education, or music for once."

Her cheeks blush. "They haven't figured out you're not set on any one type of woman?" she asks after clearing her throat. She swallows hard after getting the question out as her eyes challenge me.

"Oh, but I am," I tell her with a sly smile.

"Right," she whispers skeptically as she takes a few steps back. "Is there somewhere I can freshen up?"

"Yeah, this way. I need to wash up, too." She swings her purse over her shoulder and follows me to the hallway that branches into two separate restrooms.

"Thanks."

Once in the men's room, I stare at myself in the mirror. *Holy shit, she's actually here.*

I couldn't remove the smile from my face if I tried. No matter what happens tonight, I know that she's not lost to me forever. Unless she came with some sort of news. She said she wanted to be alone to talk to me. What if she's seeing someone? What if that's her news? My heart sinks a little at the thought, but even still... so what if she is seeing someone? Someone that deserves her, someone that's good to her and for her? She's still my best friend. That won't change regardless. I just want her in my life.

As long as she's not doing to me what I tried to do to her, I'll be fine. I can't believe I hurt her like that.

I don't deserve her.

But I'd be good to her. Of that, I'm sure.

I scrub my arms and hands thoroughly, getting off all the paint. I grab the jeans and shirt I had brought with me to change into for dinner, discarding my paint-soiled clothes in my duffel bag. I splash some water on my face and run my fingers through my hair, the smile still evident in my eyes.

I realize she's turned up the music once I make it back into the main room. She hasn't changed my playlist, and I wonder if she saw what it was called when she adjusted the volume. *For Emi.* Simple and to the point, containing all the songs that remind me of her. There are hundreds that I've collected over the years. I think I could listen to the music in that list for two and a half days without hearing a song repeated.

"I'm sorry about your dress," I apologize to her, announcing my presence. Even from across the room, I can see the paint splotches that stand out against the black fabric.

"Are you kidding?" she asks. "It's a Nate Wilson original now. Think of the resale value."

I roll my eyes and walk toward her. "Is it dried in already?"

"Pretty much," she admits, touching a blue splotch and shrugging her shoulders. "I don't really care. You look nice."

"I just look *clean*," I tell her. "You, though. You're a sight for sore eyes. How long are you here?"

"Through Monday, if you'll have me." I close my eyes for the briefest of moments, indulging in the vision of one of my fantasies of her. Thankfully, she's gone back to looking at the painting, possibly shielding herself from an unwelcome response from me. She won't get it.

"Of course. I can take the weekend off. I'm way ahead of schedule here."

"Cool." One dimple stands out more than the other with her sexy smile. "Hey, wasn't this one of our songs in that dance class... god, how many years ago was that?"

"Eight?" I ask. "And yes." She had convinced me to take a dancing class with her. She thought it would be a good way for us to meet people. I met an interesting woman... but as far as the men were concerned, if they weren't there with their wives, they weren't there to pick up *women*.

"Care to give it a whirl?" she asks, her steps sultry as she walks toward me.

"I don't know if I still can," I tell her, pulling her closer and trying to remember the steps we had learned in class. We both make more than our share of mistakes, but it's fun and we're both laughing and arguing about who's right and who's wrong. I twirl her at the end of the song, and my heart skips a beat as I recognize the song that follows on the playlist. It's about two long-time friends becoming lovers for an evening. She's still laughing and starts dancing with me again as the singing begins. My palms become sticky, my nerves shot, and I can no longer look her in the eyes, afraid she'll read every impure thought that's going through my mind. She doesn't seem to be listening to the lyrics... *yet*. My head tucked next to hers, I mouth some of the lyrics with a smile on my face.

By the time the last words of the first verse are being sung, we are in each others arms, moving together slowly. Her head is on my chest, no doubt listening to the rapid beating of my heart and my uneven breaths. Visions of her, of me, alone, touching... she will soon know exactly how I feel if she continues to cling to me this way.

"I hope we're not interrupting," Albert's voice calls to us from the door. Emi pulls away quickly, startled.

"Albert and Shannon," I announce on my way to turn the music down. "This is my friend, Emi. She's in for the weekend from New York."

Albert walks to her confidently, Shannon fast on his heels. He picks up her hand and kisses the back of it. "He's never told us about an Emi from New York," he says to her as he looks her up and down. I'd warn him to back off if he wasn't my current boss.

"To be fair," Shannon says, "he's never told us about anyone, Al." She and Emi shake hands briefly. "It's a pleasure to meet you."

"Thank you."

"Did Nate invite you to stay for dinner? We're trying to finalize the menu tonight. We could use another opinion," Albert asks.

"Yes, as long as I'm not intruding–"

"What's your poison?" he cuts her off.

"Um... do you have any pinot noir?"

"Of course," he nearly laughs, exiting the room to go downstairs to the cellar.

"So, Emi," Shannon begins. "How do you know our Nate?"

"Your Nate, huh?" she laughs. "We met in high school. We kind of swore off love together, and we've been friends ever since." I cringe inwardly, wishing there was a different ending to our story. I smile at her, though, thinking wistfully back to the last couple of months when I hadn't been such a good friend to her. At this, I'm sure she knows exactly what I'm thinking. "For the most part," she adds with a wink to me.

"Well, it's nice to see a little of Nate's secret life. And it doesn't seem as dark and scary as Albert and I had pictured it to be."

"You don't really know her," I tell Shannon, nodding to Em. "*Very* dark. *Very* scary."

Emi's eyes glint at me playfully. "I'll show you dark and scary, Nate," she warns.

"No, I've seen it," I confirm seriously as I nod toward the artwork hanging on the wall. Her attention drifts to the painting, then back to me quickly, her expression sad in recognition. My smile earnest, I mouth an apology to her while Shannon inspects the mural closer.

"Me, too," her lips form the words in silence. I walk over to her and put my arm around her shoulders.

"You owe me no apologies," I inform her quietly. I tuck an errant curl behind her ear and pull her closer, listening to Shannon's assessment of the nearly-finished piece.

"Try this, Emi," Albert says as he hands her a glass of wine and me a tumbler with sparkling water.

"Thanks. It's very nice," she tells him after a sip.

"A woman after my own heart," he announces as he touches the small of her back, guiding her to the table. "They're about to start serving." Albert pulls a chair out for Emi, then takes the seat next to her. I sit down in the chair across from her, watching my client out of the corner of my eye. I start to wonder if maybe I should have introduced her as someone other than my friend. *Hey, Albert, this is the woman I've been secretly in love with for the past twelve and a half years. Keep your wandering eyes off of her.* He can have any woman he wants, except her.

My attention shifts to Emi after a few minutes, hoping she's not falling for his charming demeanor. She's a good judge of character. Surely she can see through him. This thought settles my nerves and I smile at her across the table as a plate full of small appetizers is set in front of us. The chef brings out a bottle of champagne and pours each of us a glass.

"To Albert," I propose. "And to your first venture on the west coast."

"To Nate," Shannon add, "this piece has surpassed our expectations. I can't wait to see the next one."

We each taste the sparkling wine and start eating the samples that are constantly being delivered to the table.

The night progresses pleasantly. The food is superb and the conversation flows easily between us all. Emi, at first seeming a little distant, has had a few more glasses of wine and is more talkative than usual. She's so cute, so funny, I find myself just staring at her in adoration far too many times this evening. To distract myself, I decide to finish the glass of champagne, and I eventually start on another.

Toward the end of the evening, Emi's hand casually brushes against mine on the table, and she begins to lightly stroke my fingers with her thumb. Playfully, I capture her thumb in my hand and hold it, my eyes looking at her questioningly. There's no denying the sexual tension between us. I have to remind myself that she's probably had a little too much to drink, and that I may be reading too much into her actions.

"Were you going to stay a little longer?" Albert asks, putting on his jacket and helping Shannon with hers.

"Yeah, I've got a little more to finish up here."

"Can we give Emi a ride to her hotel?"

"Oh, uh..." I look across the table at her. "Yeah, where are you staying?"

"I don't..." She shrugs her shoulders at me.

"The suite I'm in has two rooms. You're welcome to stay in the extra room."

"You sure you don't mind?"

"Of course!"

"Did you want to go there now, or do you want to go with me? I'll just be a few minutes."

"I'll stay here," she tells Albert. "Thanks for the offer, though."

"So maybe we'll see you again this weekend?" he asks Emi, but I answer for her.

"Maybe so," I tell him, unsure what our plans might be.

"Well, Alan and his team should be out of here in a few minutes. You'll lock up behind them?"

"Sure. Have a good night. Thanks for dinner."

"Anytime. It was nice to meet you, Emi. I hope we see you again."

"Thanks, you too," she says as she stands up to shake his hand. He pulls her into a hug instead and I watch as his hand wanders a little too far past her waistline. When I look up at his face, he's gauging my reaction cautiously. Sensing my non-verbal disapproval, he nods in understanding and backs away from her. Shannon links her arm into his and leads him out of the restaurant.

"What can I help you with?" Emi asks.

"Just– come sit down with me," I suggest as I pick up two of the dining room chairs and set them up in front of the painting. "Tell me what you think it needs."

"It's not finished?" She sits down in the chair next to me and puts her hand on my knee.

"I don't think so. Something over there needs to happen." I motion to the top right corner of the mural. "It's missing something."

"Well, I don't get your process," she admits. "You're the fine artist. Not me."

"Bullshit," I joke with her. "I know you can see a gaping hole in that, graphically."

"Maybe a little. I wasn't going to say anything."

"Hey, I expect you, of all people, to be honest with me."

"I don't think you need to worry about that," she says with a sideways glance to me. "Maybe some red," she suggests. "Deep red."

"Really?" I look at the painting, considering her suggestion. Red is heat, anger, passion... *love.* "I could see that. I'll let that simmer for a few days." We'll see how the weekend goes.

The chefs wave at us on their way out, and finally, we're alone. I lock the door behind them and return to my seat next to Emi.

"How have you been?" I ask her, my elbows on my knees as I lean into her.

"Okay," she answers honestly, her posture now reflecting my own. "Just trying to stay busy with work."

"How's Chris?"

"Great," she says, relaxed. "Anna and I have discovered that we have a lot in common. She's great. I think he's going to propose on New Year's. He's planning a big party."

"Wow, that quick, huh?"

"He's very much in love. Sickeningly so," she laughs. "Not really. I'm happy for him."

"Me, too." Emi's toes tap, breaking up the silence. "Is he pissed at me?"

She smiles. "You hurt me, what do you think?"

"Emi, I'm so sorry. I was stupid."

"Maybe a little," she says. "I don't blame you. You were just trying to make things work with her."

"I was focused on saving the wrong relationship."

"Yeah, why did you do that?"

I swallow hard before telling her. "I was hurt, too. I laid it all out there for you, and you pretty much laughed at me."

"I'm sorr–"

"I meant it when I said you didn't owe me an apology. You had every right to react that way. You can't help how you feel. I can't change that."

"What happened with you and her?"

"Let's just say I realized the error of my ways at a very bad time," I hint to her.

"So it's over? For good? It's not just a long-distance-forced-separation kind of thing?"

"No, it's over."

"And you really haven't seen anyone here in LA?"

"No, I've been way too busy. What about you? Been on any dates recently? Anyone I need to belittle, or fight?"

"He would have killed you in one punch if you had started anything with him," she laughs.

"If I remember correctly, you said you didn't care if he did."

"I was mad. And unreasonable. And for that, I *am* sorry."

I nod, waiting. "You didn't answer my question."

"Oh!" she says, surprised. "No."

"Why not?"

"Well," she starts slowly. "The guy I was interested in moved to California. That made things a little difficult."

She stares at me as I search for words, try to react to what she's just said.

"Well, knowing my history with bad timing, I'll just assume you've met someone *else* who moved down here."

"Stop it," she says with a soft giggle. "I haven't met anyone else."

I shift in my chair a little, uncomfortable and suddenly anxious. "What are you saying, Emi?"

"I'm saying I want to try this."

"You're kidding me, right?"

"No," she says quickly. "I mean, if you still have feelings for me."

"*If? If* I still have feelings?" I laugh. "I don't think *my* feelings were ever the ones in question. They don't need to be now. I *still* have feelings for you."

"Then... well?"

"Well, what? How do *you* feel? About *me*?"

"I can't stand not having you in my life."

I nod slowly before dipping my head into my hands, running my fingers through my hair. "This isn't the only way, Emi. To have me in your life, I mean. I'm willing to just be friends. Whatever it takes." My eyes meet hers again as I wait for her reaction.

"I know it's not the only way. I definitely feel something more for you than I've been willing to admit. And I think this could work."

"Why now?"

"Nate, I will not survive through another one of your jealous girlfriends or pregnancy scares. I don't mean to be melodramatic, but I can't be that girl anymore. I don't want to be the girl in the periphery. I want to be the one you always see."

"You are. I've never lost sight of you, Emi. You're it. You're all I've ever seen. The rest were distractions, I swear. Since the day I met you."

"I know," she admits. "I wish I could have figured this out much sooner. I've messed up so much—"

"No, you haven't."

"I owe you this chance."

"No, you don't owe me anything. I don't want to pressure you into anything, Em."

"You're not. I *want* this. I do." She takes my hand in hers and begins to drag her finger over my palm. "If you do." My body shivers at her delicate touch. I close my hand around hers.

"Let me ask you something."

"Anything," she says. "Ask me–"

Without warning, I press my lips to hers. I pull my hands away, moving both of them up to cradle her face so I can deepen the kiss. To my delight, she inches closer to me and puts her hands in my hair, finally settling her thumbs just below my earlobes. *This* is the kiss I've been waiting for. Not the ones I've taken from her in the past. This one, she willingly gives me, and it's as amazing as I've always wanted it to be.

"How do you feel?" I ask once I pull away. Her eyes are still closed, her lips curled up in a perfect smile. She sighs contentedly before slowly opening her eyes, her lashes fluttering quickly.

"I *kiss* you," she laughs, referring to her text from earlier this morning.

"Yes, you do *kiss* me," I smile at her silliness, trying to catch my breath. "Did you feel anything?"

"My god, Nate, yes. It feels... *right*," she tells me, moving in for another. "So right," she mumbles with her lips still touching mine. "Will you give me a chance?" she asks, her eyes pleading with mine when she pulls back once again.

"I will," I vow.

"Because you still have feelings for me, right? And not because you're lonely?" She strokes my hair, and I can't help but lean into her soft caress. I can tell her question is sincere, her insecurity somewhat expected, but she has no idea how much I want her.

"Because you are the only girl for me, Emi. I'll give you a thousand chances. I'm going to make this work. God, just," I stand up and pull her into a tight hug, "thank *you* for giving *me* a chance."

"Kiss me again," she requests, standing on her tiptoes in her heels.

"Forever, Em." I start to kiss her, but pull back abruptly. "Wait, have you had too much to drink?" I ask her suspiciously.

"Maybe?" she says playfully, pulling my head to hers.

"Emi," I stop her, this time somber and concerned.

"No," she whispers. "I've been planning this for weeks. I've been sober *some* of that time."

"I'm serious."

"So am I. I know what I'm doing." I lean down to kiss her once more.

"Well, then, what are you doing?" I ask as her kiss moves to my chin.

"I'm trying to get you to take me back to the hotel," she says.

"Wow, really?" *Am I fucking dreaming?*

"Yeah," she confirms with a backhand to the chest. "I had a four-hour layover in Denver. I'm a little tired."

"Of course," I laugh, mentally kicking myself for my assumption. "I'm sorry, sweetheart. Let's get you home."

"Thanks," she says as she weaves her fingers between mine, waiting for me to lead the way out. I grab my iPod, duffel and her suitcase and guide her to my convertible, making sure I open the doors for her... making sure I do everything right.

"Top up or down?" I ask her.

"Down, definitely," she says with a smile as she kicks her shoes off, tucking her feet onto the seat beneath her. I start the car and open the top, exposing us both to the warm, fall air. "It's beautiful here."

"Yeah, it's nice. It's no Manhattan, though. The weather's good, but it's too spread out here." I accelerate quickly onto the highway, enjoying the punchy engine of the rental car and the rare open road. "You have to drive everywhere. I'm sure I've put on ten pounds since I got here."

"You look good," she says. "So you're not planning a permanent move here, then?" she asks loudly to combat the road noise.

I just glance over at her and smile with a slow shake of my head. I hold my hand open to her. She takes it in hers. "Wherever you are. That's where I want to be."

"Funny," she says. "That's why I'm here."

"Holy shit, Emi!" I yell happily, the shock of seeing her finally wearing off. "You're here!"

"I know!" she laughs. I pick up our hands and kiss the back of hers.

"My god, baby, this weekend is going to be amazing." I clear my throat, slightly uncomfortable with the nickname that just fell from my mouth. "What do you want to do while you're in town?"

"I don't care," she answers with a shrug. "What do couples do here?"

My stomach jumps a few times. "I have no idea, but we'll figure it out."

She gives me a sideways glance.

"Well, I have *some* ideas..." I admit, to which her cheeks respond with a beautiful pink blush. She squeezes my hand in hers.

"Holy shit," she mumbles with a smile. "This is happening."

"It's happening," I confirm as I take my exit. At the stop light, we meet over the console and kiss. With no traffic around, we stay there through two red lights, enjoying the company of one another. I want to tell her I love her, but I don't want to scare her away too soon. After all, she hasn't said it yet. She's been a little vague, a fact that hasn't gone unnoticed. I'll give her whatever time she needs. I have the rest of my life with her.

At the hotel, I pass the keys to the valet and grab our things.

"You sure you're okay to stay with me? I can put you up in your own room, if you're more comfortable."

"I'm sure," she says, nearly laughing at me. "Since when did you become so chivalrous and old-fashioned?"

"Since you said you had feelings for me."

"Don't act differently, Nate," she instructs as we enter the elevator. "Just be yourself. Be the man I know."

"He's not good enough for you."

"He's the man I want," she assures me as we make room for another couple in the elevator. *How did this happen, and what did I do to earn this? To earn her favor?*

As soon as the man and woman exit on their floor, Emi saunters over to me. "Don't change for me," she whispers. I drop our bags and put my hands at the nape of her neck, bringing her lips to mine hungrily.

"God, I need you." The words fall out of my mouth as soon as the elevator stops at the penthouse level. A grin spreads across her face, her eyes full of wonder and passion. She traces my bottom lip with her thumb and picks up her suitcase as she walks past me. "Last door on the left," I guide her, grabbing my own bag and jogging to catch up with her. After unlocking the door, I take her suitcase from her and welcome her into the suite. "Shit, if I had known you were coming, I would have cleaned up a bit," I apologize as I take in the sight of the messy hotel room. "Since I've been working here, I haven't allowed the staff to clean up after me."

"It's okay," she assures me. "It reminds me of your place. It feels like home." I lock the doors and watch her wander around the room. She turns around and leans against the dining room table, her hands grasping the lip of the wood. I set our things in the kitchen and go to her, unable to stay away from her now that I know how full, how soft, how generous her lips are; now that I want to explore more of her.

"*You* feel like home," I tell her after another kiss. I help to prop her up on the table. Fighting every urge in my body, I hold her knees together while I kiss her. I know I have a tendency to move fast– too fast for her liking. She's always criticized me for getting physically involved too quickly. I want nothing more than to take her on this table *right now*. Knowing how tired she is, and how badly my body is screaming for hers– and not trusting myself once I get started– I offer her some time to get settled while I clean up. She hasn't said anything, but I know I feel grungy after a full twelve hours of working on that mural.

"Wait, would you like to take a bath or something first to relax?" I suggest, reminding myself to put her needs before my own. This will be a constant struggle, but she's worth it.

"No, you go," she says. "I'll go unpack or something."

"You're sure?"

"Yeah. Which one's the spare room?"

"Oh," I answer, confused, hoping she would choose to stay in my room with me, but again, trying to be understanding of her own ideas of what should happen this weekend. "This one over here." I take her luggage and open the door to the extra bedroom that I've barely spent any time in.

"Wow, it's nice. What is that, a king-sized bed?"

"Yes, Albert likes to flaunt his money, I've found. Only the best, no matter where we go."

"Not a bad perk for the job," she comments. "Hurry and shower. We've got a ton of things to talk about."

"Right," I smile warmly at her. "Make yourself at home. Want a drink? I've only got water and champagne, but–"

"Nate," she interrupts. "Go shower," she urges me with a smile. "I'll find something, don't worry about me."

"Alright." I linger in the doorway, staring at her for a few seconds before heading to my own room and turning on the faucet. In the shower, no matter how hard I try, I can't stop thinking about all the different ways I'd like to show her I love her. My imagination free and unfettered, I keep hoping she'll walk into the bathroom with me, but she never does. Not tonight.

After towel-drying myself and combing my fingers through my hair, I pull on a pair of my boxers and an old concert t-shirt. Is it okay to wear this around her? This really shouldn't be this difficult, and I've been dressed like this a million times around her. This is no different.

Don't change for me, she had said.

I decide to grab some water on my way to her room. I peek in through the cracked doorway to see her body bathed in light from the side table lamp. She's still dressed in the pretty black dress, curled around a pillow on the bed.

"Emi?" I whisper, to which she doesn't respond. I try to rouse her once more by saying her name quietly again. I push the door open and walk over to the bed, kneeling down beside it. Even as she sleeps, her dimples reveal a faint smile. I set down a bottle of water on the night stand and gently sweep a lone curl out of her face. Just like the first night I kissed her, I watch her in wonder. Now, I know what it's like to be kissed by her, and even though every inch of my body is begging for another touch, another taste, I will never steal another kiss from this woman like I regrettably did that night. I only want the ones she's willing to give me.

"I love you," I whisper softly, happy to say the words aloud and hoping she'll wake up with no doubt how I feel about her. I pull a spare blanket out of the closet and drape it over her body. She settles into it, feeling its warmth, but still doesn't wake up.

This must be what she wants, and I'm fine with it. Because I know it's coming, and I know I am stronger than this incessant urge to consume every inch of her body with my own. I'm the man she wants.

I turn the lamp off and take one last look at her, the moonlight not quite strong enough to highlight all the beautiful features of her face. Fortunately, I'd been memorizing them for years, and I take those memories back to my own bedroom. I'd spent most nights sleeping on the plush couch in the living room. My nights spent here were no different from any of the ones in New York. I was always struck with inspiration in the middle of the night, and it was easier to keep an easel and paints set up in the main room to have them readily available if a dream stirred me into action. That's exactly how the smaller paintings came to be. Afraid I'd track paint all over the suite, I had preferred to pull a spare set of sheets over the sofa and crash there.

But tonight, I decide to settle into the bedroom I'd claimed as my own, knowing that I'd sleep well, my mind quickly getting used to the idea that the woman I'd dreamed of having for years was actually mine now.

I take out my acoustic and bring it with me to the room, wanting to practice the song I'd written for her years ago. I had always had this vision of singing it for her in a dimly-lit room, just the two of us, and I want the moment to be perfect. Slinging the strap around my shoulders, I look over the city beneath me out the small corner window and start to strum the chords as quietly as I can. The words come easily, having perfected them a long time ago. The song has danced around in my head, all this time, to the point that I knew it would be something I could never forget, even if I had tried.

My throat dry, I take a break to get a sip of the water before continuing with the second verse. Feeling confident in my feelings– and sure that she can't hear me across the suite– I sing a little louder, smiling through the rest of the song. When the last chord has been played, I let the sound linger in the silence around me. I think about what I'll say to her after. I'd never allowed myself to play out this fantasy in my mind. It was fruitless before.

The click of the door knob startles me, but immediately settles me, too. I turn to watch her enter the room.

"Did I wake you?" I ask her, my hands still fingering the strings, the song still unfinished in my mind.

"No," she says as she walks in and shuts the door behind her. Shuts us in the room together. The bedroom. Alone. All of a sudden, the room seems tiny, her presence filling the corners and all the spaces in between. She's everywhere. She's exactly where I want her to be.

She walks slowly toward me, still in her dress but now with bare feet, her toenails painted a soft pink color. She takes my guitar, lifting it how I taught her to many years ago. I pull the strap over my head, shrugging away from the instrument.

"You gonna play something for me?" I ask her as she holds the guitar awkwardly.

"Where can I set this?" I take it from her and place it on my stand in the corner. "That was lovely. What's it called?"

"Uh..." I stutter, my feet planted firmly in the floor across the room from her. "The Night You Weren't Mine." I look down at the floor, remembering that night.

"Did you write it for me?"

"I did," I admit. "A long time ago."

"Well, which night?"

"Any and all of them."

"Well... whose was I?" she asks.

"Not mine. That's all that mattered."

"I'm sorry."

"I'm not. I'm looking forward now. There's no sense in dwelling on the past."

"You're right. Because I'm yours now." She runs her hands down the skirt of her dress, straightening it. "Tonight." Her eyes are earnest, but still weary. "If you still want me."

"Emi," I sigh, knowing what she's implying. "You're tired. Why don't you–"

"I didn't come all this way to sleep alone, Nate."

I lift my eyebrows at her suggestion. "You don't have to," I tell her as I walk toward her. "You can sleep in here with me." When I reach her, I touch her cheekbones with my thumbs and lean in to kiss her.

"And to that," she begins, " I would say that I didn't come in here to *sleep*."

"Good, I guess. Because having you in here makes me not want to do a whole lot of sleeping, either."

"What would you like from me?"

"What?" I ask her.

"What do you want? From me?" Her hands dip beneath my t-shirt and push me toward the bed. I sit down when the backs of my knees hit the edge. My body shudders as her fingernails scrape lightly up my stomach to my chest, dragging the shirt up with them. She tugs on it until I raise my arms and allow her to pull the garment over my head.

The answer comes quickly. "Everything, Emi. Anything you're willing to give me. More than friendship, but more than this– more than just sex."

"So you don't want this?" she asks as she nudges herself in between my legs. She takes my hands and places them on her hips. I allow my fingers to wander, then immediately pull her into my lap, cradling her against my torso, and I'm sure she can feel instantly that it is *exactly* what I want.

"I never said that," I whisper into her ear before taking her lobe in between my lips. She exhales slowly into my own ear. With an involuntary smile, I ask, "Do you like that?"

She sighs before telling me she does, and I can't help but laugh quietly at her response.

"What?" she asks, leaning away from me with those silly furrowed brows of hers.

"I just find it fascinating that I'm learning new things about you after knowing you for all these years."

"Well, you've never known me like this."

"I've never known *anyone* like this. You have to know, Emi."

"Shhh, Nate." She presses her finger over my mouth and nods. "I know."

I press my lips against her finger and move it away, her eyes staring into my own.

"I want to know more." I place my hands behind her neck and pull her face to mine once more. She mimics my moves, and we hold each other as small, tender kisses become frantic and covetous. My hands find their way to her thighs, beneath her dress. *Silk and lace. Such a turn-on.*

She places her hand on mine, removing it from her body. I apologize, misunderstanding her. One side of her lip turns up as she moves off of my lap and once again stands in front of me.

She takes part of her dress— the ends of a ribbon around her waist— and places them in each of my hands. I look up at her questioningly.

"Go ahead," she encourages me. I sigh and laugh at the same time, in relief and disbelief. She wraps her hands around my head and pulls me into an embrace against her chest. Her fingers play with my hair. I feel her lips press a kiss to my scalp.

Pushing her dress aside, I kiss the top of her breast and feel her breathing pause with a startled gasp. Delivering kisses to her collarbone and neck, I slowly untie the ribbon and pull it from the dress. Two small snaps hold her wrap-around dress together. They easily separate under my grasp. I lean back to take in the sight of her.

She shrugs out of the dress, letting it fall around her feet. The most beautiful woman stands before me, her black silk and lace bra and panties providing little cover over her most private— most *sacred*— areas. My fingers trace the edges curiously, my hands wanting to rip them from her body.

She wears a satisfied grin when my gaze finally reaches hers.

"This is not the type of underwear I would expect Emily Hennigan to wear," I smile slyly.

"I wore them for you," she admits quietly with a blush. "I bought them with you in mind. I didn't realize seducing you would be so easy... plus, I know I'm competing with a lot of other women— one of which I've seen naked, need I remind you–"

"No, you didn't need to," I cut off her nervous banter, not even allowing my mind to go back to last New Year's Day. I focus all of my attention on the woman in front of me. "And there was never any competition, Em. You're the only one. I want you to be the only one," I breathe as I outline her undergarments with my fingers and watch as goosebumps appear where my fingers once were.

As she leans in to kiss me again, my hands travel to her back to unclasp her bra. When I start to slide it down her arms, her head bows demurely, shyly, as she clasps a few fingers of her right hand around a few on my left. As we hold one another tentatively, she affords me the time to just drink her in.

"You truly are beautiful." She adjusts her hand, resting her palm against mine. I lift her hand to my lips. "Can I just..." I take a deep breath. "Just look at you for a moment? I never thought..."

"Okay," she says with a blush, dropping her hands to her side. I study every marking, every curve, every shift of color or texture on her body. I notice a fading bruise on her forearm and kiss it. Turning her slightly, I see a familiar birthmark on her right shoulder. I kiss it, too. She puts her hand on my shoulder to steady herself, and I notice an anomaly on her skin.

"Did you know about these?" I ask Emi, brushing my finger over a grouping of freckles on her side above her ribcage, an area that would normally be obscured by her arm.

"Yeah," she says shyly. "They're weird. It's the only place I have freckles anywhere on my body."

"They're lovely," I correct her, beginning to count them. "Seventeen," I tell her.

"Really?"

"Yes. Five on the top, twelve spread out randomly below."

"I didn't realize there were that many."

Seventeen. Five on top. I get a flashback from a poetry class in college.

I begin to recite a poem as I tap the rhythm on her skin, each syllable represented by another small speck on her pale flesh.

"One transcendent kiss

That later makes lovers take

Soft breaths, holding hands"

"That was beautiful," she says, shivering when I kiss what has now become my favorite part of her. "Who wrote that?"

I look up at her, amused by her question. "That's *your* haiku. One syllable for every freckle."

"You wrote that?" I nod to her. "When?"

"Just now. Just for you."

She looks at me, stunned, before a smile breaks across her face. "Say it again," she whispers.

I clear my throat before beginning. "One transcendent kiss," I say as I rise from the bed. Standing in front of her, I lift her chin so our eyes can meet. My stomach tightens as my thumbs brush over her dimples.

She takes a deep breath. "One transcendent kiss," she repeats. I watch her closely as she moves toward me. Just another inch or two, and her breasts would be touching my torso. Her soft lips on mine, they move in sync. The sweet taste of her just makes me want more. My hands move slowly down her body. "Go on," she whispers, exposing her neck to me.

"That later—" I speak softly against the hollow beneath her ear, tracing her earlobe with my tongue. Curious, I press kisses on her shoulders, her collarbone, then finally reach my destination. My lips surround the areola on her right breast.

"That later–" she gasps headily as I suck lightly, her fingernails digging into my naked back. Not wanting to ignore her left breast, I do the same, and am rewarded with a soft moan escaping her lips. I could abandon the poetry altogether at this point, and continue to find more actions that may yield the same response. It's a beautiful sound, but I decide to continue my recitation, wanting to see her expression when I declare what we are; what we're about to be. My lips move back up her body, stopping for a gentle peck on her forehead.

She waits in anticipation for my next words. I hold her head inches from mine, watching her eyes, the skin of her cheeks, as I deliver my next line. "Makes *lovers*—" My gaze seems to move through her, and she doesn't blink as she repeats me.

"Makes lovers–" Her skin blushes a bright pink, as I had suspected it would. She would never be able to hide her reactions from me, something I had noted long ago but could never truly appreciate until now. She moistens her lips, then smiles. I lean back in to kiss her again, the passion between us beginning to boil up to the surface. Our kisses are soft and deep, fast and needing. I break away only when the need to inhale overcomes me.

"Take soft breaths—" I say quickly, drawing in the air around me, my heart racing.

"Soft breaths–" She wastes no time, either, her lips returning to mine for more. Her hands press into my flesh, traveling down my torso, pushing against my boxers. Trailing kisses down her body quickly, I stop when I reach the lacy hemline of her panties. Her breathing is expectant and shallow. I look up to her one last time. Her fingers direct mine beneath the fabric, permitting me to remove the soft garment from her body. She steps out of them as I stand back up, pushing my own underwear to the floor. She takes my hands in hers and holds them tightly at our sides. I kiss her once.

"Holding hands," she finishes the poem.

I stare at her in silence for a few seconds before concluding her haiku.

"Holding hands." I swallow hard as we stand before one another, completely exposed. Her hands still in mine, I wrap my arms around her back and pull her body tight against mine, her breasts pressing against me. I hold her wrists in my left hand, releasing the right one to explore her body. I drag my fingers slowly across her pale skin, hovering around her most sensitive area. She slowly puts her foot on the bed behind me.

"Touch me, Nate."

Fuck, I never thought I would hear those words. Before I do as she asks, I place my hands on her cheeks to kiss her. I hope she knows how grateful I am in this moment.

My fingers returning to her, I watch her closely, hoping to read each expression to learn her likes and dislikes. Her body stiffens as my fingers press against her.

"Relax," I tell her softly.

"I'm just nervous," she admits.

"We can stop–" I offer, but don't stop what I'm doing.

"No," she cuts me off. "I want this–"

"Good." I can feel the tension drain from her body as she begins to let go of her inhibitions.

"Oh, god, Nate," she sighs. "Kiss me again," she begs.

As my lips find hers once again, one of her hands moves to my hair as the other grazes my stomach, then saunters lower. My body quivers at her touch, and I can feel her smile in the kiss as her fingers wrap around me.

"Shit, Emi," I hiss in her ear before moving my tongue down her neck and across her shoulder. My fingers press against her lower back as my other hand continues to garner welcome responses from her. Her body seems ready and receptive, and I wonder how much longer I can continue our foreplay. It's been so long since I've been with any woman, but to have her here makes the desire, the need, even worse– and at the same time, *having* her, having her *here*, makes everything so much better.

I remove her other hand, feeling the immediate absence but knowing there is something much better around the corner. I put my hands on her hips and guide her to the bed, pulling the comforter and sheets back for her. As she settles in, I open the nightstand drawer, preparing myself.

"You okay?" I ask her as I climb under the covers with her. She answers with a passionate kiss, her arms pulling me closer. Eliminating any space between us, I continue my earlier exploration with my fingers.

"Oh, my god, that... where..." she breathes, incapable of speaking in complete sentences.

"Is that good?" I ask. Hitching her knee up over my hip, I want her to feel how much I want this, too. I touch her behind and pull her toward me until our bodies are perfectly aligned. She hooks her leg behind me and pulls me on top of her.

"Oh, god," she says again at the contact. I hold my body over hers, and press against her slowly, listening to the quiet moan that escapes her lips. Such a beautiful sound that I never thought I would be lucky enough to hear. I push again, just to hear it once more. I kneel back, pulling her knees up next to me and kissing each of them, trying my best to prolong the experience, but knowing I'm too weak for much more. I lean in to her navel, tracing it with my tongue before allowing it to travel further up her torso while my fingers continue to explore other parts of her body. She pulls my head up to hers. I kiss her once before telling her how I really feel.

"When I imagined this night, this was supposed to be much more romantic, but damn it, Emi, I have to have you. I don't think I can wait any longer."

"I *want* you to want me like that," she says reassuringly. "It's okay. I want to *feel* you," I stare into her eyes once more, kissing her again, hoping it communicates my devotion and assurance to her.

With my arms around her, our focus only on each other, we lie back against the pillows on the bed, and the moan from earlier suddenly becomes the second most beautiful sound as she gasps softly, our bodies finally connecting for the first time.

We move together slowly at first, but I find myself unable to contain my excitement, the many fantasies I've had of her becoming reality right before my eyes... right beneath my body. Her limbs wrapped around me, tighter, tighter still, I let go when I can't hold out any longer. She runs her fingers through my hair as I shudder into her, my tongue tracing the slope of her neck, my breath heavy and warm on her skin.

"Don't leave me," she pleads with watery eyes as I begin to pull away.

I push myself up using my elbows to look at her directly. I kiss her deeply before responding. "Emi," I vow, my lips still inches from hers. "I promise I will never, ever leave you."

"Nate," she whispers, tears now falling down her cheeks as she blinks.

"What's the matter?" I ask her, my thumbs poised to catch any more errant drops.

"I just," she says quietly, swallowing hard. "I can't believe we just..."

"Are you okay?"

She smiles through her tears and nod. "I'm completely overwhelmed, that's all." I start to kiss the tears away. "Everything was too easy. It's too perfect. Everything just coming together like this? Can you believe it?"

"Yeah," I tell her. "You were meant for me."

"I think I was," she says, biting her lip.

"You were." We kiss for a few more minutes, lazy, tired kisses, until exhaustion takes us both to sleep.

The next morning, I wake up early and carefully remove myself from the bedroom without waking her. I shower and get dressed before deciding to make Emi breakfast in bed. *God, I hope she's not regretting what happened.* Her words from last night still play in my mind. It *does* feel like everything was too easy, too perfect.

When I quietly walk in the room with a tray of food, her back is to the window. She squints away from the sunlight with a smile on her face. She reveals her bare arm from beneath the sheets and pulls the blankets up to make sure she's covered.

"Good morning," I tell her quietly from the doorway.

"Morning," she says, her voice a little hoarse.

"I made some breakfast, if you're hungry." She makes a face and shakes her head.

"Is that OJ, though?"

"Yeah."

"I'll take that. And a few aspirin, if you have any."

"Sure." I place the tray on the dresser and fetch the medicine from the bathroom. "You don't feel well?"

"It's just a little headache. And my whole body hurts." She blushes when she smiles.

"I hope you're not getting sick."

"Trust me, Nate. It's a little hangover, and the soreness... well..."

"Got it," I tell her as I sit next to her on the bed. "A good pain, then..."

"I like to think of it as well-earned."

"Okay," I laugh, planting a kiss on her lips. "Sit up."

Still holding tightly to the sheet, she sits up in the bed. I arrange some of the pillows and move into the bed behind her, running my fingers gingerly down her beautiful, exposed back. "What are you– ohhh," she says, her body beginning to relax immediately as my fingers knead her shoulders, then continue to move lower, slowly. "That's nice, Nate."

"You are so tense, Em."

"I didn't sleep very well," she admits.

"Really?" I slept so soundly, I would never have known if she had been restless. She shakes her head. "Why?"

"I was just thinking about things. I had kind of hoped we'd talk about things after... you know..." She sounds disappointed, and already I feel like a complete ass.

"Oh. What about?"

"How this is going to work, that's all."

"Well, we can talk now. I wish you had woken me up."

"See, these things, I don't know about you," she says, clearly frustrated. "If I wake you up, are you going to bite my head off, or roll over and talk to me all night? How am I supposed to know?"

"Em," I begin, massaging her tight muscles in her lower back a little harder. "We'll learn. Don't stress about that. And in the future, always wake me up. Just give me five minutes to get my wits about me."

She nods, sitting up straight so I can see the movement. I kiss her shoulder slowly, wanting to soothe her, to relax her, to get her mind off of anything stressful. I want her to feel nothing but pleasure and happiness and confidence in us for the rest of the weekend. My hands creep slowly under the sheet up to her breasts, my lips moving to her neck. She stiffens immediately, clutching my hands with hers.

"I think I had a little too much to drink last night," she blurts quickly. Knots immediately settle in my stomach.

"What?" I ask, unsure of her meaning. I drop my hands to her waist, wrapping my arms around her and resting my chin on her shoulder.

"I hadn't intended on things happening like they did," she says seriously as she dips her head toward her lap. I move her hair from obscuring my view of her face. Her beautiful green eyes are hidden behind her closed lids.

"How did you want them to happen? When you came into my bedroom last night, what did you want to happen?" I hear the anger in my voice, but didn't mean for it to show.

"Not sex. Not like that. My head wasn't completely clear."

"What? Emi, it wasn't a mistake. We are meant to be."

"It's okay, Nate," she says as she turns around on the bed to face me. She fumbles with the sheets, trying to pull them over her chest, trying to hide her nakedness from me. I was already turned on, and seeing her like this only makes it worse. Knowing now is not the time to take advantage of my desire, I take off my t-shirt and help her put it on. She thanks me quietly before continuing. "I want this. I do. It would have happened eventually. I just wish we had talked about all the consequences and risks and stuff before we just dove in, head first."

"Okay," I respond. "So we didn't have the talk. Instead, you let me show you how much I care about you for the first time in our lives, and for that, Emi, I am grateful and have no regrets whatsoever." I hold her hands in mine.

"What have we done?" she says with a quiet laugh, and my heart falters in my chest.

"Shit... Emi..." I say, all the air escaping my lungs with the two syllables of her name. After a few deep breaths, I continue. "It wasn't a mistake."

"Really?"

"It's not a mistake," I repeat. "*We* are not a mistake."

"No," Emi says. "*We're* not." I sigh, relieved. "Having a relationship is not a mistake. Starting it this way is." She looks at our hands, avoiding my stare.

"You're kidding me, right?"

"I'm not."

"Emi, we *started* this *years* ago."

"No," she disagrees. "Uh-uh." She shakes her head, looking up at me through her lashes.

"Yes, we did. Wouldn't this be the next step?"

"Um... no," she answers, speaking as if we're both using different languages to communicate with one another.

"Isn't this why you came here?"

"I came here to talk."

"About us."

"Yes, about us, about my feelings for you..."

"You said you wanted this."

"I did," she states quickly. "I do."

"Because you initiated it. I would never have taken it that far–"

"Yes, you would have," she cuts me off. "Sex is your thing."

"No, I would *not* have. Don't say shit like that." Her disbelieving stare bores into me, and I escape it by removing myself from the bed and walking to the window, considering what she thinks about me. "If you really believed that, you wouldn't be here, right now." I turn around to challenge her, see her green eyes glint in the sunlight.

"I don't want it to be true. I want it to be more."

"It is already so much more, Emi. I have feelings for you... I always have..."

"I couldn't sleep last night," she says. "I wanted to talk, but you were out cold in, like, ten minutes."

"I'm sorry, Emi." I return to the bed, kneeling beside it and pulling a pillow into my chest, suddenly embarrassed by my behavior. I got what I wanted from her, and went to sleep. I'm not even entirely sure I was able to fully satisfy her. That thought hadn't occurred to me until this moment, and I'm moderately disgusted by that. I tuck my head into the feather pillow and continue my explanation, the sound undoubtedly muffled, but I can't look at her right now. "I haven't slept well since I left New York. Every night, I've been torturing myself with thoughts of what my life would be like without you. It's been one constant nightmare for me. And it felt so good to be with you last night."

She huffs at the end of my sentence, causing me to look back in her direction.

"That's not what I meant, Em. Just to have you here, felt good. It relaxed me. I felt comfortable and settled for the first time in months. I let myself enjoy that... in kissing you, in holding you, in making love to you... in sleeping. I needed it. All of it, I needed it.

"And when I woke up this morning, it felt like everything just fell into place. Until right now."

"Have we messed this up already?"

"No," I tell her, adamant. "Why would you think that?"

"It's just... I want this to be real."

"It is real."

"I don't know," she wavers. "You just broke up with Kiersten a few weeks ago... what if you're just... I don't know, lonely?"

"My god, Emi, you *must* know that's not what's going on here."

"I should. I want to believe it. The Nate I know jumps from one woman to the next, though." I stare at her, frustrated with her assessment. She runs her fingers through my hair. "There is no down time."

"And do you want to know why that is, Emi?" I ask as I shrug away from her, the volume of my voice increasing with my level of frustration.

"Kind of, yes."

"I have had to have a constant distraction to keep myself from pursuing you."

She laughs with suspicion.

"Emi, seriously. Since I got to LA I haven't been on a single date, and I've been approached... I've been asked... but I wanted to be alone to make sure of my feelings. They've been muddled for years. Don't think for a second that I'm taking this lightly."

She nods, then asks me a question. "What happens if it doesn't work out?"

"There's a chance of that. I've been turning that over in my mind for weeks, if not months... maybe years."

"And what conclusion have you come to?"

"For me, it's worth the risk."

"I don't know," she says.

"I know, Em," I agree. "I know what you're thinking, what you're going through. But I think the chances of this working out are pretty good."

"Why?"

"Because of our history. We've been friends for nearly thirteen years. We've been there for each other through good and bad times. We've fought and we've made up, normally with our friendship getting even stronger. We never seem to get sick of each other. We're miserable without one another. It's like we're already together... like we have been for a long time. We've just never had sex... until last night," I laugh, trying to lighten the mood.

"Let's talk about last night," she demands, still serious but softer.

"Okay. What do you want to talk about?"

"Did anything stand out to you? About last night?"

"Is this a trick question?"

"No."

"Making love to you, Emi. I have wanted that for so long, and it was incredible. Wasn't that yours?"

"No," she says as my ego falls a few notches. "It was great, Nate, really. But my favorite part was... it was something you *said* to me."

"Which was..."

"No," she says. "I'm keeping it to myself."

"Emi, what was it?"

"Just something you said... I just. I don't know. It's not important."

"Of course it's important. I'd like to know."

"It'll come to you. I hope." I try to remember anything that was particularly memorable from last night. Try to remember her reaction to anything I may have said, but there wasn't a whole lot of conversation that I can recall. Even she has pointed that out.

"Was it the poem?"

Her smile is wide. "That was incredible, too, but no."

"When I said I'd never leave you? Because I won't."

"That was great, too. No." She smiles and leans over the bed and kisses me. "You'll figure it out."

"Alright." I move back up to the bed and sit next to her. She takes my hand and jostles it in hers nervously. "What is it?"

"I'm just... what happens when this doesn't work out?"

"What happens when it does? That's the question you should be asking yourself. Not this nonsense you're talking about."

"Are you sure we're ready to take this chance? I just wish we had waited to sleep together... just a little longer... just to make sure we're on the same page."

"What's holding you back?"

"Nate, I can't imagine my life without you in it. When you were busy avoiding me while you were with Kiersten, I just felt like something was missing in my life."

"Well, then it seems obvious... that we should give 'us' a shot."

"No, it's not that simple," she reminds me. "Because there's no going back. We've crossed a line now. If it doesn't work out, we couldn't just pretend like it never happened. I couldn't, at least. I mean, we could try to remain friends, but I just don't think it's possible once two people have gone that far..."

"Emi, we're going to work out."

"You can't know that."

"And you can't know otherwise. You're letting the fear of the unknown rule your life. You can't let it take over like that."

"But Nate–"

"No, listen to me. Are you willing to forego what could be the love of your life because you think it won't work out? And really, on what basis? All the signs say that we *will* work out.

"I've had a lifetime to think about all of this. And I've dated enough women to be able to say, with confidence, that I think we are soul mates. I thought it back in high school when we met. It's been reaffirmed numerous times over the years."

"Soul mates, huh?"

"That's never crossed your mind?" I ask.

"Maybe it has... back in college, I thought that once, but... Nate, this is all new to me," she says. "Really, it was when you thought Samantha might be pregnant... that's what made me start considering you as something more than a friend. I felt like I would lose a part of myself if it were true, if she had gotten pregnant. It just seemed so final... that you would belong to her, and this child would begin to rely on you and demand your time. And I was just strangely jealous about the whole thing.

"Honestly," she continues, her eyes averted, "I felt like that was supposed to be my baby. That was my place. In my heart, I always thought we would be parents together."

"I know," I agree. "I'll never forget the disappointment in your eyes that night. It nearly killed me," I explain. "If she had been pregnant, I knew that I would have forgone any chance of being with you. It tore me apart."

"Since then," she adds, "I've just been more and more envious of the women you date."

"And what is it that they have that you don't have?"

"They get a really great guy. They get the assurance that you'll be there, ready to comfort them after a bad day. They get someone who will listen to them, and share stories, and give advice."

"You've always had that from me."

"But I want to be the only one."

"I'm ready to offer you that. This isn't a casual thing for me, Emi. You mean so much to me."

She nods and smiles. "You mean a lot to me, too." She weaves her fingers between mine. "Maybe we need to set some ground rules or something."

"I don't want rules, Emi," I tell her honestly. "I just want to be with you. I want to do what feels right, and this, being with you? It feels right. I promise, I'll do anything you ask. I'll take it slow, I'll give you time, but I want this like I've never wanted anything else. Please, give me this opportunity to show you that I can be the right man for you. Let me prove that it's not all about sex for me. I am a one-woman man, Emi, and *you* are that woman for me. I don't want anyone else. There are genuine feelings underlying this, Em. Feelings I am sick and tired of denying. It is such an immense relief for this to be out in the open, finally. Let me feel. Let me show you how I feel.

"Just try. For me."

She smiles and leans toward me. "Okay," she says, her hand on my jaw, pulling me to her for a kiss.

"Emi," I begin with my lips still against hers. "Let's slow this down a bit."

"Okay."

"Can I take you out on a date tonight?"

"What'd you have in mind?"

"Well, there's an old drive-in theater that shows old eighties movies. We can binge on popcorn and Twizzlers. I heard they were showing *The Outsiders* tonight."

"That's not really a make-out kind of movie."

"Wait, weren't we taking this slow?"

"I'm sorry," she laughs as she explains her response. "I thought that was the whole point of drive-in theaters!"

I smile at her and kiss her once more. "You in?"

"I'm in. Wait, *you* are going to binge on junk food?"

"I'd do anything for you. You ever going to get out of bed?"

"I'm up," she says as she throws the blankets back and climbs out of bed, my t-shirt hanging loosely over her shoulders. "Can I wear this?"

"But it's my favorite– I mean, of course," I amend my first reaction. "*Anything.*"

She bites her lip and nods as she makes her way to the other bedroom, leaving me to find something else to wear.

~ * ~

I can't believe how quickly the weekend went by. I already miss her, and I only dropped her off at the airport ten minutes ago. I have no idea how I'll make it through the next month and a half without her while I'm in Vegas and she's in New York.

Hell, I have no idea how I'll make it through this evening alone, with the memories of last night still fresh in my mind. I still feel like shit for what happened, but she didn't say a word about it and I'm too much of a fucking pansy to bring it up myself.

I wasn't expecting us to be intimate last night after our casual movie date on Saturday. We had so much fun together pointing out the melodramatic acting and production quality of the movie. I hadn't laughed that hard in ages. I expected more of the same for our last night together. Through our conversations over the weekend, I could tell she was still a little unsure of the speed of our relationship, and I wanted to prove to her that my interest in her was more than just some idle sexual infatuation with my best friend in between girlfriends. She told me that was her greatest fear, and unfortunately, the only way to prove her wrong was to just let me show her. In time, and hopefully it wouldn't take too long, she would recognize my true affections.

But for this weekend, after Friday night, I had decided I wouldn't be the one to initiate anything more.

Last night started innocently enough. We had just gotten back from having dinner together. We brought our desserts back to the suite with us, and I was putting fruit and cheesecake on plates for us. Emi hopped up on the kitchen counter, her pale legs kicking playfully, nudging my thighs. I grabbed her leg in my hand, feeling the soft skin of her thigh from under her skirt. I picked up a berry and dipped it in cream and fed it to her. She returned the favor, then pulled my body into hers, in between her thighs. My forehead leaned against hers as her elbows rested on my shoulders, her hands fingering my hair lightly. I looked at her intently, trying to read what was going on behind her beautiful eyes. I couldn't see past her desire.

Her hand fell slowly from my hair and down my arm. She dipped two fingers in some of the fresh cream and brought them to my lips. I felt my body reacting as I sucked the sweet foam from her fingers. After she pulled them out, she noted a small dab left behind on my lips, smiled and held my head still in her hands. She closed her eyes as her tongue drew so slowly across my lips, creating the single, most erotic sensation I have ever felt in my life.

"Fuck, Emi," I breathed as she licked her own lips after pulling back. I rubbed her earlobes lightly as we stared at one another, her quickened breaths matching mine.

Before I could consciously think what I was doing, her shirt was completely unbuttoned. She giggled, knowing what she was doing to me, and then took my wandering hands into hers. "Touch me, Nate," she spoke softly. "I don't want you to forget how I feel."

"I could never," I affirmed. "Never." After tracing the lace hem of her bra, I tucked my thumb beneath it and stroked her nipple gently. She sighed as she pulled my lips to hers.

"Five and a half weeks..." she whispered.

"Huh?" Our lips continued to move together.

"That's how long you'll be gone?"

"Yeah," I said, moving my mouth from hers. I pushed the silk away to expose her breast, kissing it lightly, delicately. She moaned softly into my ear, then pushed me away and struggled to remove my shirt. I only broke away long enough to pull it over my head, swiftly picking up where I had left off.

Her legs wrapped around me tighter, squeezing my body into hers.

"Is it okay?" I asked her.

"Mmmmm," was her response.

"I'll take you right here," I warned, excited at the prospect.

"Couch," she spoke up, and not a second lapsed before I swept her up and carried her to the nearby sofa, the needy kiss continuing. "Condom," she added as I set her down.

I thought nothing of it last night as I sped to get one out of the nightstand, but in hindsight I wonder if her concern with protection is because of the amount of women I've been with or just with pregnancy. *Why did I ever waste my time on anyone else?*

When I returned to the living room, she was lying against the black couch, her milky white skin such a beautiful contrast. I slowed down, drank in the sight of her, and knelt before her, beginning to touch her again, this time with care and with reverence.

Her needy hands made quick work of removing my clothes, and even as I knew I wanted to take it slow and savor our last night together, I wouldn't deny her what she wanted, when she wanted it. She was impatient and hungry, and that was all I needed to give myself permission to continue on greedily, devouring every bit of her as soon as she revealed herself to me. And once I began on that track, there was no stopping myself.

As I look back, I can consciously recognize the old habits that seeped back in. The fact that I *had* old habits was a little unnerving. This was new. Sex with Emi was different, I could tell. It was supposed to be, and it was... but in a way, it wasn't. My internal monologue began to tell me what to do, as it always did. Touch here, kiss there. It was a routine I had practiced often, but there was nothing routine about Emi, about our attraction to one another.

I knew this, and still, I continued.

Instead of calling her by her name as we made love, I choked out the generic term "baby," a name I've undoubtedly called every woman I've ever been with, from Misty Gainor to Eva... women who mean nothing to me now, who meant very little to me then. I should have called her by her own name. Emi. Or even Emily, an attempt to show her how much I do respect her.

I pushed her to try something she never had before. She didn't protest a bit, but I shouldn't have done that. I should have let her guide me, but I didn't. I took control, as I always do.

The worst part was when I realized what I said to her our first night together, the phrase that she said was her favorite part, the words that she wouldn't reveal to me. I realized what they were as soon as I couldn't hold on any longer and blurted them out as I came.

"I love you, baby."

Another line, a string of words that I had put together for all the wrong women before her, when all that time I should have been saving them for her. For Emi. For the only woman I've ever truly loved.

Once I heard the words escape my lips, I recognized the feeling of lust that had pushed them out of my mouth. As if I could make them mean something more– make them mean what I really *did* feel for her– I said them again as I collapsed on top of her.

The telling part for me was when she didn't return the sentiment. That absence of those three words rang loudly in my ears.

It was her turn to sleep comfortably all night, and my turn to think about what had happened– about my past, and about how that could seriously fuck up my future with Emi.

She was quiet as we gathered her things this morning. She seemed sad, and she was noticeably melancholy as we discussed the length of our upcoming separation. I tried to persuade her to stay a couple more days until I left for Las Vegas, but her clients had deadlines and she needed to focus on her work to get it done. We talked briefly about her coming to visit me in a few weeks, but we didn't make definite plans.

I gave her the key to my loft before she left for the gate.

"In case you need to get away from Teresa's fiery love scenes... or, you know, maybe act out some on your own," I told her with a light-hearted laugh.

"*Nate*," she chided, blushing, as her eyes diverted to the floor. I placed my fingers beneath her chin and lifted her gaze back to mine.

"Hey," I began, searching her eyes. She blinked quickly, looking up at me through her lashes. "I wouldn't be sad if you were there when I got home." I stroked her cheek lightly with my thumb.

"We'll see," she smiled, biting her lip.

Although the kiss goodbye was long and passionate, I'm not sure it will sustain me for six weeks until I head back to New York. I will definitely want to taste her lips long before that.

And I will definitely need to know what's going on in her mind well before *that*.

CHAPTER 12

I spend the next few days packing up my things and getting ready for Vegas. I will be driving there in the convertible and I'm looking forward to the short road trip. Driving in Los Angeles has proved to be just as nerve-wracking as it is in New York City, so the change in scenery on the open road is exciting to me. Albert will be flying in on Monday, leaving me to enjoy the weekend in Sin City by myself. I will probably do a fair amount of gambling. My dad taught me how to play Blackjack at a very young age, and I spent years practicing on my mother and our service staff as I grew up. I typically end up on the winning end. It's probably luck, but I like to think of it as a learned skill.

I call Emi as soon as I'm checked into my suite at the Bellagio.

"How's New York?" I ask her.

"I think it misses you," she says.

"I miss it... and you."

"Me, too," she says. "But hey, I have some news..."

"What?"

"Chris just called, and he is definitely going to ask Anna to marry him!"

"When?"

"On New Year's Eve... he's going to throw a big party and surprise her. We'll be invited, of course."

"That's wonderful," I tell her. "New Year's Eve, huh? Wow, I can't wait to have you in my arms at midnight. I've wished for that for so long."

"Hell, I'll just be glad to have a date," she jokes.

"Well, I'm really happy for them. I'll have to call him later."

"I'm sure he'd like that... I actually thought he might have called you already."

"Did you tell him about us?" I ask.

"I mentioned that we had talked about, you know, possibly dating..."

"*Possibly?* I thought we were."

"Well, I don't want to get the family's hopes up," she explains. "They've been predicting this for years. I'm not ready to tell them all they're right."

"Yes, that makes sense, Em," I mock her.

"Shut up," she laughs. "I'm taking it slow... with them, too."

"Okay, Em, whatever you want."

"What are you doing tonight?" she asks.

"Not sure. Maybe a little gambling. Definitely some sight seeing... people watching..."

"Do you need a little luck?"

"It wouldn't hurt, why?"

"I thought you might... Check your email."

"Now?"

"I think now would be a good time." I pull out the laptop and find an outlet to plug it in. It takes a few minutes to boot up and connect to the wireless in the hotel. A flood of messages load into my inbox, and I quickly scan through them to find one from Emi. The subject is simply "Good Luck."

I save the attachment to my desktop and click it to open it up. When the file opens, I slowly inhale through my teeth, hold the breath in as I take in the gorgeous black and white photograph, and then exhale sharply. It is a side profile shot of Emi on my bed in the loft, her legs pulled into her chest, her head resting on her knee, her eyes looking into the camera, her lips slightly parted. She is holding a small four-leafed clover that is spot colored green. She is completely nude.

She laughs. "That's the response I was hoping for."

"It's beautiful. You're perfect," I say to her.

"Teresa helped me take it," she explains. I remember that photography is one of her roommate's other hobbies. Men and photography, sometimes both at the same time.

"Lucky girl," I spoke in a trance, unable to take my eyes off of the computer screen.

"I just wanted you to remember what's waiting for you back in New York."

"I was in no danger of forgetting that, but I'll take reminders like this every day," I say. "My god, baby, you'll be the death of me." I cringe as the lust invades my vocabulary again.

She sighs into the phone.

"Um... Emi, are we okay?"

"Sure, Nate," she tells me simply.

"I can't wait to kiss your lips," I say, losing myself in the picture, "or your shoulders... your arms... legs... breasts..."

"Okay," she cuts me off. "I'm going to leave you to enjoy your picture now."

"Yes, I'm going to take this to a printer to make a huge life-size poster," I tease. "I can afford a billboard..." I ponder.

"Nate, don't you dare!"

"Em, I wouldn't, don't worry. I don't want anyone else seeing your amazing body. I'm jealous enough of Teresa."

"Good, because it's only for you," she says.

"Thank you. It's unbelievable. I'm a little surprised. You've never been so... confident," I tell her.

"It's your fault," she says. "You make me feel... beautiful."

"Emi, you are."

"Alright, I'm blushing now... I need to get some work done... Like ya, Nate."

"Like you, Em," I respond automatically, the words the same ones we've always exchanged, wondering if I should go ahead and tell her I love her now. "Good night," are the only other words that come out.

"Bye."

~ * ~

"Nate, stop what you're doing!" Startled, I look up to see Shannon, Albert and another women I've never met standing in the doorway of the new restaurant. They're all dressed to the nines as they come to see my current work-in-progress.

"What do you guys want?" I ask, smiling, putting my brush down carefully and wiping the paint off my fingers. Albert shakes my hand as Shannon squeezes my arm.

"Nate, this is Cherry."

"Nice to meet you," I tell the woman with dark red hair.

"The pleasure's mine," she purrs. I shift uncomfortably.

"We want you to get out of here for a night," Albert says.

"I'm working," I laugh.

"You're working too much," Shannon informs me. "You need a break. You've been working non-stop for three weeks. Have you enjoyed the city at all?"

"A little," I tell them. "I've got a deadline, you know?"

"It's not a hard deadline," Albert argues. "That's your own self-inflicted deadline."

"True." I want to wrap this up to get back to Emi as soon as possible. Whatever it takes.

"Well, you're taking the night off and coming with us."

"No," I huff. "I'm not dressed for whatever you have in mind."

"We have time," Shannon says. "We'll close up here. You go to your hotel, throw on a suit and we'll meet you in the Bellagio bar in an hour."

I sigh heavily, not really wanting to be social tonight, but I've turned them down twice this week, and this time, it doesn't seem like they're going to take no for an answer. "All right."

I seal up my paints quickly and rinse my brushes before leaving the club. Cherry flashes a quick smile as I walk out the front door. *I hope she's not here for me.*

Albert and Shannon have made sure my stay in Vegas is nothing short of spectacular. The suite at the Bellagio is amazing, the car is fast, and they stock the club with healthy food and water, having picked up on my eating habits in LA. Albert has hinted at setting me up with women the entire time, but I've told him I'm not interested. I guess he truly believed me when I told him Emi was just a friend.

After showering and changing, I head downstairs to meet the trio that awaits me.

"You look nice," Shannon says.

"High-roller," Albert adds. "Cufflinks and everything. We're hitting the high-stakes tables. Hope you're good at blackjack."

I laugh internally.

We find two seats at a reserved blackjack table. Albert and I sit down and ante up. The women stand behind us, over our shoulders, talking amongst themselves, mostly in hushed whispers. I haven't been able to make out a single word, but then again, I'm not really interested in the conversation. As luck would have it, I get blackjack on the first two hands, and my good fortune continues through the next hour, through multiple dealers. By the time we decide to move to a craps table, I'm already up $12,500. Albert has won about

$7,000. The women are giddy with excitement.

The craps table is crowded, and someone is on a winning streak. We play through a few shooters, and then it's Albert's turn. He holds the dice up to each woman for her to blow on them for luck. His turn continues for seven rolls of the die, and we're both on a pretty big winning streak. Waitresses are serving Albert and the women drink after drink. I've been holding on to the one glass of scotch Albert ordered for me, just to keep him from incessantly insisting I drink with him. He hasn't realized it's the same glass. When he was sober, he respected my preference, but when he was buzzed, he often bought me drinks that would sit, untouched.

When it's my turn, I pull my arm back to throw the dice, but Cherry grasps my wrist and stops me.

"You need some luck," she says. *Luck.* I think back to that photo of Emi that sits on my computer, awaiting my return to the room. She is the only luck I want, the only woman I want. I hold the die up for her. I ignore the way her lips form into the perfect "o" when she blows on them. She smirks when my eyes meet hers again.

I roll a three on my first and only shot. My turn is immediately over. I pocket my chips and back away.

"Sorry," I tell the table. "Hey, Al, I think I'm gonna take a break for awhile, walk around for a bit."

"Do you mind if I join you?" Cherry asks.

"I, uh..." I stammer as I shake my head.

"Hold up," Albert says, taking me to the side away from Shannon and Cherry. "What do you think of Cherry?"

"She's pretty. Seems nice enough."

"Do you think you may want to hook up with her tonight?"

"No," I choke out a laugh. "Umm... not my type."

"I was hoping you'd say that," he says, then motions for the women to join us. "Well, Nate, if you want to meet up with us later, just call me. We'll be around."

"Sounds good," I smile, shaking everyone's hands as I bid them goodnight. I have no intention of seeing them again tonight.

I walk over to cash out my chips, and realize I'm walking away with a little over $23,000.

"That's a nice take-away," Shannon says from behind me, surprising me.

"Yeah," I laugh, running a hand through my hair. "Not bad."

"Where were you going to go?"

"Really, I just wanted to wander around the casino a bit. I've been wondering what these stores are all about."

"Oh," she says, "they're great, do you want me to show you around?"

"Sure," I tell her. "I could probably use a woman's opinion on a few things."

"I've got great taste," she boasts.

"I'm sure you do, Shannon."

We wander around the shops slowly, talking about her work and mine. Most of the stores are closed for the night, so we spend a lot of time looking at the window displays.

She waves me over to her as she gazes into a jewelry store window. I look up to see it's Tiffany's.

"How do you like these earrings?" she asks, pointing to silver posts with mesh and diamonds dangling from them.

"They're very nice."

"I'm thinking about getting them for the Vegas opening. For every club we open, I treat myself to something nice. I got this pendant when we opened LA," she says, pointing to the pink stone that hangs just above her breasts. I avert my eyes quickly back to the jewelry in the bright case. "Nice, huh?"

"Uh, yeah," I say, nodding and running my fingers through my hair nervously. A necklace catches my eye, and I can't look away from it, imagining it on Emi's neck. The choker is made of a single strand of round pearls and adorned with a colorful five-petal flower. The flower has this iridescent blue and green enamel with gold details. Each petal is highlighted with a line of small diamonds. A delicate, perfect pearl sits in the middle. It's as if it was made for Emi. I can imagine how the green would bring out the color of her eyes.

"Hey, what do think of this?" I ask Shannon.

"Which one, that pearl one?"

"Yeah."

"It's breath-taking," she says. "I've priced that, and it's way out of my budget. But I wouldn't turn it down as a gift." I nod thoughtfully.

We wander through the rest of the shops, making note of things we each wanted to come back and get when the shops were open again.

"Were you ever able to find that design book?" Shannon asks when we reach the elevators that would take me up to my suite.

"I forgot to look," I admit, remembering our conversation over lunch the week before. "I'm sure I brought it though, if you want to come up for a sec I'll see if I can find it."

"You sure?"

"Yeah, come on," I tell her, holding the elevator door open. "So, I thought you and Albert were..." I start a conversation in the elevator, easing the silence. I had always assumed they had some sort of arrangement, so I was surprised when Albert showed interest in Cherry tonight, right in front of his friend and business partner.

"No," she laughs. "We try to keep it professional. It works most of the time. He's a great guy, but he's got a wandering eye. I actually expected you to be more like him, from the way your agent talked about you."

"I don't get into a whole lot of personal stuff with Kate. I guess she's drawn her own conclusions from my past. I guess historically it may have seemed like that to her since I never brought the same woman twice to any of my shows." The elevator stops on my floor.

"So I guess Albert is to me what Amy is to you..." she says, walking next to me to my room.

"Emi..." I correct her. I've been reluctant to talk about her to my clients since it was all so new, even though the three of us had been spending a lot of time together in Vegas. I didn't want to jinx things, and the way Emi and I left things in LA was still a little up in the air. Things seem to be moving forward on the relationship front, but until I see her again, I won't truly know where we stand.

Shannon cocks her head and smiles when we reach my room, not pressing any further. "I think the book's probably in my bedroom. Just give me a minute. Sorry this place is such a wreck... when I get in the creative mode, I tend to leave shit all over the place."

"A true artist," she says with understanding as I head to the closet. "You play guitar?" I hear a cacophony of notes roughly strummed on the newly-tuned strings, making me cringe not only at the sound, but at the thought of someone unexperienced handling it.

"Yeah," I call to her from the adjoining room. She's silent for a minute or two, until I hear the sound of a cork popping. I stop in my tracks as I stumble upon the book I had been looking for in a box on the floor.

"Wow, Nate. What *don't* you do?" She startles me as I realize she's now in my bedroom. I emerge from the closet to see her sitting on the bed with two glasses of champagne in her hands.

"For starters, I don't drink." I smile, taking one of the glasses and setting it on the night stand. "Here's the book." I carry it with me to the living area, hoping she'll follow.

I wait for her in the next room, and she eventually joins me, again holding both glasses.

"Sure you do. You had scotch tonight, and I remember you drinking champagne that night in LA."

"That was a special occasion," I inform her. "We were celebrating the completion of the LA club, remember?"

"Well, surely we can think of something to celebrate tonight..."

"Shannon..."

"Come on, Nate. You seem so stressed out. Just relax," she coos, sitting down on the couch and holding the drink out to me. I grab it from her and move across the room. "Don't you ever get lonely?"

"Sure, but... I mean, no..." Flustered, I take a drink, then another, the silence in the room suffocating me. I walk into the kitchen area of the suite.

"It's good, isn't it? It's a vintage champagne... we shouldn't let it go to waste." I smile suspiciously at her and pour my glass of champagne into the sink.

"Look, Shannon, at another point in my life, this may have been something I pursued, but... it's not now." She looks at the floor in front of her, then glances at my laptop sitting next to her on the side table. I had forgotten to shut it down before dinner.

I had stared at the background so much over the last few weeks that it had begun to blend in with my surroundings, so I was startled when I realized Shannon was looking at the picture of Emi that she had sent me for luck.

"Wait, is that Emi?" I quickly cross the room and close the computer. "So there *is* something going on between you two?"

"Yeah, kind of. I think."

"That's not very definitive."

"Yes, there is something going on between Emi and me."

"When did this happen?" Shannon asks, taking another sip of her drink before setting it on the coffee table.

"When she came to visit in LA."

"I thought things were getting a little *too* friendly at dinner," she admits. "I just thought you two must be friends with benefits."

"No," I state. "We were never that. Always just friends."

"So what changed? If you don't mind me asking..."

"I don't know. I got tired of hiding my feelings for her, and she realized she had feelings for me, as well, I guess."

"Well, don't I feel silly?" she asks with an embarrassed laugh as she stands up.

"Yeah, I'm sorry if I gave you the wrong impression by inviting you here.

I really just wanted to find that book for you."

"No, I was just jumping to my own conclusions. I have to admit, not many men have turned me down."

"Well, six months ago, I would most likely not have been one of them. But at this point, I want to do right by Emi, and I respect the professional relationship you and I have. I don't want to screw any of that up."

"I can respect that," she says with a friendly smile. "She's a lucky woman."

"Trust me, I'm the lucky one in this relationship."

"Hmm..." she laughs softly, nodding. "I'm happy for you. Now I can see why you've set your deadline."

"Yeah, I'm anxious to get home."

"Well, whatever I can do to help with that, let me know."

"Thanks, Shannon. I really do appreciate it." After drinking her glass of champagne, she sets her glass in the sink and takes the rest of the bottle with her.

"You don't mind, do you?"

"I wouldn't want it to go to waste."

"Have a good night, Nate," she says as she opens the door to leave.

"You, too."

I pick up the phone as soon as Shannon leaves. It's one-thirty in the morning here, so it's four-thirty in New York. The time difference really gets in the way. Although I know she often stays up this late to work, I don't want to wake her if she is sleeping.

Alone in my hotel room, I'm reminded of another of Shakespeare's sonnets. I know she's not a fan, but the verse is too fitting, describes my feelings tonight perfectly. I decide to pick up my phone and email her the last two lines before my shower.

"All days are nights to see till I see thee / And nights bright days when dreams do show thee me."

After I take a shower, I check my messages before going to bed. There is a text from her, and I'm immediately surprised and amused at her Shakespearean response.

"Is it thy will thy image should keep open / My heavy eyelids to the weary night? / Dost thou desire my slumbers should be broken / While shadows like to thee do mock my sight?"

"So I'm keeping you awake at night?" I respond quickly, crawling into the plush bed, throwing off all the pillows but two.

"Maybe," she answers.

"Since when do you quote the Bard?"

"Since Google found a good comeback. ;)"

"You always were resourceful."

"Hey, Shakespeare, shouldn't you be sleeping, dreaming of me?"

"I was just about to go do that. I had some things to take care of."

"Like what? It's pretty late..."

"Well, I had to do things that simply involve me imagining you... and then I took a shower."

"You had to tell me that..."

"You had to ask?" She doesn't respond. *"Well, what do you do when I keep you awake at night?"*

"Wouldn't you like to know?"

"In fact, I would. Have you been to sleep tonight?"

"Nope. Can't sleep."

"What are you doing right now?"

"Right now, I'm wondering why you don't have curtains... the moon is really bright tonight... it's shining directly into your room."

"You're in my bed?"

"I am."

"And what are you wearing?"

"Such a guy response... I thought you already took care of that. :p"

"I'm just trying to give you something to do, alone, in the middle of the night, without me. Is that so wrong?"

"Well, maybe I already took care of that, too..."

"Emily Hennigan!"

"What?!"

"Next time, you'd better call me."

"In your dreams... speaking of which..."

"I miss you, Emi. I can't wait to see you in person."

"I miss you, too... but with this rock-hard pillow, it's almost like you're here."

"Rock-hard, huh?"

"Shut it, Nate. Next time I'm bringing my own pillow."

"Bring over anything you'd like. I just want you to be there when I get home."

"I may not be here, but I'll come soon enough."

"I'm sure you will. ;)"

"From poetry to porn. My, how this conversation has regressed. Go to bed, you dirty, dirty man."

"With dreams of my sweet Miranda..." When she doesn't text back, I add clarification. "Shakespeare?"

"I know, but which one was she?"

"From the Tempest. She was the one whose beauty and virtue eclipsed all others."

"Hell, I think you're already dreaming!"

I laugh quietly to myself. "Like ya, Emi."

"Sweet dreams, Nate."

I set the phone on the night stand and roll on my side, pulling the soft pillow into my body, anxious for those dreams to come.

293

~ * ~

The next three weeks fly by. I've channeled my complete range of emotions– happiness, confusion, frustration, insecurity, the list goes on– into the Vegas paintings. They're fairly different from the LA ones, but special on their own. Again, Albert is overly pleased with my work and is now even more excited to get started on the New York project in January.

Emi has been inundated with pre-holiday freelance work. She designs a lot of corporate Christmas and Hanukkah cards, and has taken on multiple annual reports this year. Although I wanted to see her– badly– and she wanted to see me, too, we were never able to find the time to fly her out to meet me. My mind was pretty wrapped up in this project anyway, so I thought, in the end, it was good to stay focused.

We've talked on the phone every day, sometimes for hours at a time. The friendship is solid, back to where it used to be, and the hopeful anticipation for something more is there for both of us. Most of our conversations have simply been about day-to-day happenings, but sometimes they do become slightly erotic, making me even more crazy with desire for her. I can't wait to hold her, to kiss her...

All of my supplies and necessities should be on their way back to New York. I land at JFK around eleven-thirty on Friday night, just a few days before my 29th birthday. Although I want to see Emi, she said she'd be unable to see me tonight because of a printer's deadline. She explained that she would leave the keys with the doorman of my building. In the back of my mind, I'm hoping that she'll be there anyway.

When I get to the building, the doorman has my keys waiting for me. I thank Marcus, but feel disappointed that he has them. *No Emi tonight.*

Upstairs, the apartment is spotless. I expected evidence of Emi when I got there. She's not one to put things back in their places, but everything looks just like I left it. It's as if she had never even been there. For a second, I wonder to myself if all of this was just a dream. Did we really make love in Los Angeles? Did we actually agree to date one another? Did I confess my feelings for her? Because looking around, there is simply nothing that proves she was here, that she is in my life at all.

I drop my luggage on the couch and pull out my phone to call her. I've missed her horribly, but it feels even worse, knowing she's just a few blocks away. I'm not sure I can *not* see her tonight. I'm just too excited. I dial her number, and hear a phone ring outside my door. A knock soon follows. I open the door to find Emi with a tote bag in one hand and Chinese food in the other.

"So much for a surprise," she says.

"What are you talking about? I'm surprised!" I take the food and bag from her and put them on the table. We hug awkwardly.

"I finished the pre-press work," she explains, "so I thought I'd come welcome you home. Marcus said that you had already come in."

"It's so good to see you," I tell her, holding her shoulders so I can get a good look. "You look amazing."

"You look tired," she says to me. "Gorgeous as ever, but still tired. And what's up with your hair?" she teases.

"I know it needs to be cut... it's on my agenda," I say apologetically, running my fingers through it.

"I'm just messing with you. I adore your sex hair," she says.

"Really?" I ask, intrigued. "I don't know if it can rightly be called that if it got that way without actual *sex*," I clarify.

"So you didn't meet a woman on the plane?"

"Well, I always meet women. That can't be helped," I tease.

"But none of them did this to you?" she asks, reaching up and putting her hands through my hair. Her hands lock behind my neck.

"None. That right is now reserved for you... and only you..." I tell her, my eyes intently focused on hers.

"Whoa," she says after a few seconds. "I think I forgot to breathe for a minute."

"Can I *please* kiss you now, Em?"

"I've been waiting," she says. She pulls me closer to her, and I cradle her lower back gently. Our lips meet, and my right hand travels up her back to the nape of her neck. I don't ever want this kiss to end. When it does, we just look at each other tentatively and smile.

"Does this still feel right to you?" I ask.

"It feels pretty incredible," she answers. "I got butterflies. I don't remember the last time I felt that."

"I'm happy to hear it," I tell her, embracing her again, satisfied that she now feels something when we kiss.

"Are you hungry?" she asks, looking up at me. "I knew you didn't have any food in the apartment."

"I could eat a little." I walk to the cupboard and pull out two plates. "What would you like to drink?"

"Water's fine." I grab two bottles of water from the refrigerator and head over to the dining room table. I set them down and pull out a chair for her.

"You know you don't have to be so polite. I've told you, you don't need to change who you are for me... don't need to impress me..."

"I just don't want to screw anything up," I tell her. "Whatever it takes to make this work, I'm going to do it."

She smiles and grabs the take-out containers, putting a portion of each ones' contents on both plates. While we eat, she tells me about her day and I tell her about the woman who sat next to me on the plane. I told Emi that I had told her about us, and she thought it was very romantic. She had wished us luck.

After dinner, I put the dishes in the dishwasher and remember the tote that Emi brought over. "What's in the bag?" I ask.

"Uh..." she stammers. "I just thought it would be nice to spend your first night back with you."

"Really?"

"Going back to what we talked about in LA... I don't know that we should just jump right back into things. I would just feel better if there were no expectations."

"I have no expectations, and I would love it if you would stay with me tonight," I assure her. "I've been wanting to just hold you in my arms for weeks. Dreaming of it, actually."

"Me, too," she says.

"Come here," I say, pulling her body against mine and embracing her tightly. "Emi, I have never been so happy. Never in my life."

"Yeah, I've been wandering around with a permanent smile, too," she admits. "The fam is on to me..."

"They're not pressuring you, are they?" I ask, imagining her mother and sister pushing her into the relationship. They were both constantly nagging Emi about her being single, asking her when she'd ever find a man that lived up to her expectations. She complained about it often to me... back when we were just friends.

"They're *encouraging* me," she says. "You know as well as I do they wouldn't be disappointed if this worked out."

"But... you're doing this for *you*, right?"

"Definitely. And I really want to keep it all for myself," she tells me. "But I just can't contain my feelings, Nate. I've managed to keep it between Chris, Anna and I, though... I can't keep anything from them."

"Yeah, Chris was very excited when I talked to him," I admitted. "He did threaten my life if I hurt you again, though."

"He wouldn't stand for it," she says.

"I have no intention of hurting you, Emi... ever." I shake my head solemnly. "That was never my intention."

"I know," she smiles and reaches up on the tips of her toes to kiss me again. "So, I know we were going to do a romantic night out tomorrow night, but Chris and Anna wanted to come along. I thought maybe we could do something, just the two of us, on Tuesday... for your birthday."

"That's fine, Em. As long as I'm with you. That's all that matters to me,"

I say.

"Good." She smiles, satisfied. "Thank you."

"You're more than welcome. Here, come and sit on the couch," I suggest, leading her to the sofa and picking up my bags. "I'll be right back." She picks up the remote and turns on the TV, finding a satellite music channel with some ambient music. I take my luggage across the room and begin to unpack a few things until I stumble upon the blue bag. I take it out and put it behind my back, returning to the living room. Emi sits up on the couch and crosses her legs, a curious look spreading across her face.

"Hey, did I mention I won at the tables in Vegas?"

"I think you said you quit while you were ahead..."

"I did. I was pretty far ahead, by the way," I tell her.

"So the lucky picture worked?"

"Well, it worked every night– wait, for what purpose were you intending it?" I joke.

"Ha ha. *Luck*," she says, crinkling her nose playfully at me.

"Oh, yes, luck. Yes, I suppose it did work for that, too."

"Good... um, are you hiding something from me? It's not a life-size poster, is it?"

I laugh. "No, Em. I left that as a tip for housekeeping."

"Nice. Really, what do you have behind your back?"

"Well... like I said, I did pretty well at the casino... and since it was your luck that got me there, I wanted to give you something in return." I pull the blue bag from behind my back, and her face lights up immediately, recognizing the distinct branding.

"Nate," she says. "What did you do?"

"I decided I would only buy something if it really said 'Emi.' And then I found this that didn't say it, it actually sang it... in, like, four-part harmony."

She stares at the bag a little longer before peeking inside and taking out the box. She turns the box around in her hand, as if the box itself were the actual gift.

"You have to open it, Emi."

She blushes and looks up at me. She unties the white ribbon slowly, and then lifts the hinged top of the box back. She gasps when she sees the necklace. "Oh, my god, Nate... what did you *do*?" She starts to pick the necklace out of the box.

"This might begin to make up for all the gifts that I've wanted to give you over the past decade... it was never appropriate before..."

"I'm not sure it's appropriate *now*!" she says, joyful tears forming in her eyes.

"Of course it is, Em. Why don't you think so?"

"It's... just... too nice... too *beautiful*... too *much*..."

"Nothing could be too much for you," I tell her. "Here, let me put it on." I take the strand of pearls from her shaking hands and clasp it around her neck. I lean in to kiss her neck on both sides. "You're beautiful."

She feels the beads on her neck, and her fingers linger on the colored flower. I take her by the hand and lead her to the mirror hanging over my dresser. She leans in to take a closer look as I admire her from behind. "You didn't have to do this," she says.

"No, I didn't. But I hoped it would help you to realize just how much this means to me, Emi."

"I'm beginning to think you might be serious," she says.

"I am very serious," I respond. I hold her shoulders and kiss her neck slowly, pearl by pearl. She bows her head down, and after a few seconds I realize she's crying. "What's wrong?"

She turns around and hops onto the dresser, sitting in front of me. "I'm just so scared, Nate." Her fingers clench the lip of the dresser.

"Of what?" I lift her chin and look into her eyes.

"Of this. I'm afraid it's all just too good to be true. That maybe... *you*... are too good to be true."

"Emi, my feelings for you couldn't be more *true*, more *pure*. You have to know that. Think about our families, our friends. They've suspected we'd end up together all along. They've seen through my past relationships, they've known who my true love was even before I was ready to admit to it. I couldn't, because I didn't think you would ever consider me in that way.

"Are you having second thoughts?" I ask.

"Yes," she says. I nod my head and attempt to stay composed, sighing heavily as if I just had the wind knocked out of me. "I'm not having second thoughts about how I feel about you. I'm pretty confident in that... I'm just so worried that it won't work, and that we'll ruin everything."

"Emi, honey," I start, "you don't have to be bitter about love anymore. Yes, your family has been peppered with some bad relationships, but that doesn't dictate *your* destiny. You are not them. You are beautiful, loving, open, generous, honest Emi... and you make decisions that make you happy. Sometimes you have to live in the present, Em, and not be so afraid of what has happened, or what may or may *not* happen."

"But if it doesn't work, I lose you for good," she says. "Are you that sure of your feelings?"

I struggle to hide the disbelieving laugh. I couldn't be more confident in knowing that I want to spend the rest of my life with this woman. I couldn't feel more confident in the trust I have in her, and in the belief she has in me. "Yes."

"Enough that you'll risk losing me?"

"Emi, this is what *we* make it. And if we want to make it work, it just... *will*. No one decides our future but us."

"But I'm scared–"

"Em, you have to get over the fear. If you don't, you'll never have any new experiences, never know what the world really has to offer you. I'm not telling you this for my benefit. I'd be telling you the same thing if you decided tonight to just walk away from this. I just want you to see what awaits you, if you just stop being afraid of everything.

"The last thing I want to do is pressure you. You know that, right?"

"I know," she sighs quietly.

"I want you to feel as certain as I am... and until you think you can do that, I don't want to go any further, okay?" She nods her head. "Because, yes, that *will* ruin everything." I smile. "We move forward when you give me the word. And I'll wait... as long as I have to. What's a few weeks or months when I've been waiting for years?"

She chokes out a laugh. "I'm getting there," she says with a sniffle. "I won't make you wait long. I just have to wrap my brain around this."

"Okay," I say, comforting her, rubbing her shoulders lightly.

"Because I do have crazy feelings for you, Nate. It's just this struggle in my head that I need to reconcile. Fear versus love. Losing you versus loving you."

"I understand." I kiss her gently, tasting her tears. *Love*, she said. It's the first time she's let on that it's more than 'like.' "You'll still stay over, won't you?"

"Of course," she says.

"Well, did you bring something to sleep in? It's getting pretty late."

"Good idea," she says. "Oh, by the way," she adds, "your jacuzzi tub–I'm in love with it."

"Great," I say, feigning jealousy.

"Mind if I take a bath?"

"Not at all." I help her unclasp the necklace and put it back in its box. While she's bathing, I finish unpacking and get reacquainted with the loft. She comes out looking refreshed, her face flushed from the heat, her skin natural and glowing. She's wearing flannel pants and a green thermal undershirt that hugs her soft curves.

"Better," she says.

"My turn. I think I'll take a shower. Get comfortable, make yourself at home," I tell her. She returns to the couch and scours the movie channels for something interesting to watch.

In the shower, I think about our conversation, but still remain confident in our future together. I know she'll choose love over fear. It's not really even a choice, especially if she feels for me even half of what I feel for her. For the first time in a long time, I realize there is a woman waiting in the next room for me, and I'm not driven to simply jump into bed with her. I can't wait to curl up on the couch with her, make fun of whatever nonsense is on TV, play with her hair, rub her back, kiss a little. I'll be ready for the next step as soon as she is ready... but right now, I just feel the need to make her feel safe... safe with me.

I pull on some sweatpants and a t-shirt and grab our water on the way to the couch. "Come here," I tell her, pulling her up to stand in front of me. I tilt her head to the side and kiss her, and I can feel her relaxing in my grasp. I steal her seat on the sofa, thanking her for keeping it warm.

"No fair!" she exclaims. I pat the couch next to me and hold out my arm. She snuggles in to me, her head on my shoulder. I stroke her hair, and she sighs heavily.

"You okay?" I ask.

"Yes," she says, and I can tell she's smiling. I pull a blanket off the back of the couch and spread it over her.

"What are we watching?"

"A Jane Austen movie..." she says as if asking me a question.

I groan, acting annoyed. "Why do you like these movies?"

"They're romantic..." she pleads.

"I'm romantic," I interject.

"And the men are dreamy..."

"You told me you had many dreams about me when I was in LA," I joke.

"And they have happy endings."

"I'm all about happy endings," I tease her. She backhands my chest playfully, then looks up at me and lifts her head. Our lips meet and my heart begins to race. I lie back against the armrest on the couch, and Emi maneuvers her way on top of me, her legs straddling one of mine.

As we kiss, she begins to move her leg back and forth, rubbing against me. "Em..." I say, stopping all activity, "what are you trying to do to me?"

"I don't know," she says coquettishly. "What *am* I doing to you?"

"You're driving me crazy," I tell her. "You're making me want to... *do things...* to you."

"Okay," she says. "I'm getting carried away. It's been a long time, I guess."

"Oh, I don't mind if you get carried away, please, be my guest."

"No, I don't want to be too much of a tease. I just want to make out tonight. I'm having fun."

"It is nice," I tell her. "I've wanted to kiss you like this for so long, Emi, it's hard to believe it's really happening."

"Well, it is happening." She brushes her hand against my cheek and chin, feeling the stubble on my skin. She looks at me directly, and again, I lose my breath. "Kiss me some more," she demands.

We make out on the couch for another hour or so– innocently, sweetly, tentatively– before we decide to go to bed. She curls up in my arms and goes to sleep quickly. I think it's the first night we've both slept comfortably together.

"So what time should I pick you up tonight?" I ask Emi before she leaves around noon.

"Chris wants to meet us at the restaurant at nine, so... eight-thirty?"

"Let's make it eight so I can spend a little time remembering what it's like to kiss you before we go."

"Sounds good," she says. "Want a preview?" I nod, and she pulls me close by the nape of my neck and touches her lips to mine. I can't keep the muscles in my face from forming a broad smile. Her mouth lingers on mine, hanging on gently to my lower lip before breaking away.

"Do you have to leave?"

"Yes, I have things to do today! And I'm sure you've got some things to take care of."

"I'll find something to keep me busy," I tell her. She embraces me tightly before picking up her things to leave.

"I'll see you in a few hours."

"See you tonight."

I stand in the kitchen for a few minutes, trying to map out my day, and eventually I return to bed in an attempt to get a few more hours of sleep. I can still smell Emi on the sheets. I hold on to the pillow she had been sleeping on and doze off.

At seven-forty-five, I grab the duffle bag that I've packed and begin the short trek to Emi's apartment. The restaurant is a low-key, trendy gourmet pizza place one subway stop from Emi's apartment, so I've opted to wear nice jeans and a white button down shirt with a blazer. The temperature is mild, probably in the mid-sixties. Teresa answers the door just a few seconds after I knock.

"Come in, she's still getting ready," she says.

"How are you doing?"

"Pretty good, actually. Emi's been in such a good mood lately that literally nothing I say or do bothers her."

I smile. "Good."

"Are you planning on staying?" she asks abruptly, eyeing the bag I'm holding, never afraid to say what's on her mind.

"If I'm invited," I tell her. "Thought I should be prepared, just in case."

"You know, we have no walls," she jokes.

"If it wasn't already obvious by looking around, yes, Emi has mentioned that a few times in the past."

"Well, we do have that screen over there," she nods, "and an ample supply of earplugs."

"I doubt that will be necessary," I smile again, this time blushing. "But thanks."

"Just looking out for you," she replies. "Nate, I'm just so happy for you both... I knew it was just a matter of time... let me go see if she's ready," she says, making her way to the restroom.

Emi emerges a few minutes later, with Teresa following closely behind. She, too, is wearing jeans, and has found a fitted green button-down shirt that matches the color in the flower on the pearl necklace perfectly. I'm happy she has decided to wear it tonight. The shirt also brings out the color of her eyes.

"You look great," I comment.

"You do, too," she says back, taking my bag from me and leading me over to her bed across the room. "Presumptive, isn't it?" she teases, lifting the duffle bag.

"Hopeful," I correct her, taking off my jacket.

"Well, guys, I've got a date with my fireman, so I'm taking off," Teresa announces.

"Have a good time," Emi says to her.

"Don't do anything I wouldn't do," Teresa instructs with a laugh as she exits the apartment.

I lean down to hug Emi and pick her up to kiss her. She wraps her legs around my waist and smiles playfully.

"How are you feeling tonight?" I ask her, propping her up.

"I couldn't wait to see you," she says. "And now that I see you, I'm a little turned on."

"Perfect," I respond, placing her on the bed and lying down on top of her. "Because I'm a little turned on, too." She repositions her legs so that mine are in between hers. I want her so badly, my mind racing with the many fantasies I've had of her. I am immediately aroused, and I can tell from her smile that she is fully aware of that fact. We kiss, and our bodies begin to move together as her breathing becomes quicker. I unbutton her blouse and kiss her neck and chest, and just when I'm about to pull down her bra strap to reveal her breast for the first time in nearly six weeks, Teresa walks back into the apartment. We both are motionless, as if we're two teens caught in the act by our parents. I bury my head in Emi's chest in frustration, sneaking in another kiss or two.

"Sorry," Teresa apologizes. "I can't find my Metrocard." I look up, but can't make eye contact with Teresa. I just smile at Emi.

"Take mine," she says abruptly, grabbing it from her nightstand and holding it out for her roommate. "We'll use Nate's."

"Okay, thanks," Teresa says, quickly grabbing the card and walking toward the door. "I'm really sorry."

"S'okay," Emi says. Teresa quietly closes the door behind her.

"Where were we?" I ask.

"I'm thinking we were getting a little too caught up in the moment," she says. "We probably need to get going."

"Just a second." I pull down the strap and catch a glimpse. My hand caresses her breast gently, my eyes meeting hers for approval. She smiles faintly and runs her fingers through my hair, silence filling the room. I first kiss her breast, then slowly put my mouth around her nipple, sucking gently. She inhales quickly, as if surprised by my touch. As I'm kissing her, I adjust the other strap and begin to massage her other breast. After a few minutes, I switch sides, and her hands are lightly tugging at my hair at this point. Instinctually, our bodies move in rhythm, Emi's setting the pace and guiding me as she begins to breathe faster, more erratically.

"Nate," she says softly as her breaths become shorter, faster, more uneven, each more audible than the last, the latter ones coupled with soft hums. Her grasp on my hair becomes tighter as her moans become louder. When I feel she is climaxing, my body still moving swiftly with hers, my kisses lead back to her wanting lips, which ravish mine on contact. "Oh, Nate," she says breathily as I feel her body calming down beneath mine. Our eyes meet and hold the other's captive. I remove a small bead of sweat from her temple and move some strands of hair out of her face.

"Emi," I begin, adding a kiss. "Emi, I lo–"

"*Like* me, Nate," she stops me from going further. "Don't say it... not yet... not now."

"But–"

"Nate," she warns, putting a finger over my mouth. "I know. Please just don't say it now." She lifts her head to kiss me again. When we break away, I bury my head in her shoulder and sigh. I am beyond frustrated at this moment for a few reasons. One is quite obvious, I'm frustrated sexually, but I didn't anticipate that we would have sex tonight. That was never in the plans, so I know that I need to exercise some self-control and move beyond the slight discomfort. I'm more frustrated with the fact that she doesn't want me to profess my love to her. It is love I'm feeling. I wouldn't have shared such intimate moments with her if it wasn't, and I want her to feel safe in knowing how I truly feel, how deeply I truly love her.

Of course, I've shared similar intimate moments with many other women, and didn't feel love for them. But this is different. *I feel different.*

"Are you okay?" she asks, continuing to run her fingers through my hair.

"I'll be fine," I mumble.

"Thank you, Nate," she says, "for, you know..."

"It was truly my pleasure," I respond.

"I need to go fix myself," she says. "We really do need to get going now." I roll over to let her off the bed, but as soon as she's gone, I just bury my head in the pillow. It's been quite some time since I got so worked up and didn't have a release. I've forgotten what this feels like. I remember quickly that I don't like the feeling... but for Emi, I'll suffer through it.

She laughs when she comes out of the bathroom a few minutes later. "Are you sure you'll be alright?"

"Yes," I say, rolling over, the erection still obvious.

"Is there anything I can do?" she asks. I raise my left eyebrow. She smiles, "Other than that?"

"Help me up," I tell her, and she uses all her strength to pull me off the bed.

"Here, let me fix your hair," she says, running her fingers through it quickly. "Perfect sex hair."

"We are getting closer to the point that you can actually call it that," I tell her, smiling. I pull her body into mine and hold her by the hips so she can feel me against her. "Emi, I cannot wait to make love to you again."

"Well, you have to," she says with a matter-of-fact tone. "A little longer..."

"Oh, alright," I say, a little disappointment coming out in my tone. "I hope I can make it till then," I joke. "I'm not entirely sure I can make it through dinner tonight. I'm going to have the image of your breasts in my mind all night..." She slaps my arm playfully, and I lean down to kiss her before adding, "...and even wilder visions of what I want to do to you."

"Nate, behave!" she says. "We have to go, and it's going to be bad enough with *one* of us fully aroused at dinner," she teases. "Don't get me all wound up again, too."

"Oh, Em," I tell her, "that will be my mission all night."

As we emerge from the subway station, I take her hand in mine and we walk down the sidewalk to the restaurant. Our fingers entwine, and I rub her hand with my thumb. As we enter the establishment, I pick up her hand and kiss the back of it.

The host greets us and asks how many are in our party.

"We have reservations for four," I tell him. "We're meeting two others. Probably under the name Chris Hennigan?"

The host whispers to a nearby waitress and nods. "We're preparing the table now, sir. It will be just a few minutes."

"Thanks," I tell him, leading Emi away from the hostess desk, out of the way. I pin her up against the wall and stare down at her.

"Nate," she laughs.

"Shhhh..." I say, leaning in to kiss her in an attempt to fulfill my mission. It is a deep kiss, long, a little frantic, and when I back off, it is as if she is gasping for air. She bites down on her bottom lip and grabs me by the waist, pulling me toward her. Our lips meet once more, this time the kiss is slower and more deliberate. I run my fingers through her hair, and, embracing me, she puts her cold hands underneath my jacket and shirt, scraping my back lightly with her fingernails. I shiver and moan quietly.

"You're not playing fair," I whisper in her ear. "This is my game, remember?"

"Well, two can play," she whispers back.

"But, see, I could carry you right out of this place and take you back to my apartment," I pause briefly, "make love to you right now. I'm already there."

"Really?" she says with an impish grin.

"Yes. It's my job to get *you* to that point."

"Well... continue..." she says, and I begin to kiss her once more before someone taps me on the shoulder.

"Your table is ready, sir," the host says as Emi and I try to appear composed. "Right this way."

Chris and Anna must have sneaked in at some point, because they are already seated near the back of the restaurant by a stone fireplace, complete with a crackling fire. They both stand to meet us.

"Nate!" Chris says excitedly and gives me a hug. "Congrats, man. I'm so happy for you guys."

"Oh, thanks," I tell him, shaking his hand. "How are you two doing?" I say, diverting my attention to his girlfriend.

"Great," she tells me. "And Emi, it's good to see you again! Where did you get that necklace?"

Emi blushes and looks at me. "Nate got it for me in Vegas."

"I won a little at the tables," I explain modestly. "I like to think she brought me luck."

"Well, you're definitely lucky," Chris says. "She agreed to date you. She doesn't just date anyone," he teases his sister.

We all take a seat at the table and begin to look at the menu. The waiter comes to take our drink order.

"We'll take a bottle of Chianti– is that okay, Em?" Chris asks.

"Perfect," she says.

"And water all around," he adds. He looks at me to see if I want to add anything, but I just nod in agreement. Emi and I hold hands under the table, and her constant touch makes it difficult for me to concentrate on anything but her.

"So, I heard the paintings are a hit," Anna says.

"I guess so," I answer. "The client loved them, and the Times is actually doing a feature on the architecture and design of Albert's club. I did a phone interview last week. I think it'll be in this weekend's Arts section."

"That's incredible," Chris says as Emi beams. I release her hand, and put mine on her knee, squeezing it lightly. She puts her hand on top of it.

The waiter brings four glasses of water and four wine glasses with the bottle of Chianti. He uncorks the bottle and lets Chris smell the cork. He then pours a small sampling, and Chris tastes it before giving his approval. Once he does, the waiter pours a glass for each of us.

"Are you ready to order?" he asks. We place our order for a medium vegetarian pizza and a medium pepperoni pizza. As the waiter walks away, Chris raises his glass.

"A toast," he starts as we pick up our wine. "To good friends and true love," he says with a smile.

"To good friends and true love," the rest of us repeat before taking a sip. I lean over to kiss Emi, putting my hand on her waist. Our lips meet and she closes her eyes as I stroke her cheek with my thumb. When I pull away, my desirous gaze meets hers and my heart skips a beat.

Shaking her head as if to clear away her current thoughts, she asks Chris what has been going on in his life.

Chris takes Anna's hand on the table and says, "Well, we've both been working a lot–"

"And seeing each other less," Anna adds. "But we think we've found a solution."

"Oh?" Emi asks. "And that is?"

Anna smiles. "We're going to move in together at the beginning of the year!"

"That's great!" Emi exclaims. "I never thought I'd see this day, Chris."

"Oh, well," he starts. "It's not just that." Anna looks at him, raising an eyebrow. "I was actually thinking..." Chris shifts in his chair, turning his body to face Anna better. He picks up her left hand and holds it in both of his. He clears his throat before continuing.

"I was actually thinking that maybe..."

"Maybe what?" Anna asks impatiently. Chris reaches into his jacket pocket and shoves his chair back so that he can get down on one knee.

"I was thinking that maybe you'd like to marry me," he says, pulling out a brilliant diamond ring. "So, Anna Cheung? Will you marry me?"

I wonder if Emi knew about the proposal tonight. By her expression, I guess she didn't, and I'm beyond happy for Chris. Anna's eyes begin to water as she chokes out one simple answer: "Yes!" He slips the ring onto her finger and they kiss tenderly. A few of the other diners who had been watching begin to clap, and we all join in.

"I thought you were going to ask her on New Year's Eve!" Emi says.

"She was on to me," Chris explains. "I started to think she might be expecting it that night, so I had to do something to surprise her. I thought tonight would be the perfect opportunity."

"I certainly didn't expect it tonight," Anna says, wiping tears from her eyes with her napkin. Emi reaches over to take a closer look at the ring.

"It's beautiful, Chris. Good job."

"Congratulations, guys," I add. When the waiter comes back with our food, they also deliver their best bottle of champagne for the table, obviously in on Chris's plan.

"So," Chris continues. "Nate, I wanted to know if you'll play at our engagement party, on New Year's."

"And Emi, I'd love you to be my maid of honor!" Anna adds.

"I'd be honored," I tell Chris.

"I'd love to!" Emi says. The thought of Emi walking down the aisle forces a huge smile on my face. I can only hope that it will be a sort of dress rehearsal for the real thing someday.

"Em, wasn't it, like, a year ago that we vowed to take care of one another in the nursing home someday? Because I'd never find the right girl and you'd never find the right guy, and we'd be destined to die alone?"

"I think it was last Thanksgiving," she says, "so yeah, a year ago."

"And look at us now, both crazy in love," he adds, raising has glass to Anna, kissing her.

"In love," Emi says as she lifts her glass, the words lingering on her tongue as she stares blankly into the fireplace. Slowly, the corners of her mouth turn up, obviously having a vision of something that makes her happy. She snaps out of her daze and turns quickly to face me. She takes a drink and smiles broadly at me, her eyes wide.

I lean in to whisper in her ear. "What are you thinking?" I ask, kissing her earlobe discretely.

"Don't do that," she laughs quietly. "That's my weakness."

"Really? What other weaknesses do you have?"

"Nate," she warns with a smile.

"Well, then tell me what you're thinking," I whisper again, taking the same earlobe between my teeth and gently tugging on it.

"Not playing fair..." she warns.

"Neither are you," I remind her.

"What are you guys whispering about?" Chris interrupts. Emi blushes and laughs.

"I'm sorry," Emi says. "That was pretty rude."

"Honestly, guys, I can't tell you how happy I am that you're finally together," Chris says. "I just always knew it would happen one day."

"I," I begin, "never thought it would." I look at Emi and smile.

"I'm very happy," Emi says and leans in to kiss me.

"We can tell," Anna comments. "I have never seen you so... smiley. You're practically glowing."

"And the PDA's are almost nauseating," Chris adds.

"Shut up," Emi says playfully.

"I saw you two against the wall before you were seated," Chris says. "I almost thought you'd just leave."

"I suggested it," I tell him, secretly putting my hand on Emi's leg. She blushes.

"She's my sister," he warns, but smiles. "Too much information."

"Sorry," I apologize, looking at Chris, but really speaking to Emi. "I can't help myself." I move my hand further up her thigh.

"I think it's sweet," Anna says. "It's all still so new for them. It's cute."

"New after thirteen years... *that's* pretty amazing," Chris says.

Emi reaches her hand under the table and grabs mine, stopping it from sojourning further, squeezing so tightly that my knuckles pop.

I smile, defeated, and pick up the champagne glass with my free hand. "Like ya, Em."

"Like you, too, Nate." She smiles with a certain self-satisfied look as we clink our glasses and drink together.

"You're still saying that?" Chris says, rolling his eyes.

"It's still true," Emi defends our exchange.

"I think Emi's afraid of the word L-O-V-E," he says to Anna. He knows his sister as well as I do.

"Chris, leave her alone," she says. "In her own time."

I kiss her on the cheek. "Yeah, Chris, leave her alone," I repeat. The look I give him lets him know to not continue with this line of conversation. He nods, letting me know that he understands. Again, Emi is staring into the fire, appearing to be deep in thought. I move my chair closer to hers and run my fingers up and down her back slowly. She is quiet for a few minutes, then excuses herself from the table.

"Is she okay?" Anna asks.

"I'll go check." I place the napkin on my empty plate and follow her toward the ladies room. Before she reaches the door, she turns around abruptly to face me, obviously knowing that I was right behind her.

"I'm sorry," she says. "I'm sorry I won't say it yet."

"It's okay, Em," I soothe her, hugging her into my chest. "It doesn't bother me."

"It kind of bothers me that you *have* said it."

"What do you mean?"

"You *do know* you've said it..."

"Yes." I catch her suspicion immediately as she tilts her head to the floor. "Hey," I say, lifting her chin. "Emi, when I said it, I meant it."

"You've never said it when we weren't being intimate, though. I've always felt like you really didn't know what real love was like. I'm still not sure you do."

"I do," I assure her. "I know now. No, I didn't, Emi, but I do now. I could tell you right now."

"I'm not asking you to. That's not what I meant. It's just... you have a track record of confusing sex and love."

"This is different. *You* are different." She stares at me with questioning eyes. "I love you." One side of her lip curls into a smile. "If you're not ready to tell me, that's fine. Don't let Chris make you feel bad about it. He's just messing with you anyway," I explain.

"Am I right to even question you? I just don't want to put myself out there if you're confused."

"I guess you have every right to doubt me. I have a fucking terrible track record. I can't change that. You're just going to have to trust me here... and not be afraid to feel something for me in return. We've been over this, fear versus love, remember?"

"Yeah, I remember."

"I'm not going to rush you. I want you to feel confident in us. If it makes you feel any better... I see something in your eyes, something that says that you love me, too."

"Do you?"

"Yes. I like to think you're warming up to the idea."

"I think I am."

"Good," I say, walking toward her until she is forced back against the wall, tucked out of view from the rest of the restaurant. My hand caresses her shoulder, then travels down her side and stops at her waist. I lift her shirt just enough to slide my hand in to touch her bare skin. I move my hand up her back and quickly pull her body into mine, leaning down to steal yet another kiss from her generous lips. Again, she is breathless, as am I. "Are you ready to leave?" I ask, again kissing her earlobe, then her neck.

"If you're really asking whether or not I'm turned on..."

"Yes," I whisper in her other ear and kiss her neck.

"I am and I'd like to do something about that," she says quickly, touching me, discovering my arousal. "Wow," she adds.

"Wow," I say, shocked at her brazen gesture, still surprised at her sexual nature since it's been hidden from me for so long. "Let's get out of here."

I button my jacket before we walk back over to the table, and before I can tell Chris and Anna good night, Emi says, "Guys, I'm really sorry, I'm not feeling well."

"Oh, sweetie, I'm so sorry," Anna says. "Are you going to be okay?"

"Yeah, I'm sure I'll be fine," she smiles. "It's just my head hurts so bad all of a sudden... I think it's a migraine. I just need to go to bed."

"Do you want us to drive you guys home?" Chris asks.

"No," Emi cuts in, "the fresh air might do me some good."

"Here, Chris," I say, offering him my credit card.

"No, it's on me, Nate."

"You sure?"

"Yeah."

"Well, thank you, and congratulations to you both," I tell them. "I'm so happy you shared this occasion with us."

"Yes, congratulations," Emi says impatiently, taking my hand, beginning to pull me away from the table.

"Take care of her," Chris says, nodding.

"Oh, I will." *Don't worry, I will.*

"Call me tomorrow, Em," Anna says loudly.

"Okay," she responds.

As soon as we hit the sidewalk, Emi pulls me by my shirt collar and kisses me once more.

"I guess I succeeded at my mission," I laugh, taking her into my arms. It has gotten considerably colder since we arrived at the restaurant.

"Let's go," she says, pulling me toward the subway station. Once we're on the train, she sits in my lap for the short ride to the next stop.

When we get to Emi's apartment, we are both pleasantly surprised to find it empty.

"I'm going to change into something more comfortable," Emi announces as she makes her way to the restroom. While she's in there, I decide to do the same. I brought sweatpants, but I debate keeping them off, opting just for a t-shirt and boxers... yes, I'll keep them off.

She comes out of the bathroom wearing tight pink shorts and a grey tank top, revealing every subtle curve. "I'm cold," she laughs.

"I suspect you might be, wearing that," I tease her. "Come here, I'll warm you up." She practically runs across the apartment in her fuzzy socks, right into my waiting arms. We hug, and I rub her back, trying to create some friction to warm her up.

"Better?" I ask.

"No," she says, her teeth beginning to chatter.

"Let's turn the heater on, then, silly," I suggest, crossing to the thermostat on the other side of the apartment. I turn off her lamp, as well. Lit only by the moonlight streaming through the window, Emi turns back the sheets on her bed, then grabs some extra blankets and throws them on top. She climbs into bed, and holds the sheets up for me to lie down next to her. We're facing each other under the blankets, and I take her leg and put it on top of mine, making it easier to warm up her bare leg. "You can put on something warmer, you know."

"I want to feel your skin on mine," she tells me. "Plus, doesn't heat transfer better that way than through clothes?"

"I guess maybe it does," I answer. After feeling her leg getting warmer, I slowly ease my hand further up her leg to her behind. "Nice," I tell her, exploring the soft skin of her backside. She laughs quietly.

"Whatever," she says. I lean in to kiss her, pulling her body toward mine and putting one of my legs between hers.

"You *are* a little turned on," I observe, whispering in her ear again, my arm now caressing her back with no space between our bodies. Our kisses are soft, controlled, but I can feel her heart beginning to race, just as mine is.

"So are you," she whispers back to me, looking me directly in the eyes. I still think I see a little doubt. She seems a little unsure.

"You do that to me," I tell her. I put my hand up the back of her shirt, beginning to massage deeply. I pull my leg up higher, and her lips find mine again, this time her kisses are much deeper. I pull her shirt up over her head and run my hands down the side of her body. After she throws her shirt on the floor, she pulls at mine, and I gladly take it off for her. My hand travels up her torso, my lips travel down her neck, chest, until they both meet at her small but ample breast. She turns on her back, and I kneel, my legs still straddling one of hers. She lifts her knee and begins to move it back and forth.

"Emi," I sigh before putting my lips around her nipple. I slowly move my hand back down to her navel, then under the waistline of her shorts, then lower still.

"Nate," she whispers, her hand reaching to stop mine.

"Guys?" Teresa's voice breaks through the haze of my mind.

"Shit!" Emi exclaims quietly. I try to analyze the way she was stopping me from proceeding. Was it because she heard Teresa, or because she didn't want to go any further?

"Uh, hey, guys," Teresa continues. "Just wanted to let you know I'm back."

"Got it," Emi says. When I hear the bathroom door close, I emerge from under the blankets. I kiss Emi, touching her cheek, which is now warm to the touch. "My shirt," she says to me. I lean over the bed and grab it off the floor. She sits up in the bed to put it back on, her silhouette visible in the moonlight. Before she pulls the shirt down, I kiss her breast one last time. I decide to leave my t-shirt off, still wanting to feel her against my skin. She lies back down and I drag the covers back on top of us. I lie down on my back and stare up at the ceiling, far more frustrated than I was earlier. Emi props herself up on her elbow and runs her fingers up and down my chest.

"I kind of wish we were at your apartment," she whispers to me.

"We can get a cab," I suggest quickly, feeling suddenly hopeful.

"No," she says. "Let's just hold off a little longer. It might make a good birthday present. What do you think?"

"Oh, god, Em," I inhale deeply, my frustration seeping out in the words. I swiftly pull her on top of me, our eyes even. I sigh heavily. "Do you promise?" I really don't mean to pressure her, but I'm desperate to savor those intimate moments with her again, and I don't know how much longer I can wait. It's been a month and a half. I mean, surely I *can* wait– and will, for her– but I just don't *want* to any longer.

"Yes," she says, giving me a kiss. "I promise."

I pull her lips to mine, and we kiss softly. Emi moves next to me, putting her head on my shoulder. Her hand continues to explore my chest, but before long, she stops moving it and her breathing becomes steady, deep.

~ * ~

Tuesday couldn't come soon enough, after the weekend we had. We decided it was best to not see each other at all until my birthday, so the anticipation has been building exponentially. I have no idea what the plans are. Emi has made all the arrangements, and is keeping them to herself. All she has told me is to dress casually, and obeying her orders, I'm just wearing khakis and a long-sleeved polo shirt.

At four o'clock in the afternoon, she knocks on my door.

"Now?" I say jokingly as I answer the door.

"No, not now," she says. "Get your jacket, I want to go for a walk."

"Okay..." I grab my jacket and keys and we head out the door, out of the building, making our way toward Central Park. The sun is already beginning to set, creating long shadows on the ground from the tall trees.

"I brought my photographer," she says, stopping on the trail. I turn around to see Teresa trailing us.

"Hey, Teresa."

"Nate," she says, smiling.

"I wanted to take some pictures, if that's okay," Emi says. "It's part of your present."

"I think it's a good idea," I say, wanting to document this time for future generations to see, see how happy we are.

"The lighting's perfect," Teresa says. "Just ignore me, I want to get some candids first." Emi and I walk hand-in-hand talking, stopping to kiss each other every now and then. We are both remembering when we were here a year ago, playing with her niece in the fall leaves. I admit to her that, on that day, I began to see myself as a father, and was imagining that we were a family.

"I was, too," she says. "I just didn't want to feel that way about you. I didn't want things to change between us. They were perfect back then."

"What made you finally change your mind, Emi?"

"When I realized that I was comparing every guy I dated to you," she says. "When I saw how you doted on your girlfriends, and I felt a little jealous." She pauses briefly. "And really, when I felt us drifting further and further apart."

"Hmmm," I say, pulling her to face me, moving a strand of hair from blocking the view of her beautiful green eyes.

"It was at that point that I thought we may never get back what we had... and I thought, if I'm ever going to take a chance on you, this is the time."

"So the fear of losing 'us' drove you to me, but it also kept you away from me."

"Kept me away when things were good between us; brought me to you when the loss was imminent."

"You *are* ruled by fear."

"I'm not anymore," she declares. "I realize, of all the things in the world I should be sure of, it's you. You're the only constant in my life– besides my family. You're honest, loyal, true... all the things a good boyfriend– a good lover– should be."

"I will never hurt you, Emi," I assure her. "And I will always treat you with respect, admiration... and love."

"I know," she says smiling, her eyes beginning to water.

"You don't have to be afraid of losing me ever again, Emi. I'm here to stay."

"I know," she repeats, two tears now running down her cheeks. I take her into my arms and hold her close as she cries quietly. I stroke her hair to comfort her.

"Why are you crying, Em?" I ask with a soft laugh. I look at Teresa as she snaps a picture of this private moment. I wonder if Emi knew where this conversation would lead when she asked Teresa to join us. I take her to a park bench and we sit down, side by side. I wipe the tears from her face. "Em?"

"I'm just overwhelmed," she said. "I've never known real happiness– until now. It's sad to think we could have had this all along."

"I like to think it wouldn't have been this way," I tell her, not regretting a moment of the lives we've led up to this point. "All the relationships we've had, that's what has made us who we are right now. And I think now, we are both in a place where this is... just... well, it's just... right.

"We were different people ten years ago, even one year ago. Don't live in the world of what-could've-been. Just live in the now, Em."

She sits quietly next to me, as if trying to form the right words to respond with. She takes my hand in hers, sits up straight, her eyes capturing me in a trance. "Love ya, Nate," she says, another tear falling swiftly down her face.

"Oh, Emi," I say, overcome with my own emotions. I stand up and pick her up to hug her, kiss her. "I love you, too, Emi. God, do I love you." I twirl her around, scattering the leaves under my feet. She wraps her legs around me as we embrace and kiss for a few more minutes. When the kisses become a little too passionate, Teresa clears her throat.

"Always *you*!" I joke with her. "Why do you always have to interrupt?"

"Sorry," she says. "Not the right place. Let's take some posed pictures. Go sit back on the bench."

After posing for what seemed like a million pictures, Teresa tells us she got enough photos. "I'm going to head back to our apartment, Em," she announces. "See you..."

"Tomorrow," Emi says, looking at me and smiling.

"That was a great idea, Em," I tell her. "Our kids are going to love this story."

"Let's not think about kids right now," she says. "I'm going to want a lot of time alone with you."

"I can certainly live with that," I assure her.

"Let's walk a little more, watch the sunset."

"Okay." I put my arm around her since the air is getting cooler as the shadows begin to take over. After another half-hour, I suggest going to get some coffee. She looks at her watch and agrees.

"Are we on a schedule?"

"No," she says, trying to hide a smile.

"I don't believe you, but that's okay."

While we are at the cafe, she gets a few text messages, but is careful not to let me see. I don't bother to ask, either.

"You ready to go?" she asks.

"Where?"

"Back to your apartment."

"And then where?"

"That's it," she says. "We aren't leaving there until tomorrow morning... or afternoon... or maybe the next day."

"Perfect," I tell her. "I couldn't have planned this better myself." She smiles and takes my hand, leading me out of the coffee shop.

We say hello to Marcus as we walk into my building and head toward the elevator. Once the door closes, just the two of us inside, I lean into her and kiss her again. When we reach the twelfth floor, I pick her up, wrap her legs around my body and carry her to the door. Unable to find my keys, I put Emi down to search my pockets until I find them.

As the door opens, I am greeted by an onslaught of friends, family members and a dozen birthday wishes. I look at Emi, confused.

"Later," she whispers in my ear, knowing the exact question that was filling my mind. "Your mom wanted to do this, and I couldn't say no."

"I curse my mother," I say under my breath, and Emi laughs. "Mom!" I smile, walking across the room with open arms to hug my mother.

James is there with Mom, next to Chris and Anna. Emi's sister, Jennifer, is also there with her husband, Michael, and little Clara, who runs up to hug me. "Nate-Nate!" she exclaims. I pick her up and swing her around, locking eyes with Emi when I stop to put her down. We exchange a knowing glance. Emi's mom and stepdad are also in attendance. Her mom always cared for me like a son.

"Thanks, everyone," I say over the noise. "Can you excuse us for a second?" I pull Emi into the rarely-used guest bedroom and close the door. There are coats and bags strewn all over the room.

"Your whole family?" I ask. I'd often spent time at her parents' homes on various birthdays and holidays, but they'd never come to my apartment before. I hadn't seen many of them in over a year.

"Not everyone," she says. "My dad would have come, but my stepmother's sister is in the hospital."

"But why?" I ask, not bothered, but simply curious.

"Your mom invited everyone," she explained quietly. "I think they're all caught up in... *us*. I think this is more a celebration of *that* than your birthday. Can you share?"

"I'll share my birthday, sure... but it's just me and you tonight, right? I don't want to share my alone time with you... no one's staying here, right?"

"No, they're all going home after the party."

"Thank God," I tell her with relief. We walk back into the open area of the loft where the party is underway. I look around to see who I missed at first glance. Eric and Jason, my band mates and friends, are also there, as are Kate and her boyfriend, Albert and Cherry, and Shannon. Teresa and Bradley, her firefighter boyfriend, are in the back, and she's still aiming the camera in my direction. I wave to the camera.

Mom has hired a waitstaff, of course, so there are two men in tuxes carrying around trays of hors d'oeuvres and champagne. I mingle with everyone, Emi at my side, catching up with people I haven't seen in weeks, months, some even years. They all wish me a happy birthday, but are more congratulatory on my relationship with Emi. "We knew it would happen eventually," most people tell us.

I ask the waiters to take a glass of champagne around to everyone, and I take one for myself. When I see everyone is ready, I clear my throat to get their attention.

"First of all," I start, "I want to thank everyone for coming tonight. I was definitely surprised... so thanks to you all, and thanks to Mom and Em for organizing it." I lift my glass and sip, and everyone follows suit. "Secondly," I continue, "I want to congratulate my friend Chris. I'm sure most of you know he got engaged to his beautiful girlfriend, Anna, over the weekend." Everyone raises their glass to them, shouting congratulatory messages, and drinks. "I couldn't be happier for you both."

"Thanks," Chris says. "And right back at you, man," he adds. "To Nate and Emi."

"To Nate and Emi," Jennifer says. "Honestly, we didn't think two soul mates could spend their lives apart, but we were beginning to think you were both going to prove us all wrong."

"To Emi," I say, "for taking the leap. I promise, it will be worth it."

"To Nate," she counters, "I hope your birthday is everything you expected and more."

"I'll drink to that," I tell her, winking at her. At that point, I'm just anxious for everyone to leave. Our parents are the first to go, followed closely by Kate, Albert, Shannon and their guests. After the two waiters leave, Michael walks over to the couch to lift up a sleeping Clara, and he and Jennifer wish us a good night. We make plans to babysit Emi's niece one weekend the following month, to give them some time to themselves. Eric and Jason invite us to join them for drinks at a bar down the street, but we take a raincheck. Teresa snaps one last picture and takes her boyfriend by the hand, leading him out of the apartment.

Chris and Anna stay behind for a bit, until Emi whispers something to Anna. She laughs and stands up, taking Chris's hand. "It's getting late," she says to her fiancé.

"Right," he says. "Thanks, Em, for getting us all together. That was fun."

"Thanks for coming," she tells him.

"Happy birthday, Nate," he shakes my hand.

"Thanks for coming," I repeat to them both, opening the door for them and then closing it softly behind them. I walk to the stereo and turn off the random party mix and choose a more soothing playlist of Zero 7 albums.

"It's eleven-thirty," Emi says. "Still your birthday, but we don't have much time."

"We're not going to rush this, Em," I tell her, taking her into my arms and kissing her cheek.

"But I promised, on your birthday," she says, her arms holding my body to hers. "And I kind of can't wait..."

"Are you just that impatient?" I laugh.

"Maybe a little," she blushes, kicking off her shoes.

"Too bad," I tell her. "I want to savor this night, take in every detail."

"I bet I can change your mind," she says, taking off her shirt and modestly covering herself with her arms crossed in front of her chest.

"I'm not an animal," I remind her. "I have some self-control."

"Really?" she asks, taking a deep breath and unclasping her bra, sliding the straps down her arms, leaving the bra to succumb to gravity and hit the floor softly. Her cheeks grow crimson as her eyes move from the floor to meet mine.

"Some..." I say, my eyes lingering on her body. I walk toward her and cup her breasts into my hands. She reaches up and runs her fingers through my hair. I kiss her neck, then her lips. She takes my shirt and pulls it over my head. She scrapes her fingernails lightly over my chest.

"Come with me," I tell her, taking her by the hand to the jacuzzi. I lean over and turn on the faucet, filling the tub with warm water.

"I do love the jacuzzi," she reminds me.

"I know you do..." I unbutton her jeans and slowly pull them to the ground, helping Emi to step out of them, my hands lingering on each calf muscle. She does the same to my pants. I kneel down and kiss her hips, then her stomach. Slowly, I ease her panties from her waist and they drop to the floor. She steps out of them and stands before me, blushing again as I watch her fidget. I hold my breath, in awe of her perfect body, perfect for me. I stand up to kiss her, and as I do, she pulls the boxers from my waist. She touches me softly, eliciting an immediate response. She lifts an eyebrow and smiles.

"Are we really doing this?" she asks.

"We are," I answer. "We definitely are."

"Are you sure–" I cut her off with a kiss. I can feel the corners of her mouth turn up.

"Get in the tub, Emi," I order with a whisper into her ear, nibbling on it after the words came out. As she turns around, I allow my hands to explore her backside, from her shoulders all the way down to her hips. She steps into the jacuzzi and quickly dips her breasts below the water line, shy, demure. My Emi...

"Fuck, you're beautiful. Don't hide." I follow closely behind and turn on the jets. We both kneel on the bottom of the tub, facing each other, the water coming about mid-way up my chest. Our hands explore each others bodies under the water as we kiss. Every touch makes me want her more, and each kiss amplifies the feelings of desire. I pick her up, and her legs wrap around my torso. She holds on to the edge of the tub, arching her back, allowing me to kiss her breasts, to begin to realize all of my wildest fantasies. Her body begins to move against mine and her breathing becomes deeper, louder. Her legs envelop me tighter.

"You are driving me crazy, Emi," I tell her, moving my lips back up to her neck. I take her earlobe in my mouth and suck gently, remembering the response I got from this action last time.

"Nate," she gasps. "It's so good... when you touch me..."

That's it, I can't hold back any longer. I want her so badly... "I love you, Emi," I remind her, overcome with my hunger for her.

"Oh, Nate," she responds. I pull her up so that her lips reach mine. We look into each other's eyes. There is no doubt in hers this time, and none in my mine. She gasps briefly as we are completely taken by each other.

I hold her tighter, pull in deeper as she calls my name over and over and over. Her voice, saying my name, awakens every part of me, every cell that has ever yearned for this woman. Just like my fantasies, only this time it's real... and how good she feels... around me...

"Nate... Nate..." She grasps my shoulder, squeezing tightly. It feels so good... so good... Completely incensed by her fragrance, I lose myself in her and feel the release coming.

"God, baby, I love you." My body shudders rhythmically as her hands begin to release me and slide down my arms. I never want this to end... am sad that it has to... take my time leaving her, and feel her immediate absence

when I pull out.   I tuck my head over her shoulder to breathe, calm...
Embracing her fully, I kiss her neck. "Did you come, too?" I breathe in her
ear, my hands exploring the soft skin of her naked back.

"Not exactly," she says.   I pull away sharply, the smile immediately
replaced with concern. I study her eyes curiously. "Um..." she says shyly. "I
was trying to get your attention... that's why I was saying your name."

"Fuck, Emi... oh, fuck, I'm sorry." I back off a little more, nervously run
my fingers through my hair. "Are you okay?"

"Umm," she hesitates. "I probably should have mentioned this before, but
I'm not on the pill, Nate."

"What?"

She just shakes her head. "I'm not. I was hoping you'd pull out."

"Emi, I am so sorry... I thought..." I stammer, having no clue what to say
or how to explain my thoughtless actions. "I didn't realize..."

"It's alright," she says. "I'm sure it's fine."

"You should have spoken up, Em," I tell her, concerned.

"I tried... It seemed like you were enjoying yourself..." *Enjoying myself?
Didn't she say that about Colin?* "I didn't want to ruin it for you." Her tone
isn't angry.

Ruin it? *She was calling my name to tell me to stop. I fucking ruined it!*
"Oh, shit..."   The reality of the situation crashes down hard and quickly.   "I
mean, I just assumed you'd be on birth control."

"No. I just assumed you'd pull out."

"Shit! Fuck, oh, my god, Emi. I *do* love you, you know that." I tell her
this as if there is any doubt of my feelings for her. I know she doesn't doubt
me. Am I trying to convince myself?

"Nate, just stop," she laughs, shaking her head again and shrugging her
shoulders. "I mean, I'm sure it's okay!"

"Oh, god, Emi, no, it's not... I was... fuck... I should have been listening to
you. I just thought... shit, I don't know what to say, Em, I'm so sorry." *I was
only thinking about myself... just say it... you know it's true.*

"Nate, trust me, it's fine, really..." she smiles as she takes my arms and pulls herself closer to me in the water. She kisses my unmoving lips. "The chances are pretty slim, right? I'm sure we're worrying about nothing. And I'll get on the pill right away. I'll go to the doctor this week, I promise. We just need to be careful in the meantime."

Fuck. Fuck fuck fuck.

"Sure, Em, yeah. I'll be more careful. I'm sorry..."

"They have those morning after pills..." she says with reservation.

"Do you think that's necessary?" I say after a few moments of careful thought, pushing a strand of wet hair behind her ear.

"I don't know... do you?"

"I don't like the idea of those, Emi. I would never suggest that."

"Yeah, I'm sure we're worrying about nothing." She stares over my shoulder before shaking her head. "This is ridiculous, Nate, I'm sure it's fine."

I pause briefly, maybe a tad too long before answering. "Of course... yeah, sure it is, Em, of course." *Fuck!*

She presses her lips against my cheek, forehead, chin, neck.

Fuck! How can she kiss me like this? I fucked her like I have fucked all the other women in my life. I just blocked out her tiny voice for my own gratification. No, I didn't even do that. I heard her, and assumed she was calling my name out of pleasure. Fucking arrogant. Pathetic. I have treated her exactly like those women before her, the ones that meant nothing, the ones I only thought I loved.... and Emi is the only woman I've truly ever loved... and I don't know how to take back my despicable behavior. I wouldn't know how to make this okay. *Grow the fuck up, man!*

"Emi, about what happened..."

"I mean it, Nate, it's fine! I'm fine... but a little *unsatisfied*," she says through her constant smile... "but fine..."

"Of course," I blush. Our first time together since I got home, and I really couldn't fuck this up any worse. She puts her arms around me and kisses me, deeper. I breathe her in and succumb to her scent again, feeling her soft, warm skin under my hands. To leave her unsatisfied... well, it's just not an option. It's the only thing I know I can make good on at this point. I can't leave her unsatisfied tonight. I won't.

"Emi, let me take you to bed... and make this up to you," I whisper through kisses.

"Yes, please," she says with a playful grin, looking at me under hooded lids, standing up gracefully in front of me. Instinctually drawn to her– because she's Emi or because she's just a woman, I can't discern– I grasp her hips tightly and kiss her between her legs.

"Nate," she sighs quietly. "Please, my knees are already weak," she laughs. "Take me to bed."

I stand up quickly, handing her a towel as I help her out of the jacuzzi. "I'll just be a second," I tell her as I close the bathroom door behind her.

My palms on the counter, I lean into the mirror and force myself to look. "Fucking asshole!" I whisper under my breath. *This is Emi Hennigan... the woman you've pined over for thirteen fucking years. What the fuck are you thinking? You can not treat her like this. This isn't just sex, this isn't fucking. I love this woman.*

I feel so much more than lust for her, but in that jacuzzi... it was the only thing I could feel. I pick up a tube of toothpaste and throw it in the water with as much force as I can muster. She's delicate, precious, everything I want to love and protect and cherish, and I fucked her.

How fucking arrogant am I to think she was calling my name out of passion? She was trying to get me to stop!

I didn't know that I could feel anything as strong as my love for Emi... but right now, the hate I'm feeling for myself is just as powerful.

"Nate," she calls from beyond the door. "I'm waiting." Her voice is soft, light, playful. She shouldn't love me. She should hate me. She shouldn't want me like she does.

"Coming," I say back to her, splashing cold water on my face and drying myself off.

CHAPTER 13

I haven't been to sleep... can't allow myself to rest. Emi, either oblivious to my unacceptable behavior toward her or incredibly forgiving, fell asleep shortly after I made amends. She went to sleep happy, satisfied... the only good thing about last night.

"I'm sorry, Emi," I whisper quietly, too quietly for her to hear, afraid I would wake her, afraid that regret would set in. I guess I hoped her subconscious would pick up on the hundreds of apologies I had whispered in her ear throughout the night. The words themselves would never be enough.

Five AM. I can't lie here any longer. Slowly, I remove myself from the bed, situating Emi on the pillow and pulling the comforter up over her. She moans softly, but turns on her side, bringing the edge of the comforter to her chest. I go into the spare bedroom and close the door behind me. A small blank canvas sits by the window on the easel next to my supplies. I pick up the brush and feverishly begin to paint, to pour everything I'm feeling into the painting.

Two and a half hours later, I feel better... it's always a cathartic experience for me, and I feel oddly inspired today... I would hate to see it go to waste. I text message Albert and see if he can meet at the New York location today. He responds and says he's there now, so I tell him I'll be there in half an hour.

I check on Emi before I shower. She hasn't moved an inch, her red hair nearly glowing in the sunrise. *God, I love her.* I watch her for a few minutes before I get ready, apologizing quietly once more.

She's sitting up in bed, rubbing her eyes when I get out of the shower. I head to the dresser and pull out a pair of jeans and a red t-shirt.

"Don't put those on," she says, her voice hoarse.

"I've got to go," I tell her, turning away from her to get dressed.

"But I thought we were going to spend the day together, in bed. Wasn't that the plan?"

"Yeah, but I forgot about a meeting I'd set up with Albert at the bar. He's expecting me in ten... I'm already going to be late." I turn around and briskly walk to her side of the bed. I run my fingers through her tangled hair, gently working out some knots, and pull her head to mine for a kiss. "You can stay as long as you'd like. Just lock the door behind you."

She looks confused, shocked even. "Well, when are you coming back? Can't I just stay?"

"Well, I guess," I hedge, gathering my wallet, keys and phone. "I just don't know how long this is going to take, that's all."

"Oh," she says, a pout forming on her lips as she traces the design on the comforter with her finger. "Okay."

"Is that okay?" I ask her.

"Are you okay?" she responds.

"I'm fine. No, great, Emi, how are you?" *Asshole... that should have been the first question out of my mouth.*

"I'm good, thanks." Her answer is terse, her brows furrowed.

"Emi, I'm sorry," I tell her. "It's work. It's a commitment I've made that I can't break. You understand, right?"

"Sure," she says, short.

"I love you, Emi. I'll call you later, I promise."

"I would hope so," she says.

"Of course I will." I walk out the door, poised, confident, but cringing on the inside. How many times have I had that exact conversation with other women? Too many to think about. Maybe I'm *not* ready for this.

When I get home in the evening, the loft is quiet, clean. Emi has left the place immaculate, something I would never ask her to do, never expect her to do. I don't deserve her. Why did she agree to this?

After my meeting with Albert– which lasted less than an hour– I spent most of the day at the Jersey Shore, thinking about how to handle the situation. I want her. I have to have her... but not like this.

And I drank today. Purposefully. I went to a bar and had a few beers... I don't like that I did it. I don't like to think that one day, many years ago, my dad went to a bar for the first time and had a few drinks, just to clear the thoughts from his head. I don't like that I did it, and yet, I want another. I hate that even more. I find the wine that I had bought for Emi and pour myself a glass. This is all wrong.

As I walk into the guest bedroom, I am startled to find Emi there. So startled, in fact, that I nearly drop the glass, sloshing wine on my shirt and onto the hardwood floor.

"Shit, you scared me, Em," I tell her, surprised. "What are you still doing here?"

"I found this painting," she says. "What's wrong, Nate?"

"What do you mean?"

"Oh, come on. I know your paintings, remember? You did this this morning, right? Because it wasn't in here yesterday... and some of the paint was still wet when I found it."

"Yeah, I did." I survey the piece of art... strokes of black and blue muddled together in my own version of organized disarray.

"Well..." she begins. "It's nice... but it's angry... or sad... I'm not sure which one. Are you going to tell me what's on your mind?"

"Nothing, Emi, I..."

"You're drinking wine? You don't drink alone... at least I didn't think you did. I thought that was reserved for special occasions."

"Yeah, I'm having a drink," I tell her directly, avoiding her obvious speculations. "Would you like one? I'd be happy to pour you a glass."

"*Why* are you drinking?" she asks. "And *why* did you paint this?" She tucks her legs in, crosses her arms over them, a submissive posture, as if she's sheltering herself for what's to come... as if she knows what's coming. I take a long sip of the wine, then hand her the glass. She takes a drink, then sets it on the nightstand.

"Emi, I can't do this," I nearly whisper to her. Hearing the words come out of my mouth nearly breaks my own heart... I can only imagine what they're doing to her.

"I'm sorry?" she asks, immediately angry. "You can't *do* this?"

"No," I tell her, sitting down on the daybed next to her, staring at my empty hands.

"What can't you *do*? Because we already *did*... and there's no *undoing* that..."

"Emi, I want you, I do..." My eyes meet hers, already moist with tears that come too quickly. "And I will commit my life to making sure you are happy, but fuck, Emi. I can't do this... I can't do what I did last night, with you, ever again."

"What do you mean?" she asks, the lump in her throat audible. "You don't want to have sex with me again?"

"We didn't just have sex, Emi. You say that like what we did was normal. And yeah, I guess it is *my* normal. Sure, we *fucked*, Emi." She cringes at my use of the harsh word to describe what happened between us last night. "And I don't want to... to... fuck you... ever again."

"Please don't say that. Don't ever say that to me." The tears stream now.

"Emi, there is so much more to my feelings for you than lust. But last night, my desire to be with you, to be inside of you, took over, and made me treat you like I would never treat someone I truly cared about." Now my own eyes begin to water, a lump forms in my own throat. The words come out quickly, loudly, every bit of the loathing I feel for myself evident in every single word.

"There. There you see how I've treated the rest of them. That's the real Nate. Do you feel like you've been missing out on something? *Really?* After last night?

"Because, really, my actions, Em? Pretty unimpressive. Pretty fucking disgusting, if you ask me. And it's weird, because that is pretty much my normal... but in all the fantasies I have ever had about you, I was never disrespectful. Never once did I not listen for and comply to every request to make you happy... or comfortable... or satisfied."

"Nate," she says loudly to stop my tirade. "You're blowing this way out of proportion. It wasn't that bad."

"*Wasn't that bad,*" I repeat with a groan before laughing under my breath. "Look me in the eyes and tell me it was everything you've dreamed of... everything you wanted it to be... and I will drop this right now. Go ahead."

Her unblinking stare holds my attention, her silence speaking louder than any words she might choose to utter. Her face crumples as she cries harder and tucks her head into her chest, a poor attempt to shield her true feelings from me.

"Thought so," I mutter, grabbing the wine from the nightstand and swallowing the rest of it on my way out of the guest room.

She suddenly tears past me on her way to the kitchen, picking up the bottle of wine and removing the cork and throwing it at my chest. "This is mine," she asserts. "You don't get any more. You don't get to feel numb about this. You're going to *listen* to every *word* I have to say and you're going to *feel* every *syllable* of what I have to say. Do you understand?"

"Calm–"

"Don't fucking tell me to calm down!" she screams before taking a swig of the wine. "Don't." We square off across the kitchen island.

"You're the one who convinced me that this would work. You told me you wouldn't hurt me. You don't get to call the shots in this relationship, Nate, not anymore. This is a partnership now. I am in this, with you. You can't break this off now, this soon. You haven't even given us a chance," she pleads.

"Emi..."

"No!" she yells, cutting me off, taking another drink. "Forget what happened last night–"

"I can't!" I yell back.

"Nate, I know you, alright? I know you better than you think I do. I know you're a sexual person, that in the past you've used sex as a way to convey emotions you may or may not have been experiencing at the time. But I know you love me, Nate. I've thought long and hard about this, and I've accepted that you can't change who you are just because you're dating me... but I know your feelings are real with me. We did not... *fuck*... last night." Her soft lips have difficulty forming the word in that context. It sounds even worse coming out of her mouth.

"I don't know how you can say that," I counter.

"I can say that because I know that you love me... I know that you love me more than you loved any of the women before me. I know that. I feel that. And *you* know that... and I love you so much, Nate... so much that I was willing to risk life-altering consequences in favor of your own happiness. Because I'd make sacrifices for you... I will... but we did not *fuck*," she repeats, angrily spitting the word at me.

"Stop believing what you want, Emi, you're so fucking idealistic sometimes you can't even see the fucking truth! I was overcome with lust, like I always am, with any woman. *Any woman!*"

She cries even harder, drinks even more.

"And you're not 'any woman.' You deserve so much more," I tell her in a hushed voice. "No, you should *expect* so much more from me."

"Would it make you feel better if I told you I did?"

"God, yes!" I answer. "Have an opinion, Emi. Be real. Get mad at me! I was completely disrespectful, completely selfish."

"Okay, then," she says, wiping her nose with a dishtowel before she realizes what she's doing. "Oh, um," she adds, blushing, holding the dishtowel out to me.

"I don't care," I laugh, batting the towel out of her hand and onto the kitchen floor. I walk to the living room to find some tissues and hand them to her.

"Okay, I did expect more from you..."

"Thank you," I tell her. "I *need* you to have higher expectations of me. I need you to hold me to your standards... to higher standards, Emi. I want to be... better... for you."

"You're not breaking up?" she asks, tugging gently on my red shirt.

"No, I'm not breaking up," I laugh. "But I don't ever want us to repeat what happened last night... especially while this is so new. I think we need to slow down. This thing?" I motion to her, then back to me. "This is entirely new to me. I've loved you forever. And I've had sex with plenty of other women. But I've never been with a woman I really truly loved... I didn't realize it until today. Sex *was* love. In my mind, it's so easy to confuse the two.

"And I love you, Emi, god, how I love you... and I really want some time to... feel that... I want to feel it with such clarity that, even when I'm caught up in the most passionate of moments, that *that particular emotion...* that *love...* will stand out above all others."

"Oh, Nate," she says, setting down the wine and coming to my side, collapsing in my arms.

"Emi, I know you said I can't call the shots... but on this... you have to let me do this my way, on my terms. I love you too much to treat you like I did last night. I have way too much respect for you."

"What does that mean, exactly?"

"It means... and I can't believe I'm even saying this... but I want to put off sex for a little while."

"But it's not because it was bad?"

"No."

"And it's not because you don't want me, sexually?"

"God, no." I hold her head in both my hands and force her gaze into mine. "God, no," I repeat emphatically, closing my eyes and remembering how beautiful she looked as she stepped into the jacuzzi last night. Just thinking about it turns me on. "Proof," I tell her as I nudge myself, growing harder, against her body. "There will probably be *lots* of proof," I laugh.

"And how long is this going to go on?" she asks, impatient.

"I don't know, Em. Until I feel like I can handle this."

"I've waited so long already," Emi pleads, her hand running down my chest, stomach, until she grabs the waistband of my jeans and pulls me into her harder.

I stare into her eyes, a slightly annoyed expression on my face. "Thirteen years, I have wanted this," I tell her playfully through gritted teeth. "I just want to treat you right. I just want to do this right."

"Just no sex? Or no nothing?"

"I can't say no *nothing*... I just hope I can draw the line."

"If I hope you can't?"

"I need your support, here, baby. Please?"

"Okay..." she returns sarcastically, pushing me away and letting go of my pants. "But can you not call me 'baby' anymore?"

"Of course, Emi. Come back here," I say, grabbing her arm and pulling her back to me. "Kiss and make up?"

"Kiss and make up *sex*?" she smiles.

"Just shut up and kiss me, damn it," I tell her. "Please?"

"Okay, *baby*," she whispers again, standing on her tiptoes to meet my lips. "I will be ready when you are."

"Thank you," I mumble as I continue to press my lips to hers, holding her head to mine.

She stayed over at the loft that night. We held each other tightly until very early in the morning. As soon as Emi left to go back to her place, I called my florist and had them send the most beautiful arrangement to her.

~ * ~

"Don't say a word, Nate," Emi warns me as soon as I open the door for her and her niece. It was our weekend to watch Clara, to give Jen and Michael a weekend to themselves. Emi would normally do this once a month for her sister, but more often than not, the two would end up at my apartment, looking for things to entertain them or escaping the escapades of Emi's roommate.

"Oh, no, of course not, Em," I smile, handing her a towel and wrapping Clara up in another one as I pick her up. "But have you heard of this new thing? This smart phone? It does more than make phone calls and record your messages. It also lets you check things like news, stocks... and even *weather*."

"Nate, I swear..." she laughs. "Just shut it. It was *sunny*!"

"It was *coming*... I warned you." She bends over in an effort to towel-dry her hair. Clara's teeth start to chatter in my ear. "Where is that little toy phone of yours?"

"You'll be happy to know that my little *toy phone* took a nose dive into a puddle," she says, pulling her small flip phone out of her front pocket and setting it roughly on the table. "If you're such a smart man, get me a smart phone, genius." Emi sticks her tongue out at me as she shrugs out of her wet sweater.

"Clara-Bee, your aunt is so silly and stubborn sometimes. Look what she did to you. She made you all cold and wet. Here," I say, setting her down and taking off her puffy down coat. "At least someone dressed you appropriately today. Maybe your smart mommy has one of these smart phones," I tell her loud enough for Emi to hear. My comment earns a wet towel thrown at my head. "Nice, thanks," I mumble. "Her hair's dry, her feet are soaked," I report.

"I'm sorry, CB," Emi says, kneeling down to her niece's level. "I know you wanted to play in the park today."

"It's okay Anni-Emi," she responds through her clicking teeth.

"Let's get you into some dry clothes."

"I put her suitcase in the guest room," I tell Emi as I get out two packets of hot chocolate and one of hot tea. I put some water on to boil before I mop up the water trails left by my impractical girlfriend and her– well, really *our*– cherished niece. She considers me an uncle. She always has. I had been in her life since the moment she was born. I had to drive Emi to the hospital the day that Jen went into labor. I held her, scared and unsure of this unfamiliar world, on her actual day of birth.

"Where's my stuff?" Emi asks once Clara is dressed in her pink and purple footed pajamas.

"On the love seat by the window," I tell her. "You still cold?" I ask Clara as she wraps her arms around herself.

"A little, Uncle Nate-Nate," she says softly with a sniffle. I walk over to the bed and pull a soft throw off the foot of my bed. I put my arm around Emi and kiss her cold lips.

"Why don't you go take a shower and warm up?"

"Can you handle her?"

"Of course."

"Okay," Emi whispers with a smile, giving me a peck on the cheek. "Thank you."

"Come here, CB." I pull out a chair for her at the dining room table and wrap the blanket around her. "Better?"

She smiles and nods. "Do you want some hot chocolate?" She smiles and nods again as I pour the hot chocolate packets and water into our mugs. "Alright, I'm just gonna let it cool for a few minutes. Why don't you pick out which marshmallows you want to put in there," I suggest after pouring part of the package in a bowl. She loves the colored marshmallows– but not the green ones. I'm a purist myself, pouring a layer of regular ones into my mug.

"Nate-Nate?" she asks after putting a few in her mouth.

"Yeah?"

"I wanted to play outside in the leaves," she says.

"I know you did, but it's raining."

"I know," she says.

"But you know what that means, don't you?" I ask her. She shakes her head at me, her little brows furrowed. "What do we normally do on rainy days?"

Her eyes widen as a huge smile spreads across her face. "Craft day!" she exclaims.

"Exactly," I confirm. I had anticipated rain this weekend– believing the weather report from my iPhone– and had already gathered up some supplies for art projects. When Jen and Michael dropped Clara off earlier today, Clara's mom had hoped for rain. With the holiday season among us, she asked if Emi and I could help her daughter make Christmas cards for her grandparents. She even left some construction paper and crayons for us to use... but those won't do. "We're going to make some presents for your grandmas and grandpas today."

Over the years, I've become much more comfortable with Clara as her creativity has blossomed. Craft day is something that the three of us have always enjoyed together. "Okay," she nods, pulling her blanket around her tighter and sneezing... twice.

"You feeling okay, CB?"

"Yeah," she sighs. I test the hot chocolate one last time before giving her the mug.

"Blow in it before you drink it, okay? Make sure it's not too hot." I go into the guest room and get out four wooden ornaments and my paint supplies. I lift up Clara's cocoa before spreading a few layers of butcher paper over the table.

"What are we doing?" Emi asks after getting out of the shower. Her skin is flushed from the hot water. She's wearing her flannel pajama pants and an old, tattered NYU hooded sweatshirt that I've had for years... since her freshman year there, probably. I don't know what Emi loves about that shirt... but she wears it every chance she gets.

"Craft day, of course," I smile. "Why did you ever give me that hoodie if you were always going to wear it?"

"It was free and it was too big for me. And you never wore it!"

"First, it's too collegiate for my style. And secondly, it always reminded me of you," I shrug my shoulders and smile. She smiles back.

"I see," she jokes. "Much too *pedestrian* for a Parson's alumni." I roll my eyes at her comment. "So..." she continues, turning her attention back to the art project, "Jen is gonna love you for this," she says, "Ornaments?"

"Painted ornaments. No crayon and paper bullshit for this one. Oops... sorry."

"Nice, Nate-Nate," Emi says in a child-like voice. Clara sneezes again.

"That's the third sneeze from your little niece-monster," I tell Emi as I grab a box of tissues and take them to the table.

"Hmmm..." she says, contemplative, feeling her niece's forehead. "Maybe a little warm. How do you feel Clara?"

"Okay," she says. "Can we paint now?"

"Of course. What colors are we going to paint with today?"

"Pink and purple and yellow... and glitter," she declares.

"Perfect."

After a few hours, we finish decorating the ornaments for Emi's parents and set them aside to dry.

"Clara, let's get you to bed," Emi says. Her niece had been growing restless and fussy over the past hour, her sneezing bouts increasing in number.

"Should we call Jen?" I ask.

"No, we can handle this. I think it's just a cold. She can kill me tomorrow. Can you put her to bed while I go get her some medicine? Maybe read her one of her books?"

"Of course. Ready, Clara-Bee?"

"Ready, Nate-Nate," she yawns and sniffles. Emi kisses me goodbye with a quick peck as I pick up her niece and carry her into the spare bedroom, pulling the sheets back and tucking her in.

"My Barbie," she says, pointing to her bag. I find her doll inside, as well as a handful of books.

"Which book?"

"Cinderella," she says.

"Cinderella, it is." I settle in next to her, tissues in one hand, book in the other, and begin to read from the pages of her storybook. She falls asleep quickly, before Emi gets back.

"Ten bucks says she'll do it," I wager her as she comes in the door.

"Is she asleep?"

"Yep."

"How long has she been out?"

"Five minutes."

"You're on. She normally does it right when she falls asleep."

"You're goin' down," I taunt her, raising my eyebrows at her.

Emi and I both stand silent, waiting patiently by the bedroom door, watching Clara sleep.

"I don't think–"

"Shhh!" I interrupt. "Hear it?"

"No," Emi says.

"She definitely is, come closer." We both move to about a foot away from the bed, listening to the funny buzzing sound coming from her small lips. "There's our little Clara-Bee," I gloat as we both giggle.

"That is so funny," Emi says. "I wonder if she'll still do that when all her permanent teeth grow in."

"God I hope so," I tell her. "It never gets old. Now pay up."

"But I don't have ten dollars," Emi whines playfully.

"Well, Emi, what do you have?"

"I have all night," she teases.

"So do I," I tell her, picking her up and carrying her to the living room. "I guess we both win."

"If you consider getting to second base winning," Emi groans.

"What does that mean?" I whisper, sitting down and pulling her in my lap, kissing her neck.

"You know..."

"Well, Emi, your niece-monster is here, so that poses some obstacles."

"You wouldn't let us even if she wasn't," she pouts.

"No, I wouldn't," I agree. "But trust me, I will make this worth your while, I promise. You will not be disappointed... but you have to be very quiet," I say softly, nodding to the guest room behind me and pulling the sweatshirt off of her to reveal a *very* thin undershirt.

"It's not fair for me to get all the enjoyment," she tries to reason with me, tracing the waistband of my jeans. I put my hands on her hips and pull her against me, push her away. "I want you to get something out of it, too."

"Oh, trust me, Em, I do. I love making you feel good."

"That's not the same. Mmmm..." she moans softly.

"This is my penance. Stop being the devil on my shoulder and let me do my time in peace."

"I forgive you," she whispers before pressing her lips forcefully against mine, pressing her hips against me just as forcefully.

"Ohhh..." I sigh at the friction as it builds, closing my eyes as her motions quicken.

"You're not... watching..." she says between breaths, my hands tightly caressing her breasts as they react to my touch. I open my lust-filled eyes, watching her body move gracefully over mine. I fight the urge to lift her shirt, claim one or both as my own with my hungry lips. I've had careful limits... but this one gives way today.

"Shit," I sigh just before my hand grabs the end of the shirt, pulls it up quickly... just before my mouth closes around one of her nipples.

"Nate, god, I've missed that."

"I have, too, baby," I answer, my lips moving to her other breast. *"Emi,"* I correct myself.

"Oh god," Emi begins. "Oh god." She gets louder.

"Clara, remember, shhhh," I warn her.

"She's still asleep," Emi answers, the view of her niece a straight-shot into the next room "Oh, Nate..." She pulls my mouth to hers. "I'm coming," I think she murmurs into my mouth, the vibrations of her lips sending shockwaves throughout my body. The tremors continue with each moan, as she's careful to keep her lips on mine to suppress her beautiful sounds.

"Oh, god, Em," I say back, feeling a familiar tightening in my abdomen that I haven't experienced– with her– since my birthday. "Fuck," I whisper, her hips fast against mine, the pleasure consuming us both wholly. She finally pulls her lips away, out of breath, but keeps her body close, wraps her arms around me, feeling each shudder that rolls through me. I hold her against me, my head pressed against her chest, so close to her pounding heart.

"That wasn't so bad, was it?" she asks as we wait for our breathing to return to normal.

I laugh quietly, tracing her neckline with my nose. "Wow, um... no... but I need a shower now." I nudge her a little, but she stays in my lap, her hands gently caressing my face.

"Thank you... for letting go."

"I didn't have a choice," I admit. "You, Emi, were too much for my willpower tonight. You are so sexy." I pull her shirt down slowly, granting my curious thumbs one more gentle pass over her breasts.

Quiet sneezes come from the next room.

"Anni-Emi?" Clara calls out. Emi hurriedly hops off the couch, straightens her clothes and goes to her niece.

"I'm gonna shower, Em," I tell her as I pass by. Under the stream of hot water, I realize how much progress I've made. I was pretty much in control, in my most out-of-control state. There's hope for me yet, I laugh to myself.

I peek in the guest room on my way back to the living room, but neither Emi nor Clara are there... not in the living room either. I peek around the corner and see Clara sleeping– no buzzing– in the middle of my bed, Emi rolled over on her side watching her and giving me an apologetic smile.

"She's not feeling well," she says.

"It's fine," I smile back. "I can sleep on the couch."

"No," she whispers. "There's plenty of room. She can share my side." She pulls her niece closer to her.

"Are you sure?"

"Yes, I'm sure. I gave her some medicine, so she should sleep through the night."

"Okay," I say, tucking my girlfriend and the cutest niece-monster under the covers. I find another blanket and pull it over myself, climbing in on my side.

"Love ya, Em," I tell her, straining across my large bed to kiss her.

She holds my face to hers, delivering the sweetest of kisses. "Love ya, Nate."

~ * ~

"You are horrible, Emi!" I say to her after she climbs on top of me one afternoon while we're watching television. "Annoying, even."

"Tell me what you got me, and I won't take my shirt off," she bargains, holding the edges of her sweater. "I need to know if what I got you for Christmas is good enough." She eyes the gifts under the small tree we picked out a few weeks ago. It was just one of the many outings we chose to do as a distraction... instead of being alone together when things got a little too heavy. We'd taken day trips, exploring every corner of the state and a few of the bordering ones. Even though I hated driving, it really seemed to be the best way for us to just talk and enjoy each other's company. I was always preoccupied with getting us from point A to point B safely. Sex was pretty far from my mind when I was driving.

Five weeks. We've gone five weeks without sex. And I'm *ready*.

"I'm not going to tell you," I laugh. "You'll find out in two days!"

"Is the little one jewelry? Did you get me more jewelry? Because you're too extravagant with jewelry."

"I am? Well, I can take the necklace back–"

"No, you can't," she laughs. "That'll buy me a car when we break up," she jokes.

"Not funny," I tell her. "And for the record, it's not jewelry."

"Why can't we open them tonight?" she asks. "It's Christmas Eve. In my family we always open presents on Christmas Eve."

"No, you don't. If that were true, you'd be with your family right now and not here, trying to seduce me."

"Well, we just postponed it this year so Chris and Anna can celebrate with her parents... it's her family's tradition to celebrate today."

"Blame it on the new girl," I tell her. "Besides, Emi, we have always had our own tradition of celebrating the day after. I like doing that. It makes the holiday last longer."

She glares at me with a pout, then quickly removes her heavy sweater, revealing a lacy camisole.

"Is it hot in here?" she says, rubbing against me. I hold her hips still momentarily and stare back. "Or is it just me?"

"Definitely just you," I say running my fingertips along the underside of her breasts, my eyes leaving hers to focus elsewhere... to watch the physical reaction happening under her shirt as I touch her. "Where'd you get this thing?"

"That little boutique on the corner. The sales lady assured me I would get anything I wanted if I wore it."

I roll my eyes at her, frustrated at her persistence. "Emi..."

The blustery winter wind and snow were our deterrents today from our typical distraction. I wasn't taking the car out in this, but I was thankful that

Emi braved the weather to come over and spend the afternoon with me anyway. I loved having her here, but it was getting difficult to say no to her advances. I wouldn't last much longer.

"Will you start a fire?" she asks.

"You just said you were hot. Put your sweater back on, silly."

"I want a fire," she pleads. "It's romantic."

I roll my eyes at her request, but give in without a fight. "Get up." I help to move her off my lap and onto the couch.

"Thanks, Nate," she sings to me sweetly.

I offer her a drink after starting the fire and get a glass of wine for her, a bottled water for me. She sits on the floor, scooting closer to the fireplace to warm up, choosing to not put her sweater back on... always so impractical. I smile as I watch her.

As the fire grows, the colors of it cast beautiful shadows on Emi, her red hair especially. Her cheeks are rosy from the heat. The vision is breathtaking, so much so that I want to document it, have it forever.

"Hey, Emi," I say, breaking her gaze away from the fire.

"Hey, Nate," she answers.

"I... you look so beautiful sitting there... can I paint you?"

She shrugs her shoulders and answers, "I don't care. If you really want to."

"I really want to." I go into the guest room and gather my easel, canvas, drop cloth and paint and set up across the room. I survey the image and walk over to move the couch out of the way. I grab the comforter off the bed and spread it on the floor in front of the fireplace.

"Would you like a pillow?" I ask her as she crawls on the blanket.

Again, she shrugs. "You're the artist. Pose me."

"Really? I can?"

"Sure," she laughs.

"Take off your shirt." The adrenaline begins coursing through my veins so quickly that it comes out as an order. "I mean, would you mind?"

"That's what I was trying to do all along," she smiles, pulling the shirt over her head and setting it behind her. I kneel down in front of her as she lies on her side, her elbow bent atop the pillow, her head resting on her hand. I mess up her hair slightly, sweeping a few strands across her forehead but careful not to cover either of her beautiful eyes. I kiss her softly as I unfasten her bra with one hand and help her out of the garment. I lean back and look at her again.

"So beautiful." I unbutton and unzip her jeans, opening the flap slightly to reveal her pink, lace panties. I run my fingers along them and inhale deeply. I drag my fingers along her curves.

"Should I put makeup on?" she asks.

"God, no," I tell her, standing up. "You don't need it, Emi."

I stand back behind the easel and look at her once more. "Perfect. Let me know if you get uncomfortable."

"Should I smile?"

"No," I tell her, opening a tube of red paint and putting a dab on the palette pad. "Just look into the fire... part your lips slightly... tilt your head down just a little. Yeah, right there. Oh, wow..."

"I better not see this in a gallery someday."

"Are you kidding? This will be my ticket to *my* new car when we break up." She throws the bra at me, and it lands right in the freshly laid out paint. "Good job," I tell her. "That may not come out. Red rarely does."

"Call it a souvenir," she says. "I didn't like that one anyway." I hang it on the tip of the easel, letting it drape over the back.

I can barely tear my eyes from her body to tend to the canvas.

Her strawberry blonde hair dances with flecks of orange from the fire. It hangs just to her shoulders, styled naturally today, just slightly wavy. When I touched it, it was soft and silky, so feather-light in my fingers.

Her milky skin, smooth, porcelain. Not a blemish on her. The only interruption of her fair complexion was the pink in her cheeks, which I was now uncertain whether it was caused by the heat or by the fact that she was lying, half-naked, on display, for me.

Her green eyes, always pale, look a translucent brown as she gazes into the fire. She flutters her lashes quickly, tries to hold her eyes open.

"Just be natural," I encourage her softly. "It's okay to blink."

She smiles and blushes deeper, glancing only briefly in my direction. Small dimples form on either side of her pink-tinted lips. The middle part of her upper lip slopes gently, evenly... Cupid's bow. That's what it's called. I remember my mother talking about her plastic surgery one day. The term stuck in my head. I close my eyes momentarily and imagine my tongue tracing her Cupid's bow. *Fuck, this is turning out to be more erotic than I had thought it would be.* I had intended a scholarly study of her body, her beauty, but she's just turning me on.

The fire apparently isn't enough to warm her, as evident in her pronounced nipples sitting atop her pert breasts, the perfect size to fill my palms. *I want to touch her.*

I take a drink of water before continuing, trying to focus, to balance the lust with the love. After a few deep breaths, I continue painting, putting as much detail as my eyes can see into every stroke. I want to remember this moment, this day... this *woman*... forever.

"Okay, I think I need to move," Emi says as I'm putting the final strokes on her jeans. Her eyes plead with mine.

"I'm finished," I tell her. "Go ahead."

"Can I see?" she asks, lying on her back on the comforter, stretching her limbs.

"No." I tell her walking briskly to her and kneeling down beside her. "Not yet." She reaches up for me, pulls my head to hers for a kiss. I pull away, looking into her eyes, now the familiar green again. I put my hand over her heart to feel it pounding, then move my hand down to caress her breast before kissing it, taking her nipple into my mouth and sucking gently.

She moans softly as my kisses travel down her body. "Thank you," I say to her as I grab the ankles of her jeans and tug lightly. She helps to push them over her hips and down her legs. I throw them onto the couch across the room.

"I'm cold," she whispers, smiling.

"You won't be for long," I tell her, smirking back at her as I take the sides of her lace panties under my fingers and pull them down.

"Nate?"

"Yes?"

"Will you make love to me now?"

"No," I answer, kissing her between her legs. "Not yet."

"When?" she barely manages to say as she exhales quickly.

"You're going to spoil all your presents, my sweet Emi." The conversation between us ends there. I bask in her sweet sounds as my tongue travels to her favorite destinations. In my head, though, we're making love. In my vision, when she calls my name, I'm enveloped inside her. Instead of her hands tugging lightly on my hair, they're wrapped tightly around my body, holding on for dear life.

"Oh, god, thank you, Nate," she says as she awaits my oncoming kiss. I grab both edges of the comforter and tuck them around us.

"You're welcome," I whisper, feeling her come down beneath me.

"So Wednesday, then?" Her breath is hot in my ear.

"Wednesday," I confirm. "Merry Christmas."

~ * ~

"Merry Christmas!" I greet my mother and James in the lobby on the way back from putting up the painting I had done of Emi yesterday. Not really safe for parental viewing... I knew Emi would be mortified if my mom stumbled across it.

"Merry Christmas, Nate!" Mom exclaims as she pulls me into a tight embrace.

"Merry Christmas, Nate," James repeats as we shake hands. He carries a bag of wrapped presents in his other hand.

"How was your afternoon?" I ask, leading them to the elevator.

"The brunch was delectable, as always," she says. "And mass this morning was lovely. I'm so glad the sun is out... and that it finally stopped snowing. It really couldn't be a more perfect day."

"It is."

"Will Emi be joining us in the park tonight?" she asks as we walk to my apartment. Every Christmas, our tradition was to watch the carolers at Central Park, bundled in our warmest coats and drinking coffee or hot chocolate. Emi had joined us many times in the past.

"Not this year," I tell her. "She's doing her family thing today."

"You're not spending Christmas with her?" she asks, disappointed.

"Don't panic," I joke with her. "We're doing our normal day-after-Christmas thing. I like that."

"Everything's okay with you two?" James asks, surprising me at his interest in my love life... or hell, in any part of my life.

"It's great," I smile, offering them both a seat. "In fact," my grin grows wider. "That little present under the tree..."

"Oh, Nate!" my mother exclaims, again throwing her arms around me in jubilation. I should have known she'd jump to marriage.

"Wait wait wait wait wait," I caution her. "Not that, Mom, for God's sake we haven't been dating that long."

"But don't you think you will propose someday?"

"Of course. But not tomorrow," I laugh. "It's a key to the loft. I want her to move in with me."

"Oh, well that's a big step, too!" she exclaims, hugging me for a third time.

"You've hit your quota of embraces, Mom," I tease her. "I get that you're happy for us. Thank you."

"Do you think she will?"

"I don't have any doubt. If nothing else, it's an escape from her current living situation, which she's never really enjoyed."

"You should redecorate or something," my mom gives her unrequested advice, as always.

"We will. That's part of the present. We're going to go on a shopping spree to make this place ours. Goodbye, bachelor pad."

"Oh, I'm so excited for you, sweetie."

"Yeah, congratulations, Nate," James chimes in.

We spend the rest of the afternoon catching up and exchanging presents before heading down to the park.

When the singers begin "Oh, Holy Night," I call Emi's number. As soon as she answers, I hold the phone up above the crowd through the entire carol. It's her favorite Christmas song. As the applause begins when they sing the final word, I duck away from my mother and the rest of the people gathered.

"Love ya, Em," I tell her.

"Love you, too. Merry Christmas."

"Merry Christmas... tell your family, too. How about I'll pick you up in the morning for breakfast... around ten?"

"I can't wait," she says. "I miss you."

"Miss you."

"Tomorrow, still?"

"Tomorrow."

"I can't wait," she repeats.

"I can't, either... good night."

"Good night, Nate."

It's another beautiful New York morning. I stop by a coffee shop and order two chai tea lattes, then head over to Emi's. She answers the door, dressed in a robe and wrapped in a blanket, her eyes a little red. I've seen these eyes many mornings after she's stayed up most of the night working or hanging out. I lean in to kiss her, and she obliges with a soft sweep of her lips before she turns around and walks to her bed.

"Hold on, Emi," I say quietly, willing her back to me, putting down the coffee. "Are you okay?" I ask. She doesn't answer... just sits on her bed with her arms crossed and raises her eyebrows ever so slightly. "Were you up late?" I ask.

"All night," she mumbles.

"And you didn't call?" I attempt to joke with her. She glares at me. "Sorry..." She forces a smile. "Why is it so cold in here?" I ask, looking over at the radiator by the window.

"The heater stopped working last night. It's just blowing cold air."

"Hmmm... you called the super?" I take her drink to her. She wraps her hands around the cup to warm them up.

"I left him three messages."

"He is such a jerk... you should move." Again, she glares, and I can't wait to give her the key to my apartment, wrapped neatly under the tree back at my loft. "Let me take a look."

"Right," she mocks me. I'm well aware I'm not mechanically inclined, but I cross the room and check the heater anyway. I flick it on and feel the blast of cold air that doesn't seem to warm up at all.

"Wonder if the boiler's not turned on?" I glance over my shoulder to see her shrug in response. Turning the radiator back off, I look down and see a small figure from a nativity scene sitting all alone on the windowsill. Shuffling it between my hands, I walk back toward the bed and sit down next to Emi. She breathes in the steam from her coffee, cringes a little and sets it on her night stand.

"Did they make it wrong? I ordered it the way you like it."

"I'm not really in a coffee mood right now." She wraps the blanket tighter around her body.

"Hey, are you okay?" Her jaw is taut as she nods her answer, not looking me in the eye. I nudge her in the side, trying to engage her in conversation. "So why do you have a baby Jesus here?"

"I stole it," she says plainly.

"From?"

"My dad's house."

"Don't you think they might miss the baby? It is the centerpiece..."

"Well, there'll be another baby soon enough to take its place." Her voice is soft, but I still hear all the words and understand their meaning even before I set the statue down next to her coffee– and the pink stick that stares back at me with a plus sign on its display.

My breathing halts as I pick it up and study it intently, as if looking at it with all my focus will change it or reinterpret it or give me the answers to the millions of questions that inundate my consciousness.

"Shit" is the first word to come out of my mouth.

"Nice," she says sarcastically. "Just the response I was hoping for."

"Let's get married, Emi," I say abruptly, the words practically falling out of my mouth, as I kneel in front of her, the test in one hand and her left hand in the other. I look up into her eyes in time to see them narrow in disbelief.

She pushes me back into her roommate's bed. "No, I'm not going to *marry* you, Nate."

"Why not?" I pick myself up off the floor and sit on Teresa's bed across from Emi.

"I don't want to get married because I'm pregnant, Nate. I want to get married for love..."

"It *would* be for love. We love each other..."

"But you're only suggesting it because I'm pregnant."

"I would have asked you anyway..."

"In time, maybe, but you don't know that. Fuck, Nate, we just started dating. We don't even know if we're going to work out as a couple."

"Of course we are, Emi."

"There's no way to tell now," she says, standing up and walking to the window. "Now we're being *forced* together by this baby, this by-product of lust–"

"*Love*, Emi."

"Oh, *now* it's love," she says snidely, her back still to me. "But at the time, it was lust, you said so yourself."

I sit in silence, trying to find the right words. "Emi, I never would have pursued you– much less slept with you– if I wasn't sure of my feelings for you first." I go to her, caress her shoulders lightly and turn her to face me. She looks at the floor between us. "Look at me." I wait until she lifts her eyes to mine. "I love you. I'm certain of that. Sure, that night, I was overcome with lust and I was disappointed in my... inattentiveness to you... and rightly so... but everything I've done for you, *with* you, is because I *love* you.

"You're my best friend, Emi. I'm in love with my best friend! How amazing is that... why wouldn't we get married and raise a family together?"

"Because this is all so new to us, and by the way, I'm not ready to be a mother!" She pushes me away and goes back to her bed, crawling under the covers and curling into herself. "It's one thing for me to carry this baby to term, Nate, but are you really ready to commit to being a father, to raising this child right now? We aren't ready for this..."

"Emi, is anyone really 'ready' for it?" I sit on her bed behind her, putting my head in my hands.

"Sure, lots of people are. We're not."

"We could be."

"Nate, I don't know that I want this right now..."

"What, are you going to *abort* it?" I ask, my heart rate picking up exponentially as I walk back to her roommate's bed and take a seat, forcing her to look at me. "Because I should have a say in this, too, this is my baby, too, Emi, and I don't think–"

"I'm not going to get an abortion, that's not what I'm suggesting."

"Well, then, what?"

"Well, there are probably people better suited for raising a child–"

"Better suited than its own parents? Its *adult* parents who love each other and would love it unconditionally, *regardless* of what happens?"

"Nate, this could all end horribly, and you know it. We either end up happily-ever-after or completely ruined. If we don't work out– if we aren't meant to be together– how would we ever have a normal relationship? It would be awkward. There'd be anger and resentment and jealousy–"

"We'd do it for our *child*, Emi. And I wish you would just stop doubting our future together. Why can't you just believe that we'll work this whole thing out?"

"Because it'll hurt less if I expect it not to..."

"Just stop being so afraid of this..."

"Don't you know that losing you would completely destroy me? I've relied on you for too long... to live a life without you... I can't even fathom that."

"You don't have to. Just stop with this worst-case-scenario shit, Emi!"

"Well, it's starting off pretty badly, don't you think?"

"No," I say, taken aback, kneeling next to her bed and again taking her hand in mine. "We were friends who fell in love and created a new life together. It's a beautiful thing."

"How can you be so casual about this? I'm pregnant, Nate! Get your head out of the clouds!"

"It's just... it's not as bad as you're making it out to be..."

"Nate, I want some time for us. I want time for us to devote to each other, to make sure we are right for one another. I really don't want a baby to be the reason we're together–"

"Emi–"

"Will you fucking hear me out, please?"

"I'm sorry. Go ahead."

"I feel like I don't have a choice anymore. I feel like we *have* to be together now, whether we want to be or not. I feel stuck..." Her eyes begin to water and for the first time, I see how unsure she truly is about us. Hurt consumes me and my stomach falls at the realization. I am forced to swallow down a growing lump in my throat.

I *really* thought we were on the same page. I *really* thought we both knew we would end up together. I *really* thought we both expected the happily-ever-after, and that we would pursue that *endlessly, relentlessly*. I had no idea she was still on the fence about us. Since we agreed to this, my future was *always* her, *only* her.

"Of course you have a choice," I say sadly. "I won't force you into anything. But, Emi, I promise to love you and provide for you. I promise I'll do anything to make you happy. But, shit, I don't want you to stay in this because you don't feel like you have any other options. I'd never want you to feel 'stuck' with me. If that's how you feel–"

"I don't know how I feel," she cries softly. "I don't know what I want. I don't know what to do." I smooth her hair down as she weeps quietly, my heart breaking that she's so conflicted, so sad, so unsure.

I find some tissues in her nightstand and begin to blot her tears. "What can I do?"

"Just give me some time to figure things out, Nate."

"Shouldn't this be something we decide together?" I ask her.

"Probably," she answers. "But I want to figure out what I want first. Can you let me do that?"

"Can we talk about things before you make any decisions? I want to be a part of this."

"Of course," she sniffles. "Of course we'll talk about things... you're right, this is something we should decide together... but I think we both need to really think about how this will affect our lives, as individuals."

"I want to be with you," I assert. "There's no question in my mind."

She squeezes my hand. "Love always clouds your judgment."

"Not this time. My feelings for you... shit," I laugh softly, more to myself since the reality of this truly isn't funny. "This is the clearest my mind has ever been. This is the easiest decision I've ever had to make. I just wish it could be as easy for you."

"I just need some time..."

"Whatever you need... but Emi, I love you. Don't doubt that. I want you to keep that in the forefront of your mind while you're considering things."

"Okay," she whispers and smiles for the first time today. "I do love you, too."

"I know," I tell her, kissing her forehead. "Why don't you get dressed and come over. We've got presents to open."

"No, Nate," she says. "I want some time... to *myself*... to figure this out."

"Okay. I understand that. But at least come over to get out of the cold. I'll give you space. I'm afraid if you stay here, you'll get a cold or something... you can't afford to be sick right now..."

"No, Nate, I'm fine. I'll be fine. I've got my electric blanket on high. Really, I'm only cold when I'm up. And I honestly don't feel like being up now anyway."

"What about food, can I bring you some food?"

"No," she laughs. "I have a ton of chicken soup, which is about all I can stomach right now. And if I really want something more, Dad and Peg sent me home with a ton of leftovers."

"You need vegetables, too. I'll bring–"

"Nate, stop. I'll call you if I need anything."

"Anything at all," I encourage her. "At any time..."

"Okay," she says. "Don't worry about me."

"I'm *going* to worry about you... *both*..."

"I'll be fine," she assures me. "*We*... will be fine."

Before I leave her building, I knock on the super's door. Hearing shuffling behind the door, I know he's in there. My nerves are suddenly shot as I already begin to worry about Emi's decision. I pound harder until he answers.

"Yeah?" asks the slight man who opens the door.

"My girlfriend's radiator isn't working. Unit 3412. It's too cold for her to be without heat. Do you think you can get that taken care of as soon as possible?"

"I got a list of tenants with problems, man," he answers.

"Listen, asshole!" I yell, grabbing his collar and pushing him against his door. "She's pregnant and she's cold, alright?"

He looks at me with fear in his eyes. Having never seen another man look at me like that, I'm shocked back into reality and quickly let go of him. "Fuck," I mutter, my hands nervously combing through my hair. "I'm sorry."

I pull out a hundred dollar bill and hand it to him. "Can you put her at the top of the list?" I ask. "Please," I plead.

"Apartment 3412. On my way," he says, taking my money and grabbing his keys.

"Thanks."

~ * ~

Two days later, after having plenty of time to consider what's happening on my own, I decide I need to talk to someone. I knock on the door to my mother's house before entering on my own. She stops mid-way down the stairs when she sees me.

"Nathan!" she smiles. "What brings you out here today?"

"I need to talk," I tell her. "Do you have some time?"

"Sure, honey, of course," she continues to walk down the stairs. "James is at work... and I'm just putting the finishing touches on things for the benefactor reception we're having here tonight. But I always have a few minutes for you. Let's go in the sitting room."

I force a smile and sigh heavily, following her quietly.

In the natural light of the sitting room, she looks me over. "You don't look too good, honey. Are you coming down with something?"

"No," I huff, wishing it was that simple.

"Well, what's going on?"

"It's Emi."

She sets down her coffee and leans toward me. "Is she okay?"

"Uhhhh..." I sigh heavily. "She's pregnant." My mother's jaw drops slightly as she reads my own worried expression. "And she's not really sure what to do about it."

"Oh," is all she can say. She picks her drink back up and takes a long sip. "Did you want a muffin? Sophia made some muffins." She gets up and heads back into the kitchen before I even tell her no.

"Sophia?" I ask when she comes back.

"New housekeeper," she explains, setting down a basket of warm pastries. They smell too good to ignore, so I take one and begin taking off the wrapper as I stare at my mother, waiting for her response. Finally, she looks at me, a strange smile on her face.

"Nathan," she says, taking a deep breath. "I have dreaded this day for a long time."

"Mom," I start, but she holds her hand up to stop me.

"I just knew that, one day, you'd come and tell me that one of your girlfriends was pregnant. Honestly, I'm just surprised it didn't happen sooner."

I nod, looking down, moderately ashamed that she expected this from me. I deserve that. Not a moment later, though, I'm grateful I'm having this conversation about Emi and not a previous girlfriend.

"That being said, honey," she continues. "I don't think this is necessarily a bad thing... because you're meant to be with her. Maybe it's not the best timing, but if it's going to happen to two people, why not two people like you, who have such a great history together. It can only mean good things for your future."

I laugh to myself. "Yeah, that's what I keep trying to tell her, but she's not speaking to me right now."

"But she will," she says with confidence. "She'll come around."

"She won't marry me. I asked."

"Well, it is a little reactionary. You just told me you weren't ready to ask her. But why isn't she speaking to you?"

"She wants some time to figure out what she wants to do."

"What do you mean? She's not thinking about an abortion, is she?" my mother asks, grasping my hand, a pained expression on her face.

"No, she assured me that was not an option."

"Good," she sighs as she places a hand over her heart. "Then what is there to figure out?"

"She mentioned adoption–"

"Out of the question!" my mother says abruptly. "I'll take–"

"Mom," I interrupt her, "I just think she needs some time to accept what's going on. I won't let her do that... but I'm going to give her space to figure this out on her own. She's a free thinker... but she always seems to make the right decision."

"So you want to raise it, then?" she asks.

"Undoubtedly. I want to be a family. She may not be ready for it now... and I can see why she has doubt... mainly about me. But *I* am certain about *her*. You know, I've been biding my time for years, but ever since I went to LA, things have just been so clear, so obvious to me. I'm sure this should freak me out, but it doesn't. I want to marry her. I will. I didn't get involved with her as a temporary thing. I was confident we would share our futures together, and I still am. It may take some time to prove to her that I'm here to stay, so I'll give her that. I'd give her anything."

"Nathan, darling," my mother says. "I am so proud of you. Just in the past few months you've become the man I knew you were destined to be. You're finally getting recognition for your artwork, and you've finally figured out the place that Emi fits into your life."

She hugs me tightly, and blots her watery eyes when she pulls back. "What did she say about moving in? Is that part of what she's trying to figure out, too?"

"I never got a chance to ask her. We haven't exchanged presents... but I already have plans for turning the spare bedroom into a nursery. I've got a few ideas... and I bought a few books... I've been doing some research on cribs and strollers... and cars. I'll have to get a different car."

"There's plenty of time for all of that," my mother says, taking my hand in hers. "Right now, you've got to do right by Emi. Just be there for her, in whatever capacity she needs you."

"I know. I've been calling her daily. She doesn't answer, but she's been texting me that she's feeling okay... and that she misses me... so that's something. She knows I'm here when she's ready."

"Nathan, if you two need anything, anything at all, you'll let me know, won't you?"

"Just don't say anything to her family yet, if you happen to see them. I don't think she's told anyone."

"My lips are sealed."

"Thanks, Mom... hey, can you spare a few of these?" I ask, motioning to the muffins. "I think she'd really like them. If she can stomach them..."

"Does she already have morning sickness?"

"A little, yeah."

"Sure, let me wrap those up for you," she smiles.

"Emi?" I call to her after knocking.

"Hey, Nate," Teresa says, opening the door. "She's not here."

"Oh. Do you know where she is?"

"I think she was going shopping. I think she was looking for a dress for Chris's engagement party."

"Okay," I smile. "Well, there are a couple of homemade muffins in here... one for each of you." Although I was hoping to split them with her. "Can you make sure she knows I stopped by?"

"Sure, is everything okay? I expected to see y'all hanging out more over the holidays." *She obviously doesn't know...*

"Fine, yeah... you'll be at the party?"

"I'll probably stop by. I have two other parties, though."

"Okay. Well, happy holidays... oh, and tell her I love her."

She looks at me curiously. "Okay, Nate, I will."

Later in the day, I get a text from Emi, thanking me for the muffins. *"I miss you,"* she adds.

"I want to see you," I reply. *"Please?"*

"I'm not ready yet."

"Love ya, Em."

"I know, Nate," she responds.

~ * ~

"What's the plan for tonight, Chris? Are we still playing for you and Anna?" I'm testing the waters with Emi's brother, just making sure there's no change in plans. Emi hasn't asked me to *not* come to the party, so I guess she's okay with seeing me later this evening.

"Of course, Nate, why wouldn't you be?"

"Nah, I was just messing with you." It doesn't seem like Emi has told her family yet. Her brother would be the first to know.

"Yeah, well, you and Em can check into your room anytime. Party starts at eight, so if you and the band can be down in the ballroom a little before to do a sound check, that would be great."

"Of course, that's what we were planning on." I sigh, hopeful. Apparently Emi hadn't asked for a separate room. "Looking forward to it."

"Me, too. Is Emi there with you?" he asks.

"No, I, uh... I think she's at her apartment."

"Have her call me when you talk to her. I have a question for her."

"Sure thing. See you tonight."

I decide to text her since that seems to be the way she wants to communicate with me these days.

"Good morning. Hope you're okay. Just talked to Chris. He wants you to call him."

I don't wait for a response, just start to gather all of my things together. My suitcase packed, my tuxedo hanging by the door, I just need to pack up my guitar before heading out to New Rochelle. I was hoping we would make the drive together.

I hear my phone ringing in the other room, the familiar ringtone I'd chosen for Emi, the one I hadn't heard in nearly a week. I run to answer it.

"Emi?" I ask, overjoyed to get her call.

"You know, Nate," she starts in immediately, her voice lilting. "We have been wasting *precious* alone time. You realize that, right?" My smile wide, I laugh and sigh at the same time.

"God, yes, Emi. I was just about to leave. Can I come pick you up? We can ride together."

"Nope," she says. "I'm catching a ride with one of my cousins. I have a surprise for you tonight, and I don't want to give anything away."

"Are you checking in before the party?" I ask her.

"Maybe," she answers. "Just leave a key for me at the front desk."

"I can't wait to see you. I have missed you so much. Just hearing your voice is... shit, I can't even catch my breath."

"Just wait till you see me," she replies. "I've missed you, too. I'll see you soon."

"Love ya."

"Love ya, too, Nate."

"Be careful. See you later."

"Bye."

CHAPTER 14

I check my watch as I pace around the room, dressed in the tux and almost ready to go... I was hoping to see Emi... in addition to my desire to touch her and kiss her, I needed help with my tie. I told Chris I'd be downstairs by now... I can't wait anymore.

"Sorry I missed you," I text her. *"I'm heading to the soundcheck."*

"I'm here in my cousin's room getting ready. I'll see you there," she answers. *"I did pick up my key, though. Hope to use it later."*

Downstairs in the ballroom, I apologize to Chris, Eric, Jason and the rest of the band we've hired to play with us. "I was waiting for Emi," I tell them.

"You weren't with her?" Jason says. "We figured you were fooling around with her... I mean look at your hair." I roll my eyes and give him a warning glance, nodding in Chris's direction.

"I'm her brother, remember?" Chris says to Jason. "I don't want to know these things."

"Sorry, man."

"We've only got ten minutes until eight... that's when the guests will start arriving. And Nate, I don't know if you've met my best man, but he is going to give a toast before the set, okay?" Chris asks.

"That's fine, and we'll be done with this in five," I assure him. I stand behind the mic and Eric and Jason assume their positions. We have decided to use our own sound system since we're familiar with it, and our tech has worked with us enough to get the sound check done promptly. We put our instruments to the side, and I see Emi's sister, Jennifer, enter at the back of the ballroom. She waves at me and walks in my direction. I step off the stage and meet her half-way.

"Emi warned me that you might need help with the tie," she says.

"Yeah... does it look okay? It's her favorite one."

"It looks perfect," Jen says, straightening the knot.

"Where is she?" I ask.

"Still upstairs getting ready... she said she'd be down soon... but she just got out of the shower."

"I can't wait to see her," I tell her.

"Yeah, she said she hasn't seen you since the day after Christmas. What gives?"

"Uh... just, uh, busy, I guess."

"You two are silly," she says. "You need to make time for each other if you're going to make this work."

"You're right. I promise to do that."

"Come with me," she says. "There's a whole slew of family members that are dying to meet Emi's boyfriend. You're a rarity, apparently. I think they need proof– they were all convinced she'd end up in a convent."

"Alright." She leads me around the room. I hadn't realized Emi had such a large family, but it will take me years to remember all of these relative's names.

Finally, around eight forty, I see her walk in wearing a short, fitted, backless red dress with matching lipstick and heels. I barely recognize her, my girlfriend, my best friend of thirteen years. I stare rudely– it *would* be considered rude if she had any idea I was ogling her, but she's immediately pulled into a conversation with some people I had spoken to earlier. Her eyes scan the room. She's undoubtedly looking for me.

I'm simply unable to peel my eyes away, even as more of her male relatives converse about music in a circle around me and my two bandmates. The dress, her wavy hair, her silky legs demand my attention as if she is standing in a spotlight. Apparently, she doesn't just have this magnetic effect on me. Eventually, the rest of the guys stop talking to see what I am looking at.

"Wow," Eric says. "I'm sorry, Nate, but your girlfriend has never looked hotter." Jason's eyes follow Eric's.

"Who is *that?*" one of her cousins asks. "She is amazing..."

"Dude, it's our cousin!" his brother tells him. "Sorry, man," he says to me. "We haven't seen her in years."

"We've never seen her like that!" his brother adds. "That's Emi?"

"Shit!" Jason exclaims. "That dress. Wow. I'm sorry, Nate. I can't promise not to stare at her all night. Her back... have you seen her back? You don't mind if I try to convince her to go out with me, do you?" he jokes.

"I do mind. Shut up, all of you. And find someone else to look at!" I tell them with a smile. "She is mine, all mine, tonight." I look her way longingly, counting the seconds until I can be with her. Finally, her eyes meet mine. Her smile is impish, her intentions obvious. I lick my lips and smile back, beginning to walk in her direction.

"Nate," Emi's mother stops me. "Nate, it's good to see you again. It was so nice for your mother to invite us to your birthday gathering."

"Yes, Mrs. Hennigan..." I say, still distracted by the beauty of her daughter.

"Rawlings," she corrects me.

"Of course, I'm sorry," I apologize at my mistake and turn my eyes to her.

"But I've told you a million times, you can call me Karen."

"I know, I know... my mother just taught me better than that," I laugh. "This is an amazing gathering. I had no idea how big the extended family was."

"That's what happens with second marriages," she smiles. "You and Emi should never have to worry about that, though." She winks and I raise my eyebrows at her bold assumption. Of course she's right. "She's never been happier."

"And she's never been more beautiful than right now," I tell her. "Have you seen her tonight?"

"No, where is she?"

I nod toward the vision in red. "Oh, my!" her mother says. "That dress is... wow... she looks so... confident... she's practically glowing." I quickly avert my eyes to Emi's mom, my face getting hot. "Don't you think?"

I laugh nervously at how correct she is. Emi *is* glowing. "I do."

"Did you have a good Christmas? How is your mother?" *I can't wait to be with her... I don't want to be rude... but god, I want to be with her.*

"It was nice, and my mother and James are both good."

"Will you be getting together with her tomorrow?" she asks, remembering our family tradition.

"Probably the day after. I think tomorrow is reserved for Em... in fact, I think I'm going to join–"

"Nate!" Chris yells to me. "Nate, come on!" I look at my watch and realize it's time to perform. How could twenty minutes go by already?

"Excuse me, Karen," I smile, anxious. "Looks like Chris is ready." I groan audibly as I walk in the direction opposite of Emi. Glancing back at her, I shrug my shoulders as she waves to me. "Nine-thirty," I mouth to her, signaling to my watch. I point at her, then point to myself, then point upward. She blushes and nods.

Chris is standing next to a man I'm pretty sure I've seen before, somewhere, but I don't think we've ever met. I walk over to them.

"So, this is my best man. You'll welcome everyone, he'll do his toast, and then you'll perform your three songs. Got it?" The man smiles and nods in my direction.

"Yeah," I tell Chris, extending my hand to his friend. "Nice to meet you," I tell him, shaking his hand, inspecting the man that will be walking down the aisle with my girlfriend, feeling somehow suspicious. I have no idea why.

"Likewise," his friend says to me as he straightens his tie.

"Right. Are we ready?"

"I'm ready," the best man says.

"Let me get the guys, I'll be right back." I head over to the bar area and grab Jason and Eric. We walk together toward the stage as the room lights dim and the spotlights illuminate the stage.

Once up the stairs, I put on my guitar and grab the mic.

"Ladies and gentlemen," I start. "On behalf of Chris and Anna, I want to thank all of you for coming out tonight. I believe, uh..." I never caught his friend's name. "I believe Chris's best man has a few words to say." I step aside and hand over the microphone to the dark-haired man.

He begins to talk, but my attention is, again, focused on the gorgeous woman in red that's running her hand down her thigh, slowly, watching my every reaction. "I want you," she mouths to me. I smile broadly, anxious to get these three songs over with.

The audience claps, and I realize the toast is over. Chris's friend steps off of the stage, walking toward Chris to shake his hand. We begin the first song, an upbeat tune by the bride's favorite band. Chris and Anna take the best man toward Emi. They shake hands, and I sense that Emi has met him before. Shortly after the introduction, Chris and Anna take their place on the ballroom floor, beginning to dance. After the first verse, they invite others to join in.

Emi and this other man continue to talk as we begin the second song, walking to the bar together. The bartender hands a tumbler of ice water to Emi, and passes a glass of red wine to her companion. At one point, she points to me, and he nods, as if recognizing me from somewhere. I just wish I could place where I had seen him. He looks nice enough, pretty harmless, but I get a strange feeling about him. I'm just anxious to hear what their conversation is about now, anxious to have Emi fill in the blanks.

I play the first few chords to the last song, and I watch curiously as this man takes Emi by the hand and leads her out to the dance floor. My heart begins to race. I don't want to think I'm jealous– after all, I know Emi and I are soul mates, *everyone* does– but something just doesn't feel right about it. She smiles, laughing with him, but she keeps her distance, doesn't let him get too close. I think she knows it will drive me insane to have another man touching her, especially the way she looks tonight... especially when she knows how badly *I* want to be touching her. When her amazing, pale, bare back faces me, I look up and make eye contact with the guy. Did he really just raise an eyebrow at me? *Prick*... and I know exactly where I've seen him.

That night when I went to pick her up from the frat party... the night Emi and I shared our first kiss. It was also the first night Emi and *he* had first kissed. When I got to the frat house, this man was with her, trying to take advantage of her. He had kissed her. *That kiss.* I wonder if she remembers who he is.

The anger I felt toward him that night returns immediately. *Dick.* It takes every ounce of my energy to stay on the stage, finish the set. *Cocky son-of-a-bitch... if he thinks he can have my girl, he's got another think coming.*

After the song, I thank everyone and begin to walk directly toward Emi and her dance partner, shaken and suddenly insecure. I'm stopped halfway there by Anna.

"Nate," she says, "thank you so much. That was beautiful."

"I'm glad you liked it, Anna," I say, trying not to look too impatient.

"It was perfect, man," Chris says.

"Good. Thank you."

"No, thank you," he says, giving me a hug and patting me on the shoulder.

"If you'll excuse me," I tell him. I can't get to her fast enough– can't get him away from her fast enough. As soon as I break away, she is the only person I see in the distance. She's looking at me, smiling, obviously ready.

372

She's still standing next to him, but I can tell that he is nowhere in her periphery at this point.

"Thanks for looking after her," I mumble to him, giving him a look, making it clear that she is mine. I briskly walk up to her, caress her face with my hand, kiss her tenderly, then take her by the hand, and escort her out of the ballroom. I am suddenly thankful that she is eager to follow me. I shouldn't have doubted her. Exiting the doors, I run my hand all the way down her back, settling it at the base of her spine.

"That's the guy that was taking advantage of you at that party in college, isn't it?" I ask.

"Was he? No, I don't think he was taking *advantage* of me," she answers as she shakes her head, pushing the "up" button once we reach the elevators.

"No, I'm pretty sure he was."

"What?" she laughs.

"Yeah," I say. "I think I remember him." *And hopefully you don't.*

"I'm pretty sure he *wasn't*," she says in his defense. "He was really nice. I think Chris had put him in charge of making sure I would stay out of trouble." The elevator door opens, and we step in, joining a woman and two small children.

"You remember that? Or is that what he *told* you?"

"That's what Chris told me..."

"Hmm," I say, not really interested anymore. "That's not how I remember it. And if I recall correctly, Chris was too drunk to know what was going on."

"You know what he said to me tonight?" The door opens on the third floor and the woman and children leave the elevator. I grit my teeth, hoping that nothing he said or anything that occurred tonight reminds her of what really happened *that* night.

"Who, that guy?" She nods. "No, what?" I pull her to me, embracing her tightly, my hands running up and down her back in an effort to keep her focus on me, on the present-day and nothing else. Her face just inches from mine, she continues to talk. I barely hear the words, concentrating on the way her lips move, how her eyes sparkle.

"He said that he knew, from that night, the first time he ever saw you... he said he knew you were in love with me."

"Really?" I laugh inwardly, somewhat surprised with his revelation to Emi. I was, of course. She knows it now, but I never knew my feelings were so obvious back then to a complete stranger. After all, I had been dating someone else at the time– even if she did break up with me a week later.

"Yeah, he said he had thought about asking me out sometime, but when he saw us together– I guess when he saw us kiss– he could just feel the chemistry or something." She starts to pull at the knot of my necktie.

"Kiss?" I comment, tucking her hair behind her ear. The only time we kissed that night was in the privacy of her bedroom. Of course he hadn't seen, but it's obvious to me now that she doesn't remember anything. "Kiss?" I repeat with a sigh of relief, moving my lips to hers, touching them lightly. "Like this?"

"Yes," she whispers, distracted, her eyes closed. We kiss until the elevator stops at our floor. I hold the door open with my shoe and keep her inside, talking to her.

"Emi, when we exit this elevator, I don't want to talk about anything– or *anyone*– other than you and me. Got it?"

She smiles and nods as I take her hand and lead her down the hallway.

"Good. Now, do you know how incredible you look tonight?"

"I tried," she says, waiting for me to open the door.

"You succeeded."

"I did it for you."

"Thank you," I tell her, inserting the key and turning the handle as we kiss, deeper. "Are we okay?" I ask her, pulling back slightly to look into her eyes.

She nods and smiles.

"What does this mean? For us, I mean?" I open the door for her and again touch the small of her back, so soft and warm and I can't take my hand off of her.

I close the door lightly behind us and wait for her answer. She removes one shoe, and then the other, then walks up to me, standing on her tiptoes so her lips can reach mine.

"I love you, Nate," she says. "And we're going to continue on just like we were before we found out I was pregnant..." She kisses me again. "And when the baby comes, we'll raise it together..." Another kiss. "In either one household or two."

"My vote is for one," I tell her seriously.

"Well, we don't have to make any decisions tonight, Nate," she responds. "I hope you're right, but let's just take this one day at a time."

"Whatever you want, Emi," I whisper to her.

"I really want you to make love to me." Her voice is soft, but I can still hear her wanting, her needing, in the inflection of her words.

"Gladly," I tell her, kissing her through my smile and picking her up, carrying her closer to the bed.

"Okay, first thing's first," she says as I gently set her down. "We have to go back down to the party by midnight," she states. "That means our clothes need to look... perfect..."

"You're being far too reasonable right now, Emi. There's no way we're going back down to that party, and you know it." My hands travel up and down her arms.

"We have to," she smiles, her eyes pleading. "Everyone will know what we're up to."

"I'm pretty sure the entire ballroom will know that we're having sex soon enough." I touch her stomach lightly. Her hands meet mine as I rub her flat stomach with my thumb. "I can't believe our baby is in there."

"I know," she whispers as I lower my lips to hers. I tug at the shoulder straps of her dress, but she stops me.

"Not yet?" I ask. "Are you okay?"

"I'm fine, Nate," she says. "There's a zipper down the side, that's all. But

I'll let you do the honors." She stands in front of me, lifting her arm to expose the zipper. I slowly pull it down, taking the strap off of that shoulder, exposing her left breast and the small batch of freckles.

I mumble against her soft skin the poem I had written for all seventeen little marks. "One transcendent kiss, that later makes lovers take soft breaths, holding hands."

"Oh, Nate," she whispers after I drop her arm.

I kiss her shoulder, and carefully pull the other strap down, kissing the other shoulder. I hold the dress by both straps as it falls easily from her body.

To my surprise, she is completely naked underneath.

"Hello, my love," I whisper, kissing her again, embracing her and lifting her to my height.

"Will you hang the dress up?" she whispers back. I pull back and look at her.

"Really?" She simply nods, her eyes shifting toward the closet. I set her down and hurry to fulfill her request.

I rush back to her naked body, quickly becoming fully aroused. I begin to undress myself, throwing my coat on the ground. "That stays there," I tell her. She smiles.

"My turn," she says. "Let me do it."

"Anything you want." I stand there, ready for her hands to remove my clothes. She starts with the tie, pulling it loose from around my neck and tying it in a bow around her own neck.

"Cute," I tell her. She removes my cufflinks next, putting them on the nightstand. Then, starting with the lowest button, she unfastens my shirt, kissing my stomach and chest with each button. She carefully pulls the shirt sleeves off my arms, and walks slowly, deliberately, to the closet to hang it up. Not able to contain myself as I watch her walk away from me, I follow her and grab her from behind, my hands gently massaging her breasts. I kiss her neck and shoulders. After she hangs up the shirt, she reaches her arms behind her to unfasten my belt and unbutton my pants. They fall to the ground, and she stands still for a second after discovering the erection under my boxers.

"You are so beautiful." I step out of the pants and walk her forward toward the wall.

"Your pants," she reminds me.

"Fuck the pants, Em," I tell her, having no intention of worrying about them at this point.

She stands facing the wall, her elbows propped up against it, and spreads her legs just slightly. I continue to kiss her neck, fondle her breasts, and rub slowly against her behind.

"Oh, god, Emi, I need you right now."

"Then take me," she says, breathless, turning around quickly and pushing the boxers to the floor. I pick her up, pressing her against the wall, pushing gently until I hear that sweet gasp. It's got to be one of the most beautiful sounds I've ever heard.

"Oh, Nate," she sighs.

"Are you alright?" I ask as she strengthens her grasp around my neck. I pause to kiss her ear, waiting for a signal to continue.

"You feel so good inside me," she says. *Thank God.* I hold on to her hips tightly, guiding them slowly, pushing deeply. When her legs wrap tighter, she pulls me into her further, gasps again. I groan quietly. *It has been far too long.*

"I want to take you to bed," I tell her my intentions as I carry her from the wall to the king size bed. She whimpers a little as we separate so I can arrange the pillows.

"Is this comfortable?" I ask her.

"Yes," she breathes desperately, "but come back to me."

She is still wearing my tie as a bow around her neck and I laugh at my precious New Year's Eve present. She smiles and lifts her finger, motioning for me to come to her. I lie on top of her, untying the tie and setting it on the night stand. I angle her knees up, kissing each one of them, sliding in between them. *There is that sound again. That glorious sound.*

377

I make sure I'm slow and gentle with her, cherishing this woman that I love. Her hands begin to pull my hair as she starts to climax.

"Oh, right there," she breathes. I'm careful to repeat the action. "Oh, yes, Nate, ohhh...." Once she begins, her arresting sounds push me over the edge, too, and we eventually come together. Our lips separate only when we both need a breath, but immediately find each others again after a few gasps.

We kiss as our heart rates return to normal. She continues to moan quietly in my mouth. Eventually, I pull away to look at her glowing, rosy cheeks, her dimples pronounced by a wide grin.

"Was that okay?" I ask, confident in her answer.

"The best," she laughs as her fingernails scrape my arms lightly. "I don't ever want to take another break from this. Ever again."

"Me neither," I confirm, pushing a few strands of hair out of her eyes and kissing the tip of her nose, then her cheek. "Never."

"God, that was sweet," she says. "I'm sorry I pushed you away this week. I was confused and–"

"Don't apologize, Emi. Just... thank you for letting me back in. We'll work this out together." I nod and smile, and she does the same. Wanting to excite her once more, my lips begin their journey down her body. She puts her knees up again, bracing herself, and my lips, tongue bring her to ecstasy once more. Her body writhes in pleasure, her moans become yells, and it's obvious she feels freer to express herself in a strange hotel than she does in our apartments, where neighbors can hear through the paper-thin walls (or roommates can hear through actual paper screens). She sits up suddenly, and I kneel to meet her lips, but she pushes me backwards, eyeing my erection, and crawling on top of me.

I've told her that this is my favorite position because I can see her beautiful body on display... we'd made out this way many times... and it's her favorite because gravity takes over, and it gives her the deepest pleasure. I take her by the hips and guide her body, oscillating wildly. I put my knees up to support her back and to give myself better leverage. She arches her back and grabs her ankles, her swollen breasts aching to be kissed. As soon as I feel the burn in my stomach starting, I sit up so I can take her breast into my mouth, feeling the release, the electric current leaving my body and exciting hers, over and over. We are breathing in unison now, moaning on occasion, as the release continues.

"Oh, my god, Nate, oh, don't stop," she begs. I keep going, faster still, not needing to stop, surprised at my own stamina. She begins to yell again, and we continue for at least a few more minutes, until I can feel the burn lessening, myself becoming more sensitive.

"Emily Hennigan, I love you," I say, completely spent. "My god," I continue, slowing to a halt, collapsing on my back. "Oh, fuck, what *was* that?"

She falls to my chest, out of breath. "I don't know," she says. "But it was the most... amazing... oh, my god."

I roll on top of her quickly, never wanting our bodies to be apart. I kiss her deeply, her legs wrap around my body tightly, pulling me closer to her.

"God, I love you, Emi," I whisper in her ear before my head collapses on the pillow she's lying on. I slide next to her on the bed as her body shifts with mine, one of her legs still covering me, her head resting on my chest.

"I love you, too, Nate." The room silent, I focus on the sound of her breathing, each breath slower, deeper. She makes the sweetest noise, a tiny sigh, as she attempts to pull herself even closer to me, gripping my arm tightly with her hand. I smooth her hair gently, breathing in the fresh smell of her shampoo. My eyes closed, my thoughts drift back over the events of the past hour or so. My smile never lessens as I recount every moment... every perfect moment with her.

Eventually, her limbs feel heavier on my body as I assume she's fallen asleep. I feel myself losing consciousness as well until I remember how she looked at me from across the ballroom. All of my senses were completely alert and attuned to her, as they have suddenly become again as I lie in bed with her.

I remember undressing her, pressing her against the wall, our bodies joining together in the bed, the intense buildup and release...

"Oh, my god," I say out loud, unable to hold in my response to what happened between us. She jumps slightly at the sound of my voice. "I'm sorry I woke you," I tell her, lightly brushing her arm with my hand. "But oh, my god," I repeat.

She laughs and lightly scratches my chest. "I know. I've never felt anything like that before."

"That makes two of us," I tell her. "I had no idea I was capable of that."

"And here I am, left wondering, how I got so lucky..." she says.

"Me, too." I kiss her once more before getting lost in those beautiful green eyes of hers. "You're by far the sexiest woman I've ever known, Emi. In the ballroom tonight, in the bedroom, in any room. You astound me. Even in my wildest fantasies, you weren't this beautiful, this alluring. It just goes beyond anything I could ever have wished for myself."

"Wow," she says, propping herself up on her elbow to lean over me. "That's a pretty big compliment."

"And yet, still, I don't think it fully expresses how I feel... how grateful I am that you've chosen me."

"Nate, please know, I feel the same about you. You've always been my best friend... and I had a feeling you'd be a good lover, but I didn't know things could be like this," she laughs as she continues to run her fingernails over my chest. "This was... unreal... that's really the only thing I can say about it. Like, out-of-body-experience-unreal."

"Exactly," I agree. "How do you feel now?"

"Perfect. And exhausted. And not wanting to go back downstairs."

"See? Didn't I tell you?" I joke with her.

"I had good intentions..."

"Well," I tell her, "it's still early, we don't have to go yet. Or at all, if you really don't want to. We're in love. They all know. I'm not ashamed."

"I'm not ashamed," she adds, "but it would be embarrassing facing the fam in the morning, you know?"

"You'd get over it," I tease. "Plus, you have sex hair right now... and I don't know how to fix that, obviously."

"Is it bad?"

I wipe a few beads of perspiration from her hairline. "No, it's good," I tell her, kissing her forehead. "You look beautiful."

"Thank you." She closes her eyes, and I watch her body, touch the warm, silky skin on her stomach. She rolls back onto the bed as I lean over to kiss her navel, my lips lingering on her stomach.

"You okay in there?" I whisper.

"I heard that," Emi laughs. "I did some research, and it's fine."

"Just wanted to talk to our child, do you mind?" I joke.

"Our child," Emi sighs. "Wow."

"Yeah, I know."

"Nate, whatever happens, I know that he or she will be welcomed and loved by us and our families... and I know we'll be able to provide for this child like no other people could. I really do hope we stay together."

"I really hope you'll soon realize that we're going to." I kneel over her legs and encircle her hipbones with my thumbs.

"Nate?"

"Yes, my love?" I place my ear on her stomach, hugging her sides.

"Let's go back to the party."

"What? No, Emi, I don't think we're... presentable."

"But you said I look beautiful."

"In my eyes, you always do... but it looks like we've been doing exactly what we've been doing... which, in all honesty makes you look even more beautiful to me."

"But they had that amazing looking chocolate cake down there... and I really, really wanted some."

"Chocolate?" I ask. "You don't even like chocolate."

"I've been craving it."

"Just the cake, or chocolate in general?"

"Any chocolate."

"Well, there's a twenty-four-hour superstore a few blocks down... I went by there earlier for some socks... the sign on the door said they were open tonight... why don't I just go get you something from there?"

"I wanna go with you."

"No, you can stay here. Rest up... midnight will be here before you know it, and I want the kiss to last all night."

"No, I'm coming. I don't want to be apart from you."

"Fair enough," I say, crawling up her body and kissing her sweetly. "Let's get dressed."

We climb out of bed and dig through our suitcases for jeans and t-shirts, hoping to sneak out of the hotel unnoticed. I call down to the concierge and ask them to have my car ready. I grab my wallet, and we walk hand-in-hand to the elevator. Once inside, she pushes the button for the lobby, and I put my arm around her, kissing the top of her head. She's silent, smiling, radiant.

We look both directions in the lobby, making sure none of the party guests are wandering around. The valet has my keys waiting as soon as we step outside.

In the car, Emi fastens her seatbelt but angles her body toward me. "I love you." She shakes her head. "Those words aren't even enough."

"I know, Em," I smile, squeezing her hand and pulling away from the hotel's driveway. "I love you, too."

"I'm sorry."

"Sorry for what?"

"For reacting like I did about the news. For acting like it's a mistake. I don't ever want our child to think they were a mistake."

"Emi, there's no need for you to apologize," I say soberly.

"Yes, there is. Just know that I will never resent you for this. I am grateful... I know it's not what we planned... but it will be the most cherished little baby in the world."

"Yes, she will."

"She?"

"Did I say she?" In my mind... it's a girl. "Seems like a girl."

"Why do you say that?" she laughs.

"I don't think anyone up there would trust a man like me to raise a boy... but He probably took one look at you and thought you would make the perfect role model for our little girl."

"Nate," she sighs. "That's so sweet... and I'm sure you're right." She giggles, squeezing my arm. I give her a sideways glance as I park the car, attempting to look offended but unable to hide the smile. "If you weren't a good man," she begins as she opens the door, "I wouldn't be with you." She shuts the door quietly and meets me at the back of the car, offering me her hand.

Once in the store, I tell her I'll meet her in the candy aisle.

"Where are you going?"

"I'm just going to get something... nothing you need to worry about."

"Honey, we don't need condoms," she jokes.

"Funny," I say, rolling my eyes at her. "Candy aisle."

"Don't be too long," she seems to sing to me. I head to the baby section and look around at the store's offerings... lots of clothes, tiny shoes, bottles, blankets... I stumble across a stuffed giraffe hanging all by itself on a peg. I look at the label, intrigued. Inside is a digital recorder... *This is the gift.*

I find an out-of-sight register and quickly pay for the toy, then head to a quiet corner of the store to record a message for our baby. It isn't hard to find a place, since we seem to be the only two customers in the entire store.

When I'm done, I wrap up the giraffe in the bag and head toward the candy aisle. There's no sign of Emi there, or on either of the aisles around it. I find an employee and ask if there's another section where they sell candy, but she tells me no.

I pull out my cell phone and call her.

"Hey, Nate."

"Hey, where are you?"

"I'm looking at some books."

"Okay, I'll be right there." I find her a few minutes later. "What did you find?"

"*The Pregnancy Book*," she says, holding on to three different chocolate bars in one hand and the book in the other, "*Month-by-Month, Everything You Need to Know...*"

"Let's get it," I tell her, taking the candy from her. She smiles and half-skips out of the book section of the store. She keeps her nose down, reading some of the pages as we walk to the register. "Pssst... she needs to scan the book," I nudge her.

"Oh, sorry," she smiles, blushing. The early-twenties clerk is careful to save her page, and hands it back to Emi in the same place. "Thank you." I give her cash and wait for the change.

"How far along?" the clerk asks.

"Six weeks tomorrow," Emi glows. "Still early..."

"I'm eight weeks. I just got that book... it's really good." She hands me my change.

"Good... thanks... and good luck to you," Emi says.

"You, too," the young woman says.

"Good luck," I add, taking the bag of candy as Emi goes back to reading. I hold on to her arm, guiding her to the car and opening the door for her. I look at my watch as I cross to the driver's side.

"Eleven-thirty," I say to her, getting in the car and closing the door. "We should be able to make it back to the room by midnight." She closes the book and digs in the bag that holds the candy, taking a bar out and opening it.

"I don't care where we are at midnight," she tells me. "Honestly, all that matters is that I'm with you."

"I'll always be with you," I vow.

"Thank you. Want some?" she asks as I pull out of the parking lot.

"No thanks," I tell her. "Hey, what's in that other bag?" I encourage her.

384

"I don't know..." She looks confused as she sees the small stuffed animal. We stop at a red light and I reach across the console, pulling the cord for her.

"*Hi, little one,*" my recorded voice begins. Emi looks at me in anticipation of the rest of the message.

"Thirteen years. One night.
Nine months. One small baby will
deliver true *love."*

"Oh, Nate," she says, stepping on my last line as her eyes tear up.

"*I can't wait to see you.*"

"I can't wait," I reiterate my recorded message aloud in case she missed it, a lump in my throat making it difficult to speak. "I can't wait for us to meet her."

"Or him," she corrects me softly, tugging the string again and holding the toy next to her stomach. "That's your daddy's voice," she says quietly, wiping a tear away before leaning in to kiss me. When she pulls back, not more than a few inches, the look in her green eyes is confident and comforting. Her dimples become more pronounced as her smile grows wider.

I tuck a strand of hair behind her ear before moving in to kiss her again, never more certain of our future together.

She sighs happily and looks at me adoringly, placing her delicate hand to my face. Her thumb traces my cheekbone lightly. I take her hand in mine, touch my lips to the soft skin of her palm and weave my fingers between hers. Clutching the stuffed toy, she moves it close to her heart. We smile at each other as I notice the traffic signal changing from red to green out of the corner of my eye.

I smile as the seemingly prophetic green light tells me it's time to go. I don't need a signal to tell me anything; I'm ready to move forward with Emi, to start our future together. Still holding her hand in mine, hoping my gaze communicates my abiding commitment to her, I stroke my thumb across her finger. Knowing someday soon she'll let me put a ring there, I smile inwardly and put my foot on the pedal, optimistic and assured and ready to go.

"Nate!"

~ * ~

WORKS BY LORI L. OTTO

Emi Lost & Found series
Not Today, But Someday
Lost and Found
Time Stands Still
Never Look Back

Choisie series
Contessa
Olivia (coming 2014)
Livvy (coming soon)
Dear Jon (coming soon)

Short Stories
In the Mind of a Dying Man
Love, Lost
Jackson
Number Seven

S P E C I A L   T H A N K S   T O

John T. Perry
Shirley Otto
Clarinda Alcalen

Christi Allen Curtis
Katrina Boone
Alex Wheelus

Angela Meyer
Nikki Haw

Melissa Dean, Annie Walsh, Audrey Kay, Casey Corn, Cheryl Dent, Christen Fiermonti, Courtney Smith, Diana Arneau, Erin Spencer, Jamie Taliaferro, Jo Ann Stevens, Kelli Spear, Lea Burn, Michelle Ochoa, Stacy Bundy, Stephanie Cobb, and Tiffany DeBlois

CPSIA information can be obtained at www.ICGtesting.com
Printed in the USA
LVOW10s2147260215

428575LV00013B/439/P

9 781453 755402